WORKING
FIRE

ALSO BY EMILY BLEEKER

Wreckage

When I'm Gone

WORKING FIRE

FIRE

A NOVEL

EMILY BLEEKER

LAKE UNION
PUBLISHING

Text copyright © 2017 Emily Bleeker

Published by Lake Union Publishing, Seattle

www.apub.com

Amazon, the Amazon logo, and Lake Union Publishing are trademarks of Amazon.com, Inc., or its affiliates.

ISBN-13: 9781542045728
ISBN-10: 154204572X

Cover design by Shasti O'Leary Soudant

Printed in the United States of America

For Elizabeth—my sister and best friend

CHAPTER 1

ELLIE

Tuesday, May 10
9:45 a.m.

Caleb & Amelia 4 Ever

Still here. Ellie ran her fingers over the blackened scratches that made up the poorly executed graffiti. The laminate in the Piggly Wiggly restroom was already ancient when Amelia forced six-year-old Ellie to act as lookout so she could carve those words into the counter. The fact that they were still here sixteen years later was either reassuring or disgusting. Back then, you weren't an official couple in Broadlands, Illinois, until you defaced property to prove it. Usually the requirement included school property, but Amelia decided she'd rather face Mr. Slattery, owner and manager of the Piggly Wiggly in Waynesville, than have the principal at Broadlands High call her father.

Unlike the declaration of their love, Amelia and Caleb only made it to the end of high school. Mr. Slattery's call and Amelia's subsequent grounding probably didn't help the budding romance much. But the evidence was etched in stone.

Or crappy old laminate countertop, Ellie thought as she slipped her phone out of her pocket and snapped a quick picture to share at next Monday's dinner. Amelia's husband, Steve, probably wouldn't find it funny, but Amelia's girls would love it. Chief Brown would make a comment about Caleb not being good enough for his daughter.

No. A year ago, her father would've made a comment about Caleb. Now they were lucky if he remembered that their mom was dead and that Ellie was twenty-two instead of six years old.

Ellie put her phone back in the hip pocket of her cargos. She'd never worn a pair of pants with more pockets, all of them full of supplies that could make or break an emergency call. It'd take a while to get used to the extra weight, like the first time Amelia made her wear a bra and it felt like it was cutting off her oxygen.

Thinking about her father was a good way for Ellie to get her mind off her partner, Chet, and the fully equipped ambulance sitting in the parking lot of the Waynesville supermarket. Her father had made this "lifesaving" thing seem far more exciting than anything she'd actually experienced in Broadlands the past six and a half months.

Then again, Chief Brown must've loved his job, because it wasn't like anything *ever* happened in Broadlands. In her senior year, Ellie was supposed to make a poster for the Broadlands Founders Day parade that would be displayed around town to advertise the event. Her father was the parade marshal and Ellie was the most successful student as well as Mr. Larue's favorite art student, so she got the job without even asking for it. But when she turned in a beautifully drawn poster of Main Street with the title BROADLANDS: THE HOME OF NARROW MINDS AND NARROW OPPORTUNITIES, Ellie was promptly banned from the parade committee, and Chief Brown grounded her for a week.

Oh great. Tears pushed at the back of Ellie's eyes, burning like slowly crawling lava. She yanked three flimsy paper towels from the dispenser and dabbed at the moisture. The last thing she needed was someone from town seeing Ellie Brown having a pity party in the supermarket restroom. Everyone else pitied her enough—poor little Ellie, her dad stroked out on the job, and she dropped out of med school to come home and help her sister take care of him. Couldn't pass the physical agility test to become a full-fledged firefighter, so she was riding in the ambulance with grouchy old Chet.

With one last wipe, Ellie blinked at herself in the mirror. The whites of her eyes were surprisingly clear, any trace amounts of red only making the few highlights of gold in her dark brown eyes stand out. Thankfully, she'd put on waterproof mascara that morning. When she worked as an EMT back in Champaign, she never wore makeup, but in Broadlands she had to keep up appearances, since half the town had known her since she was in pigtails.

Ellie smoothed back a flyaway strand of hair from her face and tightened her high ponytail. In her dark blue uniform and silver paramedic badge, she looked almost competent. If her father could see her now, really see her, he'd be proud. It had been on his advice that she even went through the paramedic training in addition to her undergrad coursework at the University of Illinois. He'd convinced her it'd be good experience before med school. He had been right, and she hated to admit that she loved the rush of the job, keeping a cool head in chaos, being in control while everyone else was losing it. Maybe she had more in common with her old man than she ever realized.

Ellie wiped her nose and put on her best fake smile. Too many teeth and it didn't touch her eyes, but it should be good enough to fool old Chet. Pausing to aim, she tossed the crumpled towels into the trash can by the door and pumped her fist when they made it on the first try. Yes, she was going to pull it together and get through another twenty-four-hour shift.

First things first: she and Chet had better get back to the station with the groceries. There were eight hungry guys waiting there, and today was her day to feed them. They ranged in age from twenty-two to fifty, but Ellie still called them "the boys" in her head just like her father always did. Chief Brown always said the reason God never gave him sons was that he already had a firehouse full of them.

A knock sounded, and the door opened a crack.

"Hey, Ellie, you in there? The ice cream is melting; we should probably get back."

Ice cream. Yeah, she'd promised to make her mom's dump cake for dessert tonight. Dump cake was never any good without a big scoop of ice cream on top. Maybe she could convince Chet to use the siren to get them back to Broadlands before the ice cream was nothing more than mush.

"Sorry! I'm coming!" Ellie squeezed in one more glance at the mirror and then opened the heavy maroon door. Chet stood on the other side, nearly a foot taller than Ellie, his once-black hair now silver. She had to pull back when she nearly collided into his chest.

"You feeling okay, L?" Chet pulled out the old nickname her father had always used for her as a child. L for Ellie and M for Amelia. He used to joke that the reason he and Ellie's mom stopped having kids after two was because Frances Brown refused to name additional children N, O, and P.

"Yeah, I'm fine. Sorry. Uh, thanks for checking out. I've got the dishes tonight."

"Huh, I'll trade dishes for flirting with Tracey Donovan any day." Chet's overgrown eyebrows wiggled at the fifty-year-old woman wearing electric-blue eye shadow and glued-on eyelashes behind register number one.

"Just ask her out already, Chet. Girls like a firefighter." Ellie wrapped her hands around the cracked plastic on the shopping cart handle and guided the full basket toward the automatic doors at the front of the store.

"Well, I was quite the ladies' man back in the day. Your dad can attest to that." Chet brushed his mustache down with one finger and gave a wink to Tracey as they passed her lane.

"Ew, I'd rather not know, thank you very much." She faked a gag and walked out the front doors into the early-spring sun. It was warm during the days, but cold enough in the evenings that Ellie had to keep a coat in the rig. The sun was low in the sky, a few storm clouds inching in and threatening to turn the day frigid. Her stomach grumbled. She'd skipped breakfast like most mornings, still trying to drop a few pounds before she gave the agility test another go. Ellie was starting to think of that grumble as a sign she was burning calories.

As Chet rambled on about his days as a ladies' man, a voice crackled over the radio—dispatch. Both Ellie and Chet stopped in their tracks.

Ambulance Twenty-One delta response, [crackle] *Lane, Broadlands. Possible shooting* [crackle] *AS-One. Police responding. Have not arrived.*

Chet picked up the radio clipped to his lapel. "Dispatch, Ambulance Twenty-One responding. Please repeat."

"Shooting?" Ellie mouthed to Chet, who was holding the radio up to his ear. It had to be a mistake. There'd never been a shooting in Broadlands, not that she remembered anyway. Maybe it was a hunting accident. Maybe a kid found his dad's gun. Maybe . . . The possible scenarios flashed through Ellie's mind. Chet grabbed the cart and pointed to the rig.

"I'll have Tracey hold this. You check the CAD. Reception's a little spotty today." Chet might have a hundred years' more experience than Ellie, but the computer in the ambulance still confused him. Nerves on edge, especially since the idea of a pediatric emergency crossed her mind, Ellie dashed to the rig.

She unlocked the passenger-side door and hefted herself into the seat, then swiveled the computer-aided dispatch screen to face her. When she hit the Responding button, a map and lines of information stared back at her. She read through the sentences on the screen, eyes flitting from one line to the next. Description of the call. A few codes she was pretty sure meant serious business. Then the address, just two miles away from her dad's house:

2318 Lark Lane, Broadlands

No.

She read the address again, and again. She didn't even need to check the map on the left side of the screen. She'd been to 2318 Lark Lane countless times, eaten dinner there, held new babies, swum in the backyard pool, cried into a soft shoulder when it became clear her father would never recover.

It can't be. It can't be. It can't be.

But it was.

2318 Lark Lane was her sister's house.

CHAPTER 2

AMELIA

Monday, April 4
Five weeks earlier

"Cora and Kate on the bus. Check. Dinner in the Crock-Pot. Check. Caleb is covering the front desk. Check. Dad at Ellie's. Check." Amelia ran through the list as she applied a second coat of plum-colored lip gloss before dropping it into the overflowing makeup bag on the counter. Not that anyone actually looked at the faces of a string quartet, but she still liked to try to break up the monotony of her all-black "uniform" with a splash of color. With her dark hair and eyes, she sometimes felt like she was fading into the background.

She stepped back from the mirror and examined her hastily applied makeup, squinting through the fingerprint-smudged mirror. One eye had too much eye shadow and the other too much eyeliner, but it was going to have to be good enough. A once-over with Aqua Net and then, despite the inconsistencies with her makeup and just a bit too much volume to her hair, she was ready. Besides, she still had the forty minutes in the car to Chandler for her hair to de-poof. Forty minutes. She checked her watch. She'd either have to speed or bend time, because the reception for the new hospital's fancy ribbon cutting was starting in thirty.

Amelia rushed out of the bathroom, then ran down the stairs and into the kitchen, where she snagged her purse off the back of a kitchen chair. After rummaging through some loose receipts, candy wrappers, and a few pennies, she still couldn't locate her keys.

Dang it. Why didn't she ever put them back on the key hooks Steve had installed right by the office door? She glanced over at the hooks just in case she'd remembered to put them there. Empty. No time to search; she'd just have to take the truck. But the keys were on the company key chain, which, dang it again, she'd given to Caleb last night.

"Caleb! Caleb!" Amelia shouted. She knocked and then peeked through the heavy steel door on the side of the kitchen that connected the house to the home office of Broadlands Roofing. Caleb, a tall, nearly bald man with fair skin, tightly cropped reddish hair on the sides of his head, and a sharply angled nose, stood up, shoving a filing cabinet closed with his foot. He smiled nervously.

"Hey, Amelia. Thought you were doin' your music stuff today." He scratched the top of his head and leaned against the filing cabinet.

"I am, I mean, I will once I find my keys."

"Oh, those keys walked away on you again?" Caleb started scanning the room. "You think they're in here somewhere?" He shuffled some papers on the desk next to the cabinet, lifting stack by stack as though they'd suddenly appear like a ball in the magician's cup trick. "You need one of them tracking devices I saw on TV. Beeps when you push a button. Unless you lose the button . . . Then you have a real problem."

Amelia sighed. She'd always been scatterbrained, which had driven organized Steve crazy from day one, but the more activities the kids were in, and the bigger the business got, and now that she was helping out with Dad, she felt like she was losing her mind.

"I don't have time to track my set down. I'm gonna take the truck. Can I grab the key from you?"

"Uh, sure. Sure." Caleb patted the pockets of his worn jeans and then fished the loaded key ring out. "Steve had me fill the tank last night, so there should be plenty for you to make it to Chandler." The key slid off the ring with a click. Amelia was always a little surprised at how well Caleb kept track of her schedule. If he weren't so genuine, it'd be creepy. "Here you go."

"Thank you. Keep your fingers crossed that there's no traffic, accidents, or rogue traffic cops on the way."

"Just flash your pretty smile at the officer, and I'm sure you'll get out of it." Caleb gave one of his rare, broad smiles, the kind that touched his eyes. That smile always brought her right back to high school before the breakup. For a long time, it had made her want to go back and figure out why he broke up with her so suddenly, but once Amelia got to know Steve, that had all gone away. Now that sporadic smile was more nostalgic than anything and made Amelia wonder why Caleb worked at Broadlands Roofing in a job where he was nothing more than her husband's lapdog and in a position where he had no conceivable opportunities for professional growth.

As a teen, he'd been a talented artist, collecting blue ribbons like Amelia collected bouncy balls from the vending machine at the Piggly Wiggly. Everyone thought he'd go into something creative, but then somewhere in the middle of his senior year, Caleb gave up. He stopped going to school, stopped going much of anywhere, and he definitely stopped painting. And even though he was the one to break up with her, she'd always felt a little guilty. Every morning that he walked into the office for his shift, a small part of Amelia was disappointed that he hadn't finally gotten up the courage to follow his dreams.

"I guess it depends on how fast I'm going," she said. "Which I'm thinking will have to be incredibly fast. Have a nice day, Caleb!" Amelia waved without looking back and bounced into the house. She collected her bag off the chair, not bothering to push it in again, and grabbed her cello in its cow-spotted case by the door.

She should set the alarm. Steve wouldn't be happy if he got home first and found out Amelia had left the house open—he thought it was important to keep everything locked down with the revolving door of day workers coming in and out of the business. But she was already late. She'd text Caleb once she got to Chandler—he knew the code and would cover for her for sure.

The white truck parked in the driveway sparkled like it'd been newly washed, a magnetic sign with the company name, **BROADLANDS ROOFING**, attached to the driver-side door. Oh great. The front left tire—flat.

"Caleb!" Amelia shouted as though he could hear her all the way around the corner of the house and through the business entrance. "Damn it."

Tears of frustration built up in her eyes. There were only small windows in her life where she was allowed to pursue her passion, to get lost in her music. This was one of those windows, and instead of jumping through it, and even getting paid in the process, she seemed to be missing the opening entirely. Trying to push back the tears, she retrieved her phone from the bulging bag still on her shoulder and sent Caleb a brief text.

Meet me out front. Emergency. I need you. After hitting Send, she briefly wondered if she'd sounded too dramatic, but the thought disappeared with the noise of the office door. Caleb's footfalls on the loose gravel were as fast and urgent as his calls to her.

"Amelia, you okay?" he shouted from around the corner, appearing just a brief moment later. He ran to her. "What's wrong? Are you hurt?" He searched her over with his eyes like he was looking for a missing appendage. Tentatively, he grabbed her elbow as if helping to hold her up.

Amelia pulled away and shook her head. "I'm fine, but I can't say the same for the truck. What the heck did you do last night? Run over a box of nails?" She gestured at the front tire, but as she followed the broad sweep of her arm, she noticed something else. The back tire was deflated and misshapen too.

"Not again." Caleb stepped away from Amelia. "I'm so tired of this shit." He took a wide circle around the truck and then stopped beside her. The hurt that had crinkled the edges of his eyes when she pulled her arm back was gone, replaced with a stillness Amelia remembered from when they were kids—anger.

With a swift and unexpected flick of his foot, he kicked the ground, sending hundreds of tiny pebbles spraying out in an arc. They tinked against the metal body of the truck and thunked against Amelia's bare legs, leaving little stinging spots where they hit. "Steve is going to flip out. They got all four tires this time."

"What do you mean 'this time'? And who do you mean 'they'?" Amelia asked, examining the tire closest to her. It looked like a typical flat tire.

"Look," Caleb said, kneeling beside the truck and sending up a burst of dust. "Right there." He glanced up, meeting and holding her gaze for a fraction of a second longer than usual as he pointed at an inch-long puncture in the sidewall of the tire. "Someone sliced these tires. Happened last week on a work site in Traverse too. Only got one of the tires, then. Steve thought it was just some punk kids, but now . . ." He ran his fingertip over the gash again. "It can't be a coincidence."

Amelia moved in closer to Caleb and mimicked his investigation with a burgundy fingernail, her urgency to leave morphing into an urgency to figure out why someone was targeting their family roofing business. Caleb was right: Steve was going to have a fit that he not only had to buy a new set of tires but that someone had come to his home to do the deed.

"We'll have to call the police, I guess." She was used to sacrificing her music for Steve, for their business, for their kids, and, more recently, for her dad. Why should today be any different? "And they'll have to live with a string trio."

"I don't think that's a real thing." Caleb stood up and stepped toward Amelia, hand in his pocket. The knees of his jeans were covered in dirt that he didn't even try to brush off. "You should still go." He withdrew his hand from his pocket and presented her with a set of keys. "Let me take care of this with Steve. He's gonna be pissed, and you don't need to deal with that. Take my car. It's no BMW, but it should get you to your performance. I can help you get Bessie in the trunk."

Caleb had been driving the same car since senior year—a black Geo hatchback with purple and green race stripes down the side. Due to an inordinate amount of attention from his skilled mechanical hands, the car looked nearly new and ran even better. But the last time Amelia rode in it was on the day of her father's stroke.

Now, she found climbing into Caleb's car one more time not only cramped, the passenger seat covered in stacks of paper, but also nostalgic. Maybe that was the wrong word. "Nostalgic" sounded positive, like the gray seats and the sagging ceiling fabric brought back happy memories. Maybe "ominous" was more accurate; the feeling was more like a sense of foreboding.

Caleb slammed the rear hatch, making the top of Bessie's case bump against Amelia's shoulder and snapping her back into the present.

He leaned against the open car window, his forehead glistening. "If you use the speed limit as more of a guideline than a hard-and-fast rule, then you should make it to the reception only a few minutes late." He leaned across Amelia and turned the keys until the engine roared to life and then pulled his arm back quickly, a blush crawling up his cheeks.

"Thanks, Caleb. I owe you one." She put the car into drive. "Let me know what Steve says. I'll be home for dinner. Ellie should be bringing Dad by to eat. Your brother is coming too. Hey, you want to join us?"

He shrugged, stood up, and took a step back from the car. "I'll see how furious Steve is first." He rubbed the top of his head, this time a small smile crinkling up one side of his face.

"Okay, just let me know so I can grab an extra steak, all right?"

"Uh, okay." Caleb put his hands into his pockets and took another step back. "You gotta go, M. You're gonna be late."

"Oh crap. Yeah." Amelia glanced at her phone, pretending not to notice that Caleb had fallen back into using her childhood nickname. "Hope to see you tonight."

She waved and pressed on the gas pedal. As the late-morning sun hit her through the windshield, she wished that she had just been grown-up enough to keep track of her keys. Then she'd be driving her own car, where she had a very useful pair of dark-rimmed sunglasses inside the middle console. Paused at the end of the driveway, she flicked down the sun visor, making an avalanche of papers pour down into her lap.

"Shoot," Amelia muttered, quickly shuffling all the papers into a pile. But one caught her eye. It wasn't just a loose piece of paper—it was a picture. Actually, a series of pictures. She'd seen them before many, many years ago.

The edges were worn and yellowed, but the image took her back fifteen years to when the fair came to town.

In the first of four photo booth pictures, teenage Caleb, with a full head of hair and twenty pounds heavier, had his arm around teenage Amelia. They were both smiling conspiratorially, like they knew a secret the photo booth did not. In picture two, Caleb was kissing Amelia's cheek, laughing. In the next photo, Amelia had turned her head, melding their lips together, in a half kiss, half laugh. The last photo was of Caleb alone in the booth, holding on to Amelia's hand as she dashed out as if the kiss had been part of a ding-dong-ditch. He was smiling but looked confused.

Amelia flipped the picture over. Written in her loopy, teenage-girl handwriting was a short message: *Love you forever and ever. M.*

The photo had been taken a week before Caleb broke up with her without explanation, a week before he began his transformation into a different person whom she never actually came to understand again.

Well, she didn't have time to figure him out today. Amelia quickly collected the papers and shoved them back into place. She'd just have to deal with squinting.

CHAPTER 3

ELLIE

Tuesday, May 10
9:58 a.m.

The first raindrop hit the rig's windshield as Chet sped out of the Piggly Wiggly parking lot. Soon the glass was covered in moisture, the drops blending together on impact into a thin film.

"Chet, turn on the wipers," Ellie ordered. What she really wanted to say was *Drive faster*, but he was already going over eighty miles per hour down Highway 12, siren blaring. When he didn't respond immediately, she reached across the cab and flicked on the wipers herself. He didn't flinch, and Ellie leaned forward in her seat, her heels pumping up and down and her mind trying not to run through the ever-growing list of maybes compiling in her mind. Chet followed the map on the screen that drew a line directly to her sister's driveway.

Ellie flipped through the contacts on her phone and pressed the Call button . . . again. It went straight to voice mail.

"Amelia, please call me. Please. I'm almost to your house. Are you okay? Dad? The kids? Call. Me. *Please*." She hung up after leaving the third message in the past five minutes. She'd tried the home phone, but it was off the hook and no one was picking up at the office. Steve's phone also went right to voice mail, and for a moment Ellie was starting to wonder if she was in some twilight zone where she was the only person who ever answered her phone.

"Still nothing?" Chet grunted, taking a sharp turn onto Exit 78 to Broadlands. Less than four miles now.

"Nothing." Ellie tapped over to texting and typed hurriedly.

Got a call from dispatch. Heading to your house. Worried about you and Dad. CALL ME. NOW!

Chet turned onto Lark Lane right as Ellie hit Send. No police cars, no sirens other than the ones blaring from their own speakers. Maybe it was a misunderstanding after all.

Chet slowed as they approached the end of Amelia's gravel driveway, stopping just short of the entrance. Ellie's heart raced along with the wail of the siren until he shut it off. The police were coming. Protocol meant that the paramedic team should be at *least* three blocks down the street until Chet got the all clear. Ellie was prepared to fight with her partner about breaking the rules, but it looked like he wasn't exactly planning on following them either.

"We should wait in the rig," he said, leaving the keys in the ignition and the lights flashing.

"I'm not waiting," Ellie said, and yanked on her blue safety gloves, making sure her protective eyewear was pushed up on her nose.

"Would you slow down and let me finish? We *should* wait in the rig, *but* if Chief Brown and your sister are in that house, no way I'm staying put." He'd put his gloves on as he spoke and opened his door as if inviting Ellie to do the same. She hopped out of the passenger side of the rig and rushed to the side door of the ambulance, where Chet was already unloading their kits.

"Chet, I could kiss you."

"Your daddy risked his life for me dozens of times through the years. What kind of man would I be if I didn't at least try to help him and his girls?"

She hefted up one of the kits that she'd spent an hour checking and rechecking that morning. Ellie didn't have a lot of details about this situation. She didn't know if there was even an emergency inside Amelia's house or if it was just a misunderstanding. She didn't know if it was true that there had been gunshots. And, as much as it devastated her to admit, if there were guns involved, sometimes EMTs couldn't do much to help.

But she'd learned in her short time as a paramedic that even though there were always unknowns, her preparation was the one thing she could be sure of. And today she had to find a way to turn her "sister brain" off and turn her "medic brain" on.

"We'd better get in there if you wanna beat the cops," Chet said, handing Ellie a second bag, this one with a hard cover. She pulled the strap over her left shoulder, and Chet threw one over his head so the strap rested across his chest.

"Let's go." Ellie brushed past Chet, leading the way over the curb, into the wet grass, not sure what she was going to find inside and not sure she wanted to find out. As soon as her feet hit the moist gravel, she hurried to a gallop, the small stones on the driveway making scratching noises under her boots and the rain hitting her face. Then she heard it. Crying, loud sobbing, swearing. The gallop turned to a sprint, and Chet gimped along behind her, slowed by the injury that had forced him off a fire truck in the first place.

"Go! Go!" He waved her forward, and Ellie didn't look back. As she turned the corner where the driveway bent, the shouting got louder, and she found a man lying prone on the driveway. He was wearing a white dress shirt nearly drenched with rainwater, half-tucked into a pair of khakis. And there was blood. Lots of it flowing from his shoulder and spreading down his sleeve. Was this the gunshot wound? The patient was moving, rolling slightly from side to side, a phone lying on the ground beside him.

"Sir, sir, you need to stay still." The man stopped rolling on the ground and then picked up his head, and Ellie was stunned. "Steve." Amelia's husband—who also happened to be one of Ellie's closest friends. "Oh my God, Steve."

The six-foot-two former firefighter was lying covered in blood and writhing on the driveway. Steve's face was coated in a pale mud, wet trails cutting through the coat of gray. More blood had soaked through the front of his shirt and dripped down his sleeve. Even with just a preliminary check, she saw there was clearly a hole in his shirt. A bullet hole. God, no . . . It *was* true. Steve started to turn onto his back when Ellie knelt down next to him and dropped her bags.

"Hey. Stop. Let's stay here for a second." She put her face close to his, assessing his breathing and hoping he didn't notice how hard she was trying to keep her voice steady. He'd been screaming just fine, no wheezing, no blood from his mouth. Airway seemed okay, but who knew what awaited them on the other side of his body. "Hey." Ellie spoke loudly and tried to get inside Steve's line of vision. "Can you tell me what happened?"

As Ellie pulled out pieces of gauze from her kit and pressed them against the hole in Steve's shoulder, he put his face into the gravel again. He was crying. Panic pounded at the back of her mind, only kept at bay by pretending the man she was working on wasn't the man who tugged her ponytail every time she beat him at cards or always picked up on the first ring when she called for advice. No, this was a random patient—someone else's brother-in-law, someone else's friend, someone else's cheerleader.

Chet approached, set down his kit, and lowered himself to his knees. "What's going on?"

"Gunshot wound, left shoulder. Airway clear," she mumbled, keeping it cool, professional. "Steve, what happened to your shoulder?"

Steve took in a shaky breath and then another, swallowing a few times like he was holding back vomit.

"Two men came into the house. They wanted money. They wanted me to open the safe. I started to, but then Amelia brought in coffee, not knowing what was going on . . . and then . . ."

"Then what?" Ellie asked, hands frozen in midair. Chet, reading his partner's emotional state, took over, adding another piece of gauze over Ellie's.

"I was getting the money from the safe, and then I heard the shots. At first I thought the men shot each other because one ran out the office door but then . . . then . . ." He hesitated as if he could see the picture every time he blinked. "I looked over the counter." Steve lifted his tearstained face again, eyes blurry with moisture. "He shot her. He shot Amelia."

CHAPTER 4

AMELIA

Monday, April 4
Five weeks earlier

Amelia tossed another steak packaged in Styrofoam and Saran Wrap onto the counter. It was going to be an interesting night. Caleb texted about an hour after Amelia's gig started and let her know that, one, he'd be staying for dinner; two, Steve was mad but not crazy mad; three, the police had already been by and filed a report; and four, the insurance company would be coming out tomorrow so Steve could file a claim. Well, that took a few worries off her mind.

The insurance money would help pay for the tires, the police would find who did it, and Caleb would give his brother, Collin, someone to talk to, since Dad wasn't exactly conversational and Steve wasn't the biggest Collin fan in the world. Amelia had already threatened Steve with no dessert if he didn't play nice, but he had always been overprotective of Ellie and, during Amelia and Steve's ten-year marriage, he hadn't taken to any of her boyfriends, starting with Trey Martin from her eighth-grade health class.

"Hey, hon." Steve walked through the office door, still wearing his button-up work shirt with an embroidered house above the breast pocket.

They'd been married ten years, but Amelia always felt a little jolt in her stomach when she saw her husband after being apart. He was still as handsome as the day they met twelve years ago.

Amelia had insisted she'd never marry a firefighter. She saw her mom live with the fear of a firefighter's wife and how the job wore on her father emotionally and physically.

She'd walked into her dad's firehouse countless times through her life. There was a legend that she'd taken her first steps across those cool tile floors and into her father's arms. But when she visited her dad at work after freshman year of college and the hunky twenty-three-year-old firefighter smiled at her in a whole new and exciting way, she knew Steve Saxton would either break her heart or steal it. Later it seemed to make sense that she'd find her husband there; everything else she'd ever loved had been a part of that place.

"Hey!" Amelia wiped her hands on a paper towel and then met Steve at the table. She perched up on her tiptoes to give him a brief kiss. The lines on his forehead worried her. Signs like that used to be subtle, but after years of experience, she'd learned the road map to Steve's displeasure pretty early. She hadn't considered that even when Steve retired from firefighting, she would still worry about him. Every day. She wrapped her arms around his waist, hoping it would calm him or at least distract him. "You get things figured out with the police?"

Steve sighed, put his arms around Amelia's shoulders, and pulled her in for a hug. "Yeah, Jackson says that there's not much they can do besides file a report and maybe send someone around to drive by the house now and then. He thinks I should put up cameras. It's at least a thousand bucks, but there's a guy in Randall who can do it pretty cheap."

More money. Steve didn't talk about the business with Amelia very often, but she could always tell when times were tight. He'd get quiet, snap at the girls if they made too much noise, and the house would turn into a mausoleum where the first question everyone asked before doing anything was, "Wait—is Daddy home?"

"Hey, whatever you need. I got paid a little something today. We can put it into a camera fund." She nuzzled her face against his chest, the buttons on his shirt rubbing against her cheek.

Steve dropped his arms and backed up, shaking his head. "You probably already spent that much on the gas getting there and back." He put his hands in his pockets like he used to after a bad shift when he had a lot he needed to talk about but couldn't bring himself to tell her.

When he'd been a firefighter, she got it. Home was home, work was work, and home meant being away from the things he had to deal with when he went into fires, or worse, what was left over when they were put out. Now that work and home were the same thing, if things were bad, she wanted to know, wanted to help. But pushing Steve to talk never got her anywhere. It was better just to let it go.

"Yeah, probably. Though I had to use Caleb's car today, and you know he won't let me pay him back for gas." Amelia turned back to the counter and sorted through her supplies. "After you get changed, can you light the grill?"

Steve's steps were heavy, and Amelia couldn't tell if he was heading toward her or toward the stairs, so she jumped a little when he ended up by her side. Her head barely reached his shoulder, and she always had a silent urge to rest her head there.

"Caleb's car? Why did you take that piece of shit?" He snagged a washed green bean out of the bowl on the counter, and Amelia playfully batted him away.

"I couldn't find my keys," she muttered, wishing she didn't have to admit her mistake to Steve.

He snorted. "Again?"

Amelia sighed and rolled her eyes, using the small paring knife on the counter to pierce the plastic wrap covering the steak. "Yes, again."

"M, you'd lose your head if it wasn't screwed on." He slid his hand under her hair and rubbed the base of her neck. She shivered and leaned into his touch.

"I know. I know."

"I'm worried about you," Steve said, but the judgment she thought she heard in his tone was erased when he kissed her temple and then worked his fingers up to the base of her skull. Amelia put the knife down and closed her eyes. "You seem distracted lately. I think taking care of your dad is wearing on you. Maybe . . ." Steve hesitated. "Maybe we need to think about a home."

Her eyes snapped open. Not this conversation again. She picked up the knife and freed the last three steaks from their packages, Steve's touch now irritating rather than relaxing.

"Ellie dropped out of med school to come take care of Dad, and I can't take care of him one or two days a week so she can work her shift at the station? Plus, we'd have to sell Dad's house to pay for it." The house where she and Ellie grew up, where all the memories of her mom lived, where she'd always imagined bringing her kids for Thanksgivings and Christmases. If it weren't for her father and that house in Broadlands, Ellie would never step foot in this town again for anything beyond a marriage, funeral, or national holiday. Amelia couldn't really blame her sister for her disdain for the little town. Ellie was an adventurer, an explorer. It wasn't that she didn't love her family; it was just that they lived *here*, or at least that was what Amelia had told herself over and over again.

"You guys are far too attached to that place." Steve dropped his hand and backed away. "All I know is that we can't go on like this. The house is a mess all the time, you're running around half-blind with exhaustion, and now you've lost a set of keys? You keep saying life will get back to normal soon, but when?"

The counter in front of Amelia was covered in half-cut-up veggies, a plate of raw meat ready for seasoning, potatoes wrapped for baking, and a cake cooling on the counter. It looked like a disaster, but it wasn't—it was the makings of a meal. It was a meal that would not only feed and sustain her family but also bring them some joy, comfort, and time together. To Steve it looked like a mess. To Amelia it looked like pieces to a puzzle.

"I don't know, but let's give it more than a few months, okay?" Amelia dusted some salt and pepper over the sirloin. "I can't give up on my dad that easily. And you know Ellie. There's no way she'd go for putting Dad in a place."

Steve took another step back and sighed. He knew Ellie almost as well as Amelia did. She'd do anything for their father and fight anyone standing in her way. He also wasn't as good at convincing Ellie to change her mind as he was at swaying Amelia.

"Yeah, I know." He pushed one of the kitchen chairs into the table and rearranged a stack of school papers that'd been collecting there for the past week. He spread his hand across the pile and then stretched his neck from one side to the other like his collar was too tight. "There needs to be an endgame—that's all I'm saying. This can't be our new life now. We've got enough going on . . ."

Steve trailed off, and Amelia picked up where he stopped, cutting the last of the peppers for the salad. "I know. You think I don't know that? I'm the one dealing with this day in and day out . . ."

"Amelia," Steve cut in. His voice was strange. She couldn't tell if it was more of the irritation she'd gotten used to hearing in nearly every conversation they shared, or if his tone was mixed with something else. Concern, maybe? Fear? Whatever it was, it sent a chill down her spine, and she spun around on her stubby black heels.

"What? What's wrong?"

Steve stood frozen by the key rack on the wall. Hanging there were his keys, the ones Caleb had been holding earlier with the keys to the truck, plus another set for the storage shed and the padlock on the garage. The final hook held a key chain with pictures of Kate and Cora, the plastic surrounding it cracked at the corners. A rectangular library card and a value-points card from the local gas station were sandwiched between three keys—one for Amelia's house, one for her father's house, and one for Amelia's car.

"My keys!" she gasped, and rushed across the kitchen. Her first instinct was to laugh at her mistake. How could she have missed them? She must've been in such a state that morning that she just didn't notice when she did a quick scan of the rack.

Then she saw Steve's face. For a moment, it was the face of a stranger, someone who was trying to figure out the person standing in front of him instead of the woman he'd been married to for ten years. Her smile dropped.

"I swear I checked here." She ran through her memory, but with the busted tires and her mad dash to Chandler, the details were hazy. Steve nodded, tight-lipped like he was trying to hold something back, and then his shoulders dropped and his forehead softened.

"I'm sure you did." He kissed Amelia's forehead and gave her another squeeze, the warm feeling in her midsection back again. "I'll go get changed and get the grill ready. You want the girls to set the table?"

"Yeah, Ellie texted a minute ago. She and Dad should be here soon." Amelia had been furious at her little sister when she put her schooling on hold to move back in with Dad, but at moments like this, when she felt alone in her own house, when the weight of life was so heavy on her shoulders that she was sure she couldn't take another step, she knew she couldn't have made it through the past few months without her.

Amelia wondered what the far-off look in Steve's eye meant. She had a feeling that he wanted to talk to Ellie about their dad when she arrived, about this "long-term solution" he spoke of. He and Ellie had always had a good relationship, more like big brother/little sister than brother-in-law/sister-in-law, and Ellie looked up to him. If anyone could convince her, it'd be Steve. But it worked the other way too. Steve was wrapped around Ellie's little finger. If anyone could get Steve to back off, it'd be Ellie.

"Go. Change." Amelia shoved him toward the back stairs that led up to the bedrooms. "And let's have some fun tonight, okay?"

"Fun? I'm the life of the party, baby." He winked and gave her a little smack on the rear before finally heading upstairs.

"Oh believe me, I know," she shouted after him. It was hard for her to stay mad at Steve. Maybe that was why he "won" nearly every argument. He'd stolen her heart in that firehouse twelve years ago, and she still didn't want it back.

CHAPTER 5

ELLIE

Tuesday, May 10
10:17 a.m.

Shot. Someone shot Amelia.

"What about the girls? Where are the girls?" Ellie asked, her throat nearly forced shut by the thought of what might be inside. Steve's eyes rolled back in his head, and Chet pushed Ellie out of the way. But she wasn't giving up. She grabbed Steve's bloodied shoulder and shook him till his eyes focused forward. "The girls, Steve. Are they inside too?"

"No," he managed to mutter, fading fast. "School . . . at school . . ."

Ellie released Steve and ran up the gravel drive, shouting behind her. "Where is Amelia? Where?" The second time it came out as a scream. Chet leaned over Steve's barely moving lips, gloved hand still pressing on his shoulder.

"The office!" Chet called out, shouting over the rain, rocking back onto his heels. "He said she's in the office. Wait!" he yelled. "You can't go in. The shooter could still be there."

"I don't give a damn," Ellie spat, water spraying off her lips, and sprinted up the cement steps to the gaping front door before Chet could stop her.

As she entered the misty dimness inside the house, the trauma and airway kits thumped against her side with every step. The room was dim, the curtains closed and the storm rolling through made it look like twilight in the silent house. Ellie flicked the light by the front door. Nothing happened. She tried again—nothing. No power.

She ripped open the pocket on her cargo pants and pulled out the small black Maglite she used to check eyes for proper dilation. As her eyes adjusted, Ellie followed the beam of light around the gray room, taking in the familiar surroundings while searching for anything out of place.

The room was tidier than usual, the dark leather couches in their customary U formation. The coffee table in the middle was free of any clutter. As far as she could tell, Amelia was nowhere in sight. She swept the beam of light around one more time but couldn't find anything in the grayness.

"Clear," she whispered, the pounding in her ears slowing a fraction. To the right were the front stairs that led up to the bedrooms. To the left was the dining room, its swinging doors leading to the kitchen, the guest bathroom, and the side entrance to Steve's company. They'd be clear too. They had to be. Maybe Steve heard wrong. Maybe it was a minor injury. Maybe Amelia was hiding somewhere and was too afraid to come out. Maybe . . .

Then she saw it, and the pounding in her ears started up again. Blood—a row of bloody footprints cutting through the carpet of the dining room. They skirted the table, a deep, nearly black crimson.

The prints lightened as they headed toward the front door, turning red and then pink and then almost disappearing. She looked closer— large shoes, large feet. The prints were not Amelia's but more likely Steve's from when he was shot and tried to escape.

But the blood—there was so much. What if it wasn't Steve's? What if it was Amelia's? What if her sister, the woman who'd taught her how to put on lipstick, who taught her how to prank-call boys she had a crush on, who was supposed to be the matron of honor at her wedding, was lying somewhere in this house, bleeding?

If Ellie turned away now because of fear and her sister died, she'd never forgive herself. She had to go forward, had to go through the swinging door to the kitchen and follow the footprints until she found their source.

In a nearly inaudible whisper, she ran through what she'd need to treat Amelia's gunshot.

"Packing gauze, IV to start a line, non-rebreather mask, twelve-gage needle decompressor just in case . . . in case . . ."

Her steps went from clacking on the tile floor to being muffled by the front room's thick carpet.

When she reached the door to the kitchen, it opened with the gentle pressure of her gloved fingers. Ellie tried to flick on the overhead light, but the kitchen remained dim. Her breathing came faster, and she had to swallow three or four times before turning her flashlight toward the kitchen floor.

The trail of red footprints snaked across the tile floor and disappeared behind the door to the Broadlands Roofing office.

In the storm-aided murkiness, she couldn't make out anything about the table beyond the streaks of red skirting it, one large swoop of blood on the tile where it looked like someone had slipped. Ellie stepped through the gore carefully, grateful for the rubber tread on her work boots.

She'd worked a lot of scenes when she lived in Champaign—lots of parties gone bad and car accidents with people who made the tragic mistake of not putting on their seat belts. She'd seen blood, but the first step as a paramedic was to find out where it was coming from. If you couldn't find the source, you couldn't stop it. She had to find the source and was terrified to find it at the same time.

Slinking past the table, chairs, and footsteps, Ellie reached the door.

The dead bolt wasn't even locked. Ellie pushed on the door gently, but it didn't budge. Then she pushed it again, harder this time. Something heavy was behind the door, heavy and unresponsive. It was either Amelia or . . . or the man who Steve said had shot her.

Shot. Amelia is shot. Ellie squeezed her eyes shut, trying to refocus and gather her strength.

With one hard shove, the door budged half an inch. Ellie flinched, hoping it was a piece of furniture but afraid she was ramming the door into her injured sister. With another shove and then another, an opening developed. She could get through, but her packs wouldn't fit. Out of breath and the seconds ticking away, she placed them in the clear spot in the kitchen, praying she wasn't destroying some vital piece of evidence, and reassessed the opening in the door.

There was no time for more finagling. Her breath was coming in rapid bursts and was infernally loud, echoing around the dark, silent kitchen. She took a breath and then held it, then another, sweat starting to stream down her face and neck.

Ellie sucked in her stomach and stuck one arm and shoulder through the crack. If anything violent was going to happen, she would rather lose her arm than stick her head through the door and be left completely vulnerable.

She held it there, shaking so hard, her elbow kept bumping against the door, making a loud thumping sound. *One, two, three, four, five, six . . .* No shots, and no one shoved the door shut.

The fit was tight. She turned her head to the side, ponytail toward the opening, cheek pressed hard against the cool metal door. With one last shove, Ellie slipped through, her paramedic's badge catching and ripping audibly as she stumbled out and into the office of Broadlands Roofing.

It was brighter in there, a splash of sun peeking in from the sloppily closed vertical blinds, and Ellie wondered if the rain had stopped. But the sun didn't make it easier to see. No. The room was filled with smoke and a sulfur smell. There was another smell too, one she was very familiar with. It was the tangy, metallic scent of blood.

As the scene came into focus, filtering through the smoke and sun, the world went still. There was no more pain in her shoulders from carrying the bags, the place on her cheek that would surely be a bruise was numb, and the ripped shirt didn't even register in her mind. All she could see, the only thing that she could even acknowledge, was a crumpled human form on the floor to her right—one leg half-bent, half-twisted, arm strewn across the face, tangled in a mess of dark brown hair, a once-yellow blouse soaked through with blood. She didn't have to get a closer look; she didn't have to see the face to know.

Lying there in a pool of blood was her sister, Amelia.

CHAPTER 6

AMELIA

Monday, April 4
Five weeks earlier

By the time Steve changed and lit the grill, it was nearly six and Amelia had most of the food on the table. Ellie, Collin, and their dad would be there soon. As much as she loved both her sister and her father, Amelia always got a pit in her stomach when she knew they were coming for dinner. Especially when other guests would be there.

Caleb was no stranger to the Brown/Saxton family, and his brother, Collin, had been around nearly as long, but still—no one could know how difficult caring for Richard Brown had become unless they lived with his condition day after day. Even Collin, the future doctor, and Caleb, the ever-present employee, had no idea.

Today they'd be using paper plates, since all the dinner plates sat in a day-old pile in the sink. Amelia prayed that the reinforced plastic would hold up to steak, salad, and corn on the cob.

"Cora, Kate!" Amelia called her girls. At ages ten and six, they were still willing helpers, still finding setting the table a new reason to play pretend rather than a chore. As she counted out eight off-white plates from the stack on the counter, a rush of footsteps spilled down the stairs.

"No fair, you started early!" Kate yelled, out of breath.

"Early? Mom called us and I went. Totally fair!" Cora shouted back between steps.

"Girls! Stop fighting," Amelia called out in a singsong voice to the girls, who jumped onto the landing in near unison. "There are plenty of plates for everyone."

"I totally won," Cora whispered to her sister before sauntering over to the counter.

"Cora," Amelia chastised in her most mom-like voice, "you are the big sister. Be kind to Kate. She's your best friend."

"I'm not her best friend. No way. Never," Kate said, her wild brown hair sticking to the corners of her mouth. Kate was pretty much a mini-version of Ellie, and as a result Amelia always felt a tiny bit of a twinge when she looked at her. Cora's hair and coloring were much lighter than Kate's, like Steve's mother, and she was almost an inch shorter than her little sister. Sometimes the girls didn't even look like they were related, more like two friends out on a playdate. Amelia couldn't believe the number of times she'd been asked if she was babysitting when Cora was a toddler.

"Girls, come here." Amelia set down the plates on the counter and put a hand on a shoulder of each girl. "Cora, Kate, I want to show you something. See this?" She fingered the delicate gold chain she never removed from her throat. Hanging off the end was a tilted *M*, also in gold. "Your grandma gave this to me when your auntie Ellie was born. She said that it meant I was a big sister now and I'd never have to be alone again."

"I know, Mommy, I know," Cora mumbled, reaching out to touch the miniature letter. "*M* for mommy."

Amelia laughed. "No, baby, *M* for Amelia. It was your grandma's nickname for me. You know Daddy sometimes calls me that. Auntie

Ellie has an *L*." Amelia rubbed the smooth letter between her thumb and forefinger before dropping it and pulling Cora in for a hug and a quick kiss on the top of her frizzy hair. "It's silly, right? But it still means the same thing. That's why I got you girls your special necklaces." She got very quiet and leaned in to her daughters. "Sisters are forever. Even after an epic stair battle. But now"—she glanced between the girls, looking deep into one set of blue and one set of brown eyes—"it's time to make things right."

The girls pressed their foreheads together and whispered, "I'm sorry." Kate's bottom lip quavered like she was about to cry. That would never do. A meltdown from Kate usually meant the loss of at least twenty minutes.

"Hey, Kate, it's okay. Sisters also forgive each other, *right*, Cora?"

"Right, Mom." Cora played along like a pro. "Maybe we should switch necklaces, Kate. We would have silly letters like Mom and Aunt Ellie."

"No!" Kate's tears disappeared, and she hopped back, her lop-sided skirt wrapping around her legs and tangling at her knees. Amelia reached out to steady her wobbly six-year-old.

"Whoa, careful there."

"Cora can't have my necklace," she said, covering the swinging pendant with her hand defensively. Amelia resisted the urge to roll her eyes. Kate was the worst at taking a joke.

"I don't want your stupid *K*," Cora added, more an adult than a nine-year-old was meant to be. She put out her hand expectantly. "Can I just set the table already?"

"Mom, Cora just called me stupid."

"I called your *necklace* stupid."

"Same thing."

Amelia opened her mouth to interrupt, when Steve cut in from the stairs.

"Girls." His voice was deep and calm, the way he probably spoke to a frantic homeowner when he arrived at the scene of a fire. The girls' eyes went wide. They never seemed to know if they were getting happy, loving Dad or grouchy, stressed-out Dad. It always took a few minutes to figure out which one had shown up that day. "Get the plates and utensils, and set the table, please." He pointed to the dining room, and Amelia passed the supplies to them silently.

As Cora went to open the swinging doors into the dining room, Steve added, "And no more fighting. You hear me? Your mom has enough to deal with. She doesn't need you two mouthing off. Okay?" There was a stern lilt to his voice at the last minute, and Amelia could see both of the girls stand a little taller.

"Yes, Dad," they said in unison like they'd practiced it, and then scooted out to the front room, arms loaded with supplies.

"I had that," Amelia protested.

"Those girls walk all over you sometimes." Steve glanced around the kitchen like he was searching for a needle in a haystack. "So, the potatoes ready to go on the grill?"

Amelia rushed over to the counter and hastily cleared off a few stray potato and carrot peels into her hand and tossed them in the trash. "Here, I just finished putting them into the foil. When everyone gets here, I'll bring you the steaks."

As if on cue, the doorbell rang.

"I'll get that." Amelia dropped the aluminum foil pouch filled with veggies into Steve's hands and then wiped her own on the dingy apron wrapped around her midsection. Just as her foot hit the tile by the front door, there was a quiet, hesitant tap—Caleb. Amelia swung the door open and held back a self-satisfied smile.

Caleb, hands shoved in the pockets of a wrinkly pair of khakis, stood on the other side, glancing over his shoulder at the van pulling up the driveway.

"Hey, Caleb. Glad you could make it tonight."

"Thanks for the invite." He hesitated like he was searching for a line in the school play. "I put up the ramp . . . for Ellie and Chief Brown. I hope that's okay."

"Oh yeah." She peeked around behind him at the black and silver ramp that fit over Amelia's front steps. She'd given in and ordered it after breaking her big toe in an attempt to get her father's wheelchair into the house on her own.

"You are just the lifesaver today, aren't you?" She hated the way she talked to him lately, like he was a child and she was his teacher. It was strange being the boss's wife, given their history together. They rarely had real conversations anymore, not like when they were younger and would spend hours on the Sangamon Bridge, tossing sticks into the water and talking about all their hopes and dreams until the sun set over the river. Sometimes Amelia wondered if she'd imagined that Caleb, made him up like a fictional character in a story.

But then she remembered how he was the only one around when the call came in from the firehouse about her dad. When she hung up the kitchen phone, the white push-button that was probably as old as the house, reality hit. Her father, who'd always been the one saving everyone else, who ran into burning buildings, was now the one who needed to be rescued.

She'd held the paper with the information Billy from the station had given her: what hospital her dad was taken to, whom to ask for, who was driving the ambulance. What she didn't have written on that notebook-paper scrap was how she was going to tell her sister that her hero had fallen. That he could die. That they could be orphans. That their lives were permanently changed in this one moment.

She'd taken no more than two steps and then collapsed onto the kitchen floor. Caleb must've heard her fall, because he was in the room seconds later. Amelia couldn't explain. It was too much to say the words out loud, so she handed him the crumpled note.

Without a word, he walked out of the room, coming back moments later with keys and Amelia's jacket. Arm around her waist, he half carried, half guided her to his car and drove her to the hospital one town over in Frampton. They didn't speak the whole way. He parked the car and took her into the hospital, but he didn't stay. Somehow his silence spoke more clearly than any small talk they'd engaged in recently.

"I'm just glad it got you where you needed to go." He shrugged, his shoulders enveloped by his ill-fitting polo. Amelia pushed the door open wide and pointed to the front room.

"Well." She paused, not sure what to say next. "Come on in and grab something to drink." Caleb gave a half smile and shuffled through the door. "There's beer in the fridge and soda in a cooler on the back porch. Steve's out there cooking on the grill if you want to join him."

Caleb nodded and headed toward the table. As Amelia stepped out the front door to greet Ellie, she could hear the girls shout their hellos to "Uncle Caleb."

Ellie already had their father lowered down from the otherwise normal-looking dark blue minivan to the gravel drive by a motorized elevator. Collin was with her as soon as the platform stopped moving, unhooking all the straps that'd kept Chief Brown immobilized. Both with quick hands and medical minds, he and Ellie worked efficiently and compassionately as a team.

Ellie waved at Amelia from the driver-side of the van as she pushed the button inside that closed up the elevator. The van cost more than Amelia and Ellie made in a year combined. The payments on it took up nearly all of their father's pension every month, but that van provided a safe, convenient ride for Ellie and Amelia when they were caring for their father.

Amelia wasn't sure if she'd ever figure out how to make this all up to Ellie—dropping out of med school indefinitely, coming back to the one town she'd been running from since she saw her first skyscraper on MTV. But when she saw her with Collin, tall, strong, intelligent Collin,

Amelia knew that there were plenty of good things lying ahead for her sister, and some of them were even native to Broadlands.

"Hey, M!" Ellie called out as she slammed the driver-side door and walked around to meet Collin by her father's wheelchair. Her dad sat half-slumped in his wheelchair, dressed in dark pants and a button-up shirt, a knitted blanket tossed over his legs.

It wasn't that he couldn't walk, but the physical therapy was slow and he tired easily. Stairs in particular were difficult, and so to spare him the embarrassment and frustration and his following outburst from both, Amelia and Ellie preferred the use of a wheelchair in public.

He didn't look up at first, just stared at the tattered notebook in his hands, shaking and mumbling to himself. The stroke had many negative effects on her father, several physical, like the difficulty walking and the slur in his speech, but the biggest blow was mental. The stroke had caused vascular dementia in her previously bright and active father. Now he was a confused, frail old man who lived more in the past than the present and didn't know the difference between a book and a shoe.

So today, if it was a good day, he'd be able to force out a few phrases and swallow some corn and potatoes. If it was a bad one, he'd grow frustrated at one of the simple tasks they were trying to reteach him, he'd refuse dinner, end up throwing a fit, and need to take one of his special pills to calm him down.

During the longer stretches when Ellie was off from the firehouse and Amelia was busy with the kids, sometimes she forgot the reality of her father's situation. He'd always been a heroic figure in her life, his white hair and mustache matching his white chief's shirt perfectly. She'd always thought he looked more like an action figure than a firefighter. But even though he looked so dignified in his dress uniform, her favorite memories of her father were of him wearing an old firehouse tee shirt and tinkering on a project in the garage, mumbling to himself while combing his mustache with his fingertips. She never quite knew what he was working on, but it always had him engrossed.

When her mother was still alive, Amelia loved to watch the way she'd float into his workspace at dinnertime and touch a small spot between his shoulder blades. Then, like she had pressed a button, he would turn and kiss her lightly; his mustache looked like it was tickling her top lip, his hands always resting lightly on her hips like too much pressure would break this fragile, beautiful thing he held in his grasp.

On the day his wife had died, Amelia's father, still shaken up from the accident and after being forced to leave his wife's broken body behind in that cold, empty hospital room, had gone straight from the car into his workroom in the garage. Amelia put six-year-old Ellie to bed alone and then spied on him from a crack in the door as he broke apart whatever it was he was creating on that workbench. Piece by piece, he ripped and threw and screamed until the room was covered in pieces of metal and wood. Then Amelia's hero cried. He cried longer and harder than she had ever known her father could cry.

When the rage had subsided and some semblance of the man she knew had returned, she quietly snuck into the room and put her small, shaking hand between her father's shoulder blades. He jumped slightly at her touch and then looked up from the table of scattered parts in front of him. She'd never forget the redness in his eyes, the evidence of pain in the trails of tears on his cheeks. She was afraid of the "broken man," afraid that she would never find the "action figure man" again.

But then he leaned forward and placed a kiss on her forehead, his mustache tickling her brow, and pulled her in for a fierce but comforting hug. From that day forward, her father wasn't her hero because he was an action figure; he was her hero because he was a man who, despite being broken, found a way to still be there for his children. He managed to wake up every morning, go to bed every night, and repeat these actions until they were a family again.

Collin pushed Chief Brown up the steep ramp, Ellie following closely behind. She carried her father's black workbag over her shoulder like a mother walking her child in to a playdate.

"Hi, Daddy." Amelia leaned over and kissed her father on his forehead and tried not to remember all the times he'd done the same to her. "I made your favorite dessert—Mom's shortcake. The girls helped."

"Um me." Chief Brown tried to speak. His head bobbed up and down, and Amelia told herself that he smiled. Ellie tried to translate like she always did.

"Yummy? Is that what you are saying, Daddy? Amelia, Daddy thinks that sounds yummy." She spoke loudly, her voice raised loud enough for the neighbors to hear. It drove Amelia a little crazy when Ellie did the whole translation thing, but there wasn't any reason to make her stop, so she just internally rolled her eyes and went with it.

Amelia readjusted her focus up about a foot. "Collin, thanks for coming. We're so happy to have you." She brushed her hand over his shoulder, and Collin gave her a broad smile.

"Wouldn't miss it for the world." His reddish-blond hair was combed to one side in a stylish swoop, his dark-rimmed glasses walking that careful line between utilitarian and stylish. Though Caleb had never had the confidence of Collin, there was something reminiscent of the Caleb from her youth in his younger brother's look.

"Dad can go over by the TV. The game is about to start," Ellie suggested, and pointed to a large flat-screen television in the corner. Collin pushed Chief Brown into the living room as Ellie pulled her sister in for a hug.

"Good day, bad day?" Amelia asked, pulling back from the embrace. Ellie shrugged with one shoulder in a way that reminded her of little Kate.

"Good day, I guess. Let's knock on wood, 'cause dinner could be interesting."

"Yeah?" Amelia tugged on her sister's long ponytail and urged her into the house. "Are you planning to announce your plans to run away with the circus?"

Ellie stopped cold and took her sister's hand. Her dark eyes were always inviting to Amelia, like there were some secrets trapped inside that she could find out if she could just look deep enough.

"Not exactly with the circus . . ." Ellie held up her left hand. A solitary diamond set in the center of a platinum band stared up at Amelia.

"What? Ellie!" She yelped loudly at first and then had to ramp down her voice when Collin raised his eyebrows knowingly at her. "When did this happen?"

"Earlier today. I'll tell you the details later. I want to surprise the girls. Caleb doesn't know either . . ." Ellie hesitated and glanced around the room before adding quietly, "Or Steve, and I know he doesn't love Collin." She mouthed the name. "So, yeah, could be an interesting night."

"Oh, Steve's a softy when it comes to you, L. He'll be ecstatic. I'm so happy for you! Have you set a date?"

"Yeah, um, after Collin's graduation next year." She swallowed hard, her smile faltering for a fraction of a second. "He is going to keep his apartment and do his rotations in Frampton."

Amelia paused, looked at her sister and then at the glittering ring on her hand. She should be happy: her sister was engaged, was going to live in the same town as her. Amelia could bring her ice cream when she was pregnant, help weed the garden in the spring, go caroling in the winter . . . They could be neighbors and sisters and friends.

But there was a problem. In all the time she'd known and loved her sister, there was only *one* place Ellie had always wanted to live.

And that was anyplace but Broadlands.

CHAPTER 7

ELLIE

Tuesday, May 10
10:36 a.m.

Amelia lay on her side, still on the floor, her dark hair partially covering her face and blood in an irregular circle around her body. Falling to her knees, Ellie took a deep breath and blew it out slowly. She couldn't be Ellie "the little sister" right now. She had to be Ellie "the paramedic." She had to turn off the voice in her head shouting that her sister might be dead and turn on the cool, practiced voice that told her what to do in this situation.

First, always first: Is the scene safe? Ellie scanned the room and jumped a little when she noticed another crumpled form on the ground. At first it looked like a pile of clothes tossed in a heap just a few feet away, but when Ellie took out her Maglite and swept it across the room and through the smoke, she could see two dark shoes sticking out from the bottom of a black pair of jeans. Shit. Steve said one of the men had run away after the shots were fired, but he didn't mention that the other one was still inside.

The beam of light started to wobble, a surge of adrenaline finally reaching her hand. Focusing the beam at the man's feet, she traced the bouncing light up his legs, torso, and finally upper body and head. That was where she saw it—the sight that would normally make a paramedic shake her head but today made her pulse lower a tick. There was a reason he wasn't moving anymore, and it wasn't because he was planning an attack. It wasn't hard to see; the man was close and facedown just an arm's reach away from Amelia's resting place. It almost blended in with the mask he was wearing, but there was a hole the size of a plum in the back of the man's head. Exit wound.

Ellie let out a shaky breath. He was dead. One of the men who'd shot Amelia was dead.

"Amelia," she choked out, then cleared her throat. "Amelia!" Ellie shouted, leaning over her sister, pretending she didn't smell her sister's favorite perfume mixed with a strong smell of blood, pretending she hadn't spent hours as a child brushing and braiding the hair she moved off Amelia's forehead. She put her face to Amelia's cheek. Shallow breathing, her sister's chest was clearly moving up and down. No. Not her sister. The *patient's* chest. She could see the *patient* trying to breathe. That was a good sign.

Ellie ran the flashlight's beam up and down Amelia's body for a blood check. She knew there'd be blood—she was already kneeling in a small pool of it—but seeing her sister's embroidered yellow blouse, her favorite clothing item that'd followed her from high school to college and then into her life as a wife and mother, saturated in it knocked the air out of her lungs. She needed to find out where all that blood was coming from. She needed her kit.

Ellie glanced to her right, so engrossed in her assessment that she'd actually forgotten dropping the cases before forcing her way through the door. Retrieving her kit from the kitchen would mean moving bleeding, injured Amelia—not exactly a best practice, but without her kit there was no way to help her. *Damn it.* The panicky little-sister voice was starting to edge back in. What if it was too late? What if Amelia slipped away while Ellie dashed into the kitchen to get her pack? What if she had to watch her sister die?

"No!" Ellie said out loud, shaking her head to refocus. There wasn't time for this. Ten minutes on the scene. One hour from injury to surgery. These were the rules she'd been trained to work by if her patients were going to live. That didn't leave any wiggle room for a full-on freak-out.

Ellie grabbed Amelia's shirt by the shoulders and dragged her to the side, careful not to flip her onto her back just yet. Now she had to retrieve the kits, find the blood, and stop the bleeding. That was as far as her to-do list could go.

Ellie pushed off the floor, when Amelia's eyes fluttered briefly. She was either waking up or having a seizure—waking up would be painful, but a seizure could be a deathblow. Faster. She needed to go faster. Nothing Ellie was doing was fast enough.

Carelessly, Ellie tossed the door open as wide as it would go without hitting Amelia and then took steady but fast steps into the kitchen. Within thirty seconds, she'd retrieved her packs, with one hanging off her sore shoulder and the other one in her hand.

Ellie grabbed at her shoulder for her radio while selecting her supplies. *If* Ellie could get the bleeding to stop, *if* she could keep her sister from crashing, *if* Chet could get through what was sure to be a circus of police and ambulances, Amelia might be able to make it to surgery at the hospital in Frampton before the one-hour window was up. *Damn it*—Amelia needed a hospital and emergency surgery, not the fumbling hands of a newbie paramedic.

Ellie talked into the receiver on her shoulder.

"Chet . . . are you there?" Silence. Ellie pressed the button again. "Chet!" she yelled, louder.

As she yanked at the receiver a third time, the cord flopped over her shoulder, bouncing against her chest. A quick check for the radio on her belt revealed an empty spot. She'd lost her radio. The electric hum of panic rushed across Ellie's arms and shoulders.

Ellie was on her own.

Find the bleeding. She had to keep moving, already regretting so many wasted minutes getting the bags and trying to contact Chet. Urgently but gently she rolled her sister onto her back and examined her bloody blouse again. Ellie let out a gasp, fear and panic pounding against the compartment she'd locked them in earlier: two holes—one by her shoulder and one in her abdomen. The one in her belly was the bleeder; she could tell that without even removing the shirt.

Her head spun and her hands shook so fiercely, she didn't know if she could continue. She squeezed her hands open and shut, open and shut, trying to force out the tremors threatening to paralyze her. *Focus, Ellie. Focus.*

Not wasting another moment, she grabbed a pair of trauma shears and cut through the thin fabric determinedly. She had to cut *around* the holes to preserve evidence, evidence that she hoped would tell the story of how and where Amelia was shot.

She started at the saturated hem of her sister's shirt and cut in a curving line, skipping past the penny-size hole by Amelia's belly button and another one just above the cup of her bra. As she shoved the drenched garment back from Amelia's shoulders, the damage became a little clearer. Holes. Red, seeping holes in her sister's skin.

Ellie put the back of her gloved hand to her mouth, pressing hard until her teeth ached. No. She couldn't let herself think about the gunshot wounds in her sister's body and what they could mean, because right now she was the only one who could help her sister—and if Ellie lost it, Amelia would die.

She snatched a neat stack of gauze. With as much control as she could muster, she wiped away the streaks of blood curling around in unidentifiable waves on her sister's midsection, chest, and sides.

When she could see more clearly, the bullet holes looked almost small, manageable. Like someone poked Amelia with a small rod or pencil. But where there were holes, there had been bullets, and bullets could kill by tearing through skin and organs and bone. Ellie tossed the drenched gauze to her side. This was going to take more than bandages.

Amelia's breathing went from shallow to struggling. Her throat strained with each pathetic breath, the golden *M* at her neck dancing with each attempt like it didn't know its owner was dying beneath it. Ellie worked mechanically, anguish tearing at her throat and begging to be free. If she let even one tear fall, she would fail.

She ripped open a large abdominal bandage and pressed it hard against the wound in Amelia's stomach and then checked to see if there was an exit wound on her back. No. Nothing. In one way it was good; exit wounds were at least twice as big as the entry, and she was already dealing with a lot of blood loss. But there was bad news too. No exit wound meant the bullet was still inside, doing who knew what kind of damage. Thankfully, the shoulder wound seemed to have gone clear through.

With one hand applying pressure and the other working fast, Ellie taped down the dressings on each injury, then placed a non-rebreather mask on her sister's face and finally grabbed the IV kit to get a line started.

Just as Ellie finished tying the tourniquet and attached the IV bag to the needle and flushed the air out, footsteps stomped up the front steps. She glanced around, remembering the motionless man on the floor for the first time since she entered the room. He was dead, right? Had to be dead.

Someone pounded on the outside office door loudly. "Police. Open up!"

"It's clear! Come in. Come quickly." Thank God. Finally, help was there. Ellie put her hands up, her blue gloves covered in blood, the IV grasped in one of them.

The door to the office flew open, and two police officers in bulletproof vests entered the room, guns drawn.

"Medic over here. Two down, one DOA," Ellie called to the officers. One of the men, the shorter of the two, leaned down and cautiously checked the masked man's pulse while the other kept his gun pointed at Ellie.

"Keep your hands up," he said in a low, firm voice. The needle in Ellie's hand was shaking. She glanced down at her sister's arm where she'd tied the tourniquet minutes earlier. The vein was ready. She needed to put the line in now.

"I . . . I'm in the middle of treating this patient." She tried to keep her voice steady, professional. She had to sound confident if she was going to convince the police officers to let her continue working. "I need to get a line started. I'm going to put the IV in now." Slowly lowering the hand holding the needle, she shifted her gaze from the officer to the arm lying in her lap. He didn't yell or shoot, so he must've believed her.

"Yup, this one's DOA," the other officer called out to his partner. The voice was familiar.

A quick check over her shoulder confirmed it. Travis Rivera was making his way across the office, checking behind desks and chairs as though someone were going to pop out and shoot them. Maybe someone *was*, but right now all Ellie could think about was getting Amelia out.

"Trav, get Chet," Ellie ordered, not even trying to be polite. She blew a strand of hair out of her eyes, but it fell right back in, this time sticking to the perspiration on her nose and cheek. "Tell him that I have a pulse but two gunshot wounds. I've started a line, but she needs to get into surgery, stat."

"Brown?" Travis asked, lowering his gun a fraction. "What the *hell* are you doing in here? Chief Plackard is going to kill you."

"Travis. Listen. Get Chet!" Ellie maneuvered the needle into the slightly bulging vein. After being tied off so long, it should've been nearly bursting. Just further evidence of how much blood Amelia had lost already. She slipped the needle out, catheter in, and shoved the sharp into the biohazard container inside her trauma kit.

"I have to check the rest of the house." Travis lifted his gun a fraction and scanned the room, distracted. "Just call Chet on your radio."

"I don't *have* my radio." Ellie put another piece of tape over the IV line coming out of Amelia's arm and then swept her eyes over her unconscious, bleeding sister. "Damn it, Travis, this is my *sister*. Get Chet!"

She hated the emotion in her voice. But it was Amelia. There was no pretending about Amelia.

Travis froze in his tracks, his black, heavy-soled shoes stopping just short of the blood arcing out around the dead man on the floor.

"Oh, Ellie," he said gently. She didn't have to look; she could hear it in his voice—he could see that her sister was almost dead, couldn't he? Ellie watched over her shoulder as Travis holstered his gun and retrieved his radio. "I'll have one of the guys put him on."

Ellie nodded, already starting to dress the less serious wound in Amelia's shoulder. When she heard confirmation come over the radio that Chet was on his way in with a stretcher, she swallowed down the sob of relief building in her throat. There would be no crying today. Today her patient would make it to the hospital, make it through surgery, would go on to have a long, stunning life full of happiness. Today was the first time since returning home that she was glad to be a member of this tiny fire department instead of off at med school. Today she was glad she lived in Broadlands.

CHAPTER 8

AMELIA

Monday, April 4
Five weeks earlier

"Well, that was interesting." Steve pulled a worn gray tee shirt over his head and let it fall over his midsection. He might not have a six-pack like he did in his firefighter days, but his stomach was still flat and firm.

"I think it was lovely." Amelia leaned back into her wall of pillows, grabbing one that sat awkwardly behind her neck, and threw it at Steve before picking up the tented book on her lap. "Collin's a nice kid. They've been dating forever, and he moved back here for her when Dad got sick. Commutes forever and ever just to be close to Ellie. And he's gonna be a doctor for goodness' sake. Give him a break."

When Ellie stood and clinked her glass with a plastic fork at dinner, Amelia knew what was coming. She watched her sister closely, monitoring all her telltale "I'm faking it" signs. But there were no stiff smiles, no nervous twists of her ponytail, and the tears gathering in her sister's eyes during the announcement seemed genuine.

Then again, maybe a piece of her was jealous. Well, the remnant of seventeen-year-old Amelia was perhaps a little jealous. Ellie was living the life Amelia thought she'd have with Caleb when they dated back in high school. Not that she imagined her life would be better with the present-day underemployed, repressed-artist version of Caleb she knew now. But back then, Caleb wasn't just her boyfriend; he was her best friend and the only person in her life who thought she could make it as a professional cellist. As a fellow artist, he knew what it meant to be passionate about your craft, and they often talked about their dreams of moving to New York and diving into that dynamic future together.

But those dreams were crushed when Caleb dumped her without explanation a week before her Juilliard audition. She canceled the audition. If she wasn't even adequate for a relationship with Caleb, how could she ever be talented enough for Juilliard?

She had loved Caleb, but the devastation was from more than failing in a teenage relationship. Losing him brought back all the pain of losing her mom. Caleb's rejection made her never want to lose anyone ever again. That was why she tried so hard with Steve, why she always wanted to please him even though she failed so often. It hurt badly enough when someone left your life because of an unexpected accident. It hurt in a whole new way when the person you loved left you because you weren't good enough.

Steve tossed his jeans into the tall white hamper by their walk-in closet and yanked off his socks one foot at a time, bringing her back to reality.

"Yeah, I know. What is with you ladies and wanting to marry a doctor?"

Amelia scoffed. "What is this, 1955? I just meant that he is smart and clearly cares about people and wants to contribute to the family."

"Yeah, I guess." Steve lifted the covers on the left side of the bed and slipped under, readjusting his head on his pillow three or four times before settling. "I wonder if this means she'll be willing to listen to some reason about Richard now."

"Steve." Amelia put her book down again, trying to measure her response so they didn't get into another fight. "This isn't just an Ellie decision. He's my dad too, and I want to help take care of him."

Steve turned onto his side, facing Amelia. His hand reached across the space between them until it rested on her forearm. "M, let's not talk about this now. It's been a long day, and I can only do one 'what to do with Dad' talk in a twelve-hour period."

"Hey, you brought it up."

Steve took his hand back and fluffed his pillow again, closing his eyes for a moment. "Yeah, I know . . . and I'm dropping it. I've got that big project in Staltsman tomorrow, and I've gotta be there at six. Hey"—his eyes popped open, head raised a little—"did you print me out that permit?"

Amelia's throat tightened. No. She'd forgotten. Again. Though Amelia wasn't an official Broadlands Roofing employee, she still helped out when she had a chance. Sometimes that meant acting as a secretary or even as an office-cleaning crew. Today she'd just ignored Steve's text when she saw it was business related. She was too busy trying to not get pulled over while speeding to her gig. Of course, she promised herself that she'd check it later, that she'd actually do something for Steve the first time he asked; she'd been forgetting his various requests so often that he'd come to distrust her follow-through on any responsibility he placed in her hands. She was unsure when she went from the teenage caregiver of a little sister and broken father to the mess she was as an adult.

When Amelia didn't answer right away, Steve shook his head like he was ashamed that he'd even hoped she'd answer in the affirmative. "I'll just do it in the morning."

"No." Amelia threw back the covers, sending her book flying across the bed. "I'll do it right now. It's only"—she checked the digital clock on the side table—"eleven forty. I don't have to get up early. You sleep. I'll find the permit."

Steve paused as though thinking through her offer and then closed his eyes again with a sniff. "Okay. It's in the Gmail account. I think I texted you the permit number today."

"Yup, I got it!" she said, almost a little too chipper as she flipped out of bed and snagged her phone off the bedside table. When her feet hit the floor, she wished she had pulled out her winter fleece pajamas instead of her summer shorts and tee shirt. April was too early to transition—the day had even been cooler than average—but all her warmer pajamas were either dirty or clean but sitting unfolded in the basement. She tried to ignore the sensation of goose bumps racing up her legs, stopping to grab her nearly threadbare sweatshirt off the back of the wing chair in the corner of the room before heading out into the dark hallway.

The house was silent and black. Her book light had kept her eyes from adjusting to the dark in her bedroom, so now the hall looked like it was bathed in ink. Every footstep sounded monstrous as she held her breath passing the girls' rooms. They'd had enough excitement for one night, planning Ellie's shower and talking about who would get to be the flower girl and who would carry the ring at the wedding. Last thing they needed was a late-night scare from a noise in the hall.

Descending the back stairs that led to the kitchen, Amelia swore the temperature dropped by ten degrees. She pulled her hands into her sleeves and let her thumbs poke out from holes on the side. She turned on the light behind the sink. A small pile of serving bowls and utensils still sat in the sink. Even after doing one full load of dishes with Ellie after dinner, there were still more waiting for her. More. Always more. That was pretty much what her life felt like right now. Everyone always wanted more. Steve, the girls, her dad, even Ellie. And now with the stroke, and the business struggling, she thought she might drown in demands. Well, too bad for them that she didn't know how much more she had to give.

She turned away from the sink and examined the steel door in front of her. Steve always locked it at night so that if someone broke into the office, they wouldn't be able to get into the main house. The single silver key hung on the key holder screwed into the wall. It rested against Amelia's set of mysteriously disappearing keys right next to it.

She unlocked the door with a familiar click and slipped into the dark office by the borrowed light from the kitchen. With less hesitation this time, Amelia illuminated the office with a click of Steve's desk lamp. The computer was about three times the size of the flat-screen computers the kids used at school. Steve found it easier and ultimately cheaper to keep the ancient pieces of machinery rather than replace them with fancy new computers and learn new software and new procedures and new . . . everything. Yeah, Steve wasn't huge on "new."

The screensaver was a series of lines and colors that chased one another around the screen in a seemingly endless game of tag. It was unusual to find a computer on after Steve had shut down the office for the night, but things had been a little mixed up that evening with the tires and the police and then having company on top of it all. A picture of Steve in his full fire gear standing in front of a blazing test house was set as the background.

Amelia clicked on the little envelope icon in the corner of the screen. She quickly scrolled through the dozen or so e-mails, checked her phone, and with just a few more clicks, the permit was printing. She listened to the whir of the printer, barely holding off a deep shiver, legs pulled up to her chest. Just as the nearly ancient printer spit out the completed document, a ding sounded on the computer.

In the screen's bottom right-hand corner, a little white-and-red text bubble floated precariously with a glowing number two hovering over it.

[Ding]

The alarm sounded again, and the number went from three to four. Who would be messaging Steve at almost—she checked the clock on the screen—midnight?

She knew she should trust her husband. She should sign him out, grab the permit from the printer, and then shut down the computer . . . but that number four was taunting her.

Before she could feel any guilt or have second thoughts, she swept the pointer across the screen to the text bubble and clicked. A chat box popped open, and four white text bubbles stared back at her.

Hey there.
What you doing up this late?
Working?

Then the last message, the only one that set off alarm bells.

I'm looking forward to meeting up tomorrow.

Amelia leaned in closer to the screen. The screen name at the top of the box read "Sue-z-Q," and the spot where there would normally be a photograph was filled with a white form with a gray background, the default avatar.

A woman. Her mind immediately jumped to all of the worst thoughts, authored by her insecurities. Maybe Sue-z-Q was a beautiful, vivacious woman. Maybe she was funnier, prettier, more adventurous than Amelia. Maybe Steve wanted to be with her more than Amelia.

With no hesitation this time, she placed the arrow over the Reply box, tried to think of how Steve would respond, and then clicked.

Working late—budget.

Her heart pounded in her ears as she wiped a hand over her face. Then, taking another breath, she added,

How about you?

The cursor blinked ten, fifteen, twenty times, and just as Amelia was sure she'd somehow given away the fact that she was a paranoid housewife pretending to be her husband, three bubbling dots blinked in the text box. Sue-z-Q was responding. She stared at those dots, trying to imagine what might pop up next, what words this woman might say that could either ease her fears or confirm them.

Working. Brad is out with his buddies. But someone's gotta bring home the bacon, right? ;)

Amelia groused at the winking smiley face. That was flirtatious. Or could it just be friendly? Amelia employed the winking smiley face with lots of people and in lots of situations. With Steve, yeah, but also with Ellie, Sandy from school, even that guy Mike who'd been in charge of setting up the function she'd played at today. She typed again, getting used to thinking like her husband.

Don't I know it!

Amelia quickly erased the exclamation point and replaced it with a period. She hit Send and then waited to see if the mystery woman would write again. When the thinking bubbles popped up, she felt almost eager.

So—Tomorrow. We still on?

A direct question. She wanted to respond with a question, maybe a thousand questions, but that'd probably give away too much. Amelia considered her options. She could give some kind of noncommittal answer and then delete the conversation. She could ask a pointed question, confront the woman who was chatting with her husband late into the night, and then wake Steve up with the conversation as evidence.

Or, she could try to get more information about the meeting, make sure she wasn't overreacting. Amelia stared at the screen for one moment longer and then typed.

I'm planning on it. What time, again?

Amelia held her breath. What was she doing? This was Steve, husband of ten years, hard worker, family man. She was letting her insecurities get the best of her. But, even though she thought it, really tried to believe it, she still waited impatiently for a reply to appear. On the edge of her seat, she rested her bare toes on the tops of the office chair wheels, her chill disappearing. Then a response popped up, and she read it anxiously.

Um, noon, by the fountain. Remember?
I'll bring the coffee, you bring the hot dogs, and we will call
it square . . . Just don't forget the hot dogs or I'll sue ;)

There was that stupid winking smiley face again. Lunch in the park in . . . April? Good things: one, public place; two, hot dogs—the least romantic of lunches ever; three, mystery woman already had a man. Bad things: one, middle-of-the-night messaging; two, winking smiley faces; three, Steve had never mentioned Sue-z-Q or the appointment.

Amelia edged the seat up closer to the screen as though she could see through it if she just looked hard enough. Her stomach was in knots, a nauseated feeling rising into her throat. She tried to calm it, push it down with logic. This woman was probably a friend. Amelia had a few male friends, a few she might even have lunch with. This was probably nothing, right? There wasn't much more probing she could do without sending off warning bells to Suze. It was time to sign off and remove all evidence of their conversation. Come to think of it . . . Amelia scrolled up to the top of the conversation, pulling down on the chat bubbles and waiting for a previous conversation to appear, but it bounced back in a double hop. No, nothing.

I'll remember. See you then.

After hitting Send, Amelia clicked on the Settings icon in the right-hand corner of the chat window and highlighted the Delete Conversation option. A warning popped up, explaining that the whole conversation would be permanently deleted if she continued. She clicked Okay, because there was no part of pretending to be Steve and chatting with one of his contacts that she was proud of. Then, she closed out the screen, logged out Steve, and shut the computer down before she could be tempted to probe any further.

Toes officially icicles, legs covered in scratchy goose bumps, she felt the shiver she'd been fighting off since leaving the warm confines of her bed finally shake through her. Steve said he was going to be in Staltsman all day tomorrow. There wasn't any fountain in Staltsman. There *was* a fountain in Broadlands Park. It'd been lying dormant all winter and would be resurrected in a matter of weeks. That had to be where Steve was meeting the mystery woman. Even if he didn't show up, even if the time and place had somehow gotten mixed up, Amelia couldn't see the harm in happening to be in that park at noon tomorrow.

Maybe Suze was a blue-haired, wrinkly ninety-year-old. Maybe she was someone from the Village office, and they were having a work lunch. Maybe . . . Amelia shook her head and wrapped her arms around her midsection. Like Ellie always said—too many maybes. As she headed back up the stairs with the permit tucked into a manila envelope in her hand, she flicked off the lights she'd turned on just half an hour earlier. Nothing had changed really, but somehow, when she slipped under the covers after placing the folder on top of Steve's dresser, Amelia couldn't bring herself to press her feet against her husband's legs for warmth.

CHAPTER 9

ELLIE

Tuesday, May 10
11:04 a.m.

Ellie ran beside her sister as they pushed her across the gravel drive. The wheels of the gurney kicked up rocks that stung Ellie's skin through her uniform. Another two ambulances had shown up from neighboring towns. The one they were hefting Amelia into was driven by Patty McDaniels and her partner, Cam Baxi. They'd work hard to save Amelia.

Ellie held the IV bag in her hands, feeling like she was doing *something* at least. She knew they weren't going to let her in the rig. No way. Amelia was too critical. Plus, when Chet showed up in the office with a stretcher and kit, he looked at her like she was the patient. He glanced at her ripped shirt, bruised cheek, the wildness she was sure lit her eyes up like a trapped animal, and then the dead man on the floor. She could see him assessing her mental state. They'd been partners for only six months, but even after a short stint, she could still predict with scary accuracy what Chet was thinking behind his fluffy eyebrows and overgrown mustache. But she didn't want him to assess her, to help *her*. She wanted him to use those years and years of experience to find a way to save Amelia.

He'd been watching her cautiously ever since as though she'd collapse into his arms as soon as Amelia was on her way to the hospital. Ellie couldn't really count that out. Collapsing felt like a very viable option right now.

Still rushing to keep up, Ellie filled Cam and Patty in on everything—the injuries, the bullet wounds, the shallow breathing, the slow pulse. She told them about what she'd done to treat each item and stabilize Amelia till they could get her out. The words came out professionally and calculated, like this was a stranger, just any other patient. She'd turned "little sister" off inside the house, but now, hearing the cold edge to her voice, she wanted those feelings back. She wanted to be the family member who sobbed after the ambulance doors shut. Who begged the paramedics to save her life. The human connection that made you, as a paramedic, work just that fraction harder.

As Patty reached up under the end of the stretcher to collapse the wheels, Ellie called out.

"Wait!" Both Cam and Patty froze in place, giving her the same look that Chet couldn't seem to get off his face. "One second." She held up a bloody, gloved finger. "Just give me one."

Patty took her hand off the latch and stepped back a fraction of an inch. Cam shifted from one foot to the other, clearly willing to be patient for a second but not much longer than that. Later, she'd be embarrassed. Later, she'd care. Right now she needed to say good-bye to her sister—just in case.

Her feet shuffled audibly through the gravel drive till she was just above Amelia's head. She kissed her forehead, that special spot that their father always claimed as his own. When Ellie's lips touched Amelia's clammy skin, the walls she'd hastily built just twenty minutes earlier collapsed in one agonizing crash. Her breath rushed out in a wave like when she'd fallen off the top of the slide in fifth grade and had felt like she'd never breathe again.

"Brown, we have to go." Cam was firm, but there was a touch of pity in his voice that would haunt her once the fuzzy blur of panic washed away. Ellie stood up reluctantly and placed the IV bag on Amelia's chest. "We'll take good care of her. I swear," he continued, and though she'd said those same encouraging words a hundred times before, she actually believed him.

As they rolled Amelia into the back of the rig, Chet walked up beside her and put his heavy, comforting arm around her shoulder. For a moment, as the red-and-white lights bounced around inside her eyes, nearly blinding her, and the sirens rang through her ears, she let herself pretend that it wasn't Chet by her side but her father and that he was going to make everything okay.

"Hey, come on. Let's check you out. Then we can follow them. Okay?"

"Check me out?" Ellie broke out of her trance and focused in on Chet's face. She shrugged his arm off from around her shoulder, wiping at her cheeks with her sleeve, determined to remove any evidence of tears before she had to face the officers and questions, the hospital, the doctors, and her father. "I'm fine. Get in the rig."

She pulled at her bloody gloves. They made a slurping sound as she ripped them off her sweaty hands. Chet took the soiled gloves and shoved them into the biohazard container inside one of the kits before adding his own and hefting it back onto his shoulder. Ellie didn't notice his heavy load, too distracted by the refreshing whiteness of her skin, like she was cleaning away the horror of what had happened so far that day.

But her hands weren't the only things covered in Amelia's blood. The front of her dark blue shirt was growing stiff with the thick crimson fluid, and two nearly black ovals were hardening on her knees. She tried to think back to when it could've gotten there. Maybe when she moved Amelia's body across the floor, or knelt by her side, or crawled around her still body to insert the IV. She wasn't positive *how* it got there; she only knew that it was unbearable to walk around wearing her sister's blood.

As Chet urged her down the curving drive toward their rig, somehow carrying all three kits and keeping her in a forward momentum, Ellie ripped the shirt off her body as though it was made of fiberglass, invisible fragments digging deeper into her skin. In just her white tank top, she balled the discarded shirt up in her hands, squeezing so hard that she hoped the fabric would just disappear.

Chet ushered her to the passenger seat. Once she settled into the familiar chair, Ellie took a deep breath. She had to phase out of "freak-out-zombie" mode fast if they were going to make it to the hospital any time soon. Chet wasn't going to let her out of his sight until he was certain she wasn't in shock.

Ellie searched her memory, trying to recall how she should be acting right now, how to look like she didn't need to be treated with kid gloves. Shifting from one side to the other, she pushed her shoulders back, legs still hanging out the open passenger-side door. When a hand touched her knee, she nearly fell off her seat. She looked up, armed with an extrabiting glare, but it wasn't Chet looking back at her. It was Travis.

"Hey, Ellie." He used her first name again. It was unnerving. She wanted the good-natured teasing back, the jokes about cops eating doughnuts and firefighters failing the police exam. "How are you doing?"

The fire department and police department crossed paths often, and Ellie had made a few friends over the past several months. There was one officer whom she always seemed to end up talking to at the end of a difficult call or who would stop by the firehouse when she was on duty, and that was Officer Rivera.

Though he seemed genuinely concerned, the part of her that just wanted to get on the road and to the hospital outweighed the polite, friendly parts she usually lived her life by.

"I'm fine! Would everyone stop asking me that? I just want to get to the hospital." Ellie leaned forward and tried to look around the back of the rig, not even caring that her face was inches from Travis's. He didn't flinch. Instead, he took in her expression silently in a way that was graver than Chet's earlier assessment.

"Chet! Let's go!" Ellie called, and then swung her legs into the cabin of the ambulance, hand on the door. "Sorry, Trav, I gotta go."

But Travis didn't move. He just stood in the way of the door, thumbs hooked into the Velcro panels of his bulletproof vest.

"I'm sorry, Ellie, but we need to talk. I need some information from you about the scene, about your sister and her husband. I know the timing sucks, but . . ." Chet slid into the driver's seat and put the key in the ignition.

"Ready?" he asked, not waiting for an answer before revving the engine. So he wasn't going to push for an assessment after all. Ellie owed a lot to Chet today, maybe even her sister's life. She nodded at Chet and then returned her attention to Travis.

"If you want to ask me questions, you are going to have to get yourself and your badge into a car and follow me to the hospital, because I'm not answering anything until then." She pulled on the handle until the door bumped Travis's shoulder. "Now, please move."

"*Brown,*" Travis said through gritted teeth, bracing his hand against the door. Something in the forceful nature of this movement reminded Ellie that he took down men with guns for a living. She tossed her soiled paramedic shirt onto the floor of the truck and put her feet on top of it. Then she wrapped the seat belt around her chest and waist. If Travis wanted to get her out of the ambulance, he'd have to drag her.

Immediately guilt tugged at her conscience. Travis was *trying* to help. He was *trying* to find out what happened inside that house. He wasn't the enemy. Ellie blinked three times, staring at the mailbox that held the tarnished gold numbers representing her sister's address. Then she looked directly into Travis's dark, stormy eyes.

"This is my sister, Trav. She's all I've got left of my family." And then her voice cracked, any attempt at sounding professional lost. "Please let me go."

Travis's fingers danced on the door panel, the thump thump thump echoing in Ellie's ears like a heartbeat. His flat palm against the plastic interior, Travis took a deep breath through his nose and then stepped back.

"Fine. You win." He put his hands up in defeat and stepped up on the soggy grass on the side of the road. "I'll see you at the hospital."

"Thank you," Ellie said, remembering to give a little nod of appreciation, since a smile was beyond her capabilities at the moment. The sound of the door slamming shut filled Ellie with a brief moment of relief. Finally. She settled back in her seat, wrapping her arms around her body, the tank top she'd been wearing as an undershirt not providing nearly enough warmth now that the adrenaline was wearing off. When Chet shifted the rig into drive, Ellie shot up in her seat. How could she have forgotten?

"Chet, stop!"

"Stop?" He looked at her from the corner of his eye, confused.

"Stop," she repeated. He put his foot on the brake, and Ellie pushed the button on her window. It lowered with a whir. "Travis!" she shouted. Travis cocked his head and took a step forward.

"You okay?"

"Yeah! I forgot something." She leaned out the window as far as her seat belt would let her. Ellie pointed toward a light pole with a black rounded box midway up. "Amelia and Steve had them installed two weeks ago."

"What?" Travis searched in the general direction of her finger and took another step toward the car.

"Those." Ellie couldn't believe it'd taken her this long to remember. Someone entered Amelia's house with guns, ammunition, and dangerous intention. Who and why were still a mystery, a mystery that could at least be partially solved by the newly installed devices she was point-ing at. She motioned for Chet to start driving, afraid that Travis would make her stop and talk if they didn't escape quickly. She shouted one more time before flicking on the sirens and lights. "They just put in security cameras."

Chet took off with a lurch, and Ellie rolled up the window, not looking back. Then she let herself get lost in the scream of the siren, forcing herself not to consider what was waiting for her at the hospital.

CHAPTER 10

Amelia

Tuesday, April 5
Five weeks earlier

Of course today had to be the coldest day of the week so far. Amelia shivered. She'd been sitting on a bench with her back to the cement fountain in the middle of Broadlands Park for twenty minutes. She knew it was crazy to show up so early, but she seemed to finish every one of her morning tasks really quickly, bringing her to this exact spot at eleven forty-five. At the time, she'd just sighed and decided it was a good opportunity to clean out her in-box and old apps on her phone, but now her fingers were frozen and the phone dangerously low on power.

Five past noon and still no sign of either Steve or the mysterious Sue-z-Q. Well, at least as far as she could tell. The old lady feeding the pigeons two benches over could potentially be good ole Suze, but Amelia highly doubted it unless she was hiding hot coffee in her quilted handbag.

Where the heck were they?

Amelia pulled her jacket up to her chin and pushed herself lower on the bench. Besides hiding from the chill in the air, she was also hiding from any prying eyes. Last thing she needed was Steve to see her there and bypass the meeting altogether. Or even worse, guess why she was at the park to begin with. She checked her dying phone one more time. Seven minutes late. Steve was usually so punctual. Maybe this was the wrong fountain in the wrong park. Maybe there was some other town between Broadlands and Staltsman with a fountain, coffee shop, and hot dog stand. She pushed the Off button on the side of the phone and shoved it into her coat pocket. Three more minutes and then she'd give up. This was getting ridiculous.

With another glance over her shoulder at an empty fountain, Amelia picked at the peeling burgundy polish on her fingernails, all that was left of the makeshift spa night Ellie had put together two weeks ago. Every time she walked into the upstairs bathroom and passed by the nail polish remover, she considered cleaning them off for real, but there was never time. Amelia shook her head. Never time, yet she was wasting half an hour sitting on a bench stalking her husband? Ugh. She was being silly.

Amelia sat up straight and rubbed her cold hands against her thighs. *Well, that's enough of that,* she thought, and went to stand up, when she saw something moving out of the corner of her eye by the fountain—a flash of yellow and red and white. She froze.

A woman with long, styled blonde hair was carrying a tray with two white travel coffee cups. She glanced around the circle and then looked down at the edge of the fountain as if considering sitting down. Then she stepped back as though sitting on that damp concrete would be the most disgusting experience of her life.

As the woman turned to scan the park, Amelia finally saw her face. With the throwback, almost eighties-esque hairdo, she'd hoped for an older woman, a lady stuck in her glory days who wore blue eyeliner and gel bracelets. But all hope of antiquity disappeared when she came into focus. "Suze" was a bombshell. Midtwenties, fine bone structure, big blue eyes, pretty much the stereotypical hottie.

Dang it, Amelia would cheat on herself with Suze. At that exact moment, Steve turned the corner off the path on the opposite side of the park. Amelia put her hand up over her face, questioning for the millionth time what she was doing there.

Steve walked briskly across the park, waving as he approached the mystery woman, a brown oil-stained bag in his left hand. When they finally met, they greeted each other with a quick side hug that made some of the tension in Amelia's shoulders lift. One good sign at least.

The pair started chatting, and two giggles and three casual touches later, they'd settled on a bench on the right side of the disabled water feature. Amelia, still trying to explain away the physical contact, strained to hear any hint of what they were discussing, but nothing carried across the park. She squinted, willing to give lipreading a shot instead, when the bench creaked as someone slid down on the seat beside her. Amelia spun around so fast, her ponytail slapped against her face. A little stunned, heart racing, she saw Caleb looking back at her.

"Caleb! You scared me." She slapped his shoulder. "What are you doing here?"

"Saw you sitting here in the cold and thought I'd say hi."

"What? 'Cause we don't see each other enough at home?" She glanced over her shoulder again just in time to see Suze laugh broadly.

Caleb shifted from side to side, crossing his arms across his chest, a little smirk working its way up his cheek. The wrinkle by his eye was the same, the texture of his skin was somewhat familiar, all reminding her of seventeen-year-old Caleb.

"Nope, never," he said, chuckling. "You looked like you needed someone to talk to." Distracted, Amelia just grunted, trying to not watch and also to definitely watch Steve at the same time. Caleb followed her eye line to the pair across the park. He let out a low "Hm" before facing forward, his ungloved hands resting on the tops of his thighs.

Amelia's cheeks flashed hot, the embarrassed heat spreading to the tops of her ears. Caleb had figured her out. Of course he had. That's what he was best at—seeing what was really going on inside Amelia. She closed her eyes, annoyed at herself more than at the man sitting by her side as she ran through ways to explain what she'd been doing spying on her husband. But Caleb spoke first.

"You okay, M?" The question was so simple, so straightforward, that it should've been easy to answer. But it wasn't.

Tears welled up in her eyes, and a lump formed in her throat that she had to cough to clear. Was she okay? Where to start? Maybe with the fact that she'd been running faster than she was able for the past six months and that she didn't see any end to the race. Or that her husband was having some sort of meeting with a beautiful young woman just twenty feet away from where they were sitting. Yeah. There was that too.

"I'm fine. I . . . I just needed some fresh air."

"Hm . . . ," he said again, the knowing sound irritating Amelia. "So, are you waiting for Steve or something?"

Amelia's eyes opened slowly, and she swallowed down the emotion creeping up and out her mouth. Without hesitating any further, she put on her "I'm great" face.

"Yeah, uh, I didn't know he was going to be here. Just went for a little walk and . . ."

"It's not what it looks like, the two of them over there. You shouldn't worry."

"Caleb, stop. I don't think it looks like anything. I'm not worried . . . I'm just . . ." She checked over her shoulder again. Steve was wiping the corners of his mouth with a napkin. A sudden pressure on her nearly frozen hand drew her attention back to Caleb. His hand was covering hers. It was warm and comforting and familiar but very unexpected. Also . . . unnerving.

"Amelia, I need to talk to you about something important. Something I've wanted to tell you for a long time." His grip tightened, and a sudden panic filled Amelia, making her skin tingle like ants were crawling up and down her arm. There was an urgent edge to his appeal, like he was either going to tell her the secrets of the universe or declare his undying love. Since she was pretty sure Caleb was not in possession of the secrets of the universe, undying love seemed far more likely. Her concerns about Steve and "Suze" dropped away in one sudden whoosh, Caleb finally coming into focus.

His face tense, he was staring at her hand in his and seemed to be considering his next words carefully. Amelia opened her mouth, closed it again, and then tugged against his grip.

"I should really go." She pulled harder, feeling like an animal with its leg stuck in a bear trap. The picture in the car, his constant presence at their home, the kids' activities, family outings, the way he blushed and stuttered every time their hands met—she'd always known deep down how he felt about her, but this, saying it out loud, taking her hand, being so forward. It changed everything.

"Stop," he said, holding on tighter. "I need to tell you. I can't bear it any longer. M. Stop." His fingernails were starting to dig into the back of her hand.

With some force in her voice, Amelia growled, "Let me *go*, Caleb." She ripped her hand away, frightened by his intensity. "And don't call me M anymore. It's been fifteen years. Steve calls me M. Dad calls me M. Ellie calls me M. *You* call me Amelia."

If she'd hurt Caleb's feelings, there wasn't a flicker of it registering on his face. Instead, he let out a deep sigh and placed his hands on the worn thighs of his jeans, his eyes growing cloudy for just a brief moment. A stab of regret hit Amelia between her shoulder blades. She was doing that thing where she took out her frustrations about something else in her life on the closest victim. Steve was well versed in this weakness, but Caleb . . . poor Caleb had no idea. She used to be more easygoing, slower to be on the defensive, with a soft place for the people she loved; but right now she felt like every time she turned around, she was doing something else wrong, and it was easier to push people away than risk letting them see how messed up she really was.

"I'm sorry, Caleb. I didn't mean to . . . ," she started to say, but Caleb stood, stopping her midsentence.

"It's fine, Amelia." She swore he put a little extra emphasis on her full name before continuing. "I didn't mean to make you uncomfortable." He stood up and put his hands in his coat pockets like he was trying to punch a hole through them. "I'll talk to you later, okay? You have a good day." With that, he turned on the soles of his work boots and walked back down the gravel path. With his head down and shoulders slumped, it looked like he was carrying an invisible load on his back.

Damn it. Amelia cursed herself. There must've been a better way to handle that situation. She bit her lip, finally taking the time to wonder what exactly he had been trying to tell her.

Just as she was about to grab her purse off the bench and rush after him, she heard her name off in the distance. When she turned to face the call, Amelia saw Steve crossing the park with the mystery woman by his side. The sight was so unexpected, it drew her attention away from Caleb's hunched-over receding form, leaping across a thin strip of grass between two parallel paths, to the pair growing bigger in front of her every second.

She readjusted her shoulders until they were held in a high, straight line and, using every ounce of self-control she could muster, Amelia forced a smile onto her face as she rushed through her mind for something other than, "Who is *this*?" to say to Steve.

"Amelia! What are you doing here? I thought you had a PTO meeting today. Was that Caleb?" His voice was friendly with a touch of concern that made her want to shout. *Damn it.* She'd forgotten about the meeting—again. This was the third month in a row her seat had sat empty while Terri Wilhouse, with her hot-pink acrylics and obnoxious gavel, banged on a desk to bring the meeting to order. She'd received a warning last month: Miss another meeting and your position as field day chairperson will be revoked. Well—Amelia grabbed her purse, annoyed at Steve's stellar memory—she never really liked sports all that much anyway.

"Terri rescheduled," she lied, far more willing to tell a little fib than give Steve another item on his growing list of reasons they should put her dad into a home. "So I thought I'd take a little walk. Caleb was on his lunch break and stopped to say hi."

At this point, Steve and the Suze woman were standing right in front of Amelia. Steve's brown work shoes were dusty from shuffling down the gravel path, but Suze's beige stilettos with a three-inch heel looked pristine as if she'd floated there.

Up close she looked a little older, some lines around her eyes and mouth giving an approximate age of at least thirty. There was some relief to Amelia in those lines but some concern too because they only made the woman look more dignified, beautiful rather than pretty. Deep down, Amelia had been questioning the possibility that Steve could even relate to someone under the age of thirty, but now . . .

Perhaps noticing Amelia's scrutiny or the worry in her eyes, the woman smiled and put out her hand. "Susan Walters, so nice to meet you."

Amelia stared at her hand briefly. The fingers were white, the skin nearly translucent, and she didn't even need to touch her to know that it was soft. Perhaps she should demand answers before taking that hand, but the longer she looked at it, the more foolish she felt. With a loud clap, Amelia took her hand and gave a strong, hearty shake that made petite Susan rock on her heels.

"You too." The shake was brief, and Susan withdrew her hand in a skilled swoop. "Steve has told me a lot about you. How is your dad?"

The question smacked Amelia upside the head and made her ears ring. Whoever she was, Steve had been confiding in her. Just how much had he told this woman? How much comfort had he received from her soft hands and gently lined eyes? Instead of asking about late-night texts and secret meetings in the park, Amelia pushed the corners of her mouth up farther, her exposed teeth growing cold in the chill.

"He's doing as well as can be expected," Amelia said, falling back onto the answer she always used with the former firefighters who would call or stop by to check on their old chief.

"I wouldn't exactly say he is doing 'well,'" Steve interjected, making Amelia's blood pressure skyrocket.

"Susan, I haven't seen you around town before. Are you from Broadlands?" Amelia put on her friendly mom face. With an ever-so-subtle step toward Susan, Amelia waited for a reply, ignoring Steve's staring eyes. In her mom jeans with a yogurt stain on the thigh and ten-year-old running shoes with the blue metallic Nike emblem peeling away, Amelia was a stark contrast to the lovely, classy Susan.

"Oh no, I'm from Jaspertown." That was nearly twenty miles away. How did Steve even meet this woman? Perhaps picking up on Amelia's growing confusion, Susan laughed in a tripping, pretty way and smacked Steve's biceps. "Steve, how have you never told your wife about me, you silly lug?"

The tone was playful and light, like they'd been friends forever. That wasn't right. Amelia and Caleb had been friends forever, and the playfulness from their friendship had slowly drained to the train wreck she'd just participated in. This wasn't an old friend. This was . . . something else Amelia couldn't put her finger on.

Steve tried to chuckle, but even with the attempt at levity, there was something heavy in his countenance.

"Amelia's been busy. She's got a lot on her plate. I was going to tell her tonight, I swear." He put a gentle hand on his wife's shoulder, and his touch relaxed Amelia in a way she hated and wished she could have more control over.

"Well, then, you give me no choice." The woman refocused on Amelia. "I'm Steve's insurance agent. You know, from George Franccoppolis's agency? We've had the unfortunate opportunity to get to know each other pretty well over the past few months with the vandalism and such. In fact"—she rummaged through her leather shoulder bag, retrieving a manila envelope—"you need to sign these. I marked the spots for you. Don't worry, I don't need it now. Just drop it in the mail in the next day or two."

When Susan held out the envelope, Amelia had several thoughts. First, relief. Insurance agent. Yes. That made sense. Lots of paperwork and red tape from, first, the vandalism on Steve's work site and now the slashed tires on Steve's truck. Second, curiosity. What could possibly be inside that envelope that Amelia would have to sign, and if it was something important enough to merit a personal visit, then why have lunch with Steve in the park rather than come to their house?

"I'm sure Steve will fill you in. Well," Susan said, closing her bag with a flip of her hair, "I need to get back to the office. Thanks for lunch. Next time I'm bringing you a calzone from Sleighford. God, what am I saying? Let's hope there isn't a 'next time,' right?"

The compelling laugh returned, and Steve joined in as though property damage and filing insurance reports were the height of fun. Amelia, determined to not be left out or made a fool, laughed along.

"Well, at least we got hot dogs out of the deal," he joked.

"Fair trade," Susan volleyed back, her eyes meeting Steve's. Their laughter slowly diminished. She glanced back and forth between Amelia and Steve and then turned on one of her heels, tossing back over her shoulder a brief, "I'll be in touch."

As Susan sashayed away, Amelia tried to decide what to ask first. Before a word left her mouth, Steve wrapped her in a brief hug. Even through his coat she could smell his familiar scent.

"Hey, you okay? You seem a little off," he asked, making Amelia bristle. She hated it when he assessed her like that. A little off? Yeah, sure, maybe, but surely these were extenuating circumstances. She stiffened and pulled away from his embrace.

"So, Susan . . ." She let the accusation trail off. She'd feel a lot less desperate if she didn't have to say the words, *Who is she, and why haven't I heard about her before?* Steve took a step back, increasing the distance between them, and put his hands into his coat pockets.

"Yeah, George assigned her to my case weeks ago. She's really good at her job. Found a few ways to get payouts that I don't think my policy even technically covered." His eye contact diminished as the explanation dragged on. He knew. He knew she was jealous. It made her cheeks flush and made her feel weak, insecure.

Or maybe he was feeling guilty. The idea made her physically ill, and she had to put it away before she succumbed to it.

He hesitated, the breeze catching in his hair like a wind machine on a photo shoot. His forehead wrinkled in that all-too-familiar way. She knew that look. He was worried about her, and he was holding back. Usually what followed was a confrontation, a major disagreement on the finer points of Amelia's stress triggers and how to alleviate them, which was the absolute last thing she wanted to happen in the middle of the park. But he didn't. Instead, his face softened, the muscles in his neck unclenched, and a familiar kindness returned to his eyes.

"I think it'd be good if I got George back on this. Susan is great, but George has more experience," Steve said, without even a hint of reluctance, then wrapped his arms around her waist and kissed the crown of her head.

A wash of self-doubt and embarrassment made her bury her face deeper into his chest. She wanted to cry from relief but knew it would only make him question her sanity further. He pulled back and looked her in the eye. His eyes were a soft brown, warm, comforting. When they'd first started dating, she used to think she could stare at them endlessly.

"Listen, I've gotta get back to work, but we can go over all the insurance paperwork tonight."

"Okay." She waved the envelope Susan had given her, less interested in insurance payouts than she'd ever been. "I'll make some caramel popcorn, sweeten the process."

"Sounds delicious." He gave her shoulder one last squeeze.

When Steve finally walked away, Amelia collapsed onto the bench. Her spot had grown cold. She examined the manila envelope—the flap wasn't sealed. It was probably something about her father's life insurance or the business, but after meeting Suze, Amelia couldn't hold back her curiosity. She spilled the pile of papers out into her palm. As she straightened the edges, carefully tapping them on her knee to make them even, something caught her eye. At the top of the page wasn't a summary of a damage complaint. It wasn't even a petition for a full-price reimbursement for the tires. At the top of the packet was one header: **LIFE INSURANCE POLICY**. Underneath that: **AMELIA SAXTON**.

CHAPTER 11

ELLIE

Tuesday, May 10
11:21 a.m.

The doors swooshed open in front of Ellie. Chet had to park the ambulance—they could only leave it in the front drive if they had a patient, and as much as Chet wanted to give her a once-over, Ellie didn't qualify. The blood that Ellie had been trying to escape when she ripped off her shirt back on Amelia's driveway had soaked through the stiff fabric, and now, running into the emergency room at the hospital in Frampton, she realized her abdomen was covered in a blotch of crimson. The blood made her flinch, but it also got the attention of the nurse behind the counter.

"Miss, can I help you? Are you hurt?"

"My sister . . . Amelia Saxton . . ." She could barely get the words out between her heavy breaths. "My sister was brought in. Gunshots. Abdomen. Shoulder. Um . . . the medics were Cam and Patty."

The middle-aged nurse, carrying more than a few pounds around her midsection in a way that made her look like she'd be nice to hug, turned her head to the side, surveying Ellie carefully.

"If you'd take a seat, I'll see what I can find out for you." She gestured to the small U of seats to the left of the counter. They were filled with a coughing toddler and his mom, a man with a bloody dish towel wrapped around his hand, and a woman half hunched over in what looked like abdominal discomfort.

"No." Ellie swooped back around and placed her hand flat on the counter where all those sick people had signed their names and hoped for a short wait. She was not waiting. Not today. "I'm a paramedic, from Broadlands. I . . . I ride with . . ." Chet broke in through the sliding doors, calling Ellie's name. To think she used to dread hearing Chet's grouchy drawl.

"Chet! Good to see you." The nurse, whose name tag read **SALLY**, greeted Chet with a smile and leaned forward, pressing her stomach against the counter.

Chet waved briefly at Sally and then refocused on Ellie. "Ellie, you okay?" And she hated to admit it, but when he pressed his fingers into her bare shoulder, she felt her knees wobble with the temptation to let him hold her up—just for a second—just until she could get this all figured out and determine if Amelia was alive or dead. Until she could fully understand what news she'd have to tell her father at the end of the night. She stretched her neck, tipping her head from side to side, and then stood up straight. No one was going to carry her today.

"I don't know. Your *friend* Sally won't tell me anything." Ellie openly glared at the nurse. She'd learned how to be hard after working in a firehouse, how to give strong and concise orders. If she didn't expect respect, if she didn't *demand* it, she wouldn't have lasted a week as a paramedic. Sally would respect her, damn it. Chet patted her shoulder briefly and then let go slowly, like he was worried she would fall down without him there.

"Ellie, hon, yelling at Sally won't help." His tone was so strongly parental, her internal child shouted that she should stick out her tongue and stomp away. Instead, she curled her lips in and looked at Chet expectantly. If he knew how to get information, then he'd better do it and fast. He nodded approvingly, his eyebrows sighing along with his chest, and then turned to face the nurse.

"Sal, can you tell me if they brought in a trauma patient, Amelia Saxton. Her husband came in too, Steve. Both shot."

Sally's countenance changed as she listened to Chet like this was the first time she was hearing this information, and Ellie had to force herself not to stomp her foot in frustration.

"Yeah, yeah, just got here. In surgery, both of them. But like I told your friend here," Sally said, replicating the tone Ellie had used just moments earlier, "I will go and find out more information if you'd please take a *seat*." She had stopped talking to Chet at that point and was focused only on Ellie.

"Fine. I'll wait," Ellie replied, taking a step away from the counter and then adding before walking off, "But could you at least try to hurry?"

Ellie heard Chet let out a gentle growl as she backed away. Tears of frustration and anger played at the edges of her eyelids, but rather than fight a losing battle with Sal, who seemed markedly less huggable at this moment, she stepped rapidly across the waiting room to a heavily decorated wall filled with pictures of doctors and administrators. The automatic doors swooshed open and closed as she stomped past them. There was one spot on the granite wall bereft of any photographs. Ellie leaned against it, the cool stone against her bare skin sending off a shock wave of goose bumps up and down her arm.

She became lost in her attempts to read what Chet was saying from under his unkempt mustache. How Sally could find any way to smile when Amelia was somewhere in this hospital, cut open, hooked up to machines, closer to dead than alive, she could not reconcile.

When Sal laughed and slapped Chet on the shoulder, Ellie thought she might lose it. Too busy holding back an angry stream of curse words she'd learned from her time in the firehouse, she didn't notice the doors open behind her till a damp breeze sent a shiver through her bare arms. Her coat was still in the rig. Once Amelia was stable, once Ellie had answers, she'd grab it. Till then, she wrapped her arms around her body, pulling herself in tighter in the hope of making the shiver building inside her dissipate.

"Hey. You should put this on." A deep voice from behind made her jump. Travis was standing by her elbow, holding out a limp gray women's hoodie.

"Oh, Trav. Hey." For the second time that day she'd slipped up and called Officer Rivera not only by his first name but also a nickname. She pushed away from the wall, forcing herself back into her "tough girl" routine as quickly as possible. "What? Did we drive too fast for you? Have a hard time keeping up?" Joking felt oddly comforting; a tiny bit of normalcy in what had already become the worst hours of her life.

"No, I needed to tell Smitty about the security cameras." Travis chuckled politely and then jiggled the shirt in front of her. "Thanks for the heads-up by the way."

Ellie reluctantly took the sweatshirt and threaded her arms into the sleeves, which came up a little short, just above her wrists. It rode high on her waist and was snug around her shoulders. Once zipped, the bedazzled embellishment across her chest read JUICY.

"Oh my God. Where did you get this? Off a stripper?"

"Maybe she was *also* a stripper," Travis said, shrugging, a bit of mischief twinkling in his dark eyes, "but let's just say that dancing wasn't the only way she made money with her clothes off."

"Ew, Rivera. I don't want it." She went to unzip the gold-toothed zipper, but Travis put his hand on hers to stop her.

"I'm kidding, Brown. Some runaway with less-than-legal money-making practices left it in my car this morning . . ." He tapped her hand gently until she let go of the zipper pull. Then Travis yanked at the golden metal and silently zipped it all the way up to her collarbone. "So don't even *think* about trying to keep it, because I'm sure Crystal will be back for it in three to six weeks."

"Tempting, but I think I'll be able to resist this time." Ellie almost laughed but then remembered she was wearing the sweatshirt to cover up Amelia's blood. The half chuckle blew away immediately, and she fought against the choke of tears for the thousandth time that day.

Travis, still holding on to the zipper pull, shuffled across the sparkly linoleum, his black boots nearly touching hers when they finally came to a rest. In an attempt to hide her emotions, Ellie stared at the matching work boots, both covered in dark slashes of blood up the side and toes. She closed her eyes, trying to refocus, but even in the darkness, she knew Travis was just inches away. His arm came around her shoulders, his fingers dragging across the worn material of Crystal's sweatshirt, close enough that she could smell the faint scent of his cologne.

Ellie didn't try to talk. Instead, she let her forehead rest against his shoulder, just above the cold metal of his badge. Travis's comfort was different from Chet's—less fatherly, more tender.

"Brown . . . I mean Ellie," he corrected himself quickly. "I'm sorry. It's what we all fear, right? The bad things that happen on the job happening to the people we love."

Ellie nodded and relaxed into him farther, turning her head to one side, eyes closed. The smoky smell of the runaway's sweatshirt mingled with Travis's musk was leaving her a little dizzy. But she liked the warmth of his arm and the fact that finally she felt like someone was strong enough to help her. She considered how appropriate it would be to ask if he could use some of his interrogation skills to get information out of good ole Sal. But before she could figure out how to ask, another rush of cold air sent a shiver through her warming body.

"Ellie?"

She stiffened in Travis's arms, glanced up, and met Collin's gaze. His face was pale, making the amber freckles smudged across his nose stand out. Just seeing someone so familiar was comforting, and without a second thought, Ellie pushed out of Travis's arms and fell into Collin's.

"Collin!" She threw her arms around his waist, the crisp button-up cool against her cheek. Collin hugged her, his embrace different from Travis's heavily toned one, but no less calming. She enjoyed the moment of safety only briefly before leaning back against the enclosure of his arms to explain Amelia's injuries.

"She was shot. Must've been a .22. Small exit wound. Two times. Right lower quadrant of her abdomen with no exit wound. And right upper chest, through and through."

Collin gently disentangled Ellie from his hold, looking through the clear lenses of his glasses into her eyes. His rich, nearly green eyes were moist and red.

"Wait. Slow down." Concern showed on his face. "*Who* was shot?" Collin asked, looking back and forth between Travis and Ellie.

Ellie wanted to scream. How had he not picked up on anything she'd been saying? She took a deep breath, closing her eyes to hide her irritation, and then slowed down. *Simplify.*

"Amelia. She's in critical condition. She was shot in her . . ." Ellie stopped herself before slipping back into her medical jargon. "She's in surgery. So is Steve. He was injured too but not as seriously. Two men came into the office and shot them."

"Shot them?" This time he addressed the question to Travis, a touch of outrage and disbelief in his voice. "Who? Who did this?"

"There is an ongoing investigation. As of right now, the man is unidentified. When . . ." Travis cleared his throat, glancing at Ellie as he said the next names. "When Mr. and Mrs. Saxton are out of surgery, we are hoping to know more."

"No one got a good look at him?"

Travis shook his head, one hand resting on the crackling radio at his side. "If you'll excuse me, I need to take this. Brown," Travis said, looking right at her, the softness in his voice from earlier replaced by a professional, almost hard edge, "we still need to talk. Don't leave the hospital without checking in, okay?"

"I'll be with Amelia."

"Anything changes, you call, okay?" Travis asked.

"Okay," Ellie said simply. Travis turned to leave, but Ellie called out. "Uh, Rivera, wait." He stopped and turned to face the pair. "This is my fiancé, Collin. If I'm not around, you can get my number from him."

Travis nodded slowly and took in Collin like he was scanning a potential suspect before putting out his hand. "Nice to meet you, Collin. Travis Rivera."

"Nice to meet you too. Heard a lot about you," Collin replied. They shook briefly before Travis's radio crackled again, an impatient voice on the other end.

"That's my cue. Brown—no running away this time. We *will* talk."

"Yeah, yeah, yeah." She waved him off, turning her attention back to Collin as Travis walked away, grabbing for his radio. Once Travis was out of range, Collin blew out a long breath.

"Whew, he's intense. *That's* Rivera?" Collin watched after him and then looked back at Ellie. "For some reason, I was imagining a two-hundred-pound forty-year-old dude. Not RoboCop."

"Don't worry. He grows on you."

Collin nodded slowly and then took Ellie's hands. "So, where is Caleb? He's got to be freaking out. You know he's always had a thing for Amelia. Was he there when this guy showed up? Oh God, is he hurt too?"

Ellie shook her head in a little flick. "No. Not as far as I know." How had she skipped this important information? "There was one other man who got away, but one of the intruders is dead. He was shot in the face." She lowered her voice so the whole ER wouldn't hear.

"Wait . . . dead?" Collin's hands tightened around hers, and he got still. Very still. The color drained from his face like someone had pulled a plug. She'd seen Collin deal with lots of things, open wounds, crushed skulls, a kid half-drowned in his backyard swimming pool, but she'd never seen him look like this. It scared Ellie, and the brief moments of comfort and safety in Collin's arms dissolved into an empty fear.

"What? What is it?"

Collin swallowed hard. "L . . . what if . . ." He swallowed again, his eyes glossed over with moisture. "What if the other man was Caleb?"

CHAPTER 12

AMELIA

Monday, April 11
Four weeks earlier

A warm breeze rushed through Amelia's dark hair, still a little damp from her postworkout shower. It was amazing what a week could do to the world. As they waited for Cora to finish her viola lesson across the street at Ms. Larson's house, and Kate took turns being "it" with the other kids on the playground in a complicated game of "Don't touch the wood chips," Amelia took a moment to just breathe. It had only been a week since she'd sat on a frozen park bench, very similar to this one, with Caleb. Back then, the world had been covered in frosty brown grass and the air tainted with hints of snow and ice. Now the world was bursting with life.

Spring had come and everything seemed brighter. It was like the color setting on the TV had been turned up several notches; the grass surrounding the playground was greener than Amelia remembered grass ever being. The tulip buds peeking through the dirt at the base of the trees in the park reminded her that good things sometimes took time and a little patience to show their beauty. Yeah. It was a good day.

As Amelia enjoyed the warm breeze, a scream broke her few moments of reverie.

"HEY! Watch where you are going." A little voice echoed through the park. Kate. Yes, definitely Kate. Then the unfamiliar cry of another child. Great. Relaxing time canceled. When it was *your* kid being the bully on the playground, the only thing to do was run up, apologize, and then run away before the parent of the child could make comments on your parenting skills.

Amelia leaped off the bench and crossed the playground, following the pained wails of a small child. On the other side of the playground equipment lay a little boy, facedown, prostrate on the wood chips, making no effort to turn his head to the side. Kate sat next to him, pieces of her dark hair stuck to the corners of her mouth. Her cheeks were red and wet like she'd been crying.

Amelia fell to her knees beside the crying mystery child. She put her hand lightly on his back and spoke in her most calming motherly tone. "Hey, sweetie. You okay? Can I help you?" Then she gave Kate a look that said, *What the HECK happened here?*

"He was kicking me while we were waiting in line for the slide. So, I told him to stop and he didn't and I told him to STOP and he didn't and I told him to stop or I'd get my mom and he didn't and then . . . I pushed him."

"Kate!" Amelia shook her head. "You don't PUSH a little kid!" She patted the boy's shoulder again. He'd stopped crying and turned his face to the side. Pieces of dirt and wood chip clung to his fair skin. "Go find his mom, okay?"

Kate nodded and ran off, searching for the mom to match with the boy.

The boy lifted his head and acted interested in the conversation for the first time. "My mom's not here. She's in San Diego. I won't see her for two more months." He had a little lisp when he said his *th*'s, and when he held up two adorable fingers, Amelia couldn't help but smile.

"Who are you with, sweetie?" The boy pushed himself out of the dirt and into a sitting position, and Amelia had to resist the urge to dust him off. He squinched up one side of his face where the wood chips were embedded into his cheek and then relaxed it.

"My daddy. His name is Randy Mraz. He . . ."

"Oh, buddy!" A deep voice came from behind Amelia, and when she turned around, she saw a tall man with black hair sprinting across the playground, Kate running behind him. The man, wearing dark jeans and a ribbed long-sleeved tee shirt, knelt right next to Amelia, arms out to his son.

"Dawson! What happened? You okay, buddy?"

"I'm not sure. I just heard crying and came around the corner, and your little guy was on the ground, and my daughter Kate . . ." Amelia swallowed, waiting for the boy to spill it all about how Kate had pushed him down, leaving out the part where he was kicking her relentlessly, but he stayed quiet and Amelia continued. "Kate was making sure he was okay. They had some kind of altercation." She tossed up her hands like she was saying, *Kids! What can you do?* and Randy nodded like he understood. "But he just wanted you. I *think* he's okay."

"Yeah, Dawson sometimes has a hard time playing nice on the playground. Don't worry. I'm sure Kate was the innocent party here." He looked up at Amelia, squinting at the sun in his eyes. Broadlands was a small town, and she'd never seen this dad before. He was handsome in a very frat-boy kind of way, not exactly Amelia's type when she was still single but cute enough that she'd have remembered him at a PTO meeting or walking through Piggly Wiggly.

"I wouldn't exactly call her innocent . . ." Amelia laughed, eyeing with a raised eyebrow the brown-haired little girl peeking around the side of the slide.

Dawson's dad coaxed him closer, and finally the boy fell into his arms. Amelia expected the child's cool exterior to break and sobbing to ensue now that his father was there, but instead he shrugged as he leaned against his dad's chest and sighed.

"I guess I'll survive," he said with very grown-up resignation. Amelia caught the father's eye and gave him a knowing smirk that said his kid was just the cutest.

"Well, I'm glad to hear that. Such a relief!" The dad laughed, raising his eyebrows at Amelia. The man's eyes were light, like Caleb's, but blue, not green. And his hair was dark like Steve's. No, darker. A Bluetooth headset hung from his ear, and Amelia couldn't get a clear idea of whether he was just a self-important weirdo or whether he needed the Bluetooth for some kind of job that also left him free to take his kid to the park on a Monday morning.

Randy kissed Dawson on the top of the head and then stood up. "Think you're recovered enough to go play?" he asked.

"Yeah, I'm fine. Can I have five . . . no, ten minutes?" He held up two hands, digits extended.

"How about *twelve* minutes?"

"What? Yeah!" Dawson's eyes were wide with exaggerated surprise at his father's generous offer. Then he turned to Kate and put out a hand. "Hey, girl, wanna go down the slide together?"

Kate looked at Amelia for permission. She nodded as Randy added, "Dawson . . . don't call her 'girl'! Ask her name . . ." as the two former enemies ran off hand in hand. They watched the pair climb up the molded rock wall, Dawson shouting out orders and Kate ignoring him like a pro.

"I give it six minutes," Randy said, glancing at his bulky silver and black watch, "maybe ten if we're lucky."

"Ten minutes sounds like heaven on a day like today." Amelia took in another sweeping glance at the park. Weather as small talk usually bored her, but right now she just wanted to soak in the spring air and try to remember what summer felt like.

Randy didn't respond at first. He seemed to be thinking and maybe also looking around the park, but when she made it back around to her new companion, she found his eyes weren't on the trees or the sky; they were on her.

"I don't think that we've met officially. I'm Randy Mraz, and that sweet angel"—he chuckled under his breath—"is my little guy, Dawson. We just moved here from Arizona not too long ago, so, yes, this break in the weather is much needed by these two desert dwellers." He put out his hand, and Amelia took it.

"Well, let me be one of the last, apparently, to welcome you to our town." Amelia laughed and took her hand back. "What brought you to Broadlands? We don't get a lot of move-ins here. Unless you work for the railroad, in fast-food management, or . . ." She looked over his neat, carefully pressed pants and designer leather shoes, their laces carefully tied in a bow. No. This man probably didn't even *eat* fast food, much less work in a facility.

"Think real estate . . . ," Randy hinted, seeming to enjoy Amelia's guessing game and half watching the kids play on the equipment.

"Ooh . . . are you rebuilding Nancy's? That abandoned store right by Route Twelve? I've always thought it would be a great place for a mall. Right off the highway. Come on . . . gotta be . . . right?"

"Wow, that is a very specific guess." He shook his head and put his hands in his pockets, no rings on any fingers. Single father? Would make sense with what little Dawson was saying about his mom. Okay. Now she *was* getting nosy.

"Well, I have very specific hopes, I guess." She tried to laugh, but she couldn't help but notice how disappointed she sounded. It wasn't the idea of Nancy's never becoming a mall that turned her suddenly sad but the idea that so many of her hopes had ended up like that burned-out old grocery store—forgotten, empty, and beyond repair. Randy Mraz seemed to sense the turn in her mood and got that searching look in his eye again that made Amelia feel like she needed to look away.

He cleared his throat and continued. "I'm sorry to disappoint, but . . . I'm just a real estate agent. Mostly residential. Some commercial, but unless you're wanting to invest in developing your old market, I'm not gonna be much help."

"You can make enough money selling real estate *here*?" She covered her mouth as soon as the exclamation escaped. "Sorry. That was not an appropriate question."

"Ha, no, it's fine. I'm actually doing quite well . . . but not *in* Broadlands. There's a lot of growth surrounding the university, and I wanted Dawson to grow up in a small town. Plus, one thing you can get out here in the 'sticks' is land. We bought the Slatterys' old place in Randall."

Amelia crunched up her nose at the term "sticks." She hated being looked at as backward because she grew up in a town of two thousand. Ellie was the first to develop this automatic response to any reference to their tiny town and limited experiences. At least Amelia left for college for a few years and experienced something outside of these invisible borders.

"Wait, some giant house is going up on that land. Is that *your* house?" Second rude question in a row. It was nearly as bad as asking about how much money the stranger made selling real estate in Broadlands. But he didn't seem to mind.

"Yeah, so much for going back to basics. I don't know, got the builders out there and everything just sounded so amazing. We are living in the farmhouse until construction is finished. I guess the house is a good advertisement. You can't exactly claim to be a great real estate agent if your own house is a hovel . . . a newly painted hovel, mind, but still."

Amelia had always adored the Slatterys' ancient farmhouse. She used to have silly dreams when she was dating Caleb that they'd buy the house one day when he was a famous painter and that she could practice her cello out on the wraparound porch in preparation for her tour with the London Symphony Orchestra.

New paint job, sure. The old place probably needed ten coats of paint and definitely a new roof with some of Steve's fanciest architectural shingles, but other than that? Amelia's dream house.

Her hand shot out and grabbed Randy's biceps, squeezing. "You aren't going to tear it down, are you?"

Randy glanced at her hand like he was trying to hide the fact that he noticed it on his arm and then continued. "No, no, I could never. That place is a part of Broadlands history. But I am thinking about turning it into a rental after I do some updating and repairs."

"Oh thank heavens," Amelia responded emphatically, making Randy chuckle and look at her a little closer. When their eyes caught—those uncomfortably unfamiliar blue eyes—she dropped her hand, blushing. She'd been holding on to his arm far longer than she'd intended, but he wasn't annoyed or mad; he was trying to hold back a smile as he watched the kids on the playground equipment.

"I'm glad to find someone else so passionate about the housing market."

"Oh yeah, you got my number. Real estate is for sure my passion . . . ," she said, trying to make a joke but worried that she sounded nearly serious. "It's not. I mean, I'm glad it is yours, but I'm a cellist. I play cello."

Only seeming to be half listening, he gestured to his little boy, mouthing, "Time to go," before responding to her.

"Well, I guess I know both now." Dawson reached his dad, out of breath and with far more dirt under his nails than when she'd seen him ten minutes earlier. "Now, all I *don't* know is your name. I can't call you 'Kate's mom' forever."

"Oh my goodness, I'm so rude." For the third time in their short conversation, Amelia felt like running away out of embarrassment. She was just too used to seeing the same two thousand people over and over again. Meeting someone new was . . . novel. "My name is Amelia

Saxton. I live just two streets over on Lark Lane. My husband and I own Broadlands Roofing. I can't believe I spaced on that, Randy." She said his name deliberately so he knew that she did remember *something*.

She put out her hand and they shook, and this time Amelia remembered to let go. By now, Dawson was hanging on his pant leg, spinning around his father's leg in circles like he was dancing the Maypole. Randy patted him on the head.

"Did you have fun, bud?" When Randy placed his hand on his son's head, it was like he pushed a button. The spinning stopped, and he looked up at his father with the same unfamiliar blue of his father's eyes.

"Yeah, Kate is funny. She knows knock knock jokes; she likes it when I make weird sounds. She taught me how to play this game called wood chips . . . Do we really have to go?"

Randy ran his hand through Dawson's loosely curled blond hair, talking to him in a deeply serious way, like he was carefully considering the thoughts and feelings of his little boy. She'd never seen Steve talk like that to their girls. He was either playful dad or grouchy dad. Pretty much no in between. Amelia enjoyed watching this sweet interaction and the way Randy's soothing tones wrapped around Dawson like a blanket.

"We've gotta get home and make lunch, and then Alice is coming over to play so I can go show some houses to some nice people. Remember, before we came, I told you we only had a few minutes to play . . ."

"But, Daddy . . ."

"Hey, how about this? Go say bye to your friend, and I'll talk to Kate's mommy."

Dawson considered the idea for a second and then muttered, "'Kay."

Randy turned to Amelia, reaching for his back pocket. He pulled out a crisp white business card and held it out to her. "Listen, these kids play really nicely together. Maybe we could do a playdate or something?"

She took the card and glanced briefly at the simple but handsome black-and-white photo of the man she'd been chatting with for the past ten minutes. Mraz Real Estate. So, he was a small business owner just like Steve. She tapped the card on the palm of her hand and then looked up at Randy. He was watching her, studying her carefully like he really cared what her answer was. Then he looked away and called out for Dawson. She must've been imagining things.

"Uh, sure. I'll text you my number, and you can tell me your schedule."

"Sounds good. We will see you soon, then . . ." He seemed to search his memory. "Amelia."

"Yeah, sounds good, Randy." She said his name nice and clear, friendly but official enough to sound like two colleagues saying goodbye at the end of a workday. As he walked away, Amelia looked down at the card one more time, a heavy feeling in the pit of her stomach telling her that saying yes to this playdate might get her more than an afternoon of fruit snacks and juice boxes. She let out a sigh and licked her lips, still unsure if she'd send that text.

When she looked up, Randy was walking away, hand in hand with Dawson. He turned back briefly and gave her one last quick wave before hopping over the wooden railroad ties that bordered the park. She smiled and returned the wave, watching the pair with curiosity. Maybe it was because of a father-son bond or because Randy was such a hands-on dad, but there was something tender there that she was jealous of. It was something she wished Steve could tap into, not just in his relationship with Kate and Cora but in their marriage too.

Amelia rolled her eyes. What was she thinking? No one was perfect. She'd known this guy for five seconds. As far as she knew, his wife left him for being a drug addict or for hitting on women in bars. She slipped his card into her back pocket, feeling surer than ever that she'd never call or text Randy Mraz.

"Kate!" Amelia called out as she headed back to the bench where she'd left her book. "Kate! We gotta go!" She tossed her book in her oversize bag and flung it over her shoulder. "Where in the world did that girl run off to now?"

Using her hand to shield her eyes against the late-morning sun, Amelia searched through the bars and tunnels with her eyes. No little brown-haired girl to be seen anywhere. A small shot of panic ran through her mother's heart.

With urgency in her movements, Amelia walked swiftly over to the side of the park where she could get a good view of the street, fearing that perhaps Kate had run to the car without her. Not safe at all. Parking lots were fraught with potential tragedy for the little girl who never ever looked both ways.

But the line of cars parked against the curb looked safely stationary, and there was no Kate to be found. Fear started to turn to full-on panic. She reached for her phone and called out one more time as she unlocked her screen, ready to call Steve and then . . . who? . . . someone who could help her find her daughter.

"Kate! Where are you! Come out RIGHT NOW!" Amelia yelled, using her angry voice, not even caring that the whole neighborhood could hear her. "I'm serious!"

Even Amelia could hear the panicky edge to her tone. She scrolled through her recent calls until she landed on Steve's number. Finger hovering above his name, she glanced around the park one last time and, as if out of thin air, Kate emerged from the tree line surrounding the far edge of the park, down by the soccer fields. Skipping along like she was Goldilocks on her way to harass the three little bears, she seemed oblivious to the terror her absence had caused her mom.

"*Kate!*" Amelia tossed her phone back in her bag, which she dropped as she ran as fast as she could toward the little skipping girl in her twisted purple skirt and worn silver ballet flats. When she reached her daughter, Amelia scooped her up in her arms, relief and anger mingling together as she nuzzled her damp, pudgy cheek. "Where were you? I've been calling and calling."

"Sorry, Mommy. I didn't hear you," Kate said, sounding remorseful enough for Amelia to drop it for a minute and make sure she was okay. She leaned back and held Kate out away from her at arm's length, looking her over carefully. No bruises or tears or dirt or . . . anything that would spell out abduction by wild dogs or bullying by random big kids. Everything was the same . . . except . . .

"Kate, hon, where did you get that lollipop? What did I tell you about ground candy? It is dirty. Don't eat it." She put out her hand, palm up. "Here, spit it out. That's so gross."

Kate turned away protectively, hand wrapped around the rolled paper stick of the lollipop. She shifted it to the side of her mouth, bulging out her cheek like a chipmunk.

"Mom, stop. It's not from the ground. Gosh. Someone gave it to me." Kate sighed and rolled her eyes like she was fourteen instead of six. The sentence was meant to comfort Amelia, but instead, it made her stomach drop. How, how had she failed so horribly as a parent that her child would accept *candy* from a *stranger*?

Every inch of her wanted to search the lollipop for hidden razor blades or some kind of drugs. Instead, she took a deep breath, not wanting to freak her daughter out any more than necessary. Already on her knees, Amelia put her hands on Kate's shoulders and looked deep into her dark eyes.

"So, Kate, honey . . . you know you aren't supposed to take candy from strangers. I know it seems like 'free candy,' but it's just not safe. Remember?"

"Moooom," she cut in, shifting the green lollipop from one side of her mouth to the other, the hard candy clicking against her teeth. "Gosh. If you'd just listen—it wasn't a stranger!"

The phrase didn't sink in at first. Not a stranger. Then . . . who?

"Oh," Amelia chuckled, relieved. She leaned back on her heels to get away from the mud seeping through her jeans where she was kneeling in the dirt and rubbed Kate's shoulders. "So, did Dawson give it to you? That was nice." Maybe they'd have to do a playdate after all. *Dang it.*

"No, Mommy. Not Dawson." Kate shook her head and looked at Amelia like she was making a huge joke. "Uncle Caleb."

"What? Uncle Caleb was here?"

"Yeah, he was in the woods, watching me play. When Dawson left, he called me over for a lollipop." Kate sucked on the diminishing sucker and then pulled it out of her mouth with a pop. "I'm hungry. Can we have mac and cheese for lunch?"

"Uh, yeah, sure," Amelia replied, distracted. She stood slowly, head raised, nerves on edge, and spun in a tight circle, her ears ringing. Caleb. Why did hearing his name come from her daughter's mouth make her heart jump?

"Come on, Mommy. My tummy is grumbling." Kate pulled at her hand, and just as Amelia was about to turn and leave, something caught her eye. Just a flicker beyond the tree line; a tall form, half-hidden by the budding tree branches . . . jeans, maybe a white shirt—not much else was visible from that distance. Then he was gone. Too far away to be sure of much, Amelia followed her daughter out of the park. Could be just about anyone out there in the woods, a random kid, someone from the park district taking a survey of the trees, maybe even the cable people installing the DSL line Broadlands had been waiting on for forever. It *could* be any of these individuals, except for one thing . . .

Before she turned away to follow Kate, there was *one* thing Amelia was certain she saw—a shocking flash of red hair.

CHAPTER 13

ELLIE

Tuesday, May 10
1:53 p.m.

"Did you reach him yet?" Ellie asked when Collin sat down beside her in the surgery waiting room. She could already decipher the answer by the scowl on his face and the redness around his eyes. Still no news.

He'd been trying to contact Caleb for the past two hours, but all his texts were unanswered and his phone went right to voice mail. No one had heard from him, and Collin was growing more and more concerned. He didn't think his brother was a criminal but considered it more likely that, through some misunderstanding, he was tangled up in the drama and now, confused and scared, didn't know what to do. There was no way that the other man Steve had seen, the one who had run out of the office, could have been Caleb, or at least that was what she kept telling Collin. But Ellie had to admit it was definitely strange that Caleb hadn't been at work that morning and that he wasn't responding to texts or calls, especially given that Amelia was involved.

"You should call your parents."

"I did." Collin ran his hand through his reddish hair and then removed his glasses so he could rub his bloodshot eyes, nearly the same color. "I didn't tell them about Caleb, though. Steve only gave one statement, right? Then he passed out? I don't want to freak them out until we know for sure that there is something to worry about. They want to know if they should come watch Chief Brown and the girls."

He put his glasses back on and pushed them up on his nose. Ellie checked her watch. Nearly two p.m. She'd totally forgotten about her dad. Yeah. He'd need to be picked up from the senior center by five. They were sticklers for punctuality, and there was no way Ellie was leaving the hospital without some news of Amelia and Steve.

"Chet's got that covered, actually. He got the girls from school, and he said he'd get Daddy tonight. Once Amelia is stable, I'll go home and take over."

Ellie couldn't help but notice a brief look of pity from Collin as he wrapped his arms around her again. The initial comfort they brought had eventually dulled, and now it felt less like he was comforting her to give strength and more like he was consoling her for a loss.

"Well, if you need them, let me know. I'm gonna check in one more time and see if they heard anything. You just stay here and relax." He kissed the top of her head and gave her another squeeze as though it were possible for her to relax in any way right now.

"Okay," she said, searching the room for the least disgusting-looking chair. It was not the easiest search. All the padded maroon chairs looked like they were saturated with body oil and food stains. Since none of them were clean, she'd have to settle for one by an outlet. Halfway into her seat, she remembered her nearly dead phone that Chet had dropped off an hour earlier before leaving to grab the girls from school. "Hey, could you get me a charger from the gift shop?"

"Sure," Collin said, waving as he headed into the hallway to make another in an unending stream of phone calls. A small part of her felt guilty that she was asking so much of him when he was just as worried about his brother as she was about her sister. At least she knew where her sister was, but the unknown? It had to be killing him.

Alone, Ellie settled back into the stained chair, too exhausted to care. She was already wearing a stranger's sweatshirt and a pair of scrubs Collin had tracked down when the blood on the knees of her pants started to harden and rub against her skin. Why not hang out in a chair that half of Broadlands had cried and sweated and slept in?

The TV dully droning in the background held nothing but news reports of foreign wars and national politics. Each time she heard about death tolls or armed rebels, her mind went to the two people she loved who were also being treated for gunshot wounds just a few rooms over. It probably made her a bad person, but she cared far more about those two small lives than the whole slew of people that news anchor was going on and on about.

Soon, the monotony of the cream-colored walls and buzzing fluorescent lights somehow silenced all the conflicting voices in Ellie's head enough to let her eyes droop and head bounce. She slipped into a restless slumber where she was a little girl in her childhood bed, the same one she now settled into each night at her father's house. The room was different back then. Posters of unicorns with pastel pink-and-blue manes lined the wall, and the canopy bed she'd begged her dad for sat like a princess's abode rather than the current drooping gray vestige that creaked every time she climbed into it. The light was different too, more amber and gold, less washed out and cold. She ran her fingers over the knitted pink-and-maroon blanket that covered her mattress, something her mother had made for her before she was born. Her mom.

Sometimes when she thought really really hard, she could remember a shadowy image of her, tall, dark haired, a smile that burst out of her face without warning. When people first started to claim she looked like her mom, Ellie would sit in front of a mirror and try to imagine what it would be like to have a mother with her eyes, her cheeks, her hair. To have a mother—period.

The phone rang in the other room. The shrill tone of the old rotary phone made a pit form in Child Ellie's stomach. It was the phone from her father's office. The sound of that metallic ring always meant one thing—fire. A fire serious enough to call the fire chief out of bed in the middle of the night—to wake his family—to pull Chief Brown away from his girls and leave teenaged Amelia to play mom to her little sister.

The ring of that phone used to make Ellie cry. Any time of day, she'd run to her father, wrap her fingers in the stiff fabric of his uniform, and nuzzle her face against the cool brass of his badge.

"Don't go, Daddy," she'd beg, tears always flooding her normally bright eyes. Her father was so big and strong back then. He'd always pull her into his arms and carry her like a little princess back to her bed. She loved being cradled there, feeling so safe and loved, but that feeling only made it worse when he'd lay her down in her bed, pull the tightly knit fabric of her blanket all the way up to her chin, and kiss her forehead good night.

Yes, she loved her father. Yes, she missed him when he wasn't around. Yes, she wanted to wake up to him making breakfast in the kitchen in his boxers, but that wasn't the reason she wanted him to stay.

She was afraid of losing him. She hadn't been able to get over that fear since that fire, the one that had killed Tim, that firefighter who hadn't looked much older than Amelia, who had been out on his first fire, who hadn't just died from smoke inhalation but, according to those women talking during his wake, had died a painful death from the heat and the flames. Tim—who had to have a closed casket. She already lived her life without a mother. Amelia couldn't fill in for her father too.

"Ellie," he'd whisper, urgency mixed with tenderness and just enough understanding to let her know that he could read her fears. "I'll be home soon, baby. I promise." He'd place his large, callused hands on the back of her small, untested ones and carefully unwind them from his neck. "This is my job, honey. I know it scares you, but I can't just not go." He'd lean her back gently on her pillow and look deeply into her wide, wet, brown eyes. "I took an oath to help anyone in trouble."

She'd sniff, considering the complications that a promise like that could imply. Which was more important? Saving people or comforting his daughter? She'd frown. Saving people, obviously.

"So, you're like Superman?"

He'd smooth the creases on her forehead and trace the tiny tears silently racing down her cheeks, trying to hide a smile.

"Yeah, sure, hon. Just like Superman."

And on those nights when she couldn't fall asleep, knowing he might be facing flames or smoke or tiptoeing through a blazing building that could collapse at any second—she'd remember Superman. The Caped Crusader couldn't die. Not without some kryptonite involved at least. Maybe, just maybe, her brave daddy had a little bit of superhero inside him that would keep him safe and bring him home . . . again.

He'd kiss her forehead again, straighten her *L* necklace, holding it for a brief moment as if it were transmitting memories, and then say good night like he was going to bed in the next room rather than off to fight—not bullies, not armies, not even criminals—but fire. Unpredictable, intense, and dangerous fire.

A shifting movement by Adult Ellie's side woke her from her fitful recollections. Neck stiff from being cricked in an odd position and just enough drool collected in the corner of her mouth to make Ellie bring the sleeve of her shirt up to wipe it away, she sat up with a start, a dark trail of saliva swooped up the wrist of her borrowed sweatshirt.

"Hello, sleepyhead," Travis said, pen and pad in hand and a soft smile turning up the side of his mouth. When he smiled like that, it made an extra crease form in his cheek, not exactly a dimple but also not a wrinkle. An intriguing smile line that gave his smirk a touch of character and briefly made Ellie's lips turn up too. She sniffed in through her nose, threw her arms above her head to stretch, and then checked her watch. All the worry that reality held came crashing in. Another hour had passed and still no news.

"So, I know this might not feel like the best timing, but I really do need to talk to you about, uh, everything." Travis was whispering even though the room was empty.

Ellie sat up and blinked several times to clear her cloudy contacts. She hadn't eaten all day beyond a few cups of coffee, which still made her stomach feel a little sour. The heavy weight of fear and the unknown settled down on her shoulders again. She didn't want to talk to Travis about what she'd seen: the blood, the open wounds, the smoke still hanging in the air. But he wasn't going to give up until she did.

"Fine." She slapped at her legs with both hands and then looked him in the eye. "What do you want to know?"

Travis flipped the black cover back, over the metal spiral, and clicked his pen to the open position.

"Tell me about Amelia. What was her job? What kind of mom was she? How was her marriage to"—he glanced over the page—"Steve?"

She rubbed her face, voice cracking a little. "First of all, let's stop talking about her in the past tense. Okay?"

Travis blinked slowly like he'd just realized how his previous statement sounded. His jaw clenched for a second, and he let the hand holding his notebook fall into his lap.

"Brown, I'm so sorry—," he started. Ellie cut in before he could fumble over his apology.

"Amelia is a stay-at-home mom, but she's also a concert cellist. She does some work for Steve's company. Her plate is pretty full, but she does it so flawlessly. She . . . takes care of my dad a few days a week while I'm working." Emotion clamped down on her throat, and though she knew she'd regret the vulnerability later, she let the feeling pour into her chest, her heart pounding against the tears like it was underwater. Words became harder to get out, and she had to really think about forming each one before saying it out loud. "And, really, she takes care of me too. She's my hero, and I can't imagine anyone wanting to hurt her."

One tear and then another raced down her cheeks, and instead of wiping them away like she was embarrassed, she let them linger. Travis scribbled in his notebook, glancing up a few times with concern but also a determination that let Ellie know he wasn't backing off any time soon.

"And her relationship with her husband? Do they fight often? Any history of infidelity?"

Ellie had been so focused on Amelia that she hadn't taken the time to really think about Steve and his injuries. Steve had always been there for her from the moment she was introduced to him when she was ten years old. When Amelia had first started dating Steve, Ellie had a huge little-girl crush on him. He seemed so tall and strong and funny, but once he and Amelia got serious, Ellie appreciated the firefighter in a whole different way.

She'd never had a brother before. No matter what was going on in Ellie's life, Steve was there for her. He was the one to bring the air horn to her graduation and nearly get kicked out for using it anytime her name was mentioned. Or he'd somewhat protectively interrogate any boy she brought home, including Collin. He tugged her ponytail and made fun of her fashion sense. Other than her father, he had been the one constant male figure in her life for the past ten years. And when her father had his stroke, Steve held her gently, rubbed her back, and let her know everything was going to be okay. Today she hoped he was right.

"No way. Steve is loyal. He loves Amelia and their girls so much."

Travis kept his eyes down, scribbling on the nearly full page almost like he didn't want to look her in the eye. Ellie shook her head and cleared her throat.

"No, seriously. They are happy. They love each other. They have the perfect marriage . . . They . . ." Ellie swallowed hard. "Steve was shot too. I saw him and his wounds. They were definitely not self-inflicted. Objectively, I just don't think he could've done it."

"Uh-huh . . ." He scribbled one last thing and then flipped to the next page before looking up, something hidden about his eyes now.

"What was his state of mind when you and your partner met him on the driveway?"

"Well, he had just been shot. So. Not great, Rivera." Ellie was starting to get frustrated. "He was rolling around in pain. I assessed him briefly, but Chet did the actual assessment."

"Because you broke protocol and went inside." For the first time his pen was still, eyebrows raised. "Right?"

Ellie hesitated, considering lying or at least delaying an answer, but if they had the cameras, they would know everything soon.

"Yeah. Sure. Fine. Put that in your report." She waved at the book, a feeling of resignation settling on her shoulders. She could get fired for this.

"Ellie, that was incredibly dangerous." He put down his pen with a click that was final, some of the judgment leaving the lines of his face.

"I couldn't wait. I couldn't." She swallowed loudly. "My sister was inside."

"But you could've been shot, Brown. You could be in there being worked on right now." He pointed with the pen at the double doors that led to the OR suites, then clenched his jaw and dropped his hand into his lap. "Or—you could be dead."

"Amelia *would* be dead if I hadn't gone in. Listen, I don't regret it. How about you ask me more about what I saw when I got into the room? Why don't you ask me about the man on the ground or the blood or the smoke in the air?" All the things she had wanted to avoid talking about moments earlier now seemed twenty times better than why she had broken every single protocol when it came to violent crime and put her job on the line.

"That's fair, I guess." Travis paused like he wanted to say something else, but instead he picked up the pen and put it to the paper again. "We'll get back to Amelia and Steve. Let's talk about the scene. Start at the beginning."

Ellie went through the call and the scene and treating Steve as well as she could remember. Then she tried to hold back her tears as she recalled, detail for detail, the door hitting Amelia's body as she forced her way through and the way the carpet squished under her feet, saturated with blood.

Travis wrote quickly and fluidly, and Ellie distracted herself by watching the words form on the page in black ink. When her narrative slowed and Travis's pen hovered above the page occasionally, she grew increasingly contemplative. The story almost hurt more being told than it had when it was happening. When they finally reached the part where Amelia went off in the ambulance, Travis put his hand up to make her stop.

"Who do *you* think did this, Ellie? Who would you look at closer if you were me?"

In all the tears and anger and worry, this was one question she had been struggling to look straight in the eye. Who would want to hurt Steve or Amelia or even steal money from them? There were the day workers, one name in particular. Sam. She'd heard Amelia mention him before. A desperate man who'd lost his cool when he was paid late one too many times, so Steve fired him. It was a silent understanding that he was most likely the one behind the slashed tires. Maybe he acted alone or teamed up with someone else who felt gypped out of a day's wage. Or . . . or . . . the name that popped into her head over and over again, the one she was trying to push away and keep from thinking, much less saying ever again . . .

Travis's eyebrows tilted toward each other, and he leaned in like he knew she was on the edge of revealing something important. She hated that he could read her so easily. Was it as a result of years of investigative instinct or something more? Could he really see through her "tough girl" façade and into her true self with so little effort?

"You know you can trust me, right, Brown?" He was leaning toward her now; with both of their heads dipped, their foreheads weren't far from touching. At that moment she knew that if she could tell anyone her suspicions, it would be Travis. He brought her help when she was helpless and stranded inside the house; he'd let her go to the hospital instead of answering his questions; he was concerned but understanding about her rule violation—he was trustworthy.

She rubbed her lips together, noticing how dry they were. She bit her lower lip, wanting to hold back but also wanting to say the name out loud. She opened her mouth, her heart pounding like it had when she walked into a dark house with no more protection than the paramedic bags on her shoulders. But, just as she was about to tell the truth, her deepest, most conflicted thoughts, the door to the waiting room finally opened and a doctor walked out, tall with a shaved head and glasses.

He glanced at the chart in his hands and then quickly rested his gaze on Ellie and Travis, the only occupants of the waiting room. Ellie didn't like the way the middle-aged doctor reset his shoulders under his starched white lab coat. He walked over to her slowly, jaw clenched, eyes flicking down to glance at the chart in his hand like he was afraid to forget the name of the loved one Ellie was waiting to hear about.

This was one of those life moments. The ones that you knew just before they happened would change everything. Like when Amelia called and said that her father had collapsed on the job. It was the two-second pause just before she said the words, "It was a stroke," that let her know something was about to change forever. The thickness of the envelope from U of I that held her acceptance letter. The tiny smirk on Collin's face just before he went down on one knee. Life forever changed.

She sat up straight; there was no use in hiding from it. No matter what the news, there was no altering it now. She might as well hear it and face it boldly, like a firefighter facing a burning building or a paramedic working on a seemingly lifeless victim. She'd face the news like her family faced everything—like a Brown.

"Are you"—he looked at the chart, wavering on trusting his memory—"Amelia Saxton's family?" He didn't make eye contact with Travis, just Ellie. His bloodshot eyes weren't exactly a confidence booster, but Ellie held his gaze and kept her chin up, realizing that she probably looked like someone pulled out of the psych ward on the fourth floor.

"Yes. I'm her sister."

He nodded slowly.

"I'm Dr. Floyd." He put out his hand, and she shook it briefly before returning her own hand to the armrest. His hands were softer than she'd expected, like he'd just put on lotion. "So, are you alone right now?" he asked, a touch of concern in his voice.

Ellie glanced at Travis, wondering if he was invisible or maybe just a figment of her imagination. She guessed that his uniform was a type of camouflage that made him seem like neither family nor friend.

"Yeah, I guess so. I mean, my fiancé is here in the hospital, but I don't know when he'll be back."

The doctor frowned. Just as she started to worry that he wasn't going to tell her about Amelia's status until Collin returned, she felt a warm, callused hand wrap around her own limp one. Travis's dark skin contrasted nicely against Ellie's ghost-white complexion, and though his touch was unexpected, it also felt soothing. She turned her hand up until their palms were pressed together, so natural it was like they'd been holding each other's hands for their whole lives. When his fingers wrapped around the back of her hand, he gave it a soft squeeze; she looked back at the doctor, this time with confidence.

"You can tell me now. I'm ready."

Dr. Floyd held the file in front of him, holding on to both sides like it could blow away in some unseen wind.

She's dead. Ellie thought as matter-of-factly as she could manage. *She's dead. She's dead. She's dead.* She repeated it over and over again in her mind, thinking that maybe if she repeated the phrase enough times, it wouldn't hurt when she heard the words coming out of Dr. Floyd's mouth.

"We treated Amelia for two very serious gunshot wounds. She'd already lost a lot of blood, but we were able to stop the bleeding and get her stable enough to work on repairing some of the damage. The surgery itself was a great success, but"—Travis's fingers tightened around her hand like he knew something bad was about to happen—"now it will just take time . . ."

Ellie went to stand up, but the doctor gestured for her to stay seated. Take time? What did that even mean?

"Wait, so the surgery went well?" Even Ellie could hear the hopeful lilt to her voice.

Dr. Floyd glanced at his chart again and cleared his throat.

"I'm sorry, but your sister is . . ." Ellie took in a sharp breath and held it. The words. She'd hear them now. Dr. Floyd started again. "Unfortunately, there were some complications. At a certain point in the surgery, her heart stopped beating and we had to resuscitate her. We were able to get her heart beating again, but you never know how someone's brain will handle being without oxygen. We can't promise that there won't be any permanent damage."

"Permanent damage? What does that mean?"

The doctor dropped the chart to his side and didn't break eye contact. "I'm sorry, Ms. Brown, but your sister might not wake up."

CHAPTER 14

AMELIA

Thursday, April 14
Four weeks earlier

"So, who is this guy again?" Steve asked for the third time as Amelia tossed her wallet into her oversize canvas purse that she'd purchased as a makeshift diaper bag when Kate was a baby.

"I told you, he's a real estate agent. Um, Randy Mraz. He is building a house on the Slattery place and fixing up the old house for tenants. Kate hit it off with his kid at the park."

Kate, hair in stubby pigtails today, bounced up and down on her toes, fully dressed and clad in her sparkly silver flats since seven a.m. Her little fingers clutched the edge of the Formica counter, little bits of red and pink still clinging close to her cuticle.

"Yeah, he's really funny, Daddy. And I'm totally stronger than him. I beat him in arm wrestling and the wood chips game."

Steve, his Broadlands Roofing shirt tucked into his belted khakis as usual with his work clothes, put up his hand, and Kate reeled back and landed a loud and hefty high five. It'd taken Amelia nearly a year to get used to Steve without his uniform. The firefighting job became such a big part of your existence that when you left, it was like leaving your family or your way of life in many more ways than just the clothes. But it was always those outer evidences that people tended to notice first.

"I'm not surprised, K. You could take down any of the boys in your class, I'm sure." He chuckled and tussled Kate's hair till she pulled away, a few strands sticking out around the rubber bands.

"Daddy!" Already imbued with a far keener fashion sense than Amelia had ever possessed on her own, she squealed and put her hand up to cover her head from further damage. "Now I need more spray on it. Oh, Daddy." She gave him a very disappointed glare and then looked to her mother for permission. "Where is the stuff, Mommy?"

"The hair spray? It's in my bathroom. I'll grab it." Amelia dropped her bag on the table and put out her hand for Kate, but she batted it away.

"No, Mommy, I wanna do it myself." Amelia put her hands up like she was in a holdup and held back a smile as Kate headed toward the stairs, covering her damaged hairdo.

"I hope she doesn't get that crap everywhere," Steve said quietly so that only Amelia could hear. "That bathroom is already a disaster."

Amelia nodded, trying not to look at Steve, afraid she'd see the frustration in his eyes. The pit opening up in her stomach reminded her that he still wasn't happy with how far behind she was on . . . everything in the house. And here she was going away for the morning, her only free morning of the week, to hang out with Randy Mraz.

Argh. Even though part of her felt like she should probably be home scrubbing the caked-on hair-spray residue off her bathroom wall, another part of her couldn't deny that she was looking forward to a few hours away from her real life. She couldn't resist the potential of a stimulating adult conversation that had nothing to do with figuring out schedules, when her dad last pooped, or how to get Cora to soccer at the same time Kate needed to be at ballet.

"I'll clean it tonight, I swear."

"No you won't. You've got your dad tonight even though it is supposed to be your night off, and now we'll have him for three days in a row." He gestured toward the calendar hanging on the refrigerator, marked up in multicolored ink. There was an edge of frustration to his voice that was becoming all too familiar.

"It's a fair trade, Steve. Ellie and Collin wanted to go out of town for the weekend to celebrate their engagement. She's taking three days next weekend so we can go strawberry picking and maybe clean out the garage." Amelia closed her purse and made sure the magnetic snap was fastened. "I need to go now. We can talk about this later." She tossed the strap over her shoulder and called up to Kate from the bottom of the stairs. Then, turning on the balls of both feet, she gave Steve a firm look, tears of anger and frustration pushing at the back of her eyes. "By the way, if the bathroom is bothering you *that* much, then maybe *you* should clean it."

The deep lines across Steve's forehead softened. He crossed the kitchen, and she tried to ignore his approach, watching up the stairs for Kate to finally come down so they could get in the car and escape all the signs that Amelia was a failure. But soon, his large hands settled carefully on her shoulders, his thumbs rubbing gentle circles on her shoulder blades, and she had to bite down hard, crushing her molars together, to keep from crying. Steve moved in closer until his lips met the soft spot under her jaw that always made her knees weak.

"I'm sorry, babe. I don't want to make you so sad. I'm sorry." His lips moved against her neck as he spoke, his breath only serving to warm her skin in a very enticing way. She leaned in to his embrace and closed her eyes, surrendering to his apology.

"It's okay. I know I keep saying it, but this *will* get better."

He pulled back a little, but then his hands traced down the silky green satin of her blouse, her shoulders covered by a loosely knit sweater, then down to her bare elbows, her hands, and then landed on her hips. From there he wrapped his arms around her waist and pulled her back in toward him, almost like he used to when they'd first gotten married and were still into snuggling nearly every minute of every night.

"I'll believe it when I see it," he whispered in her ear playfully. She jabbed him lightly in the ribs with her elbow.

"Yeah, yeah, yeah . . . you big skeptic . . ."

"I prefer 'realist' if you don't mind."

"Realist my ass . . ." The door from the office opened and shut in its all-too-familiar swoosh-bang. Steve didn't even flinch, but Amelia's gaze went right to the entrance. The sound, a sound that used to mean that Steve was home, had become one that made her heart race in the past week.

Caleb used to knock, but recently he'd been coming in at random times, stepping boldly across the threshold and into the kitchen. Sometimes she was making dinner or fitting in a few dishes, but once she'd been sitting at the kitchen table in her pj's tank top and no bra. It wasn't like he ever said anything, not even, "Sorry for freaking you out twice in the past few weeks. I swear I'm not a crazy stalker."

Amelia was still wrapped up in her worries about Caleb's overt interest in not just her but her kids. She'd been meaning to bring it up to Steve, but there was no way to be sure how he'd respond. Actually, she'd been thinking about it a lot and had concluded that there were really only two ways he'd react.

One, he'd laugh and tell Amelia she was overreacting. Or, two, he'd get angry and yell at Caleb, maybe even fire him. And Caleb didn't have much to fall back on. Barely finishing high school and then taking a few community college art courses didn't prepare you much for real life.

No. Everyone loved Caleb, so it would probably be scenario number one, and Amelia was tired of being told she was overreacting. Steve had already had a good laugh at her thinly veiled jealousy toward the insurance agent the week before.

Today, Caleb was staring at his shoes, and had his hands shoved into the pockets of his jeans, which were several sizes too big and held up only by an ancient leather belt with extra holes pounded in it, probably with something sharp like a nail. Was he losing more weight? There *were* extra lines in his cheeks and around his mouth. Obscure circles sat like the dark side of a crescent moon under his eyes. Something was off with this version of Caleb. How had she missed it earlier? He'd always been shy and a bit standoffish, but he'd never been creepy or sickly before.

Amelia kind of expected Steve to let her go and back away as soon as Caleb came through the door, but instead, he tightened his grip and kissed her neck in that spot again. But it didn't cause her weak knees this time, only embarrassment.

"Steve, Caleb's here," she mumbled, wondering if he hadn't noticed. Without looking up, Steve laid another kiss on his wife's exposed neck and then cheek.

"What do you need, Caleb? Can't it wait?" His hands were now flat against her stomach and starting to feel less like an embrace and more like a hold. Part of Amelia wanted to wrench away from what felt like some he-man show of territory that she totally didn't understand. But when she thought about the ensuing embarrassment, she tried to relax all her muscles and submit instead. Maybe Steve *had* noticed the change in Caleb, and this was his way of putting him back in his place, reminding him that although they'd been having some problems lately, Steve was still her husband. Maybe.

"I just need you to open the safe."

Steve was obsessive with security. The safe held a large amount of cash at any given time; he often had to pay workers and suppliers in cash in order to get a discount. Amelia had no idea how much was coming in, how much was going out, or how much was sitting inside that safe. He also kept all their important documents, passports, and birth certificates in it. He changed the combination once a week, usually on Monday nights, just to be careful. Every week he'd write that number on a blue Post-it with a black Sharpie and put it on the inside of his underwear drawer, and only he and Amelia knew exactly where he kept it. Steve said it was good for her to know where the information was in case something happened to him and they needed to get into the safe. It was a SentrySafe, and the only way to break into one of those lovelies was using a blowtorch or maybe the Jaws of Life.

But no one but Steve was allowed in the safe. Ever. Ever. Though she knew where the combo was, Amelia never had the nerve to spin it in herself. Even when she'd had a line of workers out the door on payday a few months ago and Steve had been running late.

When Caleb finally lifted his gaze off her dingy kitchen tile as Steve went upstairs to recheck the new combination, the cool blue of his eyes sent a shiver down her spine. She didn't want to feel this way about Caleb. Maybe, just maybe, she *was* overreacting, and she should let him clear the air.

Eyes still connecting them, she tipped her head to one side, trying to see Caleb from another angle. He worked in an office attached to her house. He was going to be family soon. Deep down, he really was a good man; she knew that without a doubt.

"Hey, can we talk?" The words were easier to say than she'd thought they would be, but her timing was bad. Steve would be back any second. How could this conversation bring closure or clarity in less than two minutes? She glanced up the stairs and then back at Caleb, who looked too stunned to speak. Then he took a step forward, a shaking hand reaching out toward her like he was trying to reassure her.

"I'm sorry, Amelia. I have a lot I need to tell you. I've been looking for the right moment, but . . . there aren't really right moments to say something like this . . ." He took another step forward, his forehead turning red and glistening with nervous sweat. Amelia's heart started to thump loudly in her chest and ears.

A tumble of footsteps stopped Caleb far better than any words Amelia could have come up with. His hand retreated, and he took one or two steps backward, and immediately Amelia knew that whatever Caleb had been trying to say, he didn't want Steve to hear it.

Caleb was already in his submissive pose, back behind the table, staring at his toes and the off-colored grout. Steve rushed down the stairs with Kate on his back, bouncing up and down like she was riding a pony.

"Faster, Daddy. More bouncing!" she shouted, pretending to smack Steve on the back like he was a racehorse and she was a tiny little jockey. Cora followed behind the raucous pair, somber, overly mature, and intentionally serious.

"Mom, I can't focus when everyone is so loud. I have to finish my homework."

Amelia always loved it when her ten-year-old acted like the one page of math and twenty minutes of reading she received every single day were equivalent to a college freshman's whole course load. Maybe it meant she'd be a natural when it came to school.

"Kate and I are headed out. You'll have sweet silence soon," Amelia reassured her daughter, who just sighed and stomped up the stairs, apparently preparing for adolescence.

Steve jumped the last few stairs, and Amelia had to hop out of the way to keep the whole tangled crew from slamming into her. She wobbled a little, and Steve, now holding Kate to his side, with one hand under her legs, wrapped his free hand around her waist and pulled her into him so she didn't fall. She tried to laugh, tried to feel safe in his arms like she always did, but something made her glance over at Caleb instead.

He was watching, very careful to hide his focus this time, and there was something on his face that she'd never seen—a toughness around his eyes, a glare that seemed to be completely involuntary and pointed directly at Steve. It made goose bumps race up her arms. She moved away from the horse and his rider and tried to slow her thoughts and pulse.

"Hey, Katie-baby, we gotta go, girlfriend." Amelia put out her arms to her daughter, and she jumped from Steve's back to her mom's arms without touching the ground. Her hair smelled strongly of hair spray, and there was sticky residue that stuck to Amelia's cheek when one of her pigtails grazed her face.

"I'm ready now. Do you think Dawson will like my hair?"

Steve growled playfully under his breath. "Uh, I don't think I like this 'going on a playdate with a boy' thing at all."

"You are so silly, Daddy. It's not a date."

"Well, that Randy fella better remember that too," Steve said, this time to Amelia, and Caleb shifted, eyes still on the ground. "You look too pretty to be hanging out at some guy's house."

Amelia looked over her dark skinny jeans, deep green blouse with buttons up the front half of the silky fabric, and an off-white sweater hanging loosely around her body. She still wore her plain old *M* necklace and hadn't put any extra effort into her outfit. Okay, not true, she'd made sure to avoid jeans with tears in the knee, yoga pants altogether, and any shirts that had stains that didn't blend into the pattern on the shirt. Which left her with only a few options.

"You have absolutely nothing to worry about, I promise you," she responded, standing on her tiptoes to give him a little kiss on his cheek. "This guy will not be impressed with my Target clearance-rack purchases from two years ago. He has a designer version of . . . everything." She picked up her oversize bag stuffed full of gluten-free, peanut-free, sugar-free munchies just in case Randy was as into designer snacks as he was designer everything else.

"You only say that 'cause you don't know what a babe you are," Steve said, almost tussling Kate's hair again but thankfully stopping short before causing a repeat of the hair fiasco of fifteen minutes earlier. Amelia placed her on the ground and patted her back.

"Run out to the car and get in your seat." Amelia clicked the Unlock button on her keys till she heard a beep. "I'll be right there."

She yanked a small purple-and-black backpack off the kitchen chair in front of her, yelling just as the storm door's hinges squeaked. "And don't forget your bag!"

Kate ran back in, her sneakers squealing against the tile, and snagged the bag with a quick "Thanks." Steve chuckled and followed the invisible trail of six-year-old energy she left behind her.

"Caleb, I got the combo." Steve flicked up a blue Post-it held between his fingers. "M, see you at dinner?"

"Yup, I'll grab Dad and then be home around six."

"Sounds *great*," Steve said, not even trying to hide his sarcastic tone. Without looking back, he pushed through the heavy door that separated the office from the house.

Alone in the kitchen with Caleb only a few feet away, Amelia didn't know what to say or do. He was still standing behind the chair at the foot of the table, the chair everyone avoided because there wasn't enough room to push it out without crashing into the oven door. There wasn't enough time to finish their conversation, but she thought he'd look up, or say . . . *something.*

But, no, he stood still as a statue, hands in his pockets, which made his sagging pants dip even lower, straining against the decrepit belt. Annoyance surged through Amelia. Fine. She could play this game. She hefted the bag back up onto her shoulder and reset her feet, determined to appear strong.

"Good-bye, Caleb," Amelia said, eyes focused on the door to the driveway. She pushed in the chair she'd been standing beside and put one ballet flat–clad foot in front of the other. At first, he was frozen, ignoring her as though she'd been the one following him instead of the other way around. But just as she was about to pass, his hand shot out and grabbed hers. A shock went through her fingers, up her arm, to her elbow and shoulder. She had to hold back a gasp.

"What the . . . ," she started to say, but Caleb interrupted, his fingertips pressing against her skin.

"Don't go." His eyes were clear and that familiar bluish green that she'd always been jealous of, like the sky before a tornado warning. She started to yank her hand away, but then he said it again, this time a little louder. His voice was thick, heavy, foreboding—full of . . . something. "Don't go."

The annoyance floated away, and the fear came crashing back down on her like a curtain dropping after a theater performance. Alone with Caleb had always been a comfortable place. Caleb was usually a place of familiarity and friendship, but there was nothing safe about the way his jaw was taut, clenched, eyes pleading with her to listen and his fingers like a vise against her own. With a surge of panic and determination, she yanked hard and fast to free her hand from his.

"You have to stop this, Caleb. We can go back to the way we were before. You can stop . . ."

"You can't go to that man's house, M." He took an aggressive step toward her, then another. If she didn't move soon, she'd be trapped; she'd have to listen. "Stay, M. Stay here and I promise to stop. Okay?"

He was close enough that she could feel his breath on her cheek and make out the fine, nearly colorless lashes fringing his eyelids. He was taller than she remembered. She stumbled backward, trying to put some space between them.

"If Steve doesn't have a problem with it, then you shouldn't either."

"Steve doesn't want what is best for you. I do." He put out his hand like he was going to grab her again. Amelia ducked away from his reach, stumbling over the leg of a chair. Feet tangled beneath her, she knew instantly that there was no stopping her momentum. She was going to hit the floor, hard. She grasped around her for anything to hold on to, feeling like she was falling in slow motion. The edge of the table slipped out of her grip, the chair tumbled down with a crack before she even had made it halfway to the ground, then air . . . nothing but air in her hands.

Just as she was about to land, her body contorted into an unnatural falling position, a strong, soft hand wrapped around her wrist. Though the grip was not enough to keep her from collapsing, it slowed her fall enough so that she hit the floor with a muffled thump. A shock went through her hip, and she was left with a sore shoulder from where her arm had taken the brunt of the intervention, but overall she was okay. Stunned and a bit dizzy, she met Caleb's gaze. The creases around his eyes that spelled worry were there, and the scary hard mask he'd been wearing for the past two weeks was lifted; for a moment she felt safe with Caleb's skin touching hers.

"Thank you," she managed to whisper. Caleb held out his other hand in an offer to help her stand. She didn't hesitate this time, placing her hand in his. He carefully pulled her to her feet, the overloaded snack bag hanging limply from her elbow. On her feet, Amelia's hands still rested in his, and she became aware of his thumb tracing a subtle circle on the back of her hand. She slipped them out of his grip. "I'd better go now."

Any softness to Caleb's features erased almost as soon as she moved her hands away from his. The set jaw, the barely disguised anger, it was all back, along with a darkness in his eyes. She was afraid he'd try to beg her not to go again, but this time he stepped back after making sure she was steady. He put his hands back in those overused pockets and let his shoulders slump, subtracting several inches from his height. It made Amelia shudder more than when he took her hand, more than when he was watching her at the park, more than when he had sat beside her on that cold park bench a week earlier. There was something so sure, so final about his demeanor that instead of running out the door like she'd planned—she paused.

"Fine," she said, wrestling the bag back into place, exasperated. "What did you want to tell me?"

This time Caleb made no effort to move closer or to give dire warnings. Instead, he shrugged and said, "Nothing. Never mind." He cleared his throat with a little cough, but Amelia didn't budge.

"All right, well, thanks for saving my life." She gave him a flick of a smile and a brief wave. "See you tomorrow," she said before heading toward the door without tripping this time. Just as she placed her hand on the nickel door handle and started to turn it clockwise, she heard Caleb's voice from behind her.

"He's not what he seems," Caleb said, being infuriatingly general about *who* he was referring to. Then, as if answering her internal question, he continued. "Trust me, you can't believe a word that comes out of Randy Mraz's mouth."

Hand still on the knob, Amelia chose not to turn around. Instead, she cracked the door open with a familiar squeal and enjoyed the crisp spring air that washed over her. She considered responding with a snarky remark or with a *Thanks a lot*, but instead she walked out the door without looking back.

For a moment after she closed it, she thought he might come after her. It wasn't until she heard the sound of gravel underfoot that she realized what was strange about what Caleb had just said to her. Randy. Randy Mraz.

She'd never said his full name while Caleb was in the room.

CHAPTER 15

ELLIE

Tuesday, May 10
3:10 p.m.

Waiting again. *Damn it.* She didn't *like* waiting. Amelia was out of surgery and headed to the ICU. Steve was out of surgery and in stable condition. She'd been told he was awake but groggy. The police wanted to talk to him before he had any visitors, and Ellie was feeling like a caged animal. At first she paced up and down the hall until Collin forced her to sit down and have a cup of coffee. She held the lukewarm cup in her hand and wondered who thought it was a good idea to give a stimulant to people already on edge. Collin ran his hand over her back again; his touch was getting more irritating the more hours that passed without any word, the longer they waited to hear back from Caleb, and the more calls she had to ignore from neighbors and friends wanting answers she didn't have.

"Mom and Dad just called." Collin gathered her ponytail up in his hand and let it fall out of his palm like he was spreading seed in a garden. "Still no news from Caleb. I'm trying not to worry them, so I'm not pushing it, but I can tell my mom is starting to freak out."

His hand went to the skin at the base of her neck, rubbing upward toward her scalp, his fingertips working in small, bouncy patterns. She leaned into his touch, finally enjoying it again.

"Mmmm . . ." Ellie tried to turn off all the thoughts in her mind and just submit to Collin's touch, but something was off today. The pressure of his hand was too light, his movements too rehearsed and bland, like he was following instructions rather than instinct. The tiny embers of relief and comfort dimmed instantly, like water being thrown on a glowing fire. She shook her head a little, hoping he'd get the message. He did. Soon his hand retreated and settled into his lap.

"I think I'm going to take a little walk." They'd been in their third waiting room of the day for going on two hours. With the coffee, Diet Coke, and a bag of spicy cheese curls from the vending machine, Ellie's stomach was a mess. Maybe the nurses' station could slip her an antacid. She slapped her hands on her knees and then stood up without even a look at Collin. He'd have to just understand that she needed a break.

"Oh," he said simply, but his confusion was spelled out clearly in the way he didn't even try to follow her, instead cocking his head to one side like he was trying to figure her out. "And if they come for you?"

If they come for me? Hm. She checked the pocket of her sweatshirt for her phone. Yeah, by now Crystal's sweatshirt was officially hers. If you cried into a piece of fabric long and hard enough, it didn't matter who it belonged to before; at that point it was yours.

"Oh, if Caleb gets in touch, text me for sure," she said, running her finger over the switch that turned her ringer back on.

Collin sighed and took off his glasses, looking worn out for the first time in that endless day. A tiny twinge of guilt washed over her. For some reason Collin's concern felt like a weight right now rather than something there to lighten the load. It made her want to run away, like when her auntie Doris, who always wore flower-printed polyester and smelled of mothballs, hugged her just a little too long and gave her one of those squishy, wet kisses that left a smear of red on her cheek.

She loved him and how much he cared, but today she needed something else. Ellie had no idea *what* that was, but it certainly wasn't this.

Jittery and completely emotionally exhausted, she glanced up and down the empty hallway. Steve was in one of these rooms. She couldn't see Amelia for another few hours, but it would be nice to at least see Steve and be reassured that one of her two favorite people was okay or at least was going to be. He seemed to be in good condition when she'd seen him before going in to find Amelia in the house, but one of the bullets had grazed his lung and caused a major bleed. After a few hours of surgery, he was doing well and recovering in his room.

It was a lot easier to hear the news about Steve than the information about Amelia's injuries. Ellie had to work hard to not think about how they nearly lost her and that her sister might actually be gone even though her body was still technically alive. She wondered if the detectives would tell Steve the truth about Amelia or wait until he answered some questions and then let the doctors come in and break the news. He would be absolutely shattered. Maybe it was better to wait a little bit, until they knew for sure what Amelia's prognosis was going to be, even though she had no idea what she would say to protect him from that information.

Ellie's feet were heavy and every step took a massive amount of effort, but a force was pulling her down the hallway toward a room with a man in a dark uniform standing outside. It was a uniformed officer. Not Travis but clearly one of his buddies. Ellie swore she could hear the murmur of voices coming from that room at the end of the hall. The rise and fall of one of the deep-toned voices was all too familiar. That had to be Steve's room. He must be awake.

Every part of Ellie wanted to run in and see him alive and well with her own eyes. She wanted to hear him say, *Hey, L!* and reach out to tussle her hair like she was twelve and not twenty-two. If anyone could make her feel better or feel safe, it was Steve.

But with the guard there, she had to play it cool and hope that maybe they'd crossed paths at some point out on a scene or parade or chili cook-off. She pulled at the waist of her scrubs, a little nervous about her unkempt appearance. It would be so much easier if she were wearing her uniform. People tended to take you far more seriously if you were wearing a badge.

She stopped in front of him, hands out of her pockets and by her side, and cleared her throat.

"I'm here to visit Steve Saxton," she said, deciding it was best to bluff her way through.

The officer put his hands on his hips like he was trying to look tough. "Uh, sorry, no visitors at this time. They should've told you that at the front desk." He took in her eclectic outfit, her unkempt hair, and it didn't take a detective to see the red rims around her eyes. "Oh, wait. I know you."

"I'm with the Broadlands Fire Department."

"Oh yeah, a paramedic, right?" He took his hand off the radio and adjusted his pants by the leather belt.

"Yup. Ellie. Ellie Brown." She lingered on her last name. When her father was still chief, it had held some power, but just seven months later, she was lucky if people remembered that Plackard hadn't always been the Broadlands fire chief.

"Ah, right . . . ," he said, seeming to catch on. But then he stood up a little taller like a shock had gone through him. "Oh my God, your dad is Chief Brown? This is your family, then, huh?"

She tried not to let the annoyed tension in her shoulders show.

"Um, yeah. Steve," she said, pointing to the cracked hospital room door, "is my brother-in-law."

"Oh man. I'm so sorry. I think they're almost done in there. Sorry, it is kinda intense, or else I'd interrupt."

"Yeah? Intense?" She took a step forward with a conspiratorial twist to her lips and breathiness to her whisper. "So, Steve is awake, I take it?"

"Yeah, he's a little loopy but awake. You know, he actually thought the nurse was you when she first came in. He called her Ellie and asked for green Jell-O or something like that."

Green Jell-O. Ellie had to bite down hard so she didn't show how the mention of that neon gelatin snack made her choke up.

When she had had the stomach flu three Thanksgivings ago and Dad had been working a double shift, she had spent the weekend on Amelia's couch and had lost track of how many times she had thrown up. Finally, seeing her so weak and dehydrated, Steve had made her a huge bowl of green Jell-O. Just the smell had made her want to yak all over again, but he had sat by her and, using his stern but gentle paramedic skills, he had fed her small bites, even when she had covered her mouth, shaking her head like a stubborn toddler. It had soon become a family joke, and each year since, Steve had made an obnoxiously huge bowl of green Jell-O to go with Thanksgiving dinner.

Suddenly she wished she were in that room, filling water cups, fetching Popsicles for post-anesthesia nausea, and watching carefully for any signs of complications. It seemed like the only thing that would keep her from obsessing about Amelia's dire situation was to have *some* control, some place of comfort and assistance in Steve's life.

"So, does he remember anything?" she asked.

The officer—Blackford, according to his name tag—lowered his voice further, still far too wrapped up in looking like he knew things to remember that perhaps he shouldn't share certain information with family members.

"Well, like I said, he's still pretty loopy, but from what I can tell, he got a good view of his attacker."

Maybe she should've been a cop. Who knew if she'd be any good at interrogating criminals, but she was doing a pretty stellar job at getting information out of this guy at least.

"I'm sure the cameras helped plenty." She knew that dropping in just enough insider information would make the officer feel more comfortable with sharing.

"Well, that's the thing. The cameras were turned off until just a few minutes before the crime. They got a good picture of all the stuff after the shots were fired but not much before that."

Ellie's mind was racing, but she had to look calm on the outside in order to keep the officer talking. She just nodded slowly as he spoke and hoped a few seconds of silence on her part would entice him to give more information. There were too many conflicting facts in his statement. The cameras were turned off. That didn't make much sense. And then they were back on *after* the crime. But, she'd been in the house; the power had been turned off at some point.

"Well, that sure is odd." Ellie tried to sound as oblivious as she could. Blackford was getting a lot of satisfaction out of acting like the all-knowing police officer talking to the less-than-knowledgeable young female paramedic.

"Right? But Rivera has it figured out. He thinks that when the power was turned off, it reset the system and booted up the emergency battery on the cameras. Would've been better to have all the footage, but really maybe it's almost as good having the recordings from when the perp didn't know the camera was on."

"Wait, you got video of the second man?" The words shot out of her mouth without her practiced cool. Officer Blackford hesitated for a second before responding. He was a little more reserved this time.

"Uh, I think we will know more soon enough."

Great, she thought. He was onto her. She decided to try one more time.

"So, did they get an ID on the body?" she asked.

"Sorry, Brown, can't really talk about it. You'll have to ask Rivera." Blackford relaxed and leaned back against the wall, and Ellie knew he was done sharing.

Disappointment flooded over her in a hot wave that made it hard to breathe. *Damn it.* She stared at the crack in the heavy door, straining to hear any clue of what was going on inside. She took a side glance at

Blackford who now had his hands on his hips in authority even though he was slouching against the wall with his bit of a belly rolling over the top of his belt.

"Well, thanks for the info." She took a slight step backward. "Tell Rivera to get me when he's done."

"Yeah, sure, not a problem, Brown," he said, waving her off.

On her second step backward, Ellie turned on the ball of her foot and, not hesitating, shoved the door open, palms flat against the polished wood door.

"Hey, Brown . . . what the . . ." His words melted away as the door flew open at her touch. A dim room stared back at her, curtain pulled around what seemed to be the only bed. Murmurs from behind the divider let Ellie know that she hadn't been discovered yet, but that wouldn't last long.

Ellie grabbed the edge of the curtain and yanked. It was lighter than she'd expected, nearly silky in her grasp, and it whipped aside, revealing two men—one totally unfamiliar and wearing a suit with a slightly out-of-date, oversize maroon tie that looked like it'd been worn by more than one generation of police detectives. The second was Travis, still in his uniform, hand hovering over what had to be a nearly full notebook at this point.

Then there was Steve—pale, drowsy, and lips in a thin line that told Ellie that he was in pain. She wanted to run to him, check his vitals, look him in the eye, and make sure that even if his physical pain level was managed, someone was tending to his emotional pain level. Unlike Travis and the detective sitting beside him, Steve didn't seem to notice or care about her entrance. He continued to stare blankly at the closed blinds that not only shut out the flashing ambulance lights from the parking lot but also cut off his view of the world and a life changed forever.

"Hey!" Blackford shouted from the doorway. He looked at Travis and the detective apologetically. "Sorry, I tried to stop her . . . She started talking and then . . ."

Travis waved him off. "Tom, no worries. Why don't you go grab yourself a coffee? I'll cover the hall for a bit."

"Yes sir," Blackford said, running his hand over his balding head and mumbling something under his breath. He gave Ellie a confused but contemptuous look as he crossed the threshold into the hallway. She'd just made an enemy in the police department for sure.

The man in the suit rolled his eyes openly once Officer Tom Blackford had disappeared around the corner. "You couldn't get anyone other than Tom for that post? God, what if she'd been the shooter, eh?"

"Who says she's not?" Steve muttered with a gravelly voice, slurring the words together as though his lips were swollen. Ellie couldn't help but smile. His voice, even coarse and tight with pain, was the best sound she'd heard all day.

"Steve!" Ellie ignored the two men at the foot of the hospital bed and lunged across the room to his side. He had IV tubes going into his arm and a nasal cannula to help his O_2 count. His hair, which she'd never seen out of place, was matted down, a few stray pieces stuck to his forehead. But even the trace of a smile on his face made her feel like a little girl again. She took his hand in hers, careful not to upset the medical equipment next to him.

"L . . . I'm so glad to see your face. Amelia . . . She . . . Someone . . . ," he started, and then abandoned several sentences, all seemingly about her sister, or the shooting or his fears for what had become of his wife. Tears welled up in his eyes, and all efforts at speech halted. Ellie took her free hand and patted his cheek, rough with stubble.

"Shhh. We will be okay. I promise. We will be okay . . ." The words tangled in her throat, and she didn't believe them even as they hit her own ears.

CHAPTER 16

AMELIA

Thursday, April 14
Four weeks earlier

She'd driven past the Slatterys' old place a million and one times during her life here in Broadlands. The old two-story colonial with a wraparound porch used to be her dream house. Every few years old Mrs. Slattery would call the local painter out to touch up the wooden siding and change the color of the shutters. Navy blue had been the color of choice when Amelia was in grade school. A brilliant red when she was in Broadlands High. They were black after Mr. Slattery died in Amelia's first year of college. They were black for a long time.

Then, just before Mrs. Slattery joined her husband in heaven, the shutters were painted a light, gauzy yellow. Not harsh or brash like the skin of a lemon or an early-spring dandelion. Not dark like gold or mustard. Yellow, like sunlight streaming through white curtains on a summer morning. Yellow, like Easter dresses and the crocus flowers her mother had planted when Amelia was a child and that still bloomed every spring.

She remembered thinking back then that this must be what houses in heaven looked like. If so, Mrs. Slattery must have felt right at home when she crossed over in her sleep just a few weeks after the paint job was done.

But once Mrs. Slattery was gone, her home went into probate and sat empty for first one year, then another, and then another. Soon, the white siding was gray and covered on one side with a thin film of algae that had crept up from the pond. And only one of the shutters the color of sunlight remained. Now it was hanging upside down, off to one side on one screw like a woman losing her fake eyelash.

Though you could see the house from the road, it still took a good three-minute drive to reach it. Another quarter mile up a dirt path was the site for the new construction that had started to go up as soon as the ground thawed enough to allow a foundation to be dug. Now, the framing and outside of the house were up. It was clearly going to be monstrous and the fanciest house within a ten-mile radius. Maybe she'd try to get Randy signed on with Broadlands Roofing. That roof would bring in enough to pay for the security cameras, the girls' recital dresses, and a whole new set of tires, heck, a whole new truck.

The house was covered in workers, like ants crawling on a dropped hot dog. She checked off in the distance to see if she recognized any of the men, their forms in dusty jackets and well-worn jeans. Sure, Broadlands was just some little town, but with cheap land and plenty of undocumented laborers in the area, it was also a great place to build whatever it was that Randy was building.

The structure was too far away for Amelia to make out any faces or really any identifiable characteristics. Amelia navigated her ten-year-old four-door SUV into the empty spot next to what had to be Randy's BMW. She had to hold back rolling her eyes. The house, the car, the clothes—what must it be like to be able to spend money like it was nothing?

But even if he imported a twenty-four-karat-gold replica of Michelangelo's *David* with a fountain arching out of it and plopped it down in his front yard, who was she to judge? He seemed nice enough last time they'd met, and it was only a silent assumption that he put so much value on the material things in life. Maybe he was a trust-fund baby, and driving a BMW instead of a Lamborghini was already a state of humility.

But it wasn't the car or clothes that confused Amelia. Now that she had met Randy and little Dawson, she wondered what in the world could entice him to build such a huge house for just the two of them. Amelia slammed her car door and headed around the back of the car to Kate's side. She was checking the top of her hair with expert fingers. Dozens of little rebellious hairs stood out around her ponytail holders, but no way Amelia would let on to the fact or even give her daughter a chance to check the mirror again.

"Kate, it looks great. Come on, we gotta get in. We're already a little late."

"That's 'cause you took forever talking to Uncle Caleb." She sighed, pushing the orange button on her lap belt and hopping down to the floor of the SUV. Sometimes her girls talked like small adults and left Amelia speechless.

"Sorry, Kate. Dawson will understand. Come on, jump into my arms!" She put out her arms, and Kate took a big leap. Amelia caught her in her arms, the warmth of her little body taking the chill off the bare skin of her wrists. She placed the wiggly six-year-old down on the gravel driveway and grabbed the bags from the passenger seat.

The smell of sawdust and paint hung in the air. It wasn't just the big house at the end of the drive that was getting work done, but the Slattery house was also under construction. It had started to transform back into the dreamland she'd created inside her head as a child.

The algae of the past few years was gone, and a new coat of paint made the house glisten white and clean in the spring sunshine. And the shutters were not yellow, not black, not even green, but a deep, rich purple that picked up the subtle hues of the climbing lilac vine trailing across the front of the porch just starting its spring bloom. The delicate scent of lilacs only added to the dream quality of the porch, the main floor planks stained a dark brown with white highlights on the stairs and railings. When the front screen door squeaked and banged, it was like Amelia had been transported into one of her daydreams. A hanging swing, maybe a wicker chair or two, and she might curl up and never want to leave.

Dawson bolted out of the front door, his eyes alive with pent-up excitement from what had probably been a morning of unbearable anticipation. His hair stood up all over, and his blue eyes danced in a way that made Amelia burst out laughing. Before she knew it, Kate was wrapped up in an awkward and aggressive embrace. Her arms hung by her side like she wasn't sure what to do with them.

"Hey, Dawson." Kate's words were nearly absorbed by the fabric of Dawson's Gap polo. He looked like a kid model from one of those all black-and-white photo spreads at the mall. Amelia could tell her daughter was starting to get a little claustrophobic with all the attention, her dark eyes glancing up pleadingly.

"Where's *my* hug, Dawson? Don't want me to feel left out, do you?"

The little boy let Kate go and leaped across the hardwood of the porch to Amelia's open arms. He landed against her so hard that she let out an "Oof," nearly knocking out all the air in her lungs. His thin arms squeezed around her neck with such strength that it felt like he wasn't just holding on to her but trying to make something come back.

Recovering from the unanticipated impact, she wrapped her arms around the boy's torso and pulled him in for a real hug—a mom hug. He smelled of pancake syrup and hair gel; she wasn't sure which was responsible for his wild hairdo. Maybe a little of both.

"Hey, buddy, good to see you again." She patted his back through the soft fabric of his shirt, but he didn't let go. "Hey, is your daddy here? Why don't you go find him?" Amelia asked softly in his ear, like she was telling a bedtime story.

Dawson nuzzled one of his cheeks against Amelia's and then backed away. She immediately grabbed his hands in hers to discourage any more "aggressive hugging" when another squeak-bang made her look up.

Randy, wearing a pair of jeans and a formfitting blue tee shirt, had his hands in his pockets. As he approached, he flinched back against the slight chill in the air. His hair was wet, and there were a few dark spots on his shirt that made her think he must've just gotten out of the shower. As he got closer, a warm cloud of shower smells, soap, shampoo, and maybe a dash of cologne or at least freshly applied deodorant followed him.

"I see Dawson found you." Randy's smile was broader and whiter than Amelia had remembered, though today he seemed nervous.

"Uh, yeah, did he ever!" Amelia let go of Dawson's hands and stood quickly before he got any more hugging ideas. Her shirt was a bit askew, showing her bra strap on one side, and her sweater was nearly hanging off her arm at the elbow. She readjusted her top until she was covered again and hopefully looked polished enough for the overly polished Randy, though a little voice in her head kept asking why she even cared what this stranger thought of her.

"Oh, sorry, did he hug you, honey?" Dawson had taken Kate's hand, and she stared at him as though he'd put a bug on it.

"A little, but he about squeezed Mommy to death," she said, yanking her hand away. "So, do you have any toys?" Kate asked as though she were starting to feel like this playdate was a trap and soon she was going to be forced to eat her veggies and go to bed early.

"Yeah, tons of toys. Come on." Dawson reached for her hand again, but this time Kate batted him away. She looked to Amelia briefly for permission, and after a tiny nod from her mom, she dashed through the screen door with her new friend, her tulle skirt trailing behind her, nearly caught in the slamming door.

Randy shivered a little and then gave Amelia an embarrassed smile. "I'm really sorry about Dawson. He can be overly affectionate sometimes. Especially with women." He tilted his head toward the door and started walking toward the entrance, sweeping the door open so fast, it didn't have time to make a sound. "He really misses his mom."

That sentence made a piece of Amelia's heart flinch in pain. That's right, his mom. Living, where did he say, Arizona? California? That had to be hard for a little child. Kate could barely make it through a school day without seeing her mom. What would she do if she had to spend weeks or even months apart? No wonder he needed an occasional squishy hug.

"Poor buddy," she said, passing by Randy into the house, excited about finally seeing inside her dream home. The smell of pancakes and bacon hit her right as she crossed the threshold.

The room was everything she could've imagined. To the left was a giant kitchen, clearly refinished with modern appliances and quartz countertops but with white cabinets and dark, mahogany hardwood all throughout. The rugs looked rustic but probably cost a small fortune. The furniture was off-white and overstuffed, making her wonder if sitting on it would be like sitting on a cloud or if it would swallow her up like quicksand.

Randy didn't seem to notice her voyeuristic observance of his home and just moved toward the kitchen, where a little blue plastic plate sat on the bar, one stool slightly askew illustrating how Dawson had gotten to the door so stinking fast. Randy took the plate and ran it under some water in the deep porcelain sink. The act seemed so normal and mundane that it made her relax a little.

"Anything I can do to help?" Her hands felt empty as she watched him move on to filling a dirty pan with water and soap.

"No, no! I'm sorry, I know this is so rude, but if I don't get these soaking, they will take forever to get clean later."

"Hey, I feel your pain! I always say that there are just some dishes that need to marinate for a day or two."

"Ha! Yes, I like that. I mean, you marinate a steak for at least twenty-four hours. Why should dishes be any different?"

It was nice to have someone get her sense of humor—even mommy humor.

"Well, I'm sure it isn't easy being a single parent."

"It is definitely not what you plan for when that little baby is placed in your arms, right?" He sounded so introspective, it was compelling to Amelia. It made her feel like there was more to this guy than the fancy things he clearly treasured. It was what she found interesting and a little frightening at the park when he connected with his son so easily, so deeply.

"I guess life takes us all down unexpected paths, huh?"

"I know. That's what I've had to tell myself every day since we lost Stella." Randy paused his washing and leaned on the sink like he was trying to prop up some broken part of himself, but the words didn't exactly make sense to her. She wiped at the countertop absentmindedly, her hand sticking in an invisible streak of syrup.

"Stella?"

Randy blew out a breath and then picked up a plate and covered it in suds.

"Yeah, my . . . wife. She passed last year. Cancer."

Oh shit. Well, there she went, putting her foot in her mouth. Amelia didn't know how to get out of this painful topic.

"I'm so sorry, Randy. I had no idea . . . Dawson said something about visiting his mom in California, and I just thought . . . I don't know."

He turned on the water and rinsed the plate clear before putting it on a rack next to the sink. With a flip, he pulled a hand towel off the bar under the sink.

"I don't know why he still says that." Randy returned the towel and closed the cabinet under the sink and then ran his hand through his hair, making it look messed up but in a really stylish way. There was a sadness that hung around Randy's shoulders and was embedded in the lines around his eyes that fascinated Amelia as he continued. "His therapist back home said it was his coping mechanism. Said it was too hard for him to understand this loss at such a young age, so . . . he just makes up stories. Sometimes it's visiting his mom, sometimes she's an astronaut and is on a trip to the moon, sometimes he was adopted and he tells people that I'm not even his dad. Anyway. He's still sad and just shows it in his own way, I guess."

He shrugged and then moved away from the sink and toward Amelia. When he reached the bar, Randy settled himself on the stool next to her, and pushed an overflowing basket of muffins and bagels and pretty much any other carb you'd expect to eat for breakfast her way. He grabbed a bran muffin from the top.

"Well, that's hard for both of you," Amelia said, making sure to avoid all the wrong things that people had said to her after her dad's stroke.

"I guess that's why I'm throwing myself into all these projects—the new house, renovations over here, my business. I think being a worka-holic is *my* coping mechanism." He popped a bite of muffin into his mouth and shook his head slowly from side to side like he'd just learned something about himself he'd never known before.

"There *are* worse things. And you are doing all the most important things right." She gestured toward the ceiling where the muffled sounds of kids playing could be heard through the floor. "I don't know. I envy you a little, I guess."

"Are you sure about that?" Randy's eyebrows rose.

"Oh, no, sorry. Not about your loss." She shook her head back and forth quickly several times. "I mean about how much you accomplish as a professional and as a parent. That's really hard to do, and you are doing it."

Randy laughed, his rich tones filling the kitchen and rattling the glassware in the cabinets. He gave Amelia a twisted smirk that reminded her of Dawson.

"It is all an illusion, I promise you. It just seems like I have this all figured out, but really what is happening is all my balls are currently in the air. When they all come down at the same time, it will look less like juggling and more like a big mess."

"Well, I think that's what we all feel like, right? Any person who actually thinks they have all their shit together is not allowed to be my friend." She let herself join in Randy's laughter, enjoying the fact that the seemingly perfect man had flaws and insecurities as big and real as her own.

Randy's laugh stopped fairly abruptly, like a thought had entered his mind and pushed out any room for humor or levity. He dragged his full coffee mug across the counter and took a deep drink as Amelia tried to read his mood. He swallowed and then licked his lips before looking back at Amelia again. This time there was something in his eyes, something she could tell he wanted to say. Usually she would smooth over the awkwardness with a joke or a change of subject, but today she just sat still, waiting, wanting to know what he was thinking. He blinked a few times and then looked back down at his coffee, and the moment was gone.

"Have you ever thought about trying your hand at real estate?" Randy asked, and Amelia was 90 percent sure it wasn't the question he wanted to ask.

"Gosh, no. I mean, I don't have a license. I wouldn't even know where to start."

"I think you'd be good at it. You have an eye for potential, you are good with people, and you know the area better than anyone I've worked with so far. I mean if you *are* interested, then I could help you get your license, maybe even give you a place to start while you build up your own client list."

"Wait, is this a job offer?"

Randy nodded, picking at his muffin, a hopeful but also reserved expression on his face.

"I think you'd be an excellent investment." He shrugged, seeming almost shy. "Anyway, no pressure, but if you ever want to know more— I'm here to answer any questions."

With a silent nod, Amelia tried not to show what she was feeling inside, but she couldn't help but let a little balloon of pride swell up inside her. Fancy Randy wanted to give her a job, and Steve didn't even think she could clean the hair spray off the door in a timely manner.

"Thanks, Randy." She held back a self-satisfied smile. No way was he serious, but maybe she *would* be good at it and she could actually help out with bills instead of dropping a piddly few bucks into a jar every time she played an event. She thought of Randy's car and house and clothes and . . . She didn't need any of those things, but in her life the financial success they represented would translate to a full-time nurse for her dad, dance classes for the girls, security cameras, and a new truck for the business.

"Hey," she added, pointing and waving with an attempt to sound casual. "Pass the muffins."

Randy chuckled and shoved the bowl across the counter, and Amelia knew she had a lot to think about.

CHAPTER 17

ELLIE

Tuesday, May 10
4:54 p.m.

Steve's eyes fluttered closed for the third time in the same sentence. He was clearly exhausted and being pulled down by the weight of the heavy pain medication. Travis had finished questioning him more than an hour earlier but still hadn't left the room even for a bathroom break. Ellie wasn't sure what he was waiting for, but if she couldn't be by her sister's side, she would most definitely be by Steve's, and no amount of police presence was going to stop her.

Collin was there too, asleep in a chair in the corner, a pillow that the nurse had brought in propped against the wall. He came in as soon as Ellie texted him her location. He'd stayed awake for all of Travis's questions and most of Steve's half-lucid conversation with Ellie. He'd been up early studying and was doing the impossible task of taking time off from his schedule to be there with Ellie. It was a sacrifice she truly appreciated, but it also reminded her every time she turned around that Caleb was still missing and she didn't know who the dead man was lying on the slab in the morgue downstairs. As Collin slept, she watched him, studied him, trying to compare her fiancé's sleeping form with the lifeless body she'd left behind in the Broadlands Roofing office.

Though Travis and the man who turned out to be Homicide Detective Michaels had let her stay during the last few minutes of his interview, the detective hadn't delved into any really hard-hitting questions while Ellie was in the room. To be honest, even with her handholding, Steve wasn't able to answer even the most basic questions about camera positioning and security software. She was pretty sure any earlier discussion and his resulting slurred answers would've been just as hard to understand.

"So, how are you holding up, Brown?" Travis asked out of nowhere, putting his phone back in his hip pocket. His tone was practiced and steady, like he was still asking about a crime.

Ellie sighed. Her hand was still entwined with Steve's and she liked the way her short fingers and stubby nails looked against the back of his hand, like a child holding her big brother's hand when she was scared. If only she could bring comfort to Steve the way he had with her so many other times in her life, like when he picked her up in his rig and uniform to scare away the bully girl who would tease her as she walked home from school. Or when he talked the director of the musical into giving her a new audition because she'd had a sinus infection during her first tryout. If only bullet holes could be healed with good intentions and strongly worded speeches.

"I don't really know how to answer that, Rivera. I . . . Thank you for letting me stay with Steve. Until I can visit Amelia . . . this helps." She gave Steve's hand a squeeze.

"Well, you should be by her side soon enough, right?" The toughness was leaving his voice again. It was like he sometimes forgot how to be human, and then when they chatted, he started to slowly remember.

"Yeah, they just want her to be stable, I guess. They promised Collin that if there was a turn for the worse, then I could come sooner. So, I guess for now the silence is a good thing." She tried to sound aloof, like every time her phone buzzed she didn't jump and have an urge to go check out who was calling or texting.

"You do know that you should probably get some sleep, right?" He shifted his gaze to Collin and then back to Ellie like he was giving her a message. "I'm sure you were well into your shift when you got the call. Maybe you should go home and get some clean clothes and grab a nap."

Ellie looked over her hodgepodge outfit and couldn't help but let out a small laugh. "I thought you *liked* my sweatshirt."

"Oh, I love your sweatshirt. In fact, I think you should keep it, but I think you might be more comfortable spending the next few days here if you've had a shower and packed a bag. What do you think?'"

"So now I smell too? Thanks, Rivera." Ellie tried desperately to sound lighthearted, but Travis wasn't buying it.

He gave her a very small, sad smile. "I'm serious about this one, Brown. You can't help anyone if you're a mess."

"But what if Steve wakes up and needs me?" She rubbed the hairy back of Steve's hand with her thumb. "Or what if something happens with Amelia and I'm not . . . I'm not here to see her?"

"I'd get in my car, lights and siren, and come get you, Brown. I swear." He leaned forward in his seat till the pad squeaked against the frame, his hands crossed in front of him, elbows on his knees. His dark eyes were soft and concerned, and she knew in that moment that he actually cared. But then he shifted back and hit the back of the chair with a thump. "Besides, don't you live super close to the firehouse? Someone there could drive you. Isn't any given location in Broadlands like no more than five minutes away from any other spot in the town? Knowing your mile time, I bet you could sprint there faster than I could make it to Broadlands from here in my car."

"How do you know anything about my mile time?"

"Um," he stuttered, and an instant blush rushed across Travis's cheeks, which was saying something because his skin was a deep olive. "Some of the guys were out for a drink, and Mitch mentioned that you'd almost passed your exam that day, and he said something about you having the fastest mile time of any man in the firehouse. I don't know, it kinda stuck with me. Remembering details is part of my job, and sometimes I don't get to pick which ones I remember."

Ellie wanted to give him a hard time about the situation but didn't for two reasons. First, because she was starting to wonder if this really was the right time to go home and get some supplies, check on the girls and her father, and then plan on spending the next few days at the hospital. But, second, because it was really incredibly nice to know that someone in a civil service career could overlook her flunking the overall score and instead focus on her great success in at least one area of her life. In fact, it was something she had a hard time remembering about herself most of the time—that one fail doesn't make *the person* a failure.

Ellie had a knot in her throat that was growing bigger by the second. She had to look away from Travis before figuring out how to respond in the most macho way she could manage.

"I'm also the firehouse arm-wrestling champion. I bet they didn't tell you that, now did they?"

"That they did not," he said. She thought she could hear laughter in his voice but didn't want to look up. Instead, she slowly released Steve's limp hand and gently laid it across his midsection.

"Well, I think I'm going to go check on Amelia and maybe go home for a bit if I can get Collin to wake up." She hitched a thumb over her shoulder at her still-sleeping fiancé, shaking her head slightly. "I'm sure he'd want to get into something more comfortable and see if Caleb called."

She wasn't sure if she imagined it, but Travis seemed to stiffen a little when Ellie talked about Collin. No, not at the mention of Collin. Caleb. She hadn't addressed her concerns about Caleb directly to Travis just yet. She'd been waiting for them to bring up his name to Steve but was surprised when no one had broached the subject. Maybe those were the questions Travis and Jackson had been discussing before she forced her way in. But now she could tell Travis had something to say, and Ellie wasn't sure she wanted to hear it.

His hands were clenched in fists on the top of his knees. "So, Brown, just one favor I need to ask you. If Caleb Thornton calls or texts or shows up or anything . . . please call me. Or better yet, call 911."

Ellie's eyes opened wide. "What? 911. Why?"

"We have some very important questions to ask him, and he's been unavailable just yet," he answered very formally, stressing the word "unavailable" as though it were code.

"Yeah, we are actually really worried about him. He's very close to Amelia . . ." Ellie paused and added, "And Steve too. I know he'd want to be kept up on what is going on." She didn't hint at any of her concerns about how closely Caleb had been watching her sister or how nervous Amelia seemed around him lately. She hadn't even told Collin that.

Travis shifted from side to side, glanced at Collin, and then smoothed over his uniform carefully till his badge lay flat again.

"Yes, we heard that Caleb and Amelia had a previous relationship. Just know that there is some indication that Caleb Thornton could be armed and dangerous. We are asking that all civilians keep their distance as a precaution."

"Wait, what?" Ellie moved to the edge of her seat. The words made sense, but she didn't actually understand them. "You think that Caleb did all this? You think he shot Steve and that dead man and Amelia?" She shook her head, not willing to consider it as a real possibility out loud no matter what the little voice in the back of her head had been screaming all day.

"I'm not saying he shot anyone, but . . . ," he said, hesitating again, "we just want to keep people safe."

"Are you seriously telling people to be on guard against Caleb? No one will believe you. He's adored in town."

"Well, I highly doubt he's still in Broadlands. That's why we went to Channel Nine in Shelby. Thought they could get the news out to more people than the local cable show."

"Caleb is going to be on the news?"

"Yes." Travis checked his watch. "It will be on at five and again at ten. I'm sure his picture will be on the morning news too."

She checked on Collin again and then looked back at Travis. "I don't know what you think you are doing going after someone like Caleb. He's not the type to . . ."

"To leave the scene of a crime covered in blood and disappear without a trace? How about to stalk and threaten your sister and her friend Mr. Mraz in the weeks prior to the crime? Does that sound like your best buddy Caleb?"

"What do you mean 'leave the scene of the crime'?" She was on her feet now, not sure how she got there but also too full of questions and anger to sit back down and take it. "Was that what you found on the cameras, or did Steve tell you that?" Even as she asked the questions, she knew she wasn't going to get any straight answers from Travis, but there was something about saying them out loud that made the scene run through her mind. Caleb, running out the side door, covered in her sister's blood.

"I've said too much already. Just know that he's not safe." Travis narrowed his eyes, head tipped up to look her in the eye from his sitting position. "But I think you knew that already, didn't you?"

Ellie thought back to that moment in the waiting room when the name "Caleb" had tickled the edge of her mind and rested heavy on her tongue. It was a different fear from losing her sister or Steve or her father. This fear was that her soon-to-be brother-in-law could possibly have been the one to pull the trigger and put those bullets there.

It filled her with a pain so heavy that it was like liquid lead being poured into every joint in her body. It made her want to double over on top of herself and squeeze the pain out.

"I don't know what you're talking about," she said, her voice cracking at the end. She looked over Steve one last time, glancing at his vitals, his coloring, his breathing. He seemed to be out cold and stable. She leaned across Collin to retrieve her charging phone and the tangled blue-and-white cord he'd purchased in the gift store, hastily shoved it all into the shallow pocket of her sweatshirt, then leaned down and gently tapped Collin's thigh.

"Collin. Hey, babe." She glanced at Travis, who was still watching her as though taking mental notes. Collin stirred slightly, and Ellie gave him a brief but deliberate kiss on his partially separated lips. Almost immediately he responded as though instinct won out over sleep, his lips pressing back against hers, his hand coming up and resting on her hip and then sweeping against the thin strip of exposed skin on the lower part of her back. The unexpectedness of the embrace surprised Ellie, who knew at once that Collin didn't remember where he was or why they were there. She pulled away from his kiss slowly, their lips releasing quarter inch by quarter inch until they shared nothing more than the breath between them.

When Collin opened his eyes, he blinked once, then twice as the room seemed to come into focus. She could only imagine what it was like to wake to a kiss, only to have the reality of gunshots, murder, and a missing brother rush in at you. Ellie swore she read the moment in his eyes when it all registered. He sat up in a rush, his hands dropping from her waist and running over the smooth fabric of the scrubs till they fell away completely.

"I'm so sorry I dozed off. Everything okay? Any word?" His eyes were bloodshot and looked just a little unfamiliar with his glasses off. Ellie ran her finger down a crease from where he was leaning on his sleeve and felt a distinct button impression.

"Still waiting to see M," she whispered, and then went down on her knees next to Collin, placing a hand on his chest till she could feel his heart beating against her palm. Ellie wished she could put her head in that exact spot and fall asleep. Instead, she bit her lip and then asked a question that made her feel nervous and a little disloyal. "Any news from Caleb?"

Collin leaned back and searched through the deep pocket of his rumpled khakis until he fished out his phone.

"Oh my God, L . . . Mom says they saw Caleb on the news. I have a million other texts here saying the same thing." He ran his thumb up and down the screen, lips forming each word silently. "He could never do this. Never. He loves Amelia. He loves your family . . . There has to be some kind of misunderstanding . . ."

His eyes flitted up and down, side to side, and it hurt Ellie to watch. She knew what this meant to Caleb and Collin and the whole Thornton family. If it was true, if Caleb was potentially armed and dangerous, that meant he could be the man who shot her sister. Even if not, his life in Broadlands was ruined, his name scarred, and his family under a hot and blistering spotlight.

Now, what she didn't know, at least not for sure, was whether she believed Collin. Of course he thought his brother was innocent and hiding because of fear and embarrassment.

But she had a growing feeling that she believed Travis, and Caleb actually was an incredibly dangerous man who was not only on the loose, but also had a vendetta against the people she loved the most.

CHAPTER 18

AMELIA

Wednesday, April 20
Three weeks earlier

"I like that one but maybe with some straps," Amelia said with as much excitement as she could muster.

It was the twenty-third dress Ellie had tried on, and all the white satin and beaded accents were blurring together at this point. Not shockingly, she looked graceful and flawless in every single one. She was going to be one of those brides who looked like she walked right off a magazine cover on her wedding day. Amelia had felt beautiful when she walked down the aisle to Steve's waiting arm, but looking back at her wedding pictures, she was pretty sure she looked more like an off-white cupcake than a glamorous bride.

Ellie scrunched up her nose. "I don't know, I was kinda hoping for something a little more . . ." She looked over the flowing satin and drop waistline, disappointment in her eyes.

"More like Mom's dress?" Amelia could read her sister so easily.

Ellie rolled her eyes and shrugged her pale shoulders. She wasn't wearing her glasses today since she'd just gotten off her shift and usually didn't like to wear them on the job, but her hair was up in a high, tight ponytail, probably once all slicked back but now with pieces curling out around her neck and temples.

"I don't know." Ellie shrugged again, and Amelia couldn't help but have a moment of sister-envy that she looked beautiful even when emotionally tortured. Ellie lifted the heavy skirt of the dress, took one step down from the three-tiered platform, and sat down with a poof. "Okay, fine. Maybe."

Amelia stood up from her spot in the upholstered armchair where she'd been sitting for nearly an hour. Her rear end was now numb and her neck screaming for one of Steve's amazing neck rubs. Stacey's Bridal Shop had been on Main Street in Broadlands for as long as Amelia could remember. She used to walk past the window and gaze at the display, dreaming of what her wedding dress would look like one day. She had purchased her wedding dress there, and now Ellie was trying to sort through the sadly outdated stock, hoping for something close to acceptable in order to keep up the tradition. They had plenty of time to find "the" dress, but Stacey's was the place to at least start.

After a quick look around to make sure she was clear of any store employees, Amelia snagged her phone out of her purse. They'd been warned that there was a strict "no pictures" policy in case you tried to find the same dress cheaper at one of those big-box bridal stores. Dressed for a casual business meeting with Randy that afternoon, Amelia felt a little awkward in her knee-length pencil skirt and loose red silk blouse. She wobbled when she walked across the soft carpet on her heels; the two complimentary glasses of champagne didn't really help.

"Scooch over, love." Amelia aimed for the empty spot next to Ellie and only ended up sitting on a small swath of the poofy dress. As soon as she was by her side, Amelia pulled out her phone and swiped across the screen through a group of pictures until she found the one she wanted. It was actually a picture of a picture. It had always hung in their childhood home just over the fireplace. The images had faded over the years, the green trees in the background now yellowed, the blacks bluish gray, and the whites browning, but when it came down to it, all Amelia could ever see in that picture was love. Her mother, dressed in a simple but elegant and slightly hippie-ish wedding dress, flowers in a crown. With her dark hair, she looked like Ellie's twin. By her side stood their father, his mustache black despite the fading. Amelia couldn't remember seeing that smile since their mother's passing.

"I look at this sometimes when I miss her and miss home. I know you see it every day at Dad's house, but . . ." Amelia paused and shifted off the crinkled material she was in the process of ruining before pointing at the picture again. "As much as I love Mom's dress in this picture, I think you need to remember that you might have your own kids one day. And they will need a picture like this to look at. Think of it like a picture book that shows them what love looks like. That should be *your* picture. Not a re-creation of Mom and Dad, right?" She passed the phone to Ellie, who had a tear running down her cheek. "That picture needs to be of 'Ellie and Collin.' Your dress. His smile." She slipped her arm around her sister's shoulder. "Your love."

Ellie blinked a few times and passed the phone back to Amelia. "Damn it, M. Stop making me cry, okay? You know I hate crying."

"For someone who hates crying, you sure seem to do a lot of it," Amelia joked, squeezing Ellie's shoulder hard and then ducking away.

"Shut up!" Ellie bumped up against her and sniffed again. Amelia lunged across the space between the mirrored platform and her seat and snagged three tissues from the box next to her empty champagne glass.

"Here, let's get you cleaned up and home. You've been awake far too long. No more dress shopping after a shift, okay?" Amelia held out the tissues, and Ellie took them.

"I think you're right. It's the lack of sleep. I'll be fine after eight or ten or maybe even twelve hours." Ellie put out her hand for help, and Amelia yanked hard to get her up. Just as she got to her feet, the door dinged with a new customer. Ellie gathered the skirt of her dress in her hands, exposing her bare feet.

"I vote for twelve hours. You work too hard!" Amelia called after Ellie as she disappeared into the changing room.

"You've been on 'Dad duty' for the past three days. No rest for me!" Ellie called out from behind the dividers. She always thought it was funny how Ellie would talk to her through the thin metal walls when she was in public restroom stalls. Then again, Ellie had no real "Edit button" when it came to issues that might cause others embarrassment. Amelia once heard Steve explaining to her that just 'cause the guys hung around the firehouse with no shirt on didn't mean she could just chill in her sports bra. Well, she *could*, but it wouldn't really help make her "one of the guys" if that was what she was going for.

"I know, but sleep is kind of a physical necessity, Ellie," Amelia shouted into the changing room, and then headed back toward her seat and purse so she could hide her phone before the manager, Bonnie, saw her with it and freaked.

She leaned over, grabbed her faded faux leather purse, and dropped the phone inside, where it settled nicely into the clutter of old receipts and appointment cards. As Amelia zipped it closed, she stood to full height and was nearly face-to-face with Collin, dressed in belted jeans and a tee shirt.

"Collin!" Amelia nearly screamed. He pressed a finger to his lips and imitated a shushing face, a bouquet of blue and yellow hydrangeas in his left hand. Amelia corrected herself and whispered this time. "Collin, what are you doing here?" She placed her fists on her hips and gave him the best sisterly stare down she could.

"My test got postponed, so I thought I'd come surprise Ellie." He had a boy-like smirk on his face, and Amelia had to fight the urge to pinch his cheeks. He'd just been Caleb's somewhat annoying little brother when she still spent time with the Thornton family, and when Ellie came home from her second week of junior year and told her that she was "going out" with Collin Thornton, Amelia told her to run, not walk, away from that boy, afraid that history was just repeating itself.

But when she brought him to Sunday dinner at Amelia's house a few weeks later, it didn't take long to see that the two teenagers weren't just messing around. They were friends in more ways than they were boyfriend and girlfriend, which was actually one of the reasons she never expected them to make it to the altar, but then they went to U of I together, both pre-med, both excellent students, and their relationship kept growing. Amelia worried that they might break up when Ellie dropped out of med school and came back to Broadlands, but Collin made every sacrifice to be close to her and claimed the ninety-minute drive to and from school was worth spending his free nights with Ellie. Those two just kept proving her wrong.

"Aren't you just the sweetest," Amelia said with a touch of actual jealousy. "I remember when Steve was working his shift back when we first started dating and he'd make his partner stop by my house on the way home from a call. Our neighbor, Mrs. Ludlow, nearly had a heart attack every time. My dad would get *so* mad at Steve, but that didn't stop him." She paused, happy that at one time Steve loved her enough to break the rules in order to see her. Then she remembered why she'd been upset at Collin's appearance. She reset her hands on her hips.

"You can't be here! You'll invalidate some poor dress by seeing it on her, and then it couldn't be 'the one' anymore because you saw it. You don't want to do that to your fiancée, do you, Collin?"

Collin laughed. "Goodness no. Who would want to do *that*?" The corner of his mouth turned up, and his cheek crinkled in a way that reminded her of his brother.

Her smile fell a little, and a cool, blank spot reopened inside her. She hadn't seen Caleb since his ominous warning in the kitchen, and every time she found herself thinking about him, it was with a mix of concern for her friend and worry about his state of mind. She'd considered asking Collin if he'd noticed anything but had never gotten the chance. This was her opening; she took a deep breath and dove right in.

"So, have you talked to Caleb lately?"

"Like five minutes ago, actually. He was talking to some guy in a suit outside of the diner. I bet you could catch him if you wanted to."

"Was the guy your height with brown, wavy hair. Kinda fancy looking?" She was just about to leave and meet Randy at the diner for their meeting.

"Yeah, sounds like the guy. They were standing by a fancy convertible BMW, but . . . Caleb works on the other side of your kitchen wall. Don't you see enough of the guy?" Collin chuckled and tapped the bouquet against his thigh, the floral paper crinkling and a few petals falling to the floor of the bridal shop, strangely blending in with the décor.

"Yeah, I mean, I see him plenty, but I wanted to know if *you* had seen him. Maybe noticed something . . . different?"

"Different?" Collin leaned in, this time forgetting the flowers altogether as they bumped into the back of the armchair she'd been a prisoner of for the past hour. More petals fell from the cluster of blossoms, making a pile on the ground.

Amelia's heart started to pound. She hadn't told anyone of her concerns about Caleb's strange and erratic behavior, but for some reason, Collin, who was as close to a stranger as her sister's fiancé could be, seemed the safest person to confide in. She opened her mouth, ready to unleash the story of the picture in the car, the strange meeting on the park bench, his appearance at the park, and then the urgent words of warning about a man he was apparently accosting in the street as they were speaking. Before she could say a word, the soft whisper of fabric and heavy clomp of street shoes made her head turn.

"Hey, you guys gotta know that these walls are paper thin and I've heard every word you've said." Ellie stood outside of the swinging curtain that separated the short hallway of changing rooms from the showroom floor. This time she wasn't wearing a wedding dress but was back in her low-rise boyfriend jeans and tight red tee shirt, hair frizzing out around her temples, a huge smile on her face. "And I agree with what Amelia said earlier. You *are* the sweetest."

Ellie looked more beautiful smiling at Collin and wearing her rumpled street clothes and day-old mascara than she had in any of the dresses so far. Yes. That was the smile her father wore in that picture. God, it didn't matter what dress she picked, did it? That smile said it all.

Amelia stood back and watched carefully as Ellie ran across the room, dropping her bag and a pair of standard white pumps covered in a soft dyeable fabric and leaving a trail of belongings behind her. With a giant leap off the top stair, she collided with Collin, wrapping her arms around his neck and legs around his waist. After an aggressive hug, she pulled her head back away from his and while staring into his eyes, leaned in for a kiss. It was just a little creepy to watch your sister make out with her boyfriend.

She'd have to wait until another time to talk to Collin about his brother. She expected to feel disappointed by this realization but ended up a little relieved. She still had her secret. Once she opened her mouth, everything would change. Her concerns about Caleb would either be confirmed and he'd have to leave Broadlands Roofing, or she'd be laughed at and never ever live it down. She looked at her watch. Six minutes to three. Barely enough time to make it to the diner without ending up with embarrassing sweat marks under her arms.

"Okay, you two. I have to go." She ran a hand through her hair, sweeping her fingers back and forth to try to regain some body. "Do I look business-y enough?"

Ellie's feet hit the floor, smile still broad, her cheeks flushed a flattering pink. "Um, if 'hot' is business-y, then, yeah. Totally."

Amelia flapped her hand toward Ellie in a halfhearted swat.

"Knock it off. I'm serious. Collin?" She struck a sideways pose.

"I'll just pretend you aren't using 'business-y' as an adjective and say, yes, you look well prepared for a business meeting," Collin added. It seemed like he was starting to get used to the sisterly banter, which was a necessity as far as Amelia was concerned. "Is this that 'real estate agent' thing?"

"Yeah. Probably getting all dressed up for nothing. Pretty sure Randy's just being nice." Amelia tossed the bag over her shoulder, getting a little nervous for the first time since she'd called Randy back, taking him up on his offer to learn a little more about real estate. "Anyway, you two have fun. And L—I still think you should try to get a nap in." She flipped her hair over both shoulders and then changed her mind, gathering it all in one hand and pulling it over to the right side.

By then, Ellie and Collin were only half listening, which made it easier for Amelia to rush out the door, running on her black high heels. She'd calculated the time it took to walk from Stacey's Bridal to Frank's Diner based on her speed in her gym shoes, not the wobbly deathtrap of her heels. The backs slipped up and down, slightly too big. The air was cool enough to keep her from sweating, but that didn't stop her heart from pounding a million beats a minute. She could perform on her cello in front of an audience of a thousand strangers and feel confident, but a simple business meeting had her about to pass out. Business wasn't her "thing"; it was Steve's "thing." What if she made a complete fool of herself? As she zeroed in on the diner, Randy's BMW sparkled in front of the restaurant like a silver dollar among a bowl full of pennies.

Steve wasn't sure about her sudden interest in real estate, but they were far enough in debt that he seemed willing to let her give it a shot. The two men hadn't met yet, and Amelia was pretty sure Steve would find Randy Mraz annoying and stuck up, but if he became her boss and helped bring in an income that included more than a gift certificate to the local nail salon as a thank-you for a performance, he'd play nice. Steve said he didn't mind her working, but it also always seemed like he was never around when she had a gig. If she could work more locally and bring in a bigger paycheck—this could possibly work out.

She always wondered why Frank and Company never repainted the dinged-up green front door. It couldn't take more than a can of enamel to refresh the whole look of the establishment. As she reached for the handle, the door suddenly opened outward, the handle hitting her palm with a crack. Pain ricocheted up her arm and elbow and into her shoulder. She pulled the wrist into her side, letting out a little squeak, the cellist inside her freaking out about how she was going to play anything if her bow arm was damaged.

Caleb rushed out from the diner, wrestling a worn ball cap onto his head. Amelia let out a little gasp, but he either didn't recognize her or didn't want to acknowledge her presence. Maybe he mistook her for a businesswoman passing through town. In the past, she would've reached out and grabbed his arm or at least called his name, asked him what was wrong, asked him to have coffee with her and talk through things. But today she let him slip by, fading into the background, worrying about him briefly but also hoping he didn't turn around and notice her.

The door opened again, and this time Amelia made sure to lunge back before getting hurt, her aching wrist still pulled into her body. Randy hurried out, rushed but still dignified in his gray suit, deep blue tie, and stylish tan shoes, his hair styled to one side with enough product in it to rival Amelia on her fanciest day.

"Oh, Amelia, there you are," Randy said, his eyes scanning the street before resting on her.

"Sorry." Amelia blushed, annoyed that Caleb's collision had made it seem like she was late. "I was just down the street with my sister. She's getting married and I'm her matron of honor and our mother died when we were young, so I'm trying to be there for her whenever I can and . . ." The information poured out of her mouth, and a horrified voice in her mind begged her to shut up.

As he listened far more intently than Amelia thought necessary for her blabbering, a pallor fell over Randy's face as if she'd said something horribly wrong or offensive. That look made the stream of consciousness she was spewing slow and then halt. She cleared her throat and ran her tongue over her front teeth just to be sure she didn't have any lingering lip gloss smeared across them.

She shuffled around again, the cute shoes getting pinchier by the minute, but it didn't seem like Randy was really looking at her. He was darting glances at the parking lot as though she wouldn't notice, like when frat guys would try to check out her boobs in college, thinking they were being all stealth about it. Then a memory flickered in her mind—the warning. Caleb's warning.

"Wait, are you looking for Caleb?" The way Caleb stormed past, the brush of red in Randy's cheek. Maybe Collin *had* seen Caleb and Randy talking earlier, and it had progressed into . . . whatever this was.

Like a switch flipped, Randy focused on Amelia's face.

"Is your wrist okay? I saw what happened through the window. That guy didn't even stop." He let the heavy door thump to a close, and then moved her out of the way of another assault. With the same gentleness she saw in him when he talked to Dawson, he took her hand and turned it over, examining her wrist. It was a completely benign action and full of genuine concern, but it also made her feel like all eyes were on her. It made her feel like Mr. Tarjan in the Sherwin-Williams was going to call up Steve and tell him about a strange man holding her hand.

But the real fear playing in the back of her mind was that Caleb could still be around somewhere, watching.

CHAPTER 19

ELLIE

Wednesday, May 11
1:37 a.m.

As Collin was outside grabbing the car, Ellie stopped by the nurses' station in the ICU with a Post-it filled with every bit of contact information she could think of. She'd been allowed to see Amelia briefly, but her time was limited because of a complication with Amelia's abdominal wound. Those were often tricky, especially on an unresponsive patient. It was almost a relief to get a few minutes to recover from the shock of seeing her sister being kept alive by machines.

In the middle of her stern warning to be absolutely certain that they knew to call her if anything happened, even a slight blip in Amelia's blood pressure or twitch of her eyelid, she heard Travis talking on the phone. He was outside of Amelia's empty room, waiting for her to return from an MRI. He was arranging for another police officer to supervise Amelia's room like Officer Blackford had been stationed outside of Steve's. Unlike the walkie-talkie, the phone provided her with only one side of the conversation, but it was enough to pique her interest.

"How long will it take her to get here?" Travis asked into the phone. He seemed to listen and then continue his thought, hand resting on his gun. "Well, as long as you can get someone here to fill in and another to replace Blackford . . . No. Blackford cannot come back. He was a disaster, and if you want me to meet the sister in the morgue, then you need someone up here with Mr. and Mrs. Saxton." He paused again, and Ellie leaned down to rummage through the plastic hospital bag with the words *This Belongs To* printed across the front, hoping he wouldn't notice her listening.

After another significant pause, he responded. "Okay, I'll meet her there at eight . . . She's pretty sure it's him, then? 'Cause of the tattoo? Right. Well, this won't be an easy one. He was shot in the face at close range . . . Yeah, I'll try to keep as much covered as I can." Ellie yanked the drawstrings of her bag and went to put it over her shoulder, when her phone slipped out of her hand with a thump. The sound of a smart phone dropping must send off some kind of universal freak-out signal, because almost immediately Travis's eyes were pointed directly at her. He pressed the phone to his face, said a quick sign-off, and headed over to Ellie.

"I've got your info in my phone, Brown. I'll call you if I hear anything."

"Well, aren't you going to need some sleep at some point, or are you Mr. Bionic Man?"

"Funny," Travis said, not laughing at all. She couldn't tell if he was entertained or annoyed at this point. "I'm on the clock; you're not."

"Rivera," Ellie added, removing all hints at humor and cocking her head to one side. "I'm glad it was you who took the call today."

She didn't know why she said it, really. But it was true. She'd thought it several times that day, and even when he'd been pushing for more information or pressuring her about Caleb, she was still glad he was the officer who found her covered in her sister's blood. He was well-known for being good at his job, but mostly it was because he always seemed to figure out the right thing to say.

Travis's hands dropped from his utility belt to his sides, where they hung limply like they'd forgotten what they were made for. In that moment, his muscles relaxed, the suspicious lines on his face smoothed, and he looked like just a guy.

"Uh, well, thanks, Brown." He took a step closer, and for a moment she wondered why he sometimes called her Ellie and at others called her Brown. Why there were times when he'd laugh at her jokes or bring her a stripper's sweatshirt and others where he would stare her down like she was the criminal he was looking for. Before she could think of anything else to say, her phone dinged. She knew without looking at it that it was Collin. His ringtone and vibration were unique.

"That's Collin. I'd better go." She looked around the shadowy hospital floor, glowing computer screens, dimmed hallways, beeps and clicks creeping out of each hospital room. The ambient light all blended together into a gray-green hue that reflected off Travis's dark eyes. He was becoming a good friend, but a part of her knew that he wasn't just a friend and colleague right now. He was also always on the watch for information. That information could turn someone she cared about into a murderer.

"Right, sounds good. See you in a while, then." Travis's hands immediately went back up to his belt like they took some comfort resting there.

"Yeah," she replied with a little wave as she turned to leave. "'Night."

She thought she could hear him echo her farewell as she walked down the hall, but she was still thinking about not just her sister and Steve or even about the strange conversation she'd had with Travis, but about a dead man lying in a cold freezer in the basement of the hospital.

If they'd found the man's sister, it wasn't Caleb, which erased a tiny, irrational worry from her mind. Steve had said a few very fuzzy and confusing things about the shooting, but nothing other than the fact that the man who shot Amelia wore a mask. He said Caleb's name a few times but never in context, and then he said, before dozing off, "I shot him. Oh my God, I shot him!"

It was moments like that one that made her glad to be a paramedic. She didn't mind picking up the pieces, both literally and figuratively, in life or death situations, but one thing she never had to do was decide who was guilty and who was not. After all, even if Steve wasn't her brother-in-law, she'd have a hard time convincing herself that this former firefighter and upstanding citizen could shoot someone.

Instead of suspicions about who shot the mystery man, all Ellie could consider was, who was this man? Without his mask and after he had been cleaned up during the autopsy, would she recognize him? She walked down to Collin's ancient Jeep where he was waiting outside the hospital in the turnaround. Any warmth that had hinted at summer earlier in the day was gone, and the cold penetrated her thin layers in one vicious gust. But even as she climbed into the familiar front seat where she had proudly etched her own declaration of love to Collin so many years ago with an *E+C* in the center of a wonky, lopsided heart, the curiosity kept nibbling at the edges of her consciousness and this new idea . . .

That maybe she'd go and take a look for herself.

~

Ellie looked at her phone again: 2:17 a.m. When she was on a twenty-four-hour shift, two a.m. was her least favorite hour. For some reason, it was at two that her eyelids would droop and her body would cry out for sleep. And if she ever dared to sit down during that predawn hour, there was no hope of staying awake.

But today she was on edge. More on edge than she'd ever been, even on the call when a man in Forestville tried to "aim" some fireworks over his girlfriend's house as part of his proposal by holding them as he lit the fuse and nearly blew all of his fingers off. It was her job to pick up all the charred "bits" to put on ice for a surgeon.

That made her heart pound; this made her heart ache; and sitting in a dark car outside of her boyfriend's apartment at two o'clock in the morning wasn't Ellie's idea of comfort. Collin was supposed to run in, grab clothes and toiletries, and be out in two minutes. But it had been nearly fifteen, and after texting five times in a row, she was getting frustrated.

If she wanted to get home, changed, and back to the hospital with a bag before the hospital became too active and she lost her nerve, Ellie couldn't imagine being gone longer than an hour. If she'd known it would take this long, she would've just showered in Collin's mildew-ridden little shower and used his Head & Shoulders 2-in-1 to get as much of herself clean as possible and tossed on a pair of his jeans. It didn't really matter what she looked or smelled like right now. It just mattered that she was there for Amelia when she returned from her procedure . . . and that she found her way down to the basement before eight a.m.

As Ellie reviewed the pieces of the case, a dark place started to grow inside her gut. The man in the mask was dead—it seemed like Steve might have shot him. Self-defense was an easy explanation.

But then why was there this whole "armed and dangerous" warning about Caleb? And why was he leaving the scene of the crime covered in blood and holding a gun? Steve needed to wake up from his drug-induced slumber soon. She hoped this time he'd have more information.

Ellie looked at her phone again: 2:22 a.m. and still not a single response from Collin to her texts. It was entirely possible that he had fallen asleep. He was always running on full speed and fitting studying in between his rounds. Then, with the stress today, he must've crashed again. Ellie dropped her phone into the armrest on the Jeep door, thumping up against the $E+C$ etched into the plastic. The lightweight door swung open easily, and Ellie's knees creaked as she jumped down to the crumbling cement driveway.

The row of small rental apartments had been built sometime in the fifties, and it showed—crumbling red brick, off-colored heavy wooden doors covered in stains and nicks that told the story of all the people who had crossed the thresholds. Back then, they housed newlyweds or the occasional bachelor who worked in the town but without the benefit of a housewife to keep house. There was one neighbor, an elderly retired general practitioner twenty years older than Ellie's dad, who had moved into the complex as a newly graduated med student and had never left.

Ellie had no desire to live in the tiny, dingy apartments filled with heavily waxed linoleum floors and a creeping mildew that had to be sprayed down weekly with a bleach-and-water mixture to prevent the fungi from taking over any damp part of the apartment. She'd already had to turn off some part of her heart that wanted to be a doctor, at least for the foreseeable future, and she wanted to live in a town where she could walk down the street and not run into anyone she knew for days on end. But it would take another huge flick of a switch to get her to live in this dingy row of apartments.

The side door was the closest to the driveway and the only entrance they ever actually used. Ellie tested the door handle, and it turned easily. The heavy door swung open with a gentle touch, and a strange chill went down her neck and through her. The darkness of the entry and the way her feet slapped against the tile brought Ellie back to earlier that day at Amelia's. She glanced around Collin's apartment for signs of distress out of reflex rather than actual fear.

The apartment was sparse and was definitely the home of a single man who was rarely home. When Collin had gotten the apartment in January, Ellie was disappointed. She knew he moved back into town to be closer to her as she cared for her father and worked at the fire department, driving the ninety minutes to and from school several times a week and crashing on couches in between. At the same time, she had hoped he would move in with his parents or somewhere more temporary. But Caleb still lived at home, and the Thornton parents were not too keen on having another child back under their roof, especially one they thought they'd successfully jettisoned. And Collin's parents were super traditional and frowned on the idea of Collin living with a woman he wasn't married to.

Now his apartment furnishings were made up of a scratchy off-white couch they'd found tossed out on a corner in Champaign, a small table—with stools instead of chairs—that also doubled as a desk, and a tiny flat-screen television that sat in the corner on a wobbly, ancient stand that had been built for the old tube TVs.

The apartment never felt quite right to Ellie, though she'd spent a few nights there and many hours just hanging out on the couch while Collin studied with headphones on. When she wasn't too tired to function, she'd make study snacks like a diligent girlfriend, and when she was too tired, she'd doze after a long shift. Today it wasn't just cold and barren in Collin's apartment; it was downright creepy, making her want to whisper when she really should be calling out to find the missing Collin.

Ellie listened carefully for any signs of what may have taken him away, but there were no breathy snores or sounds of the shower running. At first it seemed the world inside the apartment was silent and he had disappeared, but then she heard something she hadn't expected—Collin's voice.

Ellie stepped farther into the apartment, following the sound like bread crumbs. It wasn't the constant rhythm of a healthy back-and-forth but more like a brief staccato interrupting the silent landscape. Still, the sound of him talking on the phone inside the apartment while she'd been waiting in the car made Ellie both annoyed and confused, but then she remembered that Collin's family was in crisis too. Maybe he was getting an update. Maybe there was news.

Her work boots made a sharp thump on the polished tiles, and though she wanted to know what was going on with Collin, she also didn't. Sometimes, not knowing was safer than knowing.

Ellie bypassed the kitchen, where the various glowing appliances let off an unsettling blue-green hue that reminded her of the hospital, and instead she followed the thin, worn runner down the hall to the only bedroom in the place.

"Collin," she whispered, finally brave enough to call out. "Collin, you okay?"

No answer.

There was no light shining behind the bedroom door to Collin's room.

"Collin," she called again, this time letting her annoyance creep into her voice, which increased her volume several levels. Still no answer. Then the intermittent sound of conversation stopped, and Ellie picked up her pace down the hall where she shoved open the bedroom door. No Collin. The room contained nothing more than a bed and a few rows of clothes in the closet. The bathroom was unfortunately accessed only by walking through the bedroom, which was just one reason among many she hated the idea of starting her life as a newlywed here.

The bed lay unmade, a few neat piles of clothes in various parts of the room. The ratty armchair in the corner that Collin had snuck out of his fraternity was covered in a curtain of clothes still on their metal hangers in the dry cleaning bags he'd picked them up in. It was all fairly normal. Collin rarely had time to worry himself with cleaning; as somewhat messed up as it sounded, his mom would often come over to give the place a good cleaning while he was at school, using the key under the front mat to get in.

Standing in the middle of the nice-size master bedroom and spinning in a slow circle to take it all in, Ellie finally noticed a light under the bathroom door. Usually if the shower was running, the whole apartment would smell of mildew and shampoo, but tonight she didn't smell anything other than the lingering scent of Mrs. Bianca's tamales from next door.

Ellie knocked lightly on the bathroom door. "Collin, are you in there?" she asked, already knowing there was no other place that he could be unless he'd snuck out of the apartment.

The light flicked off and the door opened inward, making Ellie stumble forward. Collin stood on the other side, one hand on the doorknob and the other holding his dark iPhone. With the light from the bathroom suddenly absent, it was difficult to see more than an outline of Collin's body and facial features.

"There you are!" Ellie stared at him in confusion. "What the hell? You haven't even changed."

"Sorry, my phone died. Is . . . is it Amelia? Do we need to go back to the hospital?" Collin crossed to his bed and threw the stray bedding strewn across the floor into the center of his mattress. Reaching under the bed, he yanked out a large, empty duffel bag, the seams and edges so frayed that it looked like it'd been pushed through an X-ray machine at the airport one too many times. Then he opened each drawer of his dresser one by one, withdrawing a few neatly folded items.

Collin seemed rushed and on edge, nervous. This was a side of her fiancé she'd never seen. He was always cool under pressure, which was one of the reasons she knew he'd be an excellent surgeon one day. But this shaking, silent man was not anything like "her" Collin. In fact, the way he was behaving reminded Ellie a lot more of his brother, Caleb. The idea made that creepy feeling come back again.

"What is really going on?" Ellie asked, taking a step forward and putting her hand on Collin's back between his shoulder blades. His shirt was damp with sweat despite the cool night, and he froze when she touched him.

"I'm tired," he said, grabbing another item from a drawer and tossing it in the bag. Ellie glanced inside the open zipper.

"How long do you think we're going to be gone? Collin, we've really gotta go. I'll grab your toothpaste and brush, and then we can head over to my place."

Talking as she walked, Ellie headed toward the bathroom to collect a few toiletries. There had to be some way to get Collin moving and out of the apartment even with the stress of everything finally setting in.

Sometimes that happened after a hard call—after the adrenaline was gone and you were in your own home, it all became real. Her lacy childhood duvet had absorbed many tears from nights like that. Though Collin had plenty of experience with high-adrenaline moments, he also had never had it touch his life in such a personal manner. She tried to take a step back and not judge. The two of them would be on her own doorstep in a matter of minutes, and then maybe she'd be the one having a breakdown.

Without looking, she found the bathroom switch and turned it on. Just as she did, Collin broke from his frantic spell.

"No!" he shouted. The intensity of his call made Ellie glance back over her shoulder. Collin was headed right toward her.

"No, not the light . . . um." He hesitated, and Ellie knew Collin was hiding something. "It hurts my eyes."

He reached his hand around the wall and flicked the light off, once again bathing them in darkness.

"Why are you being so weird?" Ellie asked, pushing Collin's hand aside and switching on the light. She turned around, but instead of a bachelor's bathroom with a cluttered counter and grungy tub, red flashed back at her. Blood. Blood was smeared over the white countertop. Blood coated the stainless steel faucet and handles. There was blood on the closed toilet seat cover and even on a corner of the shower curtain.

"Ellie, stop . . ." Collin's urgent request faded away as more details came into focus: surgical scissors on the counter, surgical tape, and a strand of unrolled gauze draped over the soap dispenser like it had missed some kind of party.

"What the hell?" She stepped farther into the bathroom, her feet sinking into the area rug. Then it all fell together. The blood, Collin's sketchy behavior, the hastily administered medical supplies made Ellie think one thing: *Caleb.*

"Please, it's not what you think. I swear."

"I'm pretty sure it *is* what I think," she tossed back at him, fury building inside her. Collin had never, ever lied to her before. Not about being late for a date and not when a girl from his study group tried to kiss him after he made sure she got safely to her car when they stayed at the library till two a.m. working on a project. But all that mattered now was that, when push came to shove and Collin had to choose between protecting his brother, who may have tried to kill her sister and her brother-in-law, and being her fiancé and calling the police—he didn't pick her.

Then an even more disturbing thought hit Ellie. If Caleb had been here recently, if he was still actively bleeding and clearly severely injured, then where was he now? She gasped and backed up, bumping into Collin's chest. His arms wrapped around her, normally comforting but at this moment feeling like a prison.

"L—I had to help him. He's my brother. I thought you'd call your 'friend' Travis." She ignored the obvious jealous undertones in his comment and peeled Collin's arms off her, finding it hard to breathe, swearing she could smell the blood, remembering Amelia's blood. Collin continued to justify and apologize, but his voice turned into a high-pitched squeal, the old-fashioned fluorescent lights flickering inside their off-colored plastic casing. "I'm sorry . . . but I had no other choice . . . You would've done the same thing . . ."

Ellie's focus fell on the shower curtain. It was bloody, fingerprints up and down one side and a large stain in the corner.

She gave Collin a glare over her shoulder, grasped the edge of the curtain, and yanked hard.

CHAPTER 20

AMELIA

Monday, April 25
Two weeks earlier

"I think you're a natural," Randy said as he started the engine with a flick of his wrist.

"Well, I don't know about that." Amelia felt a hot blush across her cheekbones. "It was pretty fun, though."

Her memory flashed back to the five houses they'd looked at with a nice young couple and their new baby. Each time Randy let her type in the code and pull the key out of the lockbox and then open the door for the couple. She liked walking through those houses, dropping into a polished moment in someone else's life. Some of the houses were beautifully staged, furniture perfectly placed, polished from top to bottom. Others were not so perfect. One house in Fulton had three rooms lined with fish tanks with a green hue to the water and slow, miserable fish floating inside, barely alive.

This new idea of becoming a real estate agent was enticing. She loved working with people and the idea of bringing people into new homes. Then of course there was the money. She and Steve could always use the money.

"Listen, I know that you would be good at this. I really think that you could do very well as an agent. I wish you would consider studying for your license. That class I told you about, there are a few more days for you to enroll. Have you talked to Steve about it yet?"

Amelia had mentioned it to Steve and he'd been completely supportive, but that didn't leave Amelia without concerns of her own.

She was already struggling to keep her head above water at home with Dad around and helping with the roofing business and driving the girls all over creation. How would she be able to manage ninety hours of coursework on top of it all?

Also, it would take several hundred dollars for the classes, not to mention all the other expenses of starting up with a broker. How, when they hardly had a penny to spare, could she take on an extra expense now, even one that could lead to a steady income in the future?

And then there was Randy. What was his deal? Why would someone she had known for a few weeks be so invested in her future? Steve always accused Amelia of being naïve, but ever since dealing with Caleb's increased interest, Amelia had started to wonder about Randy Mraz's motivations.

Despite all these concerns, the day had been incredibly rewarding, and even though Amelia knew that there were more ups and downs and ins and outs to the business than she could've seen in one day, she knew that she'd probably be cool with those.

"Yeah, he's fine with it, but to be honest, Randy . . ." She hesitated. "I just can't afford it right now."

Randy, dressed in his fancy three-piece gray suit and sapphire-blue tie, brown shoes, and belt that looked stylish rather than clashing, pressed on the gas pedal, and the engine revved nearly silently. His dark hair was combed in the intentionally sloppy mess he seemed to prefer, but his expression was different. His smile had been wiped away, and instead his lips thinned against each other like he was trying to keep himself from saying something he would regret.

"Hear me out, okay?" Randy glanced sideways at Amelia and then back at the road. She wasn't sure what he was going to say, but just the idea of more pressure from another person in her life made Amelia flinch back and wish that she'd never agreed to explore this opportunity. The only thing harder than being pressured to do something you didn't want to do was being pressured to do something you desperately wanted to do but couldn't.

"Okay, but unless you have a leprechaun friend with a rainbow somewhere, I don't think there's much I can do."

"Hey, I don't think talking is a part of hearing me out," Randy joked. Amelia ran a finger over her lips and pretended to lock them with a key. "That's better. Okay, I have a deal for you. You clip coupons. You shop the ads. You like deals, right?" Amelia nodded and pointed to her lips like she still couldn't talk after their previous agreement. "Ha. Right, okay. My deal is this . . . If the Krafts buy one of the houses you helped me show today, then I will give you half of my commission to help you get started as an agent. That should cover at least your tuition and your startup fees. And I'll extend the deal further . . . If you come with me again and I make a sale, I'll give you a percentage of that sale until you've made enough to get you up and running. I get a commission from the agency for bringing you in, especially if you are as good as I know you will be. What do you think about that?"

Amelia didn't know what to say. How did someone she'd just met have more faith in her than her own husband? It reminded her of the way her relationship used to be with Caleb. He was her biggest fan and cheerleader. It was odd having that kind of support again but also flattering.

A little tickle at the back of her throat warned her that if she spoke too soon, there would be tears mingled with her words, and she didn't want that, so instead, she pretended to unlock her lips, cough a few times, and then begin again.

"I need to talk to Steve about it, but . . ." She gritted her teeth together to keep from giving away how much she wanted this, because she ultimately knew what the answer had to be. "It's too much, Randy. You hardly know me. I can't take your money; it wouldn't be right."

As she spoke, Randy nodded quickly over and over as though watching a ball bouncing across the road.

"Listen, I just know talent when I see it. I've worked in business long enough where I've learned your best assets are people, not properties. I know how to assess a deal and close it quickly before another buyer gets his grubby hands on it. I guess that's what I'm doing here."

They slowed to a stop at a four-way stop sign where four empty country highways bordering newly plowed fields of dark soil met up under a blinking light. There were no cars to be seen, no sign of human life beyond the lines in the dirt that had surely been plowed within the past few days, but he didn't move forward.

"I think you might be losing your touch if you see all that in me." Amelia laughed but then grew serious. "I mean, I'd love to work with you, but like I said, I just need to talk to Steve. I know he'd insist I pay you back once I get going on my own."

"Amelia, I guess I do have one concern." When he looked at her instead of the empty road, her heart beat a little faster, like now he was going to come forward with a list of things that made it impossible for her to ever be good enough.

"Feel like sharing?" she asked, hoping to lighten the mood.

"Yeah, uh, I'm a little worried that you'll have a potential sale on the line and you'll take a break to go call Steve and get advice." They still hadn't moved from the intersection, and the designer engine purred, nearly silent, the cabin of the car a cone of silence from the outside world.

"I wouldn't . . . ," she stammered, instantly defensive. It wasn't that she was required to check in with Steve, but it had just slowly become a habit she couldn't kick. "I think you're being a bit presumptuous." She placed her arms across her chest, wishing he'd start driving again.

"I just call it as I see it. If I go into a house and the blinds are broken and the carpet is stained, I make sure to point it out to my client. If they are still interested in the property, I make sure they're willing to accept those flaws for the price they are paying." He shrugged, unperturbed. "Maybe I'm blunt, but that doesn't mean I'm wrong."

As Randy stared her down, it seemed to all make sense. She should be able to make some of these choices on her own. She shouldn't have to run every decision past her husband. Looking at Randy, thinking about his offer, she felt like she had choices for the first time in a long time.

But this fear of making a decision without Steve's approval, this unsettled nervous feeling, it still nibbled on the edge of her thoughts like the mice that would invade the basement in the winter, gnawing through the cardboard boxes filled with old clothes and looking for a nest to birth their babies.

Rarely, one of the rodents would get brave or hungry enough to come upstairs, and that was when Amelia would put down traps and the girls would refuse to go to the basement even to retrieve ice cream from the deep freezer. But most of the time the little mice were there, stealthy, hungry, and growing. No matter how hard Amelia tried, she was never really able to free the basement from the mice. Steve said it was part of living out in the country, but she always wondered . . . what if she could just find the crack in the foundation that the mice kept nosing through and fill it, then maybe she could find a way to be rid of them—forever. What if she could be strong enough to say no more often? What if she wasn't always so afraid? What if . . .

"You know what," she said with resolve, ready to seal those cracks up in her life, "you might be good at assessing real estate, but I wouldn't get too cocky. I'm going to prove you wrong this time." Amelia offered her right hand to Randy, and after only a brief hesitation he took it.

"Sounds like a plan." Something like relief washed over Randy as they shook hands. He gave her a little smirk and placed his hands back on the wheel. "Now, I'm a bit late for Dawson's pickup. I hope you don't mind if I put the pedal to the metal a little." Just as Randy shifted his foot to the gas pedal, the familiar trill of his phone erupted from his suit coat pocket.

"Randy Mraz."

She didn't know if it was intimidating or impressive that he didn't even muss with any greetings—just his name and a no-nonsense tone.

He went first pale, then a little green. When it seemed that he might hang up without saying a word, he finally spoke.

"Okay, slow down. Is Dawson okay?"

Amelia sat up straight. Oh no. This was one of *those* calls, the ones no parent wanted to get ever.

"The police?" he asked, an edge to his voice that seemed like either anger or panic. "Is he okay?"

She didn't know Dawson incredibly well, but the idea of something happening to that child made her want to cry. Randy's hands holding the steering wheel started to tremble, and Amelia was afraid he might lose his grip. A minivan had pulled up and paused for an extra second at the stop sign ahead of them as if waiting for the BMW to make the first move. But when Randy didn't even look up, the minivan turned right toward Emmetsville.

Police. Dawson. She tried to make eye contact with Randy, tried to get some small kind of reassurance or explanation. But nothing. His trembling hands squeezed the black leather wheel three more times, his knuckles turning whiter the more frantically he gripped it.

"I don't understand a word you are saying right now. What the HELL happened to my son?" Anger didn't look good on the normally cool and collected businessman. Anger looked pale and sweaty. It looked like a restless body that shifted up and down in his seat over and over until he was nearly bouncing. "I'll be there in ten minutes, and you'd better have answers."

He batted at the earpiece in his ear until it fell out. He crushed the Answer button on the side, and the device went from glowing blue to a lifeless black. He wrapped his tan hand around the Bluetooth headset and squeezed like he was trying to kill an insect, letting out a low, guttural growl.

Amelia sat back, heart pounding, head swirling with thoughts and fears. The same thoughts that would go through her mind if Dawson were her son. Wasn't he at day care? Wasn't he safe? Why were police involved? But those were the last questions Randy would want to hear.

As she tried to figure out the *right* thing to say, Randy's growl turned into a roar, and he took the headset balled up in his right hand and tossed it across the car. It ricocheted off the windshield and landed in Amelia's lap. She picked it up off the taut fabric of her forest-green pencil skirt. The earpiece was still warm from the contact with Randy's skin, and that residual heat made Amelia shudder a little.

"Randy," she whispered, "what happened?"

Randy's face was no longer white or even green—it was crimson, which looked odd mixed with the patches of brown facial hair on his chin. He looked like he was holding something inside, more than a breath or a thought but something physical, like a gun holding back a bullet ready to be expelled. Once his hands were back on the wheel, Amelia expected him to speed ahead, make a dramatic turn toward Broadlands, tires maybe squealing a little, but he didn't. Instead, he shook the wheel violently, the veins in his arms bulging in a snake-like pattern. A guttural scream crawled up from his chest, to his throat, and out his mouth.

"Argh!" He threw his head down till his forehead was resting on the wheel. "Damn it. Damn it. DAMN IT!"

Amelia recoiled, unsure how to comfort a man who was little more than a stranger when she didn't even know the details of the situation.

But an instinct in the back of her mind told her that Randy would regret any additional delays that kept him from Dawson and whatever was going on. Time—that was something Steve used to talk about a lot as a fireman. The statistics that went along with survival rates often came down to response time. Time was the difference between a few stitches and a blood transfusion, between a limb-salvage operation and an amputation, between saying hello to a loved one coming out of surgery and saying good-bye forever.

"Randy," she repeated in a measured voice like she was approaching a wild animal or a scared child. "What is wrong with Dawson?" When he didn't respond, Amelia reached out her hand, planning to place it on his back, but just as she was about to touch him, Randy sat up. There were wet trails on his cheeks, and his well-trimmed beard was wet where the drops had soaked in.

"Dawson . . ." Randy's voice cracked when he said his son's name. He cleared his throat and swiped a hand across his face. What she saw in front of her was a broken man, the way her father looked when the doctor came in and told him that her mother had not survived surgery.

"What happened to Dawson, Randy?" She could feel tears rising in her own eyes, all of her motherly fears filling in the blanks.

Randy put his foot on the gas, hard. The forward momentum tossed Amelia back into her seat, the leather cradling her like a ball in a catcher's mitt. The speed limit was only forty-five on the highway, but the needle on the speedometer shot past fifty almost instantly. Amelia grasped at the armrest on the door.

"Dawson is gone."

CHAPTER 21

ELLIE

Wednesday, May 11
2:42 a.m.

The curtain fell back, revealing—blood. There was a lot of blood. If this was all from Caleb, then he was in bad shape. He should at least have a transfusion. Who knew what kind of internal damage had been done.

"Collin, what the HELL?" She reached for her back pocket to grab her cell phone, completely forgetting that she was still wearing a pair of scrubs and that she'd left the phone in the car.

"You are *not* trying to call the police, are you?" Collin worded it like a question, but it sounded more like an accusation. He grasped her hands and turned them up, searching for her cell phone.

"I'm not calling anyone," she said, yanking her hands away, frightened at the strength of his grip. "But I would if I hadn't left my phone in the car."

She glared at Collin and took another step into the room, trying to work out the pathology of the scene. Most of the blood was by the sink and some in the tub. Maybe Caleb had been hiding in Collin's tub all this time, bleeding and in pain from a gunshot wound instead of in surgery like Amelia and Steve. It couldn't be *too* serious if he was up and walking around, or at least that was what Ellie told herself.

"Ellie, you can't call anyone. He's really hurt and he's going to leave town, but until then, we've got to keep this a secret."

"Your brother was seen leaving the scene of a crime and carrying a gun. Leaving a crime scene where my sister was shot, and as a result of those injuries she might *die*."

"He didn't do it." Collin grabbed a handful of bandage wrappers and tossed them into the wastebasket by the sink. Then he ran the grungy hand towel over the counter, the one he always forgot to change when he did the laundry every few weeks. "Caleb said that the guy with the mask shot him and Steve. He thought Amelia was dead. I told him she wasn't . . ." The sentence trailed off because they both knew how that sentence ended. She wasn't dead . . . yet.

The white-marble counter was now streaked with red swirls. Ellie knew that as a paramedic and as Collin's fiancée she should be worried about Caleb. She should be trying to find a way to help him, protect him, or at least get his statement so she could help the police figure out what happened inside that office. But she couldn't think past the intensity of Travis's warning back at the hospital and the grainy black-and-white image Travis described of Caleb walking out the office door, bleeding, yes, but also running away from her bleeding sister, whom he claimed to love, rather than finding a way to help her.

Collin ditched the soiled towel and bits of paper into the waste bin and then yanked out the plastic bag lining the container. He knelt down to pick up a few pieces of what looked like string but Ellie knew was surgical suture. The room started to spin. Collin had been helping his brother because he was hurt, but he didn't seem to consider that he was also helping a fugitive.

"Collin! Stop. This is all evidence. You can't get rid of it. We *have* to call Travis." Ellie knelt down eye to eye with her fiancé.

"Ellie, no. You can't," Collin responded simply. In the dark, he had seemed agitated and annoyed, but in the light, she could see a smear of blood on his cheek and another splash on the lenses of his glasses. He was in this now. If she called the police, this room would be a crime scene. Collin would be in trouble for aiding and abetting. Ellie could be detained for questioning. She might never get back to the hospital. In fact, her phone could be ringing right now, right this second, with a message about Amelia.

"Damn it. DAMN IT!" She slammed her hand against the door of the cabinet under the sink. "What the HELL were you thinking, Collin? Huh?" Ellie rocked back on her heels, the devastating Catch-22 of the situation starting to sink in.

"The same thing you were thinking when you went into that call today when you knew it wasn't safe." Collin shoved the last few bits of blood-covered gauze into the Piggly Wiggly bag and then twisted the handles together in a knot. His hands were still red. "I was thinking that my brother needed help. And I don't care what your little police buddy has convinced you of—Caleb didn't hurt anybody, much less Amelia. He'd step in front of a bullet to save your sister, you *know* that. Half of Broadlands knows it. I think even Steve knew it."

She searched her thoughts on the crime, what she'd seen, where the bodies were, where the blood trail led as she spent those fifteen horrific minutes trying to keep her sister alive. Caleb didn't shoot her sister, no, probably not, but she had to admit the likelihood that he'd shot Steve. The possibilities built up like a tower in her mind, an unstable, wobbly tower that might topple over at any moment.

"I don't think Amelia was the target," she said. "Travis thinks that Caleb and the masked guy were working together. That it was another disgruntled employee, and they were trying to get what they could from the safe. And if he really was in love with Amelia, then screwing Steve probably seemed like a great idea, don't you think?"

"You and that Travis guy. You just follow him like a little puppy, don't you?" Collin yelled, and then threw the bag he'd been holding. It missed Ellie but came close enough to blow free the strand of hair she'd been putting behind her ear all day, and the discarded medical shears clanked loudly against the wall.

"Collin, what the—" Her normally calm and loving Collin, the one with gentle, healing hands, was now leaning in close enough that Ellie could tell the difference between the flecks of orange on his face that were freckles and the ones that were blood spatter. She scrambled backward, suddenly scared in a different way.

"Don't you get it? Caleb didn't *need* any money. He's got tons of it. Tons. Your loser brother-in-law is the one with the money problem. If you want to follow the money trail, I'd tell your friend Officer Friendly to start there."

"He's not . . ." Ellie started to defend herself about Travis again, but another thought crashed through her. "Wait, how did Caleb get so much money?"

Collin stood up and straightened his shirt and pants as though about to head into a meeting. They were also spotted with blood. She could only imagine that he'd tried to assist Caleb without turning on any lights. He leaned over and opened the cabinet door Ellie had just smashed with the side of her hand and pulled out a white bottle with a molded plastic handle. Bleach.

"I can't believe you don't know this already, being such a big Steve fan." Collin pulled up the silver stopper on the back of the sink and turned on the hot water with one flick of his wrist. As the steaming water started to fill the sink, he opened the child-safety cap and poured the yellowish liquid in. The sting of the bleach reached Ellie's eyes, making them flood with tears. "Steve's a bookie." Collin said it simply like he was telling Ellie about some food allergy or what college Steve had attended.

"A bookie?" Ellie asked, annoyed. She was more than done with Collin's sarcasm and obfuscation. "Broadlands doesn't *need* a bookie, Collin. There are maybe two people who would even want to bet on anything more significant than who will catch the biggest fish at the derby this year."

"I'm not making it up. Didn't Amelia know about this?" Collin glanced at Ellie, who was still keeping her distance after his outburst, then slid open one of the drawers under the sink and retrieved an old towel, dunking it in the hot, bleachy water.

"I'm positive Amelia didn't know about *any* of this," Ellie said, crossing her arms. "That's if it's even true."

"It's true," Collin responded as he climbed up on the edge of the tub and fiddled with the rings holding up the plastic shower curtain. Focused on the work of covering up all signs of Caleb's visit, Collin's report sounded so matter-of-fact that it seemed almost more convincing than if he'd sat down and seriously explained things.

"And he's not just a bookie for Broadlands. He's mostly a bookie for the college kids. But Caleb is apparently really really good at picking the winning teams. For a long time, Steve was paying him twice his salary nearly every week. He's been paying my parents' mortgage since my dad had to retire because of his back. But then Steve made a 'no employees' rule, and Caleb was back to his normal salary, not that it mattered. His bank account is pretty stuffed still. Mom told me that Caleb had started looking at places to buy in town."

He unclipped the last shower-curtain ring, and the stiff fabric fell down into his arms. He wrapped it up into a ball and tossed it on top of the growing pile of garbage. Without pausing, Collin took the bleach towel, squeezed out a large stream of pinkish water, and went to work wiping down the tub. It was more housework than Ellie had ever seen him do in their whole relationship. She found herself mentally colluding, making a list of all the things that would need to be replaced. The carpet, the towels, the toilet paper.

"Then why doesn't he just come in and tell the police everything?" she asked, not convinced but willing to dig deeper if it meant finding out what happened to her sister. It might be a wasted use of her energies, searching, questioning, hunting, but it was also the only thing that numbed her pain. "I mean, there is no reason to keep up this façade anymore, and he could break the case wide open. He could clear his name."

"I don't know, Ellie." Collin paused in his cleaning, and the tender part of the man she'd said yes to just six weeks ago was back. "He was really scared, but I don't think it was just the police he was scared of. It was . . . something else."

Ellie took a deep breath, the bleach fumes filling her lungs and burning as they settled there. She let the breath out in a loud rush, her head spinning from the confrontation and the chemicals.

"I guess we will know a lot more when . . ."

Ellie was cut off midsentence by a loud knocking at the front door and a booming voice that echoed through the tiny apartment and beat against her eardrums for the second time that day.

"Police, open up!"

CHAPTER 22

AMELIA

Monday, April 25
Two weeks earlier

Amelia didn't pray often, but when she was little, her mother would read her stories at bedtime and then teach her how to kneel down by the side of her bed and pray. Amelia never got much from it herself, but she always loved the nights when her mother prayed. They made her feel like God was there, like he was actually listening and would keep her father safe, would help Amelia grow big and strong, would comfort Ellie. When her mother was killed in a simple car accident because she wasn't wearing her seat belt and hit the windshield, when she walked out of the car and every paramedic including her father missed her concussion, when her brain gave out rather than her body—Amelia stopped praying. Her mother's God couldn't even keep her safe; why would he care about the children she left behind?

But then her father got sick, and the urge to pray came back. At first she told herself that it was just a coping mechanism, a simple way to make her feel in control when the world was crashing down around her. But the more she did it, the more she felt comfort and peace, and though there was no doubt in her mind that God would do just as much to save her father as he'd done to save her mother, she let herself find comfort in the conversations with her deity.

Today, she closed her eyes and said a quick and silent prayer. Not for some kind of miracle or an angel to scoop her out of the car. No, her adult prayers were far different, simpler, than her childhood prayers. Today as they sped down the highway, Amelia prayed for peace, that she'd know what to say to Randy and that he'd remember she was there. She prayed that she'd live to see Kate's recital and Cora's science fair. That Randy would find his center and his son.

Her eyes were still closed as the car began to slow. She doubted greatly that it was her prayer making the difference; he'd probably realized the insanity of his mad dash down Highway 12 or mentally reviewed some stats on the number of years he could spend in prison for vehicular manslaughter. He didn't stop this time; he just returned to a cruising speed that was maybe a few miles over the posted speed limit but under control enough so she could let her arms drop and the belt gave enough slack so she could sit up and put her feet on the floor.

Amelia leaned over and snagged her phone off the ground, examining it quickly for signs of damage. When she went to turn it on, Randy finally spoke.

"Don't."

"Don't what?" Amelia answered, tentatively.

"Don't make that call. Please." His voice was steady and calm, like he'd finally come to his senses.

"I'm not calling anyone, Randy. Not unless you want me to."

He shook his head, still keeping his speed at a reasonable ten miles above the speed limit. "You don't have to talk to me like I'm some crazy person. I'm not going to lose it again, I promise."

Amelia didn't believe him. Why should she? The more time she spent in the car with him since his explosion, the more she realized just how little she knew about him as a person.

"Sorry," she said quickly, and then before she lost her nerve she added, "So . . . what happened? Is Dawson okay?"

Randy flinched at the mention of his son's name but then swallowed slowly, his Adam's apple bouncing up and down under the carefully trimmed beard. "I'm sure Dawson is fine."

The sentence surprised Amelia. It was comforting because no part of her wanted that little boy to be hurt or lost or in any kind of risky situation, but after Randy's response and ominous warning that they'd lost Dawson somehow, Amelia pushed herself up a little taller in her seat, annoyance building.

"Okay," she said slowly. "Then . . . what was *that* all about?" Amelia pointed her thumb back over her shoulder in one hard pump.

"Dawson's mother picked him up early from school."

"Wait, what? I thought she was dead," Amelia blurted.

"My wife is dead," he said bluntly. "Dawson's birth mother is alive."

"Dawson is adopted?"

"No, not exactly." He readjusted his grip on the wheel, and the needle bumped up slightly but not enough to make Amelia fear for her life again. "Real estate is new to me. I used to work for JBTM Tech, recruited right out of college. I moved up the ranks pretty fast and was one of the youngest VPs in company history. Then I met Dawson's mom. I'm gonna be up-front with you—she was an intern. But it's not what it seems. There was a company party, and I got pretty wasted. I woke up the next morning in my office with this girl naked beside me. I had no memory of the night, but it was clear we'd been together. I apologized, we parted ways, and I hoped for discretion, but then the texts started and e-mails, and then the positive pregnancy test sealed in an envelope was sent to my home. My wife was already very ill, and that test nearly killed her." He stopped talking for a moment, and Amelia couldn't tell if he was emotional or angry or was pausing for dramatic effect.

"We worked it out so that Dawson came to live with me and Stella after he was born. The idea was that once Stella was better, she would adopt him officially. In return, I paid for Megan's, that's the intern, I paid her medical bills, paid for her to finish school. For a while, it was like she was part of the family, dysfunctional though it may have been. But then when Stella died last year, Megan petitioned for shared custody of Dawson and won. She won!" He punctuated his exclamation with a quick burst in speed, which slowed quickly. "She won and Dawson had to go spend time with a woman he didn't know in a one-bedroom hovel in the city. She had boyfriends in and out, and Dawson once told me in great detail about finding drugs in her room. So a few months ago when she went into the hospital for her third rehab, I moved here, to Broadlands."

He scanned the scenery. It looked so perfect, the freshly plowed fields, the rich blue sky, the fluffy skirt of clouds that drifted along like there might never be rain again. When she looked at her home from Randy's eyes, she could easily see why he thought of this place as a refuge—a town small enough to keep his secrets and big enough to provide business opportunities that could secure safety for him and his son.

There was a voice in her head at the time that said, *That is kidnapping* and *What you did is illegal,* but she tried to push those voices down, remembering how good he was with Dawson all the times she'd seen them together, how the boy was always nicely dressed and happy . . . He was such a happy boy. She wanted to believe Randy's story of being a duped savior, one who lost his wife and his son, and who wanted to keep him safe.

So instead of throwing insults or accusations, she asked, "Well, what are you going to do now?"

They sped past the **WELCOME TO BROADLANDS** sign, going at nearly supersonic speed again. Instead of slowing through the town like was expected on these smaller country roads, he hit the gas and said, "I'm going to get him back."

Amelia walked up the steps to the kitchen door, typed in the security code, and then unlocked the door while holding open the screen with her foot. They used to leave the side door unlocked like any good citizen of a small town, but with the recent vandalism and Sam, the blacklisted day worker, still showing up occasionally to beg for work . . . it was security systems and locked doors for the Saxtons.

The kitchen was dark and smelled slightly of spoiled milk. The breakfast cereal bowls were still stacked in the sink, and Amelia immediately started a to-do list in her mind of all the things she should've been doing today rather than being chauffeured around by a distraught father with a lead foot.

It wasn't that she was heartless. Amelia adored little Dawson, but after Randy's story, she didn't know whom to believe. It was almost too much for her already-packed life. Dawson was with his mom, and though Randy was anxious to get him back, he seemed far more distraught that Megan had found him than that his child was missing.

With Dad coming over that night, she had to get dinner prepared and the main-floor bedroom and half bath ready with her father's raised toilet seat. Ellie took care of the actual bathing routine, thankfully, but the more often they got him on the toilet, the fewer awkward adult diaper changes there were. Amelia was getting better at caring for her father, falling back on her mothering skills quite often. But helping him onto the toilet on good days and changing adult diapers on off days was as much as she could manage without the onset of a major anxiety attack.

Amelia dropped her bag with a thunk and took extra care to hang the keys on her designated hook. The squeaky voices of cartoon animals floated in from the front room. Steve must be working in the office. Time to get started on dinner.

Amelia flicked on the kitchen light and retrieved an apron from the drawer closest to the stove. As she turned around to assess the level of disaster she'd need to tame before dinner, an envelope on the counter caught her attention. It was one of the letters she'd brought in from the mailbox.

In the upper left-hand corner was their insurance company's familiar logo. It had been this logo that had kept her from examining the envelope closer, because anything from Country Life was always addressed to Steve. But today, her name stared up at her. She picked it up and brought it closer to get a better look. *Amelia Saxton.*

With one quick glance over her shoulder to make sure Steve wasn't watching from the door to the office or the stairs or anywhere else, she slid the folded paper out and opened it quickly. She'd signed all the papers Suze sent home a few weeks ago, but this envelope was different, confusing.

Inside was a blank piece of paper folded around a thin, rectangular sheet of paper. She picked it up and read it at least ten times. In her hands she held a check with the same insurance logo as on the front of the envelope. A check made out to Amelia Saxton.

A check for twenty thousand dollars.

CHAPTER 23

ELLIE

Wednesday, May 11
3:24 a.m.

"I can't believe you called him," Collin whispered angrily, loud enough for Ellie to hear but just low enough that there was no way the officer on the other side of the front door could make it out.

"I can't believe you played doctor for your brother's gunshot wound and then, what, snuck him out the window?" Ellie spat back, but instead of running to the front door and letting in the police, she started to pick up the last bits of evidence and shove them into one of the nearly full garbage bags on the floor. "And I told you, I left my phone in the car. It must've been one of your nosy neighbors."

The edges of Collin's glasses were starting to steam up in the stuffy, humid bathroom. A smear of blood traced the line of his right cheekbone and covered his shirt and pants in random patterns. There was no *way* he was in any state to open the door and face an officer. The pounding started up again, this time harder and more urgent.

"I'd better get the door." Ellie examined her hands and then checked her own shirt and pants.

Collin hesitated, scanning Ellie's face. "Are you going to tell them about Caleb?" Fear and apprehension showed in Collin's body movements. His eyebrows were turned in, and his hands were trembling slightly, making the plastic bag he was holding shake.

Ellie considered the question. If she told about Caleb, then they might find him. Might find out what happened in the Broadlands Roofing office that morning. Find out who tried to kill her sister and maybe even why. And Caleb would get the medical attention he clearly needed. But on the other hand, this would ruin things between her and Collin, and he could get in big trouble for hiding a known fugitive and for trying to clean up evidence.

When it came down to it, there was one question that decided it for her: Would telling the police about Caleb help Amelia get better? No, she had to admit that though it would feel good to get some answers and to be able to exact some justice, telling Travis right now about Caleb in Collin's house would do nothing to help Amelia and everything to hurt her fiancé.

"No, I won't. I promise." Even as she said the words, she regretted them, but Collin's features softened and he grabbed the spray bottle of cleaner and moved the bag he'd been holding to his side.

"I'll keep cleaning. I'll be done in ten minutes." He inspected the room a little closer and then added, "Maybe twenty."

She mumbled an okay and backed out of the bathroom. At the front door, she fumbled with the latch till it opened, revealing a figure in dark clothes—it looked like a man with his back to the door. A chill ran up Ellie's arms and quaked through her shoulders. She should've been more cautious. This could be someone pretending to be a police officer.

Her fingers searched the wall for the light switch, and she flicked it on, her body halfway behind the door for protection, but as soon as the form turned around, she recognized him.

"Brown, you okay?" Travis stepped forward. "A 911 call came over the radio from one of your neighbors here. Domestic dispute. Recognized Collin's name. Told dispatch I'd check it out."

"Rivera, you're supposed to be at the hospital." Now no one was there to keep her informed of Amelia's condition. Her sister could be awake. She could be worse. Ellie could have missed her chance to say good-bye.

"I left another officer with her. He has my number and yours." Travis looked over Ellie's head and into the dark hallway behind her. She instinctively pulled the door closer to her back to keep out his prying eyes. "So want to tell me why I got called out here?" He took a step closer, his dark eyes sweeping over her, making her relieved that she'd done the blood check before answering the door.

"I have no idea," Ellie answered, searching for a reasonable explanation. "Collin was upset about his brother. We got in a little argument. He's sleeping now, no big deal."

Travis leaned in and put a hand on the door she was trying to keep closed like he wanted to push it open. "Do you mind if I come in for a moment? Grab a glass of water."

"Actually, I'm on my way out. I need to get to my dad's house, pack up, and head back to the hospital." She stepped out the door and pulled it closed behind her. When the lock clicked shut, her stomach dropped. The keys. She'd left the car keys inside. She turned and shook the handle. It was locked again. "Damn it," she cursed under her breath, and rested her head against the door.

Travis came up right behind her, his body only inches from hers as he reached around and lightly swept her hand off the knob and gave it a turn. He still smelled faintly of his cologne and brought her back to the morning when he'd held her while she cried. He didn't back away, even when she turned slightly in an attempt to get some space and instead their shoulders touched. That look came over him again, the one from when she'd first opened the door and the one from the hospital when she got the news about Amelia, a look of concern and something else that seemed like a desire to make it better.

"Maybe you should call your boyfriend," he said, his breath tickling past her ear and ruffling her unkempt hair. She swallowed and tried to move away but instead bumped into the corner of the brick wall behind her.

"Uh, my phone is in the car and, anyway, he's really tired and I probably should let him sleep." She felt like she was rambling between the proximity, her worries that he'd smell the blood or the bleach on her, and how this close she was able to see that he had fine lines around the corners of his mouth that must come from having such a broad smile.

"I'll take you to your dad's house and the hospital. I have to go back there anyway."

Though he'd let go of the doorknob, he was still standing close, and it was as distracting as it was intimidating. She could call Collin and have him come out and take her home, but then he'd still need to drop her off at the hospital and head back home to finish cleaning up the bathroom. Plus, she was sure that Travis would wait for Collin to show his face before he was willing to leave Ellie outside by herself at three thirty a.m. She didn't have enough confidence in Collin's ability to double- and triple-check his appearance before facing Travis's practiced scrutiny.

"Yeah, I'll go with you," she said, making the decision at the same moment she said it out loud. "Let me grab my phone and we can go."

Ellie looked at him directly. She'd read somewhere that when you felt guilty, it was hard to look authority in the eyes, so she thought it was a good bluff. But when their eyes met, Travis didn't feel like an authority figure, and she forgot he was wearing a uniform. He didn't step aside like she thought he would. He just stood there for a moment longer, connected by nothing more than their matched gaze. She swallowed slowly and licked her lips, suddenly aware of how dry they were. Both anxious to leave and desperate to put as much space as possible between

Travis and Collin's bathroom, Ellie put her hand on his shoulder and pushed him back lightly.

"Ready?" she asked simply, hoping he would finally let her go without some kind of interrogation. He blinked a few times and took a big step to the right, making plenty of room for Ellie to get through to the hedge-lined walkway and then back to the car. She walked as fast as she dared, grabbed her phone and the hospital bag with her belongings from the Jeep, slammed the car door, and looked around for Travis's cruiser.

"It's around the corner," he said, making a good guess as to what she was looking for. Hands on his utility belt, he took one more glance at Collin's door. When no one emerged from it, he tipped his head toward the dark street where she could make out the form of his car by the light of a lone streetlamp.

Ellie flung her bag over her shoulder and clasped the phone tight to her side as it buzzed. It was on Silent, but that was Collin's vibration pattern. She slipped the phone into the loaner sweatshirt's pocket, after declining the call. It was only a mile and a half to her dad's house. She would turn it back on then, text Collin, explain the situation.

CHAPTER 24

AMELIA

Monday, April 25
Two weeks earlier

"Daddy, I know you don't like it, but you have to eat something. If you don't eat the meat, then I have to give you the protein drink, and I know you don't like that nasty stuff." Amelia sat in front of her father in her living room. His favorite spot when he came to her house was the recliner just in front of the TV. He'd watch any channel with sports, had come to love watching golf and fishing shows, and regularly forgot how to use the remote.

She usually tried to get her father to eat at the table with the family. There were still days that he was lucid enough to talk about his day and ask the kids if they were finishing their homework on time and a few other grandfather-y things, though his speech was slurred. The girls would always look at their mother with concern whenever their grandpa said anything to them directly, and Amelia would have to translate to the best of her ability.

Today she fed the kids first, since Steve was out late at a work site. It worked better, eating in shifts. Plus, there was always the added pressure of having Steve there, silently displeased with the current "Dad situation."

"One more bite, Daddy." Chief Brown gave her a look of displeasure that reminded her of Cora when she didn't like the dinner she'd made and was swallowing it just to be nice and so she could be excused. "Then we can put on the news, and I'll brush your hair," she added.

That was always a good motivator. He used to love it when she would run his old horsehair brush through his hair, and when she was a child, he'd pay her a dime to retrieve the brush from his bathroom counter and play hairdresser. She later thought it was his effort to make up for the loss of her mom at such a young age or to give an example to Ellie of how to sit nicely when he was trying to do her hair. It was a silly little bonding activity that went by the wayside as the girls grew older.

But a week after his stroke, Amelia brought the brush to his hospital room along with a bag of other personal items to help him feel more comfortable as he worked toward recovery. That day she sat down beside him on his bed, adjusted the pillows so she could reach the crown of his head, and spent a few minutes brushing his hair. He was still nonverbal and was only at the point of relearning how to swallow, and some part of Amelia wondered if the father she knew and loved had died the day of his stroke, but as the brush whispered over his thick, white hair, tears ran down his cheeks and she knew he remembered. Some part of her father was still in there, waiting until he could find the path back out again. After that night, she and Ellie swore they'd never let a night go by without brushing their father's hair.

Chief Brown swallowed and reached for the glass of water on the wooden side table beside him. His hand shook, and Amelia had to quash her desire to just pick up the glass and bring the straw to his lips, but his physical therapist insisted that it was important for her father to do as many daily activities as possible by himself. Ellie was the best at this kind of measured patience. She'd spend an extra hour getting their father dressed if it meant he figured out how to fasten even a single button or found a way to adjust the Velcro on his waistband. Amelia was always bogged down with guilt at her irritation when her father spat out his food or spilled his juice.

Amelia leaned forward and as noninvasively as possible placed a towel under his chin to catch the streams that dribbled down the corners of his mouth. His stubble was as white as his hair, and he was in desperate need of a shave. Usually this was Ellie's job, though once a month they'd take him to Stan's Barbershop to get a good shave and a haircut. It was Dad's favorite day of the month. Well, Amelia was unsure if he kept track of days in a linear way anymore, but it was a day where the one half of his mouth that could still smile would turn up more often than down. He never refused to eat on barbershop day and sometimes the old sparkle was there, the one that said *I love you* with no words. Maybe barbershop day was Amelia's favorite day too.

"You need a shave, Daddy. Want to see Stan tomorrow?" she asked, whisking away the cup when he pulled the straw away from his lips one last time and then swiped the damp towel up to take care of the remnants of his drink and dinner that clung to the corners of his mouth. Chief Brown nodded eagerly.

"Try to say it. You know Patty says that's the only way you're gonna learn again. Try: Let's see Stan." Her father set his lips, and she knew that meant he was annoyed. "Come on, Daddy. You can do it."

Amelia placed the glass down on the side table next to her and scooched up closer to her father. She reached out and scratched his stubble with her fingertips, eyebrows raised playfully.

"Or maybe you want a beard. I've always known how much you *love* beards. It'd look so nice and burly with your mustache." She'd never seen her father without his neatly trimmed and now pure-white mustache.

"Let's . . . see . . . Stan . . ." The phrase came out halted, his *t*'s and *l*'s sounding like mumbled *d*'s. Then he added one last phrase, this time in his own voice, clear as though he'd never had a sick day in his life. "M."

Amelia's throat felt thick, and it was difficult to swallow. There were so many memories when he said her name that way. Memories of when he woke her up early to get to orchestra practice before school or when he squeezed her hand and said he loved her one last time before he handed her off to Steve on their wedding day. With tears blurring her vision, Amelia leaned in and wrapped her arms around her father's once burly and now thinning shoulders.

"I'll call Stan in the morning. I promise. I love you, Dad." She kissed his stubbly cheek and pretended not to notice that he had a tear gathering in his right eye. As she sat back, Chief Brown raised his right hand up in front of him, trembling with the effort and then extended two fingers. He remembered.

When she was a teenager, she hated public displays of affection; even an "I love you" was too embarrassing for the teen who was still mourning her mother by shutting off those emotions in other areas of her life. So her father started a code for good-byes. One finger meant *I love you*. Two fingers meant *I love you too*.

His hand fell, and the moment of clarity was gone.

"I know you do," Amelia whispered, and kissed her father's forehead in the special spot. She put a blanket on his lap and passed him the four-buttoned remote that was supposed to give Chief Brown some autonomy when in their home. It was time to put the kids to bed before she started a similar but supersize routine with her father. But the kids could wait for a few minutes while she texted Ellie about her father's progress. They shared enough of the lows in this caregiving life that it was always a glorious moment when they could share a victory.

Amelia started to type, when the back door slammed shut. Steve was home. Her stomach fluttered. He was going to ask for her decision about the real estate training. It was impossible to know what to say. If she told him the truth about Randy and their wild ride, she knew Steve would never let her spend time with him ever again. Then again, she didn't know if she wanted to have anything to do with Randy anymore anyway. Plus, there was that check—twenty grand in her name. How to bring that up without sounding like she was accusing him of some kind of error or manipulation?

Amelia slipped her phone into the back pocket of her jeans and swiftly tucked the lap quilt around Chief Brown's legs. He was already dozing. She patted his hand and rushed into the kitchen, hoping to catch Steve before he went up to change.

As she pushed through the swinging doors from the dining room to the kitchen, she found him rummaging through the refrigerator.

"I made you dinner. It's on the second shelf. Just pork chops, potatoes, and peas. Kate thought it was hilarious that they all started with *p*. Said we were having a *P* dinner, which Cora hated because she thought it sounded like we were having pee for dinner . . ." Steve didn't laugh. He closed the door to the refrigerator, only retrieving a beer. The bottle made a gasping sound as Steve wrenched off the cap. "Hard day?" she asked.

Steve took a long drink from the frosted amber bottle and smacked his lips before speaking.

"Yeah, pretty shitty actually. Lost another one of my best workers to that Talbot's Roofing in Carterville. And some stuff was stolen from our work site after Tom left the doors unlocked. Problem is, wasn't just our stuff. Some of it belonged to the homeowners. Anyway, shitty. How about you? The girls already asleep?"

Amelia glanced at the clock. It was nearly nine and the girls were still awake on a school night. Wow, she'd gotten more distracted with her dad than she'd realized.

"The night has been nice and calm. Girls did their homework. Dad got his dinner down and did the most amazing thing—" Steve cut her off.

"Ohhhhhh. Forgot your dad was coming tonight." He took another sip of his beer and wiped the remnants off his lips with the back of his hand. She knew that tone. He was trying not to let on that he was annoyed or disappointed or whatever he wanted to call it that her father was there on a night where he felt stressed out and tired. It was better to not linger on her father's presence for very long.

"Yeah, switched with L, remember?"

"I guess," he responded, short, gruff. She couldn't tell if he was annoyed by remembering that her father was there or because of his bad day. Amelia decided to change the subject.

"So I think I decided about that offer," she stated, trying to think through how much to share with Steve and how much to edit out.

"Yeah? You get a gig or something?" Though distracted, Steve still reached out and put a hand on his wife's shoulder, squeezing slightly. Amelia tried not to be annoyed that he had no clue what she was talking about.

"Uh, no. The training with Randy, remember?"

"Yeah, yeah, sorry, babe. Forgot about that. What do you think?" He seemed actually interested and gestured for Amelia to take a chair at the table as he pulled out the one in front of him.

"I really want to do it, but my thing with him today was so . . . strange. Things were great at first. He offered to pay for my license and share profits on some sales till I get on my feet in the business." She hesitated for a second and remembered that this was the part where she needed to tread lightly.

When they'd gotten back into Broadlands, Randy had driven directly to the day care without even asking if the detour was okay with Amelia. She'd stayed in the car as he ran inside without looking back. He'd been gone only for a short ten minutes, and when he returned, he was white and angry instead of the mess of worry and tears she'd been expecting.

"Well, what do you think? Sounds like it might work out after all, right?" Steve asked, licked his lips, and put his bottle down again, the watermark pattern overlapping the old one, leaving Mickey Mouse ears on the table. He took a second to unbutton the last two buttons on the collar of his polo.

"I don't know that I'm ready to be gone that much, and I still have Dad to take care of and I'd need a whole new wardrobe and . . ." *and Randy scares me a little,* she wanted to add at the end but resisted.

"Well, if he thought you'd be good at it, maybe it is something to look at. I mean, you don't get that many jobs playing weddings or whatever anymore. This could be a good new career for you."

"Maybe," she said, feeling strange about the support he was show-ing and then guilty that she was surprised. "But I don't think it is going to work out. There was some drama with Randy's kid, and he had to cut our day short. Honestly, I'm not sure he will even be in Broadlands much longer."

"What kind of drama?" Steve asked, resting his forearms on the edge of the table, hands clenched in front of him.

"Something with custody. I'm not totally sure, but from what Randy said, it doesn't look good for him. And some other legal issues that we didn't really talk about. But I bet he'll sell the Slattery place. Bet you a million dollars."

Steve finished off his beer as Amelia was talking. She grabbed the empty bottle, headed over to the counter, and dropped it into the recy-cling bin under the sink. Then she turned, arms folded across her chest, and looked at Steve a little closer. He seemed to be thinking about something, sitting with his thumb to his lips and biting the tip.

"Well, babe, don't give up on this idea. I think it is a good one," he said.

His quiet encouragement was touching and reminded her of the early days of their relationship, when she was going to auditions and long trips to and from Chicago for various jobs. Back then, he was her biggest fan, and it wasn't about earning a couple of extra bucks but about following her dreams. In a rush of gratitude she hadn't felt in a long time, Amelia hurried around the table, took Steve's face in her hands, and pressed her lips against his.

"I love you," she whispered, and kissed him again before she slowly pulled back, their lips separating slowly.

"I love you too," he echoed, tracing the lines of her face with his eyes, serious, solemn. "Amelia, I need to tell you something." He took her hand and guided her into the chair she'd just vacated. She let him put her into her seat, and he pulled her across the tiles.

"What is it? Are you okay?" She put her hand on his face and rubbed the dark stubble on his chin like it was a symbol of how tired he must be and how hard he worked for their family. Steve shook her hand off, the lines on his face growing deeper.

"Don't be worried about me, Amelia. I don't deserve it."

"What . . . what did you do?" Amelia asked, rejected and scared. She leaned back and away from his reach. She had brief flashes of the insurance woman, that weird check in the mail for so much money with her name on it, Steve's recent interest in insurance for everyone in their family, including her father. "So help me, Steve, if this is about Suze from Country Life, I'm gonna lose it."

"Suze?" Steve's mouth quirked up on one side, confused. "You mean Susan Walters?"

"Yeah, you said you weren't going to use her anymore, and then I got this check in the mail, signed by your friend Sue-z-Q." Amelia retrieved the envelope from her back pocket and slapped it on the table.

Steve picked up the opened letter, unfolded it, and peered inside. With a slow blink and a deep sigh he refolded the envelope and put it on the table, his fingers curled on top of it.

"This is part of it, but it has nothing to do with Susan. Well, not exactly. Not what you are thinking at least. Like I said . . ." His skin ashen, he paused, hardly able to make eye contact with Amelia. "I'm in trouble . . ."

CHAPTER 25

ELLIE

Wednesday, May 11
3:39 a.m.

The light was on inside the two-story bungalow. It was one of those houses that looked like it was a ranch but had a hidden staircase to a large upper room that was about the size of the living room. That was Amelia's room growing up.

Ellie got the small office-size room right next to her parents'. The room size used to be a bone of contention between the two sisters, but once Amelia moved out and Ellie had the opportunity to live in the coveted upstairs room, everything changed. She tried it out for one week, moving her stuffed animals and pj's up to Amelia's abandoned abode. She loved it while she was listening to Pearl Jam as loudly as she wanted or doing her homework sprawled out on the hardwood floor, but then night would come and the openness felt less like freedom and more like loneliness. Each night sleep came slower and slower until on night seven she watched the morning sun peek through the small window at the crest of the wooden arches where she'd been staring as each minute of each hour ticked by in a seemingly never-ending night. She moved back into her box-like bedroom that very day.

As Travis's police cruiser pulled up to her house, all the lights were dark except for a faint flicker of the TV in the front room. Chief Brown often fell asleep on his recliner in front of the television, and Ellie would leave him there for the night, tossing a light blanket over him and wishing she were strong enough to carry him to bed like he used to do for her as a child.

Chet was probably sound asleep right next to him. The men had always been friends, and Ellie was pretty sure that Chet chose to be her partner for that reason. He'd never, ever admit it, of course.

The police cruiser was heavy and thunked loudly as it turned into the cracked-cement driveway. The converted minivan she drove her dad around in was parked on the right side of the driveway. It was all decked out in the latest tech, including a wheelchair lift, and every kind of hook and harness one could think of. It was also her only vehicle. She'd sold her nearly broken-down Kia in order to get up her half of the down payment.

"Sweet ride," Travis said, taking a long glance at the van she'd taken to calling Big Bertha.

"Thanks," she said, rolling her eyes. "It's for my dad's wheelchair, so it might be kinda tacky to make fun of me for it." She opened the passenger-side door as soon as he stopped the car.

"Sorry, Brown. I didn't mean . . ." Travis tried to apologize, but she slammed the door, tired of playing nice with everyone. She had to be with her sister this morning. She might lose her. She saw her brother-in-law, shot up, drugged after surgery. Her fiancé lied to her face, and now she had to check on her dad, who probably had no idea what was going on. Then she had to check in on her nieces, who might lose their mother at an even younger age than she had. It was too much to manage all that and try to be nice at the same time.

The sight of her front door, so close and so familiar, made Ellie break into a sprint. A part of her thought that if she could just get through the door, maybe she would be transported back to the days when her father would gather her up in his arms and swing her around the kitchen, his mustache tickling her ear as he whispered, "I missed you."

Travis's car door shut loudly behind Ellie and his footsteps rushed closer, but she kept pushing forward, the peeling black door the closest thing to a finish line she could imagine that horrible day. When her hand landed on the tarnished brass knob, the cool metal sent a shiver of relief through her body that raised goose bumps over her arms and legs. She shoved the door open and crossed the raised cement threshold onto the octagonal tile landing. The subtle smell of beef stew and Lysol that always seemed to linger in the air wrapped around her in the closest thing to a hug her house could give her, the only constant, unaltered item still in her life.

Ellie was half-tempted to close the door on Travis, who she knew couldn't be too far behind. Instead, she shoved it backward hard enough to make it close but lightly enough to keep the latch from catching. Ellie glanced around the dark entry.

The TV was glowing, and, as she had suspected, her father was sound asleep and snoring lightly, the mustard-yellow, orange, and brown blanket her mother had knitted pulled up to his chin. Chet was sitting up on the couch, still dressed in his paramedic uniform, his head tipped back like he'd intended to stay awake but finally gave in to the pull of sleep. To the left was the kitchen. The cup from her coffee that morning was still sitting in the sink. The only unexpected sight was two little backpacks hanging on the back of one of the bar stools.

The door swung open behind her, and Travis let himself inside. It must have been part of being a police officer, but he seemed like he belonged there, like he didn't need an invite. He closed the door and flicked the dead bolt as though he'd done so a million times.

"Okay, what do you need? Can I help?" He glanced at his watch and whispered, "We can get you back to your sister in fifteen minutes if I use my lights."

Ellie dropped the hospital bag on the floor and stripped off the smoky sweatshirt, then leaned down to untie her boots. They came off one at a time with a loud clunk. Next she peeled off her socks and added them to the pile. Just as Ellie reached for the drawstring in her pants and yanked at the bow to untie them, she remembered that Travis was standing there.

"You can leave, Rivera," she said, gathering the items off the ground and heading for the back bedroom.

"You gonna take that blue monstrosity out there? How's your dad going to get anywhere? How about Chet and the kids? Are they all going to ride in his ambulance? Have your boyfriend . . ."

"Fiancé," Ellie interrupted.

"Fine. Have your fiancé meet you at the hospital or whatever. Okay?"

Ellie sighed. He was right. She couldn't take the van, and with Collin out of commission for a while, she needed a ride back to see her sister and to the morgue before eight a.m. She wrapped her arms around the collected clothing, the rubber soles digging into her forearm.

"Fine," she agreed, perturbed. *"Fine,"* she said again, this time with more actual anger deepening the volume of her reply. She had no idea why, but it made her blood boil that he wanted to help. She could only think of one possible reason—the fear that he was pumping her for information rather than actually caring about her. No one liked being used.

"Well then, hurry," Travis replied, the empathy on his face not matching his words and impatience.

Without another word, Ellie marched back into her bedroom, opening the door carefully in case there were little girls sleeping on the floor. Instead, both girls were curled up in her bed under the off-white lacy polyester duvet that had covered her bed since she was six. That was when her mom had helped her redecorate it into a princess room, to be more specific a unicorn-princess room, thus the canopy bed and unicorns on the wall. Both girls were wearing Ellie's casual tee shirts, one from her dad's days playing softball for the department team on Kate and a worn Cardinals jersey on Cora. Those poor girls, no clothes here of their own, no Puppy Moto for Kate to sleep with, or Cora's ever-so-secret but still very real blankie she snuggled every night. Everything in their own house was a piece of evidence for now. Ellie wondered how much they knew and who told them. What was going to happen to those little girls?

Ellie placed her collection of clothes on a chair in the corner that was already filled with various items of clothing. Then she went over to see the girls closer. Cora had her arm across Kate's body, hand encompassing her sister's little fingers. That was when it hit.

What was Ellie going to do without her big sister?

Amelia and the girls living in this town was the *only* upside to moving back to Broadlands. Everything else was merely bearable. Sure, when Collin moved into town at the beginning of the year, life seemed to brighten up a bit, but he had such a steady course load and often had to crash at friends' houses off campus when his study schedule became too intense. But Amelia and her family were a lovely constant in her life. They were her picture of domestic felicity and a goal for what she wanted in the future even if it meant living in this crap-tastic town. She'd always thought that even if coming back home meant putting off being a doctor, at least she had her sister.

But watching Cora comforting Kate in her sleep, Ellie couldn't help but feel an emptiness in her own hand where Amelia's used to be during the hard times. Ellie ran her fingers over the swooping *L* at her neck, wishing she'd thought to ask the hospital staff if they had Amelia's *M*. She'd like to wear it at least until Amelia recovered, because watching her nieces sleep, Ellie decided that she needed to stop wondering if her sister was going to die and instead start planning for her to live.

A few silent tears rolled down Ellie's cheeks as she rummaged through her drawers and shoved item after item into a small pink duffel bag she kept hanging in the closet. Then she stripped off her borrowed clothes, and though she wanted to throw them in the garbage can in the kitchen, she tossed them into the white wicker laundry basket so she didn't have to touch them for one moment longer.

She even changed her underwear and bra, on which a smattering of blood had dried in an odd pattern. She'd cleaned up the best she could at the hospital but now wished there was time for a shower to ensure that every molecule of blood and fluids was off her. But the glowing red numbers on the alarm clock on her bedside table read 4:06 a.m., and Ellie knew it was more important to keep moving forward.

Without looking, she put on the first thing from her drawer, a V-necked plum-colored shirt, soft from multiple washes. Then she tossed on her favorite pair of jeans, the ones that were more comfortable than her yoga pants even if they were a size or two too big. Almost willing to skip a belt, she yanked one off the hook anyway with a tiny clank, pausing a second to check the girls and make sure she hadn't woken them.

The old, worn belt threaded through the loops on her jeans easily. With a rush across the room, Ellie placed a gentle kiss on each of the girls' foreheads, taking an extra moment to try to memorize their individual scents. Cora smelled of bubble gum and the chief's shampoo, which Chet must've had the girls use for their baths. Kate smelled of spit, the fingers of her right hand shoved into her mouth, a small trail of drool sprawling across her cheek, and strongly of Ellie's rosewater perfume. Ellie had loved the stuff as a kid, thinking that smelling like roses was the most romantic notion ever. Amelia would always tease her, saying the scent smelled more like decaying flowers than a blossoming rose. Little Kate always begged for a spray or two, and Ellie, perhaps with a tinge of mischievous revenge, would acquiesce.

A quick trip to the bathroom and Ellie's bag was packed, enough for a few days. She glanced in the bathroom mirror. Her once-high ponytail hung limply to one side, and what was left of her eye makeup was smudged under her lower eyelashes like she'd been going for a smoky look but failed. She'd already packed her brush, but she grabbed her dad's comb and unwound the tie that had been holding her hair in place all day. It took several tries to get the flimsy plastic to straighten her tangled mess, but once she got through the biggest snags, the teeth slipped through easily, and the feeling of the comb against her scalp was refreshing and relaxing.

When the rat's nest was tamed, she used a tissue to wipe away the makeup residue under her eyes, and washed her face vigorously with the strong-smelling Zest soap they kept on the bathroom sink. She'd rather go without makeup than continually worry about her tears making her look like a bedraggled clown. She rinsed her face with cold water, dried quickly, and reassessed.

She didn't think of herself as a beauty. Her sister always said she was the gorgeous one, but Ellie knew she was average at best. Her body was round where she'd like it to be flat, and she had hips that she usually would rather hide than accentuate. Her face without makeup looked young and childlike. Normally she used makeup to hide behind, not just her flaws but also her age and to play down her appearance of vulnerability. But standing there in her street clothes with not a stitch of makeup, she looked just as young and scared as she always felt.

Tempted to put on a quick layer of foundation and some mascara after all, Ellie stopped herself. She didn't have time. Instead, she grabbed her makeup bag, slipped it inside the jumbled mess of her duffel, and headed out to the front room.

Travis was facing away from Ellie, sitting on the couch and talking to an awake Chet. Chief Brown stirred at his side, and it seemed like he might wake up. It was hard to tell what state her father would be in when tossed out of his routine and schedule. Ellie couldn't imagine anything going right at the moment, so it was probably going to be rough. She quickly crossed the room and put her hand on Travis's shoulder, which made him jump.

"Oh, you ready?" he asked, stopping for a moment when he laid eyes on her. "You look . . ." He looked her over head to toe as though she were a stranger.

"You look cute," Chet finished the statement with his own assessment.

"Not exactly the look I was going for, but thanks, Chet."

"I was going to say—different. You look different," Travis said before Ellie had a chance to open her mouth and ask Chet about the day.

"Yeah, well, come find me one day when you aren't in uniform, and I'll tell you the same thing." She patted his shoulder firmly like she would another firefighter. His shoulder was solid, and that made her remember crying there earlier that day, so she rested her hand on the back of the couch when she put it down again.

"How is our little M?" Chet stood and shuffled tiredly around the couch to wrap his arms around her, the stiff fabric of his uniform shirt bringing back too many memories. "Rivera here said she's still in a bad way."

"Yeah, she's, uh . . ." Ellie's rib cage shook. Chet pulled her in tighter, and Ellie closed her eyes and pretended again that her father, not her coworker, was the strong one holding her up. But her father was sleeping through the whole thing. Honestly, he probably wouldn't even understand if he were awake.

"So, are you okay staying till Steve's parents get here?" Ellie asked, freeing herself from his arms. "They're going to stop by the hospital first thing tomorrow, but they said they'd take the girls to their hotel and talk to them a little about what happened. You kept them away from the TV like I told you, right?"

Chet nodded, rearranging himself into his divot on the couch. He ran a finger under his nose and sniffed loudly, like his mustache made him want to sneeze.

"I kept the girls away, but while I was putting them down, Chief got the remote and the news was on. I don't know, Ellie, I think he saw something, 'cause I heard him making some noises, and I came out here and he was shifting in his seat like he wanted to stand up. I turned it off and he was so upset, I had to give him one of his pills. He was scaring the girls, and I was afraid he was going to hurt himself."

"What was he saying?" Travis asked, now sitting on the edge of the couch.

"I couldn't really tell. He was just getting worked up. I saw the ten o'clock replay of the news, and they don't say Amelia's name or anything, but they did have a picture of Caleb and a warning."

"Yeah, I know about that." She eyed her father, who was stirring in his chair. "So, he doesn't know, then?"

"No, I didn't know what to say. Just told the girls that line you said about the emergency, and then Chief . . . I just couldn't do it, Ellie. I was hoping you would know what to say so he would understand . . ."

She should be happy with this news. She'd wanted to be the one to tell him, and a part of her whispered, *Now you can wait until you know.* But another part of her was disappointed because she didn't know how to tell him so he would understand.

"That's fine." Ellie walked behind the back of the couch, skirting the tile of the entryway without crossing over, a habit from when she was a child and played lava with Amelia on rainy days. Chief Brown's armchair was fully reclined and looked more comfortable than his ancient full-size mattress in the back bedroom. He shifted again in his sleep, and Ellie wondered what he was dreaming about. "I guess I'll have to come back tomorrow. Or if things are better, maybe you could bring him by the hospital."

"Of course, hon. You keep me updated, and I'll do whatever you want." Chet patted his shirt pocket where he kept an outdated flip phone.

Ellie lowered her voice a fraction. "I'll pay you for your time. I promise. Thank you for helping out. It means everything to me."

"You will not pay me a penny. I owe your dad my life ten times over. I can help out one measly time, right, Chief?" Chet said to a sleeping Chief Brown. Ellie swore he smiled under his mustache.

Travis stood, readjusted his belt, and then put out a hand toward Chet.

"Thanks for giving your statement to Detective Conrad earlier. He said it was extremely detailed."

Chet took Travis's hand and gave it three strong shakes. "I've given enough statements in my day that I should know what I'm doing by now." Then, with a meaningful glance at Ellie, Chet let go of Travis's hand and gestured to Ellie's duffel on the ground.

"Here, I'll help you out." Chet pushed himself off the couch slower this time like he'd used all of his energy the last time he got up. But whatever amount of exhaustion he was experiencing, he pushed through and snagged Ellie's bag before she could protest. The sight of Chet carrying her childhood overnight bag she'd used for nearly every slumber party she'd attended was enough to make her have to hide a smile behind her hand.

"I've got it," Travis said, putting out his hand for the bag and gesturing for Chet to sit down. The crusty old paramedic clenched his lips together so they disappeared under his impressive facial hair and gave a pointed look to the officer standing in her father's living room. Something seemed to click. "Ah, yes. Thank you for your help," Travis added as he headed out the door with Chet. "I'll see you in the car, Brown."

The two men exited quickly and without another word, conspiring to give Ellie a few moments alone with her father. Standing close to the arm of his chair, she ran her fingers through his thick, white hair, wishing she had his brush. As she repeated the action, she watched her father sleep. He looked like his old self, and she was glad he was asleep tonight so she could pretend that he would wake up and know what to do. She was so tired of being the only one holding their disintegrating family together.

"Daddy, M is hurt bad," she whispered, playing along with her fantasy of his ability to hear her and understand, and to fix the brokenness all around them. "She can't wake up, and they don't know if she will." She placed her hand on the side of her father's face, his stubble scratching at her palm. "What am I supposed to do, Daddy? How did I end up the only one left? Mommy, then you, then M." The weight of her loneliness came crashing down on her shoulders in a nearly physical way. She closed her eyes, trying to fight the drowning feeling pulling her under. "I can't do this alone. I'm supposed to marry Collin and Mom was supposed to help me pick a dress and you walk me down the aisle and Amelia be my matron of honor, but now . . ."

Before she completed her sentence, a warm, familiar hand wrapped around hers and she opened her eyes in shock, almost wondering if she'd imagined it. But what she saw was her father, his eyes open wide and clear, his hand on hers. When they made eye contact, he smiled a little and patted her hand like he'd heard everything and was telling her everything was going to be okay.

She gasped. "Daddy!" A harsh voice in the back of her mind told her that the fantasy of a healed father would soon be broken by reality, but she couldn't help lingering in it for a few moments longer.

As soon as she spoke, Chief Brown's forehead wrinkled, eyebrows pulling together like he'd just remembered that he left the oven on after leaving for a week-long trip. He started to shift back and forth in his seat, his hand no longer a gentle caress but a strong vise around hers.

"Ouch!" Ellie gasped, and tried to pull her hand away, remembering what Chet had said about her father after watching the news—overexcited, active, upset. Whatever the medicine made fall away from his consciousness earlier was back, and he wanted to say something.

"What, Daddy? What?" She leaned in closer. His lips were moving, soft whispers of something important escaping but imperceptible. Now on her knees, her hand behind his shoulder with him propped up on the edge of the recliner, Ellie put her ear up to his mouth; she closed her eyes and listened intently.

"Caleb." He said the name as clearly as anything he'd said in the past seven months. "Caleb . . . Caleb . . . Caleb," he repeated over and over again, the volume escalating quickly and the clear quality to his speech disappearing. Ellie tried to back away, but her father held her shoulder tightly, the sound of Caleb's name pounding against her eardrum in her father's frantic voice.

Chet ran through the front door after hearing the commotion.

"Not again," he muttered, and rushed forward, putting his experienced hands on Chief Brown's frail ones. Her father held strong, her face against his, his breath on her cheek. He said one last phrase, quieter this time, so quiet she could barely make it out. Then his hands went limp, and she stumbled backward, away from her father and away from the secret he had just whispered in her ear.

Chet waved at her like he was asking her to leave rather than giving her permission. Ellie's heart was pounding fast and hard, and this time there was no hesitation. She breezed past Travis, who had been watching from the doorway with his sad eyes and unreadable features, and stomped across the lawn to the police car in the driveway.

Once they were inside the car, Travis turned on the engine, backed out of the driveway, and pointed the car toward Frampton and the hospital there. He didn't ask what her father had said, though she knew he wanted to. She was mute because it saved her from lying. They drove in silence, but for Ellie the car ride was loud, blaring even. As they drove through the dark, past houses of sleeping people and fields of newly planted grain, Ellie could hear it, her father's last message, clear and pure:

"Caleb is a murderer."

CHAPTER 26

AMELIA

Tuesday, May 3
One week earlier

"Tired" was the wrong word. Yes, Amelia was tired, but there was something more there, exhaustion or devastation or a complete loss on how to keep moving forward in her life. At least her father was at the senior center for the day. Well, they called it that, but it really was an elder-care facility where Ellie and Amelia could feel safe putting their dad on the days when they both had other obligations. It was always with a wave of relief followed quickly by another wave of guilt that she left him there.

Usually, she had a day of chores or errands or practicing for a gig, but today she was headed over to the firehouse to pick up Ellie and head out to lunch. She didn't know what she was going to tell her. Ellie thought they were meeting to discuss venues for her wedding, not the bombshell that Steve had laid at her feet more than a week earlier.

After she presented him with the check from Susan at Country Life, Steve slowly explained that he was in trouble because he was in debt. But not because of the business or the vandalism around the house—he'd started taking bets again. Amelia was both shocked and relieved. Steve had been running a small sports-booking business when they started dating. She hated it and made him quit eventually, but at least it wasn't an affair.

She shouldn't have been surprised. Steve's father had always run a sports-booking business that the local law enforcement in their hometown of Chadwick, Tennessee, overlooked because many of them participated. Steve learned from his dad and brought the time-honored tradition to Broadlands with him as a young firefighter. By the time she and Steve got married, he'd built a complicated network that reached all the way to the University of Illinois campus and brought in three times as much cash as anything he made as a public servant.

At first Amelia did what everyone in the firehouse, police station, and town seemed to do—ignore it. And when she did get the courage to ask him about the "business," Steve explained that he would keep it going only until he had enough to retire as a firefighter and start his own legitimate business.

By the time Cora was born, he did just that. It was hard at first to live without the steady, albeit dishonest stream of income, but Amelia slept better at night and soon the jobs started pouring in, and running an illegal gambling business on the side would've been downright inconvenient. But in the past few years, the jobs were sparser, the workers needed more money, and things just kept going wrong.

When Steve explained his reasoning for starting up the business again, she could almost see the logic in it. It was tempting to go back to something that used to bring instant money and security, especially when at first it brought in tons of cash. But then, Steve explained, everything went wrong. He wasn't super clear on why, but he was losing money hand over fist and that was when the vandalism started.

He didn't have the cash to pay out a big client, and . . . soon things started to disappear off the work site. And then the tires were slashed, and even more recently a small warehouse several towns over that was insured in Amelia's name burned down. Even with the insurance payout that just came in the mail, Steve couldn't make up the loss from the accidental fire.

But no matter what he did, Steve's luck never turned around. And now he was in a hole that included not just the business, for which he could at least declare bankruptcy and save a little face, but also in a more dangerous game of owing money to the wrong people. Lots of money. And that was where he left off; they were on the cusp of declaring bankruptcy, and he had no idea how to ever pay back the money he owed.

What was she supposed to say to any of that? Amelia wondered. And what would she say to Ellie? Poor Ellie, who thought her brother-in-law was the best guy on the planet, who had no idea that Steve had ever done anything illegal now or in the past. But Amelia needed to talk to *someone*. This sorrow was too much to keep and carry on her own.

When Steve dropped the bomb, she nearly said the first words that came into her mind: *I'm leaving you* or *How dare you do this to us?* or *I'll never forgive you*. But instead she said, "It's okay. We will figure this out. I forgive you."

Why? Why did her mouth continuously say things her mind didn't agree with? Well, today when she talked to Ellie, she was determined to tell the truth or at least as much of it as she could bear. Ellie would know what to do and was strong enough to help Amelia stand up to Steve.

Ellie was sitting on the steps outside of the station. The building was old; a simple stone carving at the crest of the three-door garage spelled out *1901*. Ever since she was a little girl, the tan bricks and triple-wide driveway made her feel nearly brand-new.

Inside, the tile floor was black and white and always sparkling clean. Her father had always been fastidious about the firehouse, and though he knew how to encourage his men with friendship and humor, he had high standards and was willing to help out to keep the place in good shape. Even with his seven-month absence, his years of attention to detail still showed.

Amelia didn't know how Ellie came here every day. There were too many memories creeping out from behind the well-built walls when she saw this place, like her first time sliding down the brass fire pole with her father's hands keeping her safe from falling, or when at seventeen she walked into the lounge and saw a handsome young Steve sitting there and he fell into her life like he belonged there.

As Ellie made her way down the front walk and across the cement drive, Amelia blinked rapidly, knowing that if she started to get emotional *now*, there was no hope of keeping things under control as she broached more difficult subjects. Okay, *if* she talked to Ellie. The idea was becoming more and more overwhelming, panic crawling up her spine and shoulders and neck in a prickly heat. She shifted in her seat, her faded blue yoga pants feeling sticky and hot rather than comfortable. Nervous, she pressed the button to unlock the car doors several times.

"Hey, long shift," Ellie said, her voice dragging with exhaustion as she jumped into the passenger-side seat. "Got called to a fire in Frampton, and there was this little boy who hid in his toy box when he got scared. The guys found him and got him out, but he's so burned, M. Like, seventy-five percent of his body burned."

"Oh my God." A shiver went through Amelia, cooling the fiery nervousness that was invading moments before. It was the same chill she always seemed to get when someone in her family talked about the things they saw on the job. She was proud of their service and sacrifice and all that other stuff, but she wasn't one of them. She didn't run into burning buildings or put dressings on burned flesh or look into the eyes of a child who was burned beyond recognition and tell him that everything was going to be okay.

In fact, at this point in her life, Amelia had come to believe that rarely did everything turn out okay. Amelia pulled away from the station as Ellie continued to share her difficult call.

"I . . . I don't get why people don't make those stupid fire-escape plans. It's not even that hard. They talk about it in school, and now Carl won't . . ." She trailed off, and Amelia recognized the reaction. Steve used to get this way too after a hard call, wanting to talk but not wanting to share too much, the emotion finally hitting and becoming overwhelming. That was when Steve would go for a run or grab an extra bottle of beer or kiss her in that *I want you* way that always made her knees wobble.

"I mean, you guys even have one of those flexible ladders in all the bedrooms, right? I remember when Steve got it, he said, 'God, can you *tell* a former firefighter lives here?' And the kids know a plan to get out, right?"

At the cheerful mention of Steve, Amelia found her own emotions getting heavy. It usually made her feel proud when Ellie gushed about Steve—she loved that her sister looked up to her husband and felt like he was a brother to her—but not today. Today it just reminded her that she was going to break that vision of him into a million pieces, and then Ellie would have to figure out a way to put it all back together into a new picture that made sense.

"Yeah, we had a family meeting like two months ago. Why don't you ask them about it sometime? It might be helpful to run through the basics." Amelia turned onto Main Street and without asking, slowed in front of Frank's. "Want to have breakfast with me?" Amelia glanced at her phone. It was nearly noon. "Okay, breakfast for lunch?"

She tried to put as much excitement into the question as possible, eyebrows raised playfully. Ellie, despite the hard call and the exhaustion that hung heavy on her shoulders, nodded and smiled.

"I'll never turn down breakfast at Frank's." Her smile quirked to one side. "But I thought we were going to your place. Steve said he had a book on treating burns I could grab."

Amelia's foot came off the brake, and though it was not exactly legal, she did a giant U-turn in the middle of Main Street, crossing the double line and swooping so close to the line of cars parked on the other side of the road that Ellie clenched the armrest, her unpainted nails blanching white.

"We can go home," Amelia said, righting the car and starting to understand why Randy manhandled the car on the day that Dawson was taken. Control over something so big made her feel less like she was losing it.

"Whoa, hello, crazy driver." Ellie stared at her sister. "What's up, M? You seem off. Was it the kid? Sorry, I know you don't like those kinds of stories."

Amelia kept her eyes forward, not wanting to have this conversation in the car.

"No, it wasn't that. Steve and I just had a fight, and he isn't my favorite topic of conversation. So, I'm glad he's your BFF that you text after a hard day at work, but we are going through a rough patch."

She hit her driveway at full speed, which made them both bump out of their seats. If Steve had been in the car, his head would've crashed into the ceiling. Amelia slowed the car as they sped up the gravel drive.

"Dang, M, he got you mad." Ellie unbuckled her seat belt and looked over her sister one more time. "We didn't have to come here first. I wasn't asking that. You know that, right?"

Amelia's gray crewneck collar was starting to feel tight. It was easier to keep things secret. Telling was too hard. Why tell Ellie? Why ruin her vision of marital bliss right as she was starting to envision her own?

"I know. I'm being a baby. You go get your book. Steve and I will be fine. It was just a little fight, nothing big." She explained it all away with a few sentences and a wave of her hand. Lying was easier. Ellie's fingers played against the door handle before they stilled and wrapped around the smooth silver surface.

"I'm sure you're not being a baby, but let's talk about this over breakfast." She cracked the door open and let one foot hang out. "I might as well get the book, right?"

"Of course," Amelia said, feeling sick that she'd almost told Ellie, that she'd made the mistake of thinking she could tell anyone.

"I'll be fast, I swear." With a swoosh of her messy ponytail and a slam of the door, Ellie ran the short distance up the drive toward the office door. The first few steps looked painful to Amelia, but soon her strides became regular, and she leaped up the steps.

Amelia, who'd been clenching the steering wheel since her spontaneous U-turn, collapsed against it as soon as Ellie was out of sight. Those moments, as she sat in darkness, eyes closed to the light, were the most peaceful and refreshing she'd had since Steve said those words, "I'm in trouble." If she was honest, she was exhausted, and it wasn't just the one night of no sleep. It was life. No matter how hard she tried, Amelia could never catch up, and just when she thought she had a way out of the crush of debt and the heavy weight of feeling never good enough, Randy also turned out to be someone she didn't even know. In fact, she didn't recognize any of the men in her life.

Her father was trapped or lost inside his injured mind. Steve had been lying to her for who knew how long about his business and debt. Caleb was still a confounding mirage that she was afraid of one minute and laughing with the next. As least she had Ellie—steady, strong, hardheaded Ellie.

The tempting fingers of sleep tugged at Amelia even with the stitched leather of the steering wheel pressing into her cheek. Her body started to relax inch by inch, a nice change from her head spinning from lack of food and sleep. If only she felt calm and safe enough to walk into her house, up to her bed, and flop down under the covers. Soon she would. She'd find a way to hush the worries inside, to put away all of the disappointment, and just go back to normal. Okay, maybe no part of her life was normal right now, but at least she could return to the status quo.

Just as Amelia was about to drift off into a deep sleep, a loud pounding on her driver-side window sucked her back from the quiet comfort nearly encompassing her. She raised her head without opening her eyes, ready to grouse at Ellie for playing a totally immature joke on her, but as she peeked out from behind her heavy eyelids, she didn't see Ellie laughing at her on the other side of the driver-side glass.

Instead, she saw an angry and agitated Randy.

CHAPTER 27

ELLIE

Wednesday, May 11
4:27 a.m.

What the hell *is my problem?* Ellie asked herself as she pushed the glowing B button and then stepped back against the scuffed stainless steel walls. She worked with injured, dying, and sometimes dead individuals, but there was still something inside her stomach that wouldn't stop fluttering at the idea of sneaking into the morgue. It wasn't just the challenge of getting past security and getting out before Travis showed up with the dead man's sister. It was also the idea of a room full of people who were alive not too long ago and had families crying for them somewhere. It was a hard reminder that everyone ended up the same way—dead.

When the elevator hit the bottom floor, the butterflies in her stomach flew into her heart and throat. It would be her luck that a guard would be sitting on the other side of the doors and she'd have to use her hastily created excuse about getting lost or something like that. But as the doors opened, nothing was standing on the other side but a dim hallway filled with flickering fluorescent lights. It was like the design team had watched too many horror movies and modeled the morgue after the scene where the serial killer stalked his victim in an abandoned hospital basement.

This was crazy. She was sneaking into the morgue in the same hospital where her sister was on life support, bullet holes in her tender flesh, machines keeping her alive. She should be sitting by her side, holding her hand and watching the monitors for signs of life. But this made her feel like she was actually *doing* something rather than waiting for the worst. She knew that finding out who shot her sister wouldn't make the wounds seal up or her eyelids flutter, but it would help the narrative of how, and more important, *why*, fall into place.

A pair of silver doors stood in front of her, two parallel rectangular windows lined up side by side. Her palms itched to shove them open in one broad, swift move, but, eyeing a well-hidden security camera covered by a glass dome, Ellie considered a more cautious approach. She forced her eyes down and watched her feet peek out from under the hem of her jeans with each step. With a gentle touch, she pushed open only one of the two doors, which opened silently. She'd expected some kind of creak or swoosh, but the silence was more unnerving.

The whole floor seemed abandoned. There was a second hallway with a windowed office on one side and a blank wall on the other. A part of Ellie that knew someone's sister was going to be in that office in a few hours to identify the body of her brother. Even though she didn't know this woman and even though her brother may have shot her sister, Ellie's heart broke for her.

The door to the office butted up next to the giant picture window that revealed a computer with a repeating screensaver that scrolled the words Frampton Memorial Morgue over and over again as though it were a surprise.

The second set of double doors stood in front of Ellie to the left of the office. This was where she finally hesitated. Usually you'd have to check in with the morgue attendant, sign something, and then be escorted into the morgue itself, but today the office was thankfully empty and, honestly, she'd been banking on it. The hospital was notoriously understaffed, especially on the night shift. If they didn't have enough employees to take care of the living, then there was no way they'd have a full staff taking care of the dead. But just in case, Ellie was prepared with a cockamamie excuse for needing to be in the morgue.

It was too late to turn back now. This time she inched up to the doors instead of stepping boldly. Heart pounding in her ears, Ellie tested the door by pushing with her fingertips. It gave, and she pushed a little harder, this time the door swinging open to a dark, cavernous room. Scales hung from the ceiling, and the ambient light from giant computer screens reflected off the highly polished metal surfaces, including four long silver autopsy tables. The floor was damp, and when she stepped inside, her feet echoed as they slapped against the tile that gently sloped to a drain in the middle of the room. She shivered in the dark and pulled her arms in closer, wiping away rows of goose bumps with her palms.

To her right was a large rectangular window that looked into the same office she'd spied from the hallway. On the left wall were six silver squares that filled the space. She already knew that each went six feet into the wall and they were refrigerated. One of them held a dead man. Well, maybe more than one held a dead man. Ellie hadn't fully considered the idea of multiple dead people.

With a quick glance over her shoulder, Ellie crossed to the refrigerator doors. She decided to start in the middle and work her way out. Trying not to think too hard, she grabbed the long, narrow handle and pulled. There was a lot of weight behind the latch, and she had to pull harder than she'd expected. The door unsealed with a pop, and she leaned back to get the leverage to swing it open.

Unlike what you'd normally see on TV, the body wasn't lying there naked, covered by nothing but a sheet. Instead, the deceased was zipped up in a body bag, an identifying tag by the feet. Though hard to decipher in the dim light of the sleeping morgue, it clearly said *Female*.

Ellie slammed the door. These poor people didn't ask to be in a box in a hospital waiting to be cut open and weighed and measured from the inside out. It seemed worse than those naked dreams where you show up at school feeling pretty sure that it is totally normal you've got no clothes on until everyone else points and laughs at your nakedness. What was more exposing and intimate than another human looking through your insides?

Ellie pushed the door closed until the seal swooshed and the latch clicked. Her hand remained on the latch for a moment longer as one tiny part of her brain wondered who this woman may have been and why she was here.

With a step to the right, Ellie put her hand on the next door. This one she opened with less ceremony and yanked hard. The door swung open and her stomach dropped. It was empty. She glanced at her watch; this was taking far too much time. She slammed the door closed, this time without any attempt at silence.

The colossal stupidity of this whole scheme was settling on her shoulders; she realized that because she had spent the day and part of the night with Travis, he might have been willing to share the information about the dead man's identity. She should've at least asked.

One more door. She'd give herself one more door. It was becoming more routine, the cool touch of the metal, the heavy clunk of the latch, the swoosh of the seal, and the satisfying swing of the door. This one was full. Her hands were shaking as she reached out to flip over the manila tag, bending closer to read the handwritten words on it. *Male. Unidentified. Gunshot wound.* And then her sister's address.

This was it. She wasn't going to hesitate or turn back now. Glad that she lifted people on gurneys day in and day out, she used all the strength in her upper arms to roll the heavy drawer all the way out until it bounced as it ran out of track. The big black bag was cold to the touch, and the metal zipper pull stuck to her finger pads. Ellie unzipped the bag like she'd been doing it her whole life. There was no real smell since the body was fresh and newly washed to help with identification.

She didn't need to see much more than his face. Hopefully he would be somewhat familiar despite his wound. Ellie had some guesses as to who was on the other side of that black plastic. She now knew it wasn't Caleb, and something inside her urged that it wasn't some random stranger. Maybe Sam, the day worker Steve believed was behind the vandalism on their work site. Or that Tom guy they fired for leaving their last work site open. Or maybe . . .

Ellie slid her hand in between the open sides of the zipper and pulled it back slowly, exposing one side of the man's face. There was a large wound taking up the majority of the right side of his cheek. At first the wound drew her eye because it was bigger than you'd expect for a gunshot victim, and her paramedic mind started to work through where the bullet entered and exited, how much blood was involved, and whether there would have been any hope for survival if she'd gotten there sooner. But the professional assessment of the man's wound ended when her phone buzzed in her pocket.

An unknown ring at five a.m. meant one thing in her mind—Amelia.

She'd just seen her. Her vitals were strong—she wouldn't have left otherwise—but to get a call this soon . . . It couldn't be good. Ellie wanted nothing more than to pick up the call; instead, she reached into her back pocket, and rather than pulling it out and hitting Talk, she pressed the side button that sent the call to voice mail.

Ellie's hand hovered over her back pocket for a few seconds longer after she discontinued the call. Part of her worried the phone would ring again right away, and another part of her completely regretted hanging up. All she'd wanted since sending her sister off in the ambulance yesterday morning was to stand by her side and hold her hand. And now that she could be holding vigil over her unconscious form, Ellie was chasing answers. That realization alone should have been enough to refocus her, but it wasn't. She'd come this far. She wanted to know who was inside the bag.

Wasting no more time, Ellie gathered all her courage and pulled the bag apart, splitting it in the middle like she was ripping open a shirt. She'd only pulled the zipper down to the man's midchest area, but when she yanked at the edges, it opened to his waist. She may not have been able to recognize him by the injured side of his face, but she knew him once she saw the familiar tattoo on his stiff, graying forearm—an arrow pointing to his wrist, a name written down the shaft. *Stella.*

"Randy," Ellie whispered, her breath making his hair ripple. She'd only met him once, and it had been very . . . memorable to say the least. It was just over a week ago, and now Ellie felt guilty she hadn't thought to mention it to Travis earlier. Well, that wasn't true; she had thought of mentioning it, but it put Caleb in a bad light, and with all the complexities of the situation, she'd avoided any anecdotes about her soon-to-be brother-in-law that made him sound unhinged. But now she wondered if Randy's mental state on that day should've been a clue at things to come.

"Randy," she whispered, not sure how to fit him into the narrative that had been forming in her mind. Now, it was all blank. "My God, it was Randy."

A light flicked on in the office and Ellie clamped a hand over her mouth, frozen as though lack of movement would make her disappear. She could see into the office as clearly as watching the attendant on a TV screen. It would be a little harder for the woman on the other side of the glass to see her unless she was looking closely.

The woman looked young, a short blonde ponytail hiked up on the crown of her head. She seemed preoccupied with a bowl of oatmeal in one hand and tossing papers and pens into a gray-and-white bag sitting on one of the two office chairs in the room. She was probably at the end of a twelve-hour shift and ready to leave, and though that worked to Ellie's advantage as she packed up, it would soon turn into a disadvantage when she came to do a final check before she handed the reins over to the day crew.

"Damn it," Ellie whispered. This time she forgot to be quiet and slammed the door shut with a click that resonated through her arms and around the room. Her sneakers squeaked on the floor made up of tiny tiles as she turned quickly. She needed speed over silence.

With a hand on her back pocket to make sure the phone didn't fall out, Ellie dashed for the doors, her right foot slipping and causing her to stumble. Her knee cracked against the floor, and a sharp stab of pain raced through her knee and femur. Adrenaline taking over, she leaped up as though the floor were made of rubber.

Limping now, she burst through the first set of doors like she was running into an emergency, forgetting about the hall window with the speaker hole that allowed direct access to the morgue office where sane people would sign in and wait for someone who knew what they were doing to go inside. Thankfully, the room was still empty, and though that could mean that the woman inside might be waiting for her on the other side of the second set of doors, it also meant that Ellie had a moment to recover.

Ellie walked through as calmly and naturally as she could manage. The hall was empty still, one of the twin fluorescent lights in the ceiling flickering.

The elevator was just a few steps away, and Ellie felt a surge of relief and also a tiny thrill of victory. She'd just seen a man, who had once been a friend to her sister, dead and disfigured—but it was also the first time in the past twelve hours that she felt like she'd actually completed a task she'd set out to accomplish.

As she pressed the Up button on the elevator, a jingle of keys down the hall distracted her. That part of the basement held the laundry and sterilization equipment, the laundry detergent smell covering the smell of formaldehyde and bleach that accompanied the morgue. A man in pale blue scrubs was pushing a large basket of folded linens down the hall. Ellie stared at her feet and then pushed the button again, hoping he wouldn't ask why she was in the basement or why she didn't have an ID badge.

The elevator doors slid open and Ellie dove inside, pressing the lobby button seven times in a row and the Close button even more ferociously. It wasn't fast enough. The man rolled the giant basket into the elevator by backing in through the doors. When he noticed Ellie inside, he jumped but then smiled and nodded like there was nothing out of the ordinary.

"Could you push LL for me, please?"

"Uh, sure," Ellie responded, and pushed the button for the lower lobby, still trying not to make eye contact. Then her phone started to buzz again. This time she couldn't help herself; she needed to know the news.

Ellie slipped the buzzing phone out of her back pocket and was surprised and relieved to see Chet's name staring back at her. She let out a sigh of relief and sent him to voice mail; it could wait until she was out of the elevator. Moments later the orderly exited on LL, and Ellie was finally alone. A message had buzzed through.

Still nervous that someone would pick up on the fact that she'd been snooping around the basement, Ellie found a quiet corner by a large ficus and a decorative remake of an ancient statue. She wanted to call Collin, tell him that Randy was the dead man, that he might be right, Caleb might be innocent, but first, she had to call Chet. Instead of listening to the message, she just touched Chet's name in her Recents list.

"Hello?" Chet answered, as though any one of ten million people could be calling him.

"Hey, Chet, it's Ellie. Everything okay?"

Chet hesitated. "Did you listen to my message?"

"No. I just saw you called."

"Oh, Ellie, I kinda wish you'd listened to the message."

"You're making me nervous. What is going on? Is it Amelia?" she asked.

"Ellie, it's not about Amelia," Chet said, sniffing like he always did when he was trying to figure out what to say. "It's your dad. He's missing."

CHAPTER 28

AMELIA

Tuesday, May 3
One week earlier

"Randy!" Amelia jumped in her seat, heart racing as she took in the sight of Randy on the other side of her window. He was dressed down, tee shirt and jeans, hair unkempt. He looped his finger in circles, urging her to lower the window.

After the crazy day in the car, he'd been calling her endlessly. She didn't know what to say to the increasingly frantic man. Talk of the town was that most of Randy's image was under lease or loan, and when he had to pay a crapload of back child support and legal fees, he had to cash it all in after Dawson was picked up from preschool by his very normal-looking mother. It wasn't an abduction. It wasn't dramatic. The law was not on Randy's side, and that in and of itself made Amelia question everything he'd ever said. She wasn't really sure what to think about the whole Dawson situation, but one thing was becoming increasingly clear—Randy was not what he seemed.

So last night she called his phone in the middle of the night and left a voice mail that explained that she was honored by his offer but needed to decline. She thought that oh-so-brief chapter in her life was closed, but now it was looking at her through the smudged window of her SUV.

"Can we talk?" he asked, his voice loud enough to be easily understood through the glass.

She wanted to know how Dawson was doing, and she'd been friends with Randy before the whole business thing started, so Amelia put all her personal issues in a well-worn box inside her that kept all the problems and dysfunctions she tried to ignore or explain away, and rolled down the window.

"Where did you come from? I didn't see your car."

"Yeah, I had to trade it in. I need to downsize until I get Dawson back." Randy tried to give a small smile, but it didn't reach his eyes. He looked tired, and the lines on his face and dark circles under his eyes made him look ten years older. "I just wanted to come see you and apologize in person for what happened the other day. I wasn't myself, and I know I upset you."

He clasped his hands in front of him, resting them on the door. A long, black arrow tattoo ran down his forearm and pointed to his wrist. A word that Amelia couldn't really decipher was scrawled along it.

"Hey, no apology needed."

"No, apology totally needed, and I was hoping you could rethink my offer. I think you and I would make a great team." He gave one of his bright, sparkly smiles, and Amelia couldn't help but smile back.

"Randy, I think you have more important things to worry about, don't you? Dawson ring a bell?"

"I'm working on that, but this offer—it has an expiration. I need to know . . . now."

"Listen, it's such a generous offer, but I'm honestly too busy in my life already. I'd just be a burden. And I'm pretty sure you have enough to worry about right now."

He stared at her intensely, eyes never wavering, the blue in his casual cotton tee catching some of the blue in his eyes.

"I don't think you understand. I am leaving town for a while, but I'll need you to take over for me when I do. You can start by listing my place." Amelia shook her head, hoping she could find the magic words that would make him back off.

"I can't, I'm sorry. I thought I could, but it is too much right now." Steve wanted her to do the job. Randy wanted it for her. Ellie thought she'd be great. But it wasn't time. Not now. Not with this man.

Randy gritted his teeth at her response and leaned into the window so she could smell his soap. She leaned away, trying not to offend him but getting nervous and hoping Ellie would return. Another smile, this one clearly his most charming.

"Amelia, I signed you up for classes online, and I'll lose the deposit if you back out."

"Randy," Amelia said, speaking slowly and with more than a touch of frustration, "that is not my problem. You really overstepped there. I can't do this right now. I can't."

Randy's smile melted away like wax dripping down a candle. He took a step back from the car.

"Damn it, don't you get it? Your life isn't going to get any better. Not till you get out of this shithole town. I thought you were smarter than that, but you can't even see it, can you?" He glared at her as though she were the most invalid human on the planet. With a closed fist he swore and punched her door, hard, and then walked in a small circle, shaking his hand.

Randy's reaction was so over-the-top, she couldn't even make any sense of it. And now she might have a dent on the side of her car. Steve would want to know where that came from. He'd want it fixed. Another expense in a pit of expenses. Amelia opened the door and hopped out, scared of Randy, who was still muttering to himself and walking in a small circle, kicking up dust from the gravel drive, but she was more worried about what Steve would say about damage to the car. She examined the paint on the driver-side door. There was a scuff and slight dent but nothing obvious from a distance. Then her fear tripped over the thin line to anger.

"What the heck was that?" Amelia shouted, pointing at the dent. Randy rushed over and put his hands on her shoulders. She immediately regretted getting out of the car. His grip was tight and felt like a trap. When she tried to pull out of his grasp, he held on tighter.

"Ouch, stop it." She pulled back again, but he didn't relent.

Noticing her panic, he tried to put on the charm again, but something was off, like when she wanted to be She-Ra for Halloween in third grade, but the mask had warped and sat awkwardly on her face, making her look like something from a horror movie.

"Amelia, you deserve more than this. I know you know it. Let me help you get out of this. We can work together. I can help you, and you can help me get Dawson back. Get in the car, and we can leave right now and never look back. I know things . . . We can get the girls . . . They can be with us."

"Us?" Amelia gasped, and wriggled against his grip. His eyes were wild, pupils dilated, body heat rolling off him and soaking into her skin like fire. "Randy, let me go. I have no idea what you are talking about."

"Yeah, you do. I see how you look at me. You want it too; you just aren't being honest with yourself. Let go of this"—he pointed at the house and cars and lawn and her car—"and we can be free."

"No," she said, clear and strong as she put her hands on his chest, trying to put some space between them, fear morphing into anger. She was tired of being pushed around. "I know that your story about Dawson is a lie. Everyone in town is talking about it. His mom isn't a drug addict; she was just too young and naïve to fight you in court when he was born. I'm not falling for all of this. My sister is coming back out. You should leave."

"I don't care what anyone says. Dawson is *mine*, and that girl gave up her rights years ago. Now she wants to take me to court?" Randy paused and reset like he knew he was getting off track. "I'm not leaving.

Not until you say you'll work with me. Please, Amelia. Please." His body was against hers now, and the Randy she thought she knew was gone. Her arms curled against her chest, and a scream balled up inside her throat. She swallowed it down, wrestling against his unbreakable embrace, trying to stay calm, trying to think as though she were the hunter, not the hunted.

"You need to leave," she said simply with a cutting edge to her voice, but before he could respond, a deep yell came from the house.

"Get your hands off her!"

Both Amelia's and Randy's heads turned toward the voice. It was Caleb, and he was running. Randy released Amelia and charged toward Caleb, not seeming to care that his fists were clenched or that he was ready to fight.

"Leave her the hell alone!" Caleb yelled again, shoving Randy against his chest.

"What I do with her is none of your business. I don't know who you think you are. You are just some loser who gets paid barely more than minimum wage so he can moon over his ex-girlfriend and is under the thumb of her husband. You are pathetic. Absolutely pathetic," Randy spat back at Caleb, far more aware of his history than Randy ever let on. Amelia, now free of Randy's arms, trembled, barely able to take one step before her knees gave out and she braced herself on the car.

"I'm pathetic? You put on a good show, but I could buy and sell you ten times over." Though he was thin, Caleb also stood a good six inches taller than Randy and used that height to his advantage.

"Then what are you doing working for Steve-o in there, huh? A Mr. Moneybags like you shouldn't be living in his mommy's basement."

She'd already figured out that Randy and Caleb had some sort of history, but the depth of knowledge Randy spewed about her lifelong friend shocked Amelia.

"I'm not the one about to go bankrupt. Does bankruptcy cover debts to your bookie, I wonder? Hm . . . probably not." Amelia's ears perked up. Randy was one of Steve's clients? Steve always acted like he didn't know who he was.

"Oh my God," she said out loud, quietly at first and then one more time, her voice rising. "Oh my GOD!" she shouted, taking in both men with new eyes. "You didn't want me to work for you because you thought I'd be a good partner . . . You were . . . laundering money for Steve, weren't you?"

Randy half turned toward Amelia, glaring. "No, I thought a frumpy housewife from Broadlands would be the perfect associate for me to waste my time on. You're a nice lady but not exactly the brightest bulb." Randy's tone had turned nasty, and without warning, Caleb's fist landed squarely on Randy's cheekbone.

"Take it back, asshole," Caleb growled. Randy held his face in his hand, stunned and in pain as Caleb grabbed the collar of his shirt and said it again. "Take it back."

"Caleb!" Amelia screamed. "Caleb, stop!"

Randy was limp in Caleb's grasp, as if the punch had left him dizzy. He spit blood onto the ground, a trail dribbling down his chin, and then looked up at Caleb with a mocking smile.

"You think you're so much better than me, don't you? You're just as trapped as I am. Maybe I should tell your precious Amelia about *all* of your work duties. Maybe I should tell her what you'll be doing next Tuesday. I bet she'd *love* to hear about those plans."

"Just you try," Caleb said, pulling Randy in close and saying something Amelia couldn't decipher under his breath. She rushed forward, partially in an effort to hear and partially from worry that Caleb was going to hit Randy again. What the hell was going on? Steve knew Randy. Steve was the puppet master. Her husband—Steve. And the man defending her, sheltering her, trying to warn her? Caleb.

"Caleb." She tried to speak calmly, noticing over his shoulder that Ellie was on her way out of the house and rushing toward them. Amelia needed answers, but she needed them without Ellie around. "Let Randy go. He's a total ass, but he's an ass you don't want to go to jail for assaulting."

Caleb's eyes connected with Amelia's, and an ancient thrill went through her. For one moment, the green highlights in his eyes took her back in time, and she remembered how much she used to care about him. One blink broke the spell, and Caleb shoved the stunned man onto the ground.

Ellie was there moments later, crouched on the ground as she assessed Randy's injuries. He was calm and talking normally to Ellie as she played paramedic to his minimal bumps and bruises. To any outsider, it probably looked like the well-mannered businessman had been attacked by the quiet and withdrawn blue-collar employee. While Ellie tended to Randy's wounds, Amelia took a step toward Caleb and pointed to his bruised right hand. He tested his fingers and then put his hand out in front of him where she took it in hers. His palm was rough, callused, but there was also something beautiful about his long slender fingers and the flecks of paint caught up in his cuticles.

"Are you still painting?" she asked, running her finger over a fleck of paint on his wrist. He glanced at it and then at his feet. There were so many other questions she should be asking, but this was the one that danced on the tip of her tongue and refused to retreat.

"Yeah, sometimes," he responded, suddenly shy, a stark contrast to the man who'd towered over Randy and spoken with more force than she even knew he possessed.

With one last sweep of her thumb over his knuckles, she carefully loosened her grip until his hand dropped. He immediately put it into his pocket. Amelia couldn't be sure, but he looked like he wanted to say something, so she spoke first.

"Caleb, what is happening next Tuesday?"

CHAPTER 29

ELLIE

Wednesday, May 11
5:26 a.m.

It was a bad sign when the nurses knew you well enough to wave you through at ICU. The floor was pretty empty: one car accident, one head injury, one unidentified illness that meant the nurses suiting up in what looked like hazmat suits before entering. Then, in the back corner was Amelia, the lights on full blast and three figures filling the space and one officer sitting sleepily on a chair just outside. Two were nurses doing their hourly check on Amelia, but there was also a man in a wheelchair pulled up close to Amelia's bedside.

"Steve!" Ellie ran through the door, knowing she was both talking too loud and moving too fast for the ICU. She rushed to put her arms around his shoulders, still broad and taut under the hospital gown, but then she remembered his injuries and took his empty hand in hers. "You look so good! How are you feeling?"

Steve turned his hand so his palm pressed against Ellie's, and she relaxed immediately. At least he was okay. It didn't make anything better with Amelia, but if she could at least lean on Steve, she would make it. She wasn't alone.

"I'm all right. It wasn't very serious, just in and out. It grazed my lung, but they fixed it. I'm trying to convince them to let me leave soon. I'm sure the kids are a mess, and my parents don't know how they are going to comfort them. My mom is here." He gestured to her purse sitting on one of the open chairs to the left of Amelia's bed. "She needed some coffee. She'll be right back."

"I'm so glad they came. I had to leave the kids with Chet and Dad last night."

Steve shook his head. "You were right to be here. M needs you." He placed his other hand over their clasped pair. "I need you."

Ellie squeezed Steve's hand, and they sat there in silence for a moment. It was good to know she was needed, wanted, loved. Then the nagging urgency in the back of her mind reminded her why she was there.

"Dad is missing." Chief Brown meandered frequently, sometimes turning up at the fire station or Amelia's house or just wandering around town, dazed and confused. She'd occasionally joke that they should fit him with a tracking device, but even with all the experience, it was scary whenever he went missing. "I need to go look for him but only if Amelia doesn't need me. She seems pretty stable, right? It's okay if I go?"

Steve looked over at Amelia's monitors, the lines beeping and waving in some kind of steady rhythm.

"She's as good as can be expected, I guess." He got somber fast, tears in his eyes before Ellie could even ask what was wrong. "This is all my fault. Those men, they just wanted my money. I shouldn't have hesitated. I should've just given it to them."

"They were robbing you?" Ellie asked, dragging a chair across the room so she could sit at his level.

"Yeah, they both had masks on. They came in and demanded money from the safe. Amelia came in from the kitchen to bring me a cup of coffee, and, boom, the guy shot her. Then the second man got angry and said something about this not being the plan and started to leave, and the guy with the gun just up and shot him as he was running out the door. Then he pointed the gun back at me, and I said I'd give him the money. I thought it was the only way to get him to leave so I could get help for Amelia, but then I remembered that I had a gun in my safe. So, I went in, I pretended to grab cash, and then I turned around and held up the gun. That's when he shot at me. The bullet hit me in the shoulder, and I couldn't help it . . . the pain, the fear, Amelia on the floor . . . I fired back. I pulled the trigger till it wouldn't pull anymore. I shot him, Ellie. I shot him in the face, I think."

During the narrative, Steve had put his hands on his face to hide his tears or embarrassment. Now he looked up, his cheeks moist and eyes a deep red in a way she'd never seen, not when he'd gone into a house where the whole family, including the six-month-old baby girl and her three-year-old brother, was killed from carbon monoxide poisoning, not from joy when his kids were born, and not from fear when Amelia was so distraught over her father's stroke that she completely shut down and walked around like a zombie for two whole days. This was a new Steve—a devastated Steve. She waited as he tried to form another thought sticking somewhere in his mind like peanut butter to the roof of the mouth.

"I don't know how to tell you this, L, but I know who the guy was that got away." His shoulders shuddered under his gown, shaking it with each movement. She knew what he was going to say, and she wanted to stop him, relieve him of this trauma. But then the words spilled out. "It was Caleb."

She knew it was true. Caleb. She could see Caleb wanting to rob Steve. It all came together. Randy and Caleb must've been working together. You didn't punch a stranger in the face. The whole question for Ellie had always been why Caleb would ever want to hurt Amelia. The answer—he didn't. He wanted to hurt Steve.

"I know," she said, patting his hand reassuringly. "And the other guy was Randy, that real estate agent Amelia had been working with."

"What?" he asked, his mouth gaping open like his own best friend had betrayed him. "Why? Why would they do this? Why would anyone hurt Amelia?" And as her name came off his lips, Steve broke down, curling over into himself and pulling Ellie's hand into his chest as he wept.

Ellie felt so helpless with her hands held there, no way to comfort and no promises of improvement for Amelia. Seeing Steve heartbroken was more painful than feeling her own heartbreak. "This is all my fault," he sobbed, and then a fire rose in Ellie's stomach. All night she'd been trying to figure out who was to blame and, yes, she'd even considered if it was Steve, but with everything she'd seen and heard in the past twenty-four hours, she couldn't stomach this.

"Did you shoot M?" Ellie asked, trying to get him to look at her. He didn't meet her gaze, but he did shake his head, his face red and a mess of tears. "Well, then, let's stop with all this 'my fault' stuff. Randy is dead and they are out looking for Caleb, so soon enough the real culprits will be taken care of."

Ellie's phone buzzed in her pocket. It was Collin. Finally.

"Sorry, I've been waiting for Collin to call me back. I need a ride to look for Dad, and Collin has been MIA." As soon as she said it, Ellie knew she shouldn't have. Steve didn't like Collin, didn't think he was good enough for her, and this description of his behavior didn't exactly put him in a positive light. "I'll be right back."

She nearly dropped the shiny phone as she tried to hit the Talk button and pressed the phone to her ear.

"Hey! There you are. I was worried about you. Everything okay at home?" She tried to speak in generalities, almost through the door where the police officer in the hall was sitting.

Ellie was dying to tell Collin the truth about his brother, but finding her father was more important.

"I have your dad," a deep, gravelly voice responded—a voice that was definitely not Collin. All the muscles in Ellie's back and shoulders tightened, and she held the phone tighter.

"Caleb?" she asked as soon as she was far enough away from listening ears, lowering her voice just in case.

"I have your dad," he said simply, his voice strained and wobbly. "He's okay," he rushed to interject, "but I need you to come see me."

"Put Collin on." Ellie tried to rid herself of the idea of her father hurt or alone and scared.

"He's not here. He's coming to find you. I told him everything. He's gonna take you to me and Chief Brown."

"I don't like this idea, Caleb." The fury was building, and it took all of Ellie's nearly depleted reserves of strength to keep from losing it and screaming through the phone. She took a deep breath and tried to sound cool and measured. "My father is a sick man. He needs medicine and proper care. You can't just pluck him up off the streets and think he's going to be okay."

"You need to stop talking. We are running out of time. Your father is safe. You have nothing to worry about, I promise you. Whatever you've been told about me is a lie. Meet Collin at the hospital entrance. He will drive you to my location. I'll explain more then."

"Why do I need to come to you? Why don't you come to me? I'm at the hospital. Turn yourself in and get some real treatment and you can explain everything." Ellie was now pacing the small hall that connected Amelia's ICU room to the main hallway. Still aware of the officer outside and Steve inside, Ellie worked hard to keep her voice down as much as possible, but it was getting increasingly difficult to not scream into the phone.

"Are you with Amelia?" Caleb asked, ignoring Ellie's suggestions.

"Yes, I'm with Amelia," she responded, trying to soften her tone since she knew that Amelia was Caleb's weak spot and maybe the only way to get him to come to safety. "She's in bad shape. You should come see her. She might die, Caleb."

There was a long pause and then a deep breath on the other end.

"Is Steve there?" Caleb asked, this time sounding less concerned and more anxious.

Ellie could see into Amelia's room. She focused in on Steve, who was curled over his wife's limp hand. Every thirty seconds or so he would lift it to his lips and place a light kiss on the back of it.

"Yeah, and he told me what happened. It's okay, Caleb. You didn't hurt anyone. We'll all testify and help you, I promise. You'll be safe."

Caleb coughed out a rueful laugh on the other end of the phone.

"Yeah, I'm sure he told you *everything*. Did he tell you about all the secrets he keeps in his safe? Probably not. Don't trust that man, Ellie, and don't leave him alone with Amelia." Then, before she could ask for clarification, he said, "Collin will be there soon. If you care about your family at all, you'll go with him." And then he hung up.

"Caleb," Ellie tested, whispering into the receiver. "Caleb." But he was gone. She was tempted to call Collin's number back but had a sinking feeling that it would be a waste of time. Instead, she put the phone in her pocket and stood up straight. She took another look at Steve, finding Caleb's warnings disturbing enough to try to understand. But this time Steve wasn't pouring care and love onto his injured wife. This time he was watching Ellie. She acknowledged his attention with a tip of her shoulder. He gave her a little smirk that brought her back to all the times they played board games on a Sunday night and he'd come up with an awesome plan to win the whole game in just two or three moves. For half a moment she considered telling him about the call and the invitation to meet Caleb, but that smirk . . . that tiny quirk of his mouth to one side . . . made her pause.

She wouldn't tell him. Not yet. Not until she heard what Collin and Caleb had to say and she knew her father was safe.

"Ellie, so good to see you." Steve's mom, Shelly, stood behind her, holding a cup of steaming coffee in each hand. Despite driving through the night from Tennessee, she looked flawless, as always, dressed in a flowing silk blouse and perfectly fitted gray slacks, and she smelled of some kind of imported perfume. Ellie was relieved to see another familiar and comforting face.

"Hey, Shelly." Ellie gave Steve's mom a half hug and tried to sound chipper, but she knew it came out wrong. The smell of hot coffee made Ellie's stomach growl, and she quickly backed away to keep from being tempted by the idea of food. She didn't have time to eat even though she was running on empty. She chased away the question of how long she could go on like this before she'd break down.

"This is so scary, isn't it?" Shelly said. Ellie nodded somberly and glanced back at her sister again.

"Hey, could you do me a favor?" Ellie touched Shelly's shoulder and spoke quickly, sure she was anxious to get the coffee inside the hospital room before it went cold. "Could you tell Steve I have to go find my dad? He knows what I'm talking about."

"Sure, hon." Shelly's Southern accent gave a softness to her response that mellowed the confusion that was clear on her face, even through the thick coat of flawless makeup.

Ellie took two steps away from the hospital room before turning back and adding, "And, Shelly, can you stay with Amelia for me until I get back?"

"Of course, darlin.' I'll never leave her side," Shelly answered, emphatic in her response. Ellie's knees buckled slightly with relief.

"Thank you." She turned, glad she was wearing sneakers, and walked as fast as she could to the elevator. Okay, she'd do it. She'd go with Collin, she'd talk to Caleb, she'd get her dad back.

And if Caleb wouldn't come to the police, she would bring the police to Caleb.

CHAPTER 30

AMELIA

Tuesday, May 10

Tuesday, the ominous day that Randy and Caleb were fighting about, had arrived. Immediately after the confrontation, Amelia tried to get information out of both men, but they seemed to have come to their senses and clammed up. Caleb returned to work, Randy to the electric-blue economy rental he was driving now. Ellie shooed Amelia into the car, talking a mile a minute about the possible reasons Caleb and Randy had been fighting in the driveway. She'd only seen Caleb nearly knock Randy out and thankfully hadn't heard any of the previous conversation. Ellie was a little shaken up and went on about how weird Caleb was and how calm Randy seemed. All of it was too much for Amelia to process. She retreated into her shell and hid there, putting on the well-worn masks of "I'm okay" and "Everything is normal."

Amelia and Steve never spoke about his confession or about the two men who had claimed to be working for him in less-than-legal ways. She didn't know how to bring something up to Steve head-on. He always had some magic way of explaining it away or even convincing Amelia that it was all her fault. So for now, she kept it in the box she reserved for her marital issues. Out of sight but never out of mind.

In fact it was so heavy on her mind, she could barely find room to do simple things like keep up a schedule or make a complicated meal. Either she'd find a way to stop worrying or she'd find a way to bring it up to Steve, but she wasn't ready to do either just yet.

Lying in bed together after they'd made love early Saturday morning, Amelia had been seconds from asking him why he lied about knowing Randy. Then the girls started knocking on their locked bedroom door. Steve groaned and got up to shower while Amelia dressed in silence, wishing she didn't feel like the bad guy for asking her husband about his mistakes. But that was where life had led them.

Amelia used to think she held back because of respect, but lately she realized it was something else—fear. He'd never hurt her, not physically, but she never felt good enough, and the chains of his judgment and anger were enough to keep her in line.

Amelia didn't know what to do. She was a passenger in her own life, and even though she made very few decisions and had very few options in her personal and business life, some extremely treacherous consequences were headed her way if Steve was ever found out. Her name was on everything, including the business and insurance policies.

Trapped. That was the word that kept scrolling through her mind as she went through the motions every day. She was trapped, and she didn't know how to get out or even how to take any control back. Randy's career opportunity could've been a chance if it had been real, but it was another one of Steve's manipulations. That level of deception shattered any idea Amelia had that she could make it on her own. But still . . . it was Tuesday.

She had watched her father wheeled into the senior center and then had swapped out the van for her car. She looked at the clock on her dashboard: 9:15 a.m. She was planning to do some grocery shopping before running to see Cora perform in the school's Spring Fling concert. The precocious nine-year-old had picked viola rather than cello, which didn't bother Amelia as much as her family thought it would. They could barely get Bessie around town without a trailer hitch, so there was no way their cars could take two cellists in the family.

The closest decent supermarket was two towns over, which was why she always wished they'd rebuild Nancy's. But it was just a dream, and though Randy had shown interest in her business scheme, she now knew it was all part of a ploy to use her. Amelia shook her head, embarrassed that she ever believed him. She wished that box would stay closed and stop leaking out all her worries. It used to work so well, but now it seemed like that mental container was overflowing and nothing she could do would keep the anger and frustration down for very long.

She'd lived through most of her relationship with Steve being paralyzed with fear that he'd leave her, but lately she wondered why she'd never considered another option—leaving him. No. That idea was still too overwhelming, but just considering the option filled her with equal parts panic and optimism.

As she headed to the interstate, Amelia passed by the burned-out shell of Nancy's Emporium, which almost seemed to be mocking her. The front of the building looked nearly the same as before the fire. Across the front, large red block letters spelled out **NANCY'S**, and then smaller slanted letters whispered *Emporium* underneath.

It was during the ascent up the ramp to the highway that you got a good view of the rear of the building. It was still blackened and burned out from the fire fifteen years ago. Steve had been on that fire. He told her all about it after they'd been dating for a while. He was there when the building caved in and when the young firefighter, Tim Ray, was pulled, dead, out of the ashes. Steve called it the worst night of his whole fire career, and pinpointed it as the moment he decided he couldn't do it forever.

Amelia always thought the building looked like it had been stepped on accidentally by a giant who, walking through the open corn and soy fields of Central Illinois, hadn't noticed the market sitting there. She told Ellie a story like that once, but then her father heard it and got angry. He said that a good man died in that fire, and there wasn't any use in telling fairy tales to make it better.

Richard Brown had seen a lot of death and destruction in his career, but she'd never seen him cry in public until her mother's funeral. Amelia never told the giant story again, and Ellie never asked about the shell of a building. They'd heard rumors every year since of the building being torn down or a farmer buying out the land, but so far no one had ever made good on their plans.

Instead of turning onto the on-ramp, Amelia turned into the Emporium's parking lot. The asphalt was cracked and covered in a lacy pattern of prairie grass and wildflowers poking through. Sitting there, staring at the ruins, she wondered how to remake her life instead of dreaming of remaking the destroyed supermarket.

The first thing she had to do was find out what Tuesday held in store for Steve, Randy, and Caleb. She wasn't completely convinced that she had the nerve to do it, but it was time to retake control of her life, starting with this moment.

Amelia crept the SUV up to the edge of the road and turned on her blinker, which pointed toward home—back to Broadlands and back to the old Amelia, strong Amelia, the girl who helped raise her sister, who comforted her father, who dreamed of beautiful houses, happy children, and playing music, real music, because it filled her soul and not only her pocket. Back to the Amelia who knew what she wanted in her life and didn't back down for anything or anyone.

CHAPTER 31

ELLIE

Wednesday, May 11
5:52 a.m.

Collin's Jeep pulled up in the circle drive as soon as Ellie walked out the door. Unlike the last time she crawled into his passenger seat, the morning wasn't nearly as cold and the sun was peeking up over the horizon. The sunrise over Broadlands' newly plowed fields and the neighboring apple orchard was always a beautiful sight, the warm reds and pinks and oranges spilling all over the sky as if God were playing with watercolors.

But this morning she couldn't look or even care about the sunrise or colors or God. She could barely even look at anything beyond her feet. Once she was inside and buckled, Collin spoke as he drove away from the hospital and back toward town.

"How is Amelia?"

"She's fine," she responded tersely, knowing it wasn't true but also not ready to talk to Collin about anything having to do with her sister while he was still aiding and abetting one of the individuals responsible for putting her in that condition.

Collin sighed loudly. "I knew you'd be pissed," he started, staring at the road, defensive rather than apologetic.

"Seriously? You're mad that I'm mad?" Ellie turned toward Collin. "God, Collin, take a look at how this has gone down. My sister was shot, and the whole time you are worried about where your brother is. At first I got it, but once they started telling everyone he might be armed and dangerous, I think it might have been wise to let the police take care of the situation." Ellie glanced around as they got on Highway 12. "Where the *hell* are we going, and how in the world did you think it was okay to take my dad anywhere? I'm just baffled here. Baffled." Ellie tapped her forehead with her fingertips, more angry with Collin than she had ever been.

"You are doing that thing you do, Ellie. You are jumping to conclusions, and you are getting overly protective. Your dad is safe. Actually, he's far safer than when I found him wandering around town. You need to hear Caleb out. I'm positive you're not getting the whole story from Steve-o in there." He tipped his head back toward the hospital.

"Steve is sitting by his wife's bed, holding her hand because she might be dying. Caleb is hiding somewhere and using my dad as bait because he's evading arrest. Who do you think is more trustworthy here?"

Collin took a sharp right and then a left onto Main Street. No one was out this early other than Frank sweeping in front of his restaurant and a few early risers heading in for some coffee and doughnuts. The town flashed by, and they were on the other side of Broadlands. If Collin took a right, it would mean they were headed toward the residential area of the town; a left would take them to the highway and from there, who knew where. When Collin got to the blinking red light, he slowed but didn't stop. He turned left.

"I'm not going to try to convince you," Collin said, walls a million feet thick going up around him. "You have to talk to Caleb."

Emotion suddenly overwhelmed Ellie, and her eyes filled with tears for the tenth time in the past twenty-four hours. This time it wasn't because she was scared or worried about her sister or Steve or because she was frustrated with her circumstances. This time the tears were for her and Collin.

"How are we going to survive this?" she asked, one tear racing down her cheek.

"Talk to Caleb and you'll understand. That's all I'm going to say."

"No, Collin, how are *we* going to survive this?" she asked again, spinning her engagement ring around her finger two times, wondering how long it would be there. Would they make it a week or a month before the trauma from this day would settle in and they'd realize they couldn't get past the betrayal or the bitterness? Or would they make it a year or two, pretending this day never happened, before it would all come crashing in to ruin their lives?

Through smudged lenses, Collin looked at Ellie. His eyes were wide. He glanced back at the road and then back at her several times before speaking.

"Nothing's changed for *me*," Collin clarified, and stared at the side of her face again. "Don't base our future on this, L. You'll regret it. I know you will." He spoke with such conviction that Ellie stopped fiddling with her ring and placed the stone back toward the middle of her finger.

"I don't know, I just feel like . . ." Her voice trailed off as Collin made one last turn. It wasn't onto the highway—it was into the parking lot for the abandoned Nancy's Emporium. "What? Why are you taking me to this dump?"

Collin didn't answer right away; instead, he picked up speed and angled the Jeep toward the back of the abandoned supermarket. When he turned into the docking area, he slowed to a crawl and then angled up beside the building between an old cement wall and the outbuilding that used to store dumpsters. Though the sun was already above the horizon, the shadow thrown by the half-crumbled wall made the interior of the car dim, a weird twilight-like shadow descending over them. No one would see the vehicle there, not from the front of the store and definitely not from the highway.

"Come on, L. They're inside." Collin opened his door a few inches until it tapped the wall on his side of the car. The way this building looked, Ellie knew it wasn't safe. Even a small impact like a door opening or closing could make whole sections of concrete fall. And a man who might be a thief and a murderer was waiting inside, basically holding her father hostage. It sounded like a trap.

"You have my dad in *there*?" Ellie asked, opening her door and ignoring the heart and letters carved into it. Collin didn't respond. He kept walking toward the blackened vinyl paneling at the back of the store where a giant cement ramp plunged into the ground next to the building. As Ellie jumped down from her seat onto the chunks of cement on the ground, she heard a clunk. Her phone. The shiny silver rectangle was easy to find among the rubble. She picked it up and dusted off the screen, inspecting it for scratches. When her thumb hit the Home button on the bottom of the touch screen, the lock screen appeared along with three glowing texts from Travis.

Brown—checking in. At ICU in ten minutes.

You okay? Mrs. Saxton said you ran out. Let me know if you need help.

Then the third one:

I know you were in the morgue this morning. Call me.

Once again, the texts were a strange mix of concern and investigation. His motivations were so mottled, it was hard for Ellie to trust him. She slammed the Jeep door, the noise echoing off the building and bouncing back and forth until it flew off into space, a chunk of concrete falling from the vibrations.

This is not safe, Ellie thought, even more concerned about her father's safety than before they'd driven up to this cesspool. *I need help.*

She'd been toying with an idea since she left the ICU, but if she followed through on it, Ellie knew it would be the end of things with Collin. It wouldn't be the scenario she'd just been contemplating—their relationship tapering off in a week or two months. No. If she did this one simple thing, it would end their relationship as soon as the blue-and-red lights turned into the parking lot of Nancy's Emporium. Ellie glanced at her ring one more time, memorizing what it felt like and considering the future she and Collin had planned.

They'd had five and a half years of something. It wasn't something overwhelmingly bad, but it wasn't something great either. Outside of his questionable actions that day, Collin was steady and predictable. He was loving but not passionate. He was enjoyable but not exciting. Her relationship with Collin was like Broadlands—it was familiar and ultimately the only relationship she'd ever known. And when the thing you'd counted on being dependable and safe suddenly turned on you, there was little reason to stay. Not if it meant risking more lives.

She stared at the small stone she'd just gotten used to wearing, and then she took it off. Ellie opened the car door again, leaned across her spot, which was still warm from her body heat, and dropped the diamond solitaire into the cup holder with a clink. Then, before she could think better of it, she reemerged from the car, closed the door carefully this time, and then pulled out her phone and started typing.

CHAPTER 32

AMELIA

Tuesday, May 10

The driveway looked the same as it did on any normal workday. Two trucks were parked at the top by the oversize garage where the roofing supplies were stored during the winter. Amelia parked at the end of the gravel drive like she always did during roofing season. It was the best way to keep her car from being nicked by the constant stream of vehicles coming in and out and to ensure she could leave at a moment's notice if she needed to grab the girls from school or run an errand.

She had been on the lookout for Randy's rental car but didn't see it in the street or by the house, and she was starting to wonder if maybe whatever ominous event had been planned for the day had been canceled after last week's altercation.

Well, she might as well go inside and take a quick look around. Maybe this big thing wasn't even going to happen in Broadlands. For all she knew, Randy could be off somewhere robbing a bank, *that* being the crazy thing planned for this Tuesday. Amelia laughed out loud at the thought.

She ascended the back stairs and unlocked the door to the kitchen. She placed the keys on her hook like she'd been sure to do since that day six weeks ago when she somehow overlooked their existence. The kitchen was dark. Not sure what she was even doing here, Amelia flicked on the light in the hall next to the key hooks, but nothing happened. She flicked it up and down a few more times and still nothing.

Instead of making Steve change the bulb and get a lecture on how it probably burned out because she and the kids always forgot to turn off the hall light when they left the house, Amelia took off her Nikes and headed toward the pantry where they kept the new bulbs. She reached up to pull on the string hanging down from the bare lightbulb in the ceiling. Once again, the light didn't turn on.

"Damn it!" she swore under her breath. The power must be out. Sometimes the kitchen breaker flipped if the coffee machine, Crock-Pot, and the microwave were running at the same time or pretty much any other combination of appliances. Broadlands Roofing shared a wall with the kitchen, and the breaker box remained there, even after what used to be a utility closet was expanded one hundred times to be the new business office. Amelia did occasional jobs for Steve, a lot of it organizing or delivering papers and obtaining signatures, but in general she stayed out of the office unless it was empty or she was invited.

Usually she'd send him a text about the breaker. She rarely entered the office during the workday without asking first, but after checking her back pocket, she realized she'd left the phone in the car. She batted at the hanging string and wished she could do one thing right, that one time, just once, she could try to take a stand and be successful. How could someone fail so very often?

She walked out of the pantry and closed the door carefully, tempted to go back to her car and ignore the tightly wound cocoon inside her. It was filled with some sort of winged creature ready to break free from the silken walls it had settled on as its home, walls that now she understood were ropes that kept it from flying.

Sometimes when a stupid thing like this happened while she was in a moment of boldness, Amelia wondered if it was a sign that she was as forgetful and useless as she always felt. In the past, she'd rush to correct the error, hoping that no one had seen, that no one would be able to tell the story of how silly Amelia forgot her phone in the car on the same day she decided she was going to be independent and responsible.

The cocoon seemed particularly tightly wound lately, but when, resigned to returning to the car and forgetting it all, she felt her fingers land on the cool metal of her key chain, Amelia froze. The breaker box was on the other side of the office door to her right, a door she hated and had never wanted in her kitchen. How much of her life had been decided for her over the past twelve years since meeting Steve? He had gotten good at making them feel like her decisions too, but they weren't, were they?

She didn't want the ugly white door in her kitchen and she didn't want Steve playing bookie in his spare time to make money, she didn't want to give up her real dreams of music, and she didn't want to put her father in a home. She'd already decided this: today was day one in the life of New Amelia. If the light was out in the kitchen, her kitchen, and she needed to flip a simple switch, then, starting today, she wasn't going to play by Steve's unwritten rules. She would flip the breaker herself.

Releasing the keys, Amelia wrapped her fingers around the cool nickel doorknob, letting the warmth of her palm soak into the metal ball. She could hear the murmur of voices on the other side. With a quick twist of the knob and a set jaw, Amelia opened the door. It swung in toward the office and felt lighter than usual. With a deep breath, she picked up one foot and stepped over onto the office's thin gray carpet.

"Don't worry about me. Just need to flip the switch. Light in the kitchen is out again." Amelia spoke as she walked, her eyes on her feet. The door slammed shut behind her.

"Amelia. Why are you home?" Steve returned her pleasant greeting with a growling reprimand that made the room come into focus.

Steve was standing by the safe, which was in the back of the office behind all the desks. It was open. Randy stood just a few feet away from

Amelia in front of Caleb's empty desk. Both men looked shocked, like she'd caught them looking at porn on their office computers. But this wasn't something as juvenile as pornography. No.

Randy looked . . . different. He wasn't wearing a nice suit and a hundred-dollar tie. He wasn't even wearing a pair of designer jeans. He was dressed all in black and had dark gloves on. In front of him on the desk was a dark blue ski mask folded in half and a silver handgun with a black handle. Amelia's eyes widened and an immediate flood of fear made her head feel light. The room was just as dark as the kitchen other than the horizontal streams of light coming from between the blinds covering the large picture window that overlooked the driveway. The rest of the room was dark and stuffy, and it smelled slightly of gasoline or lighter fluid or something equally pungent.

This was bad. Really bad. She didn't know what she'd just walked into, but there was no way that Amelia was supposed to see it.

She should want to demand answers. She should want to know what the hell was going on. But she didn't. Knowing wouldn't be safe. Knowing would hurt too much. Instead, Amelia did what she had learned to do over the past twelve years—she pretended everything was fine.

"The lights in the kitchen are out," Amelia started to respond, still heading toward the breaker box.

"Shit. *Shit!*" Randy ran a hand over his face and glared at Steve. "You said no one would be home." He moved in front of the desk, obscuring her view of the gun.

Steve, unlike Randy, didn't panic. He stood slowly from his crouched position in front of the safe and shook his head slowly. It was his "How could you be so stupid" face. She was used to seeing it when she washed a red sock with the whites or when she locked her keys in the car with the car running. Today the look was more somber than angry.

"The power is out, M. I've called the power company. We've got it under control," Steve said calmly in the voice he used with her when he was trying to convince her of something. The voice worked like a hypnotist's swinging locket—and, usually, she couldn't resist it for long.

"Okay," she responded out of pure instinct, used to accepting Steve's pronouncements, and turned to leave. But then she felt it, those little flapping wings inside her, the ones that had been fighting for so long to get out, to be free. She kept promising she would let them out soon . . . soon. Twice already today she'd tried to make them stop, twice she flinched away from her resolve, but as she went to walk through that steel door back into the kitchen like a good little wife, the last silken strands holding in the magnificent creature inside her snapped.

She turned around and put her back to the door, the slats of light hitting her across her body and warming her in a zebra-like pattern of light and dark.

"I'm not going anywhere till you tell me what is going on." The words were easy to say, but the panic that rose inside her after they escaped was harder to hide. She straightened her shoulders and stood up taller.

Steve closed his eyes and sighed like she was a child asking for a lollipop before dinner. "Oh, Amelia, always sticking your nose where it doesn't belong."

She'd really done it now. She almost wished she could shove the words back in and run away. She could've called the police. She could've grabbed the girls from school and stayed a few days at her dad's house till she figured things out. There were *guns* involved, for goodness' sake.

Then he shifted from annoyed to sorrowful, his voice heavy like he was ready to cry. "I tried to keep you out of this, M. You can't say I didn't try, but if you insist on knowing, then . . . that's fine. You're on the line for all of this"—he pointed to the room and the filing cabinets and the safe—"if I go down, so if you really want to know, I'll tell you. Anyway, we really could use another set of hands."

CHAPTER 33

ELLIE

Wednesday, May 11
6:09 a.m.

Although 911 response times in Broadlands were excellent, with just one text to Travis—Caleb @ Nancy's. Meeting in the basement. Come ASAP—Ellie couldn't predict how long until backup would be here. So, she followed Collin down the cement ramp to a doorway with no door. Instead, a piece of plywood stood up over the opening with a giant **DO NOT ENTER** sprayed in orange paint across it in a diagonal.

"Collin, it says 'Do Not Enter'; maybe we should listen," Ellie said, mostly to herself. The plywood was shifted to one side, leaving enough room for Ellie to squeeze through.

Inside, there was a massive open area, empty and vast, rays of light breaking the darkness in a few areas where the high windows were clear of debris. Off to one side, a burst of light cascaded from one giant gash in the ceiling, the jagged edges of the floor blurring into a celestial outline that resembled a sun in the damp gray of the basement. A large puddle of standing water reflected light around the room, its sparkling surface almost beautiful in the morning light.

But as Ellie's eyes adjusted, she realized that the world was not exactly gray in this barren dwelling. The walls, though lacking any kind of shelves or framed pictures, were not completely empty.

Top to bottom they were covered in a beautiful mural. Some scenes were done with spray paint in a style that seemed to mimic graffiti, others with a brush and some kind of acrylic. These paintings were not words or gang tags like you might expect in an abandoned basement; they were works of art. The first ceiling-high painting was of a day worker crying, his face covered by his dirt-coated hands. His child lay by his side, either sleeping or dead.

Ellie gasped, taken in by the beauty of the pictures on the wall. As she turned in a small circle to view the whole scene, she noticed a shift in the art. First it was dark and sad, images of the transient workers who not only filled Steve's roster but many of the farmers' come harvest. There was something captured in the eyes, especially of the children, a happiness that comes from knowing you are loved but always with a tinge of sadness that could only be produced by hunger and poverty. She swore she could recognize some of the faces—maybe not exact representations of people she had known, but a familiarity that made her want to reach out and ask how she could help.

Then the pictures started to shift. Less darkness, more bright colors, more landscape, and then a nearly perfect replica of the Slattery house, this time with yellow shutters and climbing vines of blossoming lilacs. And then there were children. Unlike the more devastating paintings, these warm ones never showed faces. In these paintings, the children were playing, dancing, a boy and girl running down lanes and through fields. If there was a sound track to this part of the mural, it would be laughter.

Then, as Ellie reached the farthest wall from the entry, there was nothing but color, blacks and reds and oranges and . . . fire . . . It was a fire, and in the fire was a man's face. It wasn't like the fire-man was burning; it was more like the fire-man *was* the fire and his scream was sorrow at what he had destroyed. Around this mass of color and soot and pain was a blackened landscape of a burned-out world, nothing but rubble.

It took a moment for Ellie to move again. She knew Caleb was an artist, but this . . . She couldn't tell if this was genius or insanity. How many hours had he spent making this basement his masterpiece? More important—in which direction did the pictures go? Did his artistic progression start at the fiery inferno and transform into the deep, moving, poignant art that made a statement about social injustice? Or was it the other way around—starting with the mind of an artist full of potential and then descending, as many geniuses did, into madness?

"He's amazing, right?" Collin whispered as though they were looking at his brother's artwork in a gallery rather than in the devastated basement of an abandoned supermarket.

"Yeah, it's stunning." Ellie wanted to be sarcastic but couldn't, not about this. She was willing to give space to the idea that Caleb was some kind of artistic savant, but she quickly changed the subject back to her main concern, the well-being of her father. "Where is he?"

"Close, close." Collin gave Ellie's shoulder a quick rub that made her understand that he hadn't noticed she wasn't wearing her engagement ring. Then he followed the perimeter of the basement, skirting the giant puddle of stagnant water and climbing over a large chunk of concrete to shout Caleb's name into the blackness beyond the walls of art.

"Shhh!" Ellie flinched, sure that the right vibration could make everything come tumbling down on top of them. Collin waved her off and called again. He must've heard something, because after a sizable pause, he came running back. When he reached her, Collin stood close enough that she thought he might put his arm around her waist. Thankfully, he didn't touch her again, but that was the least of her worries as soon as she saw Caleb emerging from the darkness.

He walked slowly from a doorway she hadn't noticed at first, nursing his right arm and holding it to his side. If Ellie hadn't known that he was recovering from not only a gunshot wound but also a backroom patch job, she wouldn't have thought much of it. He was dressed in fresh clothes, a dark gray tee shirt with a crisp flannel unbuttoned over it. Ellie recognized it as one that Collin wore last fall along with a dark blue pair of jeans that Caleb's frail frame swam in. Other than that, he looked a lot like the Caleb she'd gotten used to seeing in the back of every family event, nearly a piece of furniture or a light fixture that you came to expect and only missed when he wasn't there. His face did look pale and drawn. He probably had a lot of blood loss if the amount of residue in the bathroom was an indicator. In fact, it was likely that even if Collin had managed to treat the wound effectively, Caleb still needed a blood transfusion.

But even with Caleb's appearance, she couldn't see her father anywhere in the basement.

"Collin, where's my dad?" she asked, panicking.

Collin didn't respond, but Caleb did.

"He's sleeping." Caleb pointed at the dark doorway he'd emerged from. "Don't worry, he's fine. Let's let him sleep until it's time to leave."

"Hell no!" Ellie said, and rushed across the room, aware of Collin's hand trying to stop her but slipping off.

"Ellie! Stop!" Collin shouted, rushing after her, but Caleb put up one hand, halting his brother's pursuit. Then, as Ellie brushed past him, about to enter the doorway he was blocking, Caleb got his hand around her upper arm, his grip tighter than she would've expected for someone who looked so frail.

"Ellie, he is resting." He was calm but firm, and the strength in his voice made her hesitate. His eyes were the color of prairie grass that filled all the empty spaces in Broadlands. They were also calm in a way she hadn't expected. This man was the artist who painted the moving portraits by the entrance of the basement, definitely not the creator of the burning man on the opposite wall. It was that calm, steady gaze that made her stop. "You and I need to talk."

"Let me go first," she said, looking at her arm where his hand held tight and then back up at Caleb's prairie-grass eyes. "Then we can talk."

He nodded and released his fingers one at a time. Ellie stretched her arm, sure that she would have another bruise. So many bruises in one day, but the only injury she worried about was the permanent kind, the kind that was internal and would never fade and eventually heal. Losing her sister. Losing her father. Those were the pains she couldn't ever fully heal from.

"Thanks for hearing me out," Caleb said, still calm but this time with a quick rub of his injured arm. "I don't exactly have anywhere to sit." He glanced around the room as though waiting for a living room set to appear out of nowhere.

"I don't care about sitting, Caleb. Do your talking, give me my dad, and let me get out of here. Better yet, add 'turn yourself in to the police' to the end of that list and my life would be complete." At that, she moved herself out of range just in case she decided it was time to retrieve her father and he tried another grabbing maneuver to stop her.

Caleb sighed and shuffled over to a large chunk of what used to be the ceiling. He sat down carefully, adjusting his whole body into several different positions before settling. Ellie refused to sit. She preferred to keep her options open when facing a man who had just committed armed robbery.

"I'm sure you have a lot of questions and I will answer all of them, but first I want to tell you a story," Caleb began, bending his arm so it rested limply on his lap.

"The only story I'm interested in hearing is what happened to my sister. You want to tell me that?" She was being rude and demanding, but she didn't know if there was a Miss Manners column for this particular experience.

Ellie could hear Collin's annoyed sigh in the background. Just like she knew his personalized ringtone, she knew what that sigh meant without looking. He wanted her to shut up and listen. Well, he'd never say it that way, but it was exactly what he meant. Ellie couldn't let herself care about Collin's wants anymore.

"I'll tell you that story, I promise, but first I need to tell you something that happened when you were just a little girl. Do you remember when this store burned down?"

Goose bumps ran up Ellie's arm from her wrists to her elbows. Of course she remembered that day. Everyone in Broadlands remembered the day Tim Ray died. Up until the stroke, her father still mentioned Tim's family in their family Thanksgiving and Easter dinner prayers, and Amelia had told her that Steve still walked around in a funk, snapping at everyone in his house, on the anniversary of the fire.

Once she asked her father about the firefighter they always prayed for, and her father told the story of a giant fire at Nancy's Emporium, an enterprise already out of business and abandoned. It was started in the basement by some hitchhiker from the highway who broke the lock to the basement with a rock. Later, it was determined that the vagrant lit a fire in one of the no-longer-functioning stand-up freezers. But because of the nature of the freezer, it burned and burned and burned until it got so hot that it exploded, causing a whole section of the floor to collapse. It just so happened that Tim, wearing only half his gear, was navigating the fire against his supervisor's orders, and when the building collapsed, Tim went down with it. She once heard Steve talking about how they pulled him out of the rubble three hours later once they had gotten it under enough control that no other lives would be risked. By then, he was long dead and so horrifically burned, there was not much left to retrieve.

"I don't know what that has to do with any of this besides being the location of your super creepy art studio."

Caleb steepled his fingers together and stared at her over them like a supervillain with some kind of evil plan.

"Ellie, it has *everything* to do with this."

CHAPTER 34

AMELIA

Tuesday, May 10

"Arson?" Amelia gasped, still standing with her back to the door, not sure she'd heard Steve's convoluted plan correctly. "You have lost your mind. My goodness. What in the *world* are you thinking?"

"What am *I* thinking? I'm thinking that someone has to take care of this family, especially now that we have your dad weighing us down too. And you, my dear," he said, shooting the term of endearment at Amelia like a spear, "owe me. I've given and given and given so you could do your music stuff while I sit around in this crappy office day in and day out. So, today, you are going to give back to me. You are going to help us."

Amelia forced herself not to respond. No way in hell she'd help burn down the office. Why would she perpetrate fraud and put her own home and belongings at risk, not to mention her good name, just because Steve had gotten them into debt? There had to be a way other than guns and gasoline and committing actual crimes.

Randy, who'd been standing silently tapping his foot back and forth in a rat-a-tat pattern, finally spoke up.

"We don't need anyone else. Let's just do this." He shifted his attention from Steve to Amelia, a building panic shown through the tension in his shoulders and restless fingers. "You won't tell anyone, right, Amelia? You know how to keep a secret. She knows how to keep a secret, Steve. I'm sure of it."

This lapdog version of Randy was disconcerting and such a strange contrast to the real estate agent she'd considered as a potential business partner. She didn't know who was more disturbing—the manipulative criminal mastermind her husband turned out to be or the sniveling crony Randy transformed into.

"I can keep all kinds of secrets when I want to, Randy," she replied, saying his name like she was speaking to a child, "but . . . I don't think I want to keep this one. You two have a blast setting the house on fire. I'm going to go." Amelia pointed her thumb over her shoulder toward the kitchen, the moment feeling too surreal to be scary.

As Amelia turned to leave, Steve spoke loudly.

"You aren't thinking of doing anything stupid, are you?" His nostrils flared, and his muscles seemed puffed up like feathers on a bird preparing for a fight. "You'll be arrested too, you know, and then you'll leave our children with no parents. What kind of mother would do that?"

Those words, they had power. When Steve spoke to her like that, Amelia's mind would grow cloudy, and things she thought she knew suddenly became unsure. She knew she was a good mother; she knew it. Her children loved her. They felt safe and cared for. They were fed and clothed and clean, but when Steve questioned her parenting, all of those sureties faded into gray and then black.

"I don't believe you," she responded with a firm resolve even though every part of her mind was racing through a cloud of questions.

"Remember what it was like to grow up without a mom? You want to do that to our girls? You want little Cora and Kate to have to tell the kids at school that their mommy and daddy are in jail? What kind of mother are you? You are so selfish, Amelia. Pure selfishness."

It was hard to stand up against the barrage of words. He hadn't touched her, he hadn't even raised his voice, but she felt as though she were being held down and hit repeatedly. They made her wonder if perhaps she was a bad mother and wife. Maybe she *was* the selfish one. Look, Steve was willing to risk everything to make life better for her family. All she ever did was play at a few stupid wedding receptions, ribbon cuttings, and the occasional festival. She refused to take the job with Randy. She insisted on keeping her father out of a home. She never had the laundry folded and put away, dinner on the table, floors washed, house decorated like everyone else's wife did. And then here she was again, standing in the way of Steve taking care of their family.

"No, it is wrong. This is wrong," she said out loud as she worked through the swirling thoughts that threatened to down the winged creature inside her. "I'm not selfish. He's selfish." She looked up and saw Steve for the first time in years. He wasn't the same twenty-something who made her heart thump when he looked her in the eye or flirted with her over the other girls who constantly chased the handsome firefighter. He definitely wasn't the man who ran into burning buildings and saved lives in the back of an ambulance. That man was gone.

But it wasn't just physical. This man, he had stopped caring about other people. He'd flirt with and manipulate an insurance agent to get her to cooperate with his fraud, he'd hold old debts over Randy, who, she learned from the neighborhood gossip, was desperate to get his son back but spiraling into bankruptcy, in order to force him to do Steve's dirty work, and Caleb . . . Where was he? Was he involved in this plan too? If he was, who knew what Steve was holding over his head, but it had to be big. Really big. And here he was, doing it again. Using this skill to control and manipulate and to force his own wife into a scheme that could destroy her home at best and could land her in jail at worst. This was not the man she married. This was no longer the man she

promised to honor and obey. This man was a stran[
going to sacrifice everything for him.

She was tempted to call the police. It might put Ste
nifying glass by the officials, or he might actually get in t.   ...aybe
even go to jail, but then she and the girls would be safe from Steve and
he would be safe from himself. It was time to stand up and do what
she'd always done—protect her family.

"You are the selfish one." Amelia pointed an accusatory finger at
Steve; it was trembling with anger and fear. She didn't know how to
stand up to Steve, not permanently. She might stand up to him occasionally, but she always ended up apologizing for pretty much everything. "You. Not me. I won't participate in this. Randy, you should get
out. Anything that takes a ski mask and a gun and whatever way you
plan to burn this place down without getting caught . . . it isn't just
selfish—it is *stupid*."

Steve rolled his eyes, his lips blanching white. White, it turned out,
was the color of fury. Before meeting Steve, she would've said red, but,
no, when he was angry, truly "gonna lose it" angry, he went white, not
red. His hands tightly clenched at his sides, Steve looked not at Amelia
but at the one person in the room he still had control over: Randy.

"Shoot her." He said the words as easily as an order at McDonald's.
The words were so casual that at first they didn't register with Amelia.

"What the . . . ?" Randy looked at Amelia with wide eyes, like he
hoped she'd tell him this was a joke. "Shoot her? I'm not going to shoot
her."

"Take that gun"—Steve looked meaningfully at the gun on the
counter—"and shoot her, and then we'll be even."

"What are you talking about? You've lost your mind! I'm your *wife*."
She took a step farther into the office, drawn in rather than repulsed by
his order. She put out her hand, palm down. "Randy, he's not serious."

But Steve didn't flinch. He also took a step toward Randy and said
it again.

"Shoot her. Shoot her and we're even. I'll take care of the cleanup and the office. Shoot her, and you can walk away a free man with your money. Don't look at her. Look at me. Look at me, Randy."

Randy gave Amelia one last look that seemed to say, *I'm sorry*, and then turned his full attention to Steve.

"Oh my God. Oh my God. Oh my God!" Amelia's extended hand dropped and then went to cover her mouth. This was real. Steve's voice droned on in the background, turning from a suggestion to an order to a growled demand. As the men went back and forth about ending her life, Amelia backed up slowly, ready to dash through the door, knowing that the most dangerous moment would be when she turned her back to the men.

"DO IT NOW!" Steve screamed, and Randy picked up the gun.

Just as she was about to pull the door open and risk her escape, the outside door of the office opened, letting in a flash of light and a gust of spring air. Caleb.

CHAPTER 35

ELLIE

Wednesday, May 11
6:31 a.m.

Ellie liked the way Caleb talked—calm, measured, succinct. He was silent so often that even with dating Collin and having Caleb in Amelia's home nearly all the time, she'd never gotten used to the gentle tenor of his voice. It was hard to listen to him and keep her guard up at the same time. Though his injured arm remained by his side, he used his other arm for simple gestures.

"I did this." Caleb flipped his finger around in a giant circle. "This was all me."

"I kinda guessed. Nice art." She punched the *t* with a strong and sardonic staccato.

"Nah," he said, waving his good hand. "Not talking about the paintings. That's just a hobby. I'm talking about this." He did the finger thing again but with a more encompassing circle gesture. "All this. Nancy's. The fire. Everything. This is all because of me."

"Wait, what?" Ellie had no clue this would be the topic of conversation when she agreed to talk to Caleb. In fact, her grand plan was to keep Caleb talking until backup could come and take care of things, but now her interest was piqued. "My dad said that a vagrant started the fire."

"That was the story, but it's a lie." He winced and rubbed his right arm and then continued. "I started the fire." Then he laughed, a loud, shaking laugh that was in stark contrast to his gentle tone. "Man, I've kept that secret for so long. It feels amazing to get it out." He took a deep breath and shouted this time. "I STARTED THE FIRE!"

His voice ricocheted off the walls back and forth like an audio Ping-Pong game. A rush of rocks or gravel tinked in the distance, and Ellie's immediate instinct was to cover her head with her arms as though they could protect her from five tons of concrete falling on top of her.

"You probably shouldn't be that excited, Caleb. A man died in that fire," Ellie said, growing angry at his enthusiasm.

Caleb quieted, readjusting on his concrete slab.

"Yeah, I know all about Tim Ray. I know he was just a kid and that he played football at Broadlands High and that he loved Twinkies in his lunch and that his favorite subject was actually poetry even though he told his buddies it was woodshop. I know that he shared a room with his baby brother who cried every day for a year after his brother was buried. I know that his mother turned to drinking and got arrested for one too many DUIs and his dad moved away because he couldn't deal with all the memories of Tim around town. So, yeah, believe me . . . I know."

Caleb recited the list with a heavy, knowing tone, all shadows of a smile gone with the first mention of the young firefighter.

"The fire was an accident. I was using the basement even back then for my studio. I used to make a fire to give me light at night, but that night, some rags caught fire and I couldn't put it out, and with all the flammable paint supplies . . . it spread so fast, but it wouldn't have been so devastating if I hadn't kept all my supplies in the empty freezer." He pointed at the dark, cave-like area her father was apparently sleeping in. "The heat grew and grew and grew until it was like a bomb, and just, kapow"—he extended his one usable arm as if to illustrate—"it blew. And poor Tim was inside the building."

"Wow." Ellie was nearly speechless. It all made sense. Well, how the fire happened and even how Tim died made sense, but not what it had to do with her father or her sister being shot. "So, my dad . . ."

Collin had snuck past them as Caleb told his story and disappeared into the room where her father was sleeping. It was a relief to know Collin was checking on him because, even if she wasn't ready to trust him as her fiancé, she would always trust him as a doctor.

"Your dad. Yes. Okay, I'll get to that part now." Caleb seemed to sense her urgency. It wasn't just getting her father out; actually, it was this new desire to know what else was different about this story she thought she knew verbatim. "Your dad was barely chief back then. When the call came in, it was just a smoke sighting, and they'd had problems with homeless using the Emporium as a temporary shelter when the days got shorter and colder. So he sent two firefighters to check it out. That was Tim, of course, but you probably don't know who the other one was."

"No, this is the first I've heard any of this." Ellie gave up on her defensive pose, sincerely invested in hearing Caleb out. She stumbled backward over a few small rocks until she found one large enough to sit on.

Caleb nodded. "Yeah, Ellie, that was on purpose. No one's heard this before. No one but your dad and me and the other firefighter who was there that night—Steve."

Steve. She had expected to hear his name mentioned that morning as Caleb tried to explain away his participation in that crazy robbery plan, but not in conjunction with a fire. Especially not *this* fire. Why hadn't he mentioned this before? Why hadn't Amelia? Then a strange sour feeling developed in Ellie's stomach. Amelia probably didn't know either.

"Steve and Tim came out to check the smoke report. Steve saw me running away and chased me through the Carters' fields and tackled me. We were fighting when, apparently, Tim went inside to check out the source of the smoke. He wasn't wearing full gear. He wasn't even fully trained. The floor fell in, and Steve and I saw it from the field. We didn't know about Tim yet.

"Steve let me go and I ran away, but Chief Brown showed up on my doorstep the next morning with Steve by his side. They both explained that if the real story ever got out about the fire, we would all be in trouble, your father for not following procedure and meeting his men at the call, Steve for letting Tim go into that building alone, and me for inadvertently causing the death of a firefighter. I think your dad would've taken the blame if it wasn't for you girls. He agreed to Steve's plan to protect you and Amelia, I'm sure of it.

"So, your dad and Steve both had copies of an official report, the real official report about what happened at the fire. They both agreed to keep them under lock and key, and I promised to never tell with the understanding that I had the most to lose. So I kept quiet. And I've done whatever Steve Saxton told me to do every day from that moment forward. Until yesterday when . . ."

"When Randy shot Amelia, right?" Ellie didn't wait for a response. She could tell from the look of confusion on his face that she had stolen his big reveal and it was time to do what she came here for—to bring Caleb in. "I know it wasn't you. I think you'll be treated very fairly if you stop running away." She took a gamble and stood up, bypassing the rocks she had tripped over earlier.

Caleb didn't make eye contact, and the closer she got, the more his spine curved in and his healthy hand curled into a fist. She continued with her attempt to convince him to turn himself in. "Look, you ran away the night of the fire, and it changed your whole life and not for the better. Don't run anymore. Walk out of here with me, and we will make all of this right."

Ellie batted at a strand of hair that had broken loose and was sticking to her forehead. Somehow she was cold and hot at the same time. Then she put out her hand, close enough that Caleb could take it. The idea of his hand in hers was unnerving but also the only way she thought she could possibly get him out of the safety of his underground dwelling and into the open air. He didn't take her hand. He didn't even acknowledge it before Collin emerged from the other room, supporting her father's frail form.

"Daddy!" she called out, forgetting her fear of loud noises in the unstable structure. Ellie's father looked up like he remembered her by just her call. Maybe he did. Chief Brown was still wearing his BFD sweatpants and had a loosely knit yellow-and-gold blanket from his house wrapped around his shoulders. His feet were bare, and with each step Ellie wanted to cry, knowing the floor was filled with rubble and sharp bits of metal that could pierce her father's tender skin.

She was about to run to him but instead fell to the ground and untied her shoes, each set of laces needing a hard pull to get them to release. Her shoes would be too small for her father's feet, but he could at least wear her socks. She peeled them off her feet, glad she'd worn the ones that went up to her midcalf rather than the ankle socks she used when she worked out. Her sweaty feet were difficult to wedge back into her athletic shoes, so she pushed as hard as she could but then let her heels press down the back lip. The socks were still warm when she scrunched them into a ball and rushed over to where Collin and her dad were making very slow progress across the room.

"Stop. Let me put these on him," Ellie ordered. Collin's feet stilled, and he gave a few short nods. She'd been around him enough to know that he was concerned but not rushed or annoyed. Chief Brown smiled as Ellie wrapped her arms around his neck. "Hi, Daddy," she whispered in his ear as she gave him an extra squeeze and kissed his stubbly cheek. "I sure missed you."

There were tears in Chief Brown's eyes. He patted the top of her head as Ellie knelt at his feet. First, she flattened the socks on her thigh, smoothing each one down. Next, she ran her hand down his flannel pajama leg till she reached his foot, which she pulled gently. He wobbled when she lifted it, but Collin held him tight around his waist so he didn't fall. Ellie looked at his foot, white and smooth, the same feet her mother used to playfully push off the coffee table, the feet that would turn red when he'd run outside in the snow to grab the paper in the middle of the winter. That was the hardest thing about being her father's caregiver. It wasn't the time or the exhaustion; it wasn't living in Broadlands. It was knowing who Richard Brown used to be, and then to be confronted with the reality of where his life had landed them after the stroke.

Ellie sighed and gently dusted off her father's sole, dislodging a few embedded pebbles and concrete residue. Without looking, she selected one of the socks from her thigh and wiggled it onto his foot and up his slender calf. She put it down and let his pant leg drop till it hit the floor and then repeated the process with his other foot.

"There you go." Ellie stood and put her hands on her father's shoulders. "Be careful where you step, Daddy. It's dangerous in here."

"Ah no," Chief Brown responded, and Ellie translated in her mind. *I know.* Yeah, no way her father had forgotten this place.

"Ellie, we're not done yet." Caleb spoke in his calm, soothing voice. "We need to talk about Steve."

"You can talk while we walk. I'm not staying in here another minute and, I'm sorry, but I don't think you are going to hurt any of us, so you can't stop me." Ellie slipped her arm around her father's waist on the opposite side of Collin. Their arms overlapped, and though just twenty-four hours ago she'd woken in his arms, now it felt like she was touching a stranger.

Caleb must have known that he'd have to either muster a violent side or start talking fast. As Ellie and Collin urged her father forward,

Caleb stood, wincing in pain when his body weight fully registered as he lifted himself.

"Fine, so Steve has both of the reports now. He took one from your father's house a few weeks ago. He took Amelia's keys and somehow got into his safe. Right, Chief, do you remember Steve asking you about the report and the combination for your safe?" Caleb's voice rose, and he slowed his speech when he talked directly to her father. Chief Brown was so focused on putting one foot in front of the other, he didn't seem to fully comprehend that Caleb was talking to him.

"The safe," he repeated. "Seven, twenty-two, forty-nine." Though the numbers were difficult to make out, they soon clicked together for Ellie. Her mother's birthday. Her father had suffered from aphasia as well as several other speech disorders since the stroke, not to mention the vascular dementia, but this . . . these numbers in the right order and with such deep meaning, it made her want to look in her father's eyes and ask, *Are you in there, Daddy?*

"Yes, you told that to Steve, didn't you, Chief? Do you remember what happened here with Steve?" At first, Chief Brown shook his head back and forth in broad strokes like he had to think extra hard about each action, but then he paused and his feet stopped their forward momentum. He looked Caleb right in the eye.

"You . . . ," he managed to get out, the word coming out thick and dropping off before he finished the vowel sounds. "You killed . . ." Ellie could feel the anger building in her father. He never used to be an angry man, but anytime he was frustrated or confused, anger now seemed to be his default emotion. Now she had a good barometer for his risk of explosion.

"Shhh . . . Daddy . . . it's okay. Keep walking." Ellie tried to calm her father and get him moving again. "Back off, Caleb. How about you turn yourself in and I'll get you your precious reports." As she said the words, it all fell together. The robbery wasn't about money for Caleb. It was about getting the report and, simultaneously, freedom.

For a fraction of a second, Ellie felt bad for Caleb and the guilt he must have lived with every day, but then when she thought about how another one of his stupid decisions caused another death and two serious injuries, she wanted to scream. If Steve or her father had done the right thing years ago and turned Caleb in . . . none of this would've happened. It was hard to be furious at the shell of a man her father had become. It was almost like he was suffering from his own punishment each torturous day of his life. Goodness knew that Steve had plenty to answer for, but ultimately, according to the law, the guilt for a death in a fire always lay with the one who set it. And that was Caleb.

"You selfish son of a bitch." Ellie swatted at Caleb, wishing she had both her hands free. "Leave us alone. Haven't you already hurt enough of my family? God. Just let us go." She shoved his shoulder as hard as she could, finally close enough to touch him.

"ELLIE!" Collin shouted, and tried to reach across Chief Brown to stop her assault on his brother. "He's trying to *help* . . ." But Collin couldn't finish his thought. A loud pounding from the doorway they were headed toward echoed through the basement, and Ellie swore she could hear cracks erupting all around her.

"Police, demand entry!"

"HELP!" Ellie screamed. "He's in here!"

Within seconds, the plywood exploded backward, and two officers with guns drawn rushed through the door and split up as they ran along opposite walls. Collin covered his face with his arms, but Caleb stood perfectly still, as if he'd been expecting the intrusion.

"Hands up," the voice continued, and immediately she knew who was behind the SWAT gear. She'd been waiting for him since she pressed Send on that text message, and if she was honest, she'd nearly given up hope. But now she felt a weight lift nearly immediately, and instead of being scared of the yelling officers, Ellie was relieved because Travis was finally here.

CHAPTER 36

AMELIA

Tuesday, May 10

"Caleb!" Amelia screamed, wanting to run to him. If he responded, she never heard it because a loud crack turned all sound into static, and then a hot searing pain in her shoulder let her know that sound . . . was a gunshot. Shock overriding the pain of the wound, Amelia covered the burning spot with the heel of her palm and slumped back against the door when another devastating blow hit her stomach like someone had shoved something hot and hard through her belly button.

This time there was no shocked calm. She fell to her knees and then hard onto her side, her other arm wrapped around her midsection as though she were trying to keep in the warm gush of blood that ran down the front of her shirt and soaked into the thirsty fabric of her jeans.

As the light in the room started to flicker like someone was covering and uncovering her eyes, she heard one more shot. She flinched and waited for more pain, more blood, wishing she could move or hide, but instead she heard a man groan and then a thump across the room.

"You weren't supposed to really shoot her." It was Steve's voice. He sounded far away, down a tunnel or a hallway. She wanted to call out, maybe he could help her, but then she remembered—he wanted this.

"What do you mean?" His voice was high and full of panic. "You know you wanted me to! Oh God, I shot them. OH GOD!"

"Whoa, Rambo, you might want to put that thing down." Steve sounded like he was joking. How is was joking? Amelia wondered. She couldn't ponder it long. She was so sleepy. The pain was disappearing, but this tempting darkness was pulling at her with luscious, dark tentacles. "It doesn't matter what you *think* I said. You are in this deep. So you need to stop flipping out and start focusing."

"Oh, I'll focus. Give me my money." Randy's voice wobbled, high-pitched and frantic, the gun still extended in front of him, not exactly pointing at Steve but not pointing away either. "I'm not doing anything else till you give me the damned money."

"You'll get your money. Hold on." Steve knelt back down in front of the safe and disappeared out of Amelia's eye line. Her drifting mind wondered what her life was worth to Randy and why Steve didn't just use the money he was going to pay for his "services" to pay off their debts. Why? That was a question she never seemed to have an answer to in her life. But her pondering didn't last long. Since she couldn't see Steve, Amelia watched Randy as he waited for Steve to count his payment, his defenses falling down around him, the gun slowly lowered to his side.

Even in his monochrome outfit, the jeans tapered into a nearly skinny cut, and the black tee shirt rolled at the sleeves and hugged his muscles in a very complimentary way. It was like she was watching a movie rather than real life. Part of her mind said, *You've been shot . . . Save yourself . . . Save Caleb . . .* , but mostly her mind and body were telling her to be still and close her eyes.

"Could you hurry?" Randy bounced on the edge of his toes.

"Keep your cool, dude." Steve's voice was steady and sure, and Amelia could see its controlling effect on Randy. "Already have enough messes to clean up thanks to you."

"I think I cleaned up your mess today," Randy said, placing the gun down on the desk again and picking up the ski mask. "When do those cameras come back on?"

"The backup generator for the cameras kicks in after fifteen minutes of power loss. That's what the brochure said anyway. Too bad we didn't get to test it before you got all trigger happy," Steve responded, sounding distracted.

"I'm not going down because of your shitty cameras." Randy slipped on the ski mask and adjusted it over his nose and mouth. "Next time you want to commit insurance fraud, maybe don't point cameras at your house." He picked up the gun again and this time pointed it right at where Steve would've been crouching. "That's long enough. It doesn't take that long to count out twenty grand. I want the money, now."

It was like the anonymity of the mask gave him some kind of power. The gun didn't shake this time, and Amelia knew that if Steve didn't produce a payment soon, he would be added to the list of Randy's victims.

An unnerving amount of blood surrounded Amelia in a crimson halo, and when she tried to fight all of her instincts to drift asleep and turn to watch Randy, the carpet squished like it did when the front window broke during a storm and flooded the office. Bile burned at the back of her throat as she moved one inch and then another, with no real plan for how she could stop Randy or help Steve.

Then she remembered Caleb. Caleb had come in, right? And then there was the shot. Oh, Caleb, trying to help her, trying to save her, and look what it got him. She was afraid to look but needed to know if her old friend was alive or dead. Amelia cocked her head to one side, the pain in her shoulder returning with the movement. But it was worth it. From that angle, she could see Caleb. He was alive. Relief washed over her, and she spent an extra moment checking his body for injury.

On his side facing her, he didn't seem to be moving, but he was awake and watching the men argue. Her slight movement caught his eye. Amelia tried to speak, but no sound came out and it was becoming more difficult to breathe, like a pair of steel hands were around her lungs, constricting. Caleb, who had blood on the floor beside him and on his clothes and smeared on his face, seemed more with it than Amelia. He put up one finger to his lips, leaving a line of red. Then he mouthed, "I'm sorry."

She didn't understand very much right now, like why time seemed to be going by in slow motion, and she definitely didn't understand why Caleb would be apologizing to her. As she closed her eyes to ponder these things and escape into the warmth of the darkness, one more loud bang made her eyes open in a flash, panic flooding through her. Steve. Did Randy shoot Steve?

The darkness fell back away from her eyes, painful like pins and needles after your foot falls asleep. The room came into focus and she did see Randy, and he was very, very close to her now, and though there were a lot of things Amelia didn't know, what she did know was that Randy was dead. His body lay within arm's reach, blood pouring out from a wound in the back of his head. It was half-covered by the ski mask but still made her stomach turn. The bile in her throat built to a tipping point, and she couldn't fight the nausea any longer. It burned in her throat and nose, and the smell as she spit onto the floor made the bile creep up again, threatening to cause another involuntary reaction.

The safe clicked closed, and Amelia could see through the blurring darkness that Steve was not only alive when he emerged from behind the desk, he was also unharmed. He had a large silver gun in his hand, much bigger than the one Randy had been using and that was now resting just a few inches away from Amelia. Steve surveyed the scene and shook his head like he was sincerely sorry that things had gone so horribly wrong. Then he walked over and checked Randy's pulse, careful to only touch him with two fingers. Steve's work boots squished with each step, the carpet of the office nearly to the point of saturation from the three injured, dead, or dying.

Without a second thought, Steve stepped over Randy's body and approached Caleb, who was now lying still on the ground, eyes closed, incredibly pale. After seeing Randy go from living to dead in a matter of seconds, Amelia was scared that Caleb, the only person in the room who hadn't been involved in some kind of scheme, was already gone. But when Steve leaned down to place his fingers on Caleb's jugular, checking for a pulse, Caleb's eyes flashed open and he grabbed onto Steve's arm like he was trying to pull him down.

"Don't worry about me. Call 911. Amelia is in bad shape. Save Amelia." At first she'd thought Caleb was fighting with Steve, but it turned out he was begging him. Amelia was even more confused at Caleb's pleadings until she remembered that Caleb hadn't seen everything, getting there just as the shots were fired.

Steve's back was to Amelia, so she couldn't see his face, but she could hear his voice.

"You've always had quite the thing for my wife, haven't you?" The hefty gun was by Steve's side, but now he carefully pointed it in front of him right at Caleb. "Don't worry, I won't tell."

"What are you doing?" Caleb released Steve's arm and shielded his face as though mere flesh and blood could save him from a bullet.

"I'm finishing what Randy started. If you had been here today like you were supposed to be, none of this would've happened. Amelia is dead because of you, you spineless asshole." Steve's voice swelled with emotion as though he were sad Amelia was shot and dying, which, once again, didn't make sense. How could Steve, her husband of ten years, leave her so clouded and unsure even after what she'd witnessed today? How could she know so clearly one minute that he was driven by purely narcissistic values but then question her own sanity the next?

Though she couldn't see if Steve was crying, she knew Caleb was. He took his arm off his face and looked up at Steve, tears streaming. He reached up and put his hand on the gun but didn't try to wrestle it away; instead, he pulled it down until it rested against his forehead.

"Do it," he whispered. "Just do it already. I can't live like this anymore. Shoot me."

Caleb's willing participation must have stunned him, because his finger left the trigger momentarily. Amelia knew this was her last chance. Either she climbed out of the fog of pain and blood loss and years of emotional manipulation to do something, or she watched her friend, a man who deep down she knew loved her more than Steve ever could, be shot in the face.

Randy's gun. The thought entered her mind like it was sent there by another source. Randy's gun was only a few inches from where Amelia lay, and though even the thought of moving that far made stars play at the back of her eyes, she knew she could do it. She'd had two babies. She'd pushed through pain. Pain didn't always equal bad . . . Sometimes it meant a new life was starting.

With her last ounce of energy, Amelia rolled forward, holding back the yelp of pain that gathered in her throat. More blood filled her shirt and ran down her side as she crawled just far enough to wrap her fingers around the hilt of the gun, put her finger on the trigger, and point.

"Do it already," Caleb repeated, almost begging. Steve sighed and repositioned his finger on the trigger.

"No!" Amelia called out, gun drawn and pointed at her husband. "Leave him alone."

Steve didn't say a word; he just raised the gun and pointed it at Amelia, but before he could shoot, she tugged on the trigger, one, two, three times, until the gun was empty of any remaining bullets. Then she collapsed. The darkness could not be evaded any longer, and though she could hear the external office door open and close and felt Steve nearby, moving the gun, checking for remaining bullets, and then rubbing it down, she knew her time was over. She was floating now, the pain gone, awareness gone. In her last moments, all she could think about were her girls and how Steve was right; they'd end up without a mom or a dad now. She rolled onto her back, the cool metal of the door feeling good against her burning shoulder.

The only comfort she had as she fell into what felt like the deepest sleep of her life was that Ellie was safe. Little Ellie would take care of her babies, be their mom, teach them how to put on lipstick and study for calculus and, when it was time, how to kiss boys. Yes, Ellie. Ellie would save her family.

CHAPTER 37

ELLIE

Wednesday, May 11
6:48 a.m.

Ellie looked over at Collin's Jeep. She rarely drove it, but as Collin walked off with the detective who had questioned Steve, he handed her the keys. In that moment she could see that he knew she was the reason the police were there. He was disappointed in her but seemed resigned, as though he knew what she would do long before even she did.

The only sign of anger Ellie could detect was when Collin passed Travis on the way to the squad car. Travis greeted him with a small two-fingered wave, but Collin kept his eyes forward, refusing to acknowledge the officer. Ellie swore Travis had a little self-satisfied smirk on his face once Collin couldn't see him anymore. He was by her side as soon as Collin drove off, with Caleb already ahead of him in a separate squad car.

Travis had peeled off his gear and was wearing street clothes underneath. He looked so normal, the maroon tee shirt a nice contrast to his olive complexion. He must've showered recently, because his face looked newly shaved and he smelled faintly of fresh deodorant.

"So, you went home after all," Ellie said, flipping through the keys, ready to go back to her sister's bedside and not leave. Travis had already given her an update. Amelia was asleep but still stable. Now that her father was in an ambulance on the way to the hospital and her sister already ensconced there, she knew where she had to be. The girls were under Mr. and Mrs. Saxton's care for now, and soon Steve would be released and be by their sides. Ellie had plenty of questions for Steve after Caleb's wild story, but those could wait. The girls needed their father now.

"I got in trouble." He shrugged with a mischievous grin on his face that made a dimple sink in on one side. "You're really not supposed to work more than ten hours, twelve at most. Chief had a fit when he realized I was still working this case." Ellie started walking toward Collin's Jeep, listening and flipping the key ring in a circle around her finger repeatedly. "I'm just glad I got your text. I must've been in the shower when you sent it, because I didn't get it when it first arrived. I'm sorry, Brown."

Ellie stopped flipping the keys and turned to face Travis, already at the rear of the car. She studied his expression. He was sincere, and there was relief there in his soft brown eyes. She reached out and put her hand on his arm and gave a squeeze. She meant for it to be brief, but he placed his hand over hers and took a step closer, their bodies not far from touching.

"I think you should start calling me Ellie, what do you think?" She looked up into his eyes.

"It might take me a while, but, yeah, I think I like that. Need anything else from me today? Sweatshirts? Emergency arrest warrant? Coffee?"

"Mmmm, coffee sounds great." She gave his hand one last squeeze and then slipped her hand out from under his, refocusing on who was really important right how—her family.

"I'll grab some and meet you at the hospital if that's okay?" He put his hands in his jeans pockets like he wasn't sure what to do with them anymore. "Hope they let you in after that whole morgue fiasco. You have any problems, you tell them to call me. I'll figure out a reason why you were sneaking peeks at dead people in the middle of the night."

Ellie's cheeks burned. She still couldn't believe half of the things that had happened since she and Chet got the call from Lark Lane.

"Glad you've got my back, Rivera," she said, laughing and faking a salute.

"One day you are telling me that story, deal?"

"Deal," Ellie replied, and picked out the key to the ignition. "See you soon."

"Sounds like a plan, Brown." He stopped himself, twisting his lips up to one side. Ellie was pretty sure he was blushing. "Sounds like a plan . . . Ellie." He completed the sentence, shook his head like he was laughing at himself, and then waved a good-bye before taking off across the back lot of Nancy's to his truck. He hefted himself into the driver's seat and started the engine with a loud roar. Ellie gave one last wave and climbed into the Jeep alone.

The car started, and everything about the experience was familiar at the same time as it was unfamiliar. The sound of the engine, the smell of the exhaust, the way the upholstery scratched against the back of her arms every time she readjusted her position, all things she'd come to find comforting over the past five years with Collin. They'd made love for the first time in the back of that Jeep. She cringed, wishing it sounded more romantic and less like a pair of amorous teenagers. But at the same time, she was the one in the driver's seat now, and the wheel felt foreign to her touch. She wondered, briefly, if the car would even move with her pressing on the gas.

As she worked the car into reverse, she ran through what had just happened inside the Emporium. It was disturbing, this idea that her father had taken part in a grand deception. He'd always seemed so strong, so perfect, so full of unwavering integrity. She never wanted to let her dad down; it was why she became a paramedic at U of I on top of her already-packed course schedule, why she was determined to become a firefighter even after failing the agility test twice, and ultimately it was why she came home.

So what if Caleb's stories were true and her father wasn't the perfect superhero she had always thought he was? She'd decided that it didn't make her love him less. In some ways, it made her love him more. He wasn't a superhero—it turned out he was a man.

She still wanted answers from Steve, but for now she'd lean on this strange type of relief, that if her father wasn't perfect, then she didn't have to be either.

Ellie shifted the car back into drive and turned the corner that would take her to the front side of the Emporium and eventually to the road. Ahead, Travis's truck sat at the edge of the parking lot, waiting, most likely, for Ellie to pass by so he could be sure of her safe exit. With a big wave, which Travis immediately returned, she turned left, hoping he wouldn't follow her. She needed to get a few things for her dad, but they weren't at his house. They were at Amelia's. In her rearview mirror, she watched Travis take a right turn and get on the highway; she pressed on the gas, hoping to get to her sister's house before the Broadlands police caught up with their day and headed over for further investigation. All she needed was Dad's brush.

It never took more than five minutes in a car to get anywhere in Broadlands, and she was at Lark Lane within two. The house looked like it was decorated for Halloween with police tape strung across the driveway. She wasn't supposed to be there, but at this point in her day she'd done enough things she wasn't supposed to do that the nervous thrill that should've kept her from parking down the block and sneaking through the shrubs to the kitchen door disappeared.

She lifted up the edge of the welcome mat and pulled the black backing material away from the stiff fibers. A silver key fell out and clanked onto the cement step. As quickly as possible, Ellie unlocked the door and slipped inside the dark house.

The smell in the room was thick and heavy, the smell of day-old blood and that same gasoline smell from the day before mixed together. It was a strange scent and so different from the ones that usually greeted her inside that door. The room was still covered in blood, but numbered signs traced along the floor like yellow trail markers, and Ellie was relieved to know what areas to avoid. Her head spun, and her empty stomach turned with the smell and sight of browning blood. Fresh blood reminded her of her job, but old blood reminded her of death.

Ellie skirted the bloody footprints and evidence markers, pressing her body against the kitchen cabinets and remembering that her father's brush was usually in the front room by his favorite TV chair. In an increasingly comfortable state of heightened stress, she tried to focus only on getting the brush and getting back to the hospital so that the images in front of her didn't bring back any memories from her last visit to the house.

Once she'd passed the area of the house still under investigation, Ellie searched the side table by her father's recliner and quickly grasped the brush. The wooden handle was reassuring in her palm, and when she slipped it into her back pocket, she finally felt like she'd done something helpful.

Following approximately the same path back to the kitchen, Ellie rushed toward the back door, ready to leave the crime scene and determined to never break the law again—not even for a good reason. Glad that she'd been working on her balance skills, she made it back to the kitchen door in less than a minute, slightly out of breath but also relieved to be done so quickly. Though she'd become accustomed to the feeling of adrenaline rushing through her veins, she still hadn't acquired a taste for it.

As Ellie readjusted the brush to keep it from falling out, a thump sounded behind the steel door that led to the Broadlands Roofing office. Nerves shot, she jumped and let out a little yelp; then she peeked through the downturned blinds on the kitchen door to see if a squad car was parked outside. The driveway was empty, the yellow caution tape whipping in the spring air, the threat of more rain in the sky.

Another thump sounded from the other side of the wall, and Ellie pulled her hand away and pressed her back against the door. Part of her wanted to run away, take a chance, and dash across the gravel drive and into the safety of Collin's Jeep. Then the rebellious part of her that was so tired of being scared wanted to fling open the door and confront what was sure to be a fallen file box. Ellie paused, holding her breath and listening.

Time was flying by, and Ellie's nausea was reaching a peak. She put her head between her legs, her breathing closer to panting. Each breath brought in the same smell she was trying to escape, making her gag. Oh God, she was going to vomit all over the crime scene. She swallowed again and again, craving the cool air outside. Just as she gathered herself enough to take another look out of the blinds, a loud crash and a muffled cry sounded in the office.

She stood up, her senses on edge, the nausea lifting and replaced with panic. Someone was in the office, someone else who was hiding. She should leave, she should run, but that cry, it sounded like pain. It sounded . . . familiar. Just like when running into a burning building or wrapping a tourniquet around a gushing artery, Ellie made a decision based on instinct more than intellect. She let the adrenaline drive her forward until her hand was resting on the silver knob of the office door.

Surprisingly, it wasn't latched, much less locked. All it took was a hard push forward, and the door whistled open. If it weren't for years of pushing past the discomfort of panic and anticipation, she would've closed her eyes as though the thin protection of her eyelids were enough to keep the monsters in the closet from getting her. But when the door smacked against the rubber doorstop and the light from the room flooded in, she didn't see a monster. At the back of the office, kneeling on the floor in front of a ripped-up segment of carpet and a rectangular hole in the floor was Steve. Ellie was surprised and relieved at the same time.

"What the HELL are you doing here?" Ellie asked, letting out a long breath. He was probably there for the same reason she was—to get something.

Steve stood with effort, his face showing the briefest flash of pain but otherwise calm as though he were attending a family party rather than hiding in a roped-off crime scene filled with priceless evidence.

"Hey, L," Steve said like he had a million times before, his eyes holding on to hers. A soft smile turned up the corners of his mouth in a way that was familiar but not comforting. "I think it's time we had a little talk."

CHAPTER 38

AMELIA

Wednesday, May 11
7:11 a.m.

Ellie needs to get to school. Late, so late.

Why couldn't she wake up today? Usually her alarm would go off, she'd wake up Ellie, make Dad coffee, throw a few frozen waffles in the toaster oven, and then take a shower before heading to school. But today, today it was different. Her alarm was beeping, but she couldn't force her eyes to open.

Wake up. Wake up. Wake up.

The darkness was heavy, but she could sense the light in her room. It didn't feel warm like sunlight, and the more she focused on her body, the more odd sensations she found there. She couldn't move her arms or legs; they were heavy as if they were filled with lead. There was a faint nibbling of discomfort or maybe pain in all the heaviness. It was hard to know for sure; maybe her leg had fallen asleep. Maybe she'd slept funny.

The beeping again. God, she wanted to make that beeping stop. And Ellie . . . Ellie . . . Ellie . . .

Ellie. The beeping increased and her fingers twitched, wanting to slap the Snooze button. Then there were hands touching her. Not

Ellie's hands, not little-girl hands, bigger, stronger. The hands made her struggle, her numb arms and legs tingling like they'd fallen asleep. The beeping came faster and faster, making Amelia want to scream.

"Is she okay?" a deep voice asked. Not Steve. Someone else.

"Her pain medication must be wearing off. Sometimes that can cause stress even in a coma patient. Let me check her chart, and then we can give her some relief." Then in a sweeter tone: "We're gonna get you some medicine, honey. Don't worry. You'll be resting nicely in no time."

No. She didn't want to rest. She wanted to wake up. *Wake up, Amelia. WAKE UP.*

Her eyes opened. It was bright, so bright, and the pain that seemed distant before started to flood in. There was one woman in scrubs rushing around the room. She didn't seem to notice Amelia's eyes following her as she searched through a metal chart that she'd retrieved from the foot of her bed.

But behind the woman was a young, attractive man sitting on the edge of his seat like he wanted to help but didn't know what to do. He was typing frantically into his phone, and Amelia wondered who was on the other end of this stranger's urgent texts. He pressed a button with finality and placed the phone in his jeans front pocket. When he glanced up to take in the scene, they made eye contact. The man jumped to his feet, his hands waving at the nurse still working hard in the room.

"Look. Look." He pointed toward Amelia without breaking their connection. The nurse finally took notice.

"Good morning, sweetheart," she crooned with a slight Southern twang. "Good to see you awake. How is your pain, hon? One to ten." She placed a cool hand on Amelia's forehead and glanced at the numbers listed on the machine by her bedside.

Amelia tried to focus in on the throb in her midsection and shoulder. She knew what she wanted to say, but the words seemed to jumble in her mind.

"Six," she responded after two attempts.

"Okay, I'll get the doctor." The nurse rushed out of the room, and the man hurried over to her side.

"Where am I?" she asked, the words stumbling as they came out. "Who are you?"

"You're in the hospital. I'm going to let the doctors talk to you about the medical stuff, but you've been asleep. I'm Travis. I'm a police officer and a friend of your sister."

Your sister. The phrase made her pulse rise and the beeping on the machine next to her go wild. Amelia wrestled against the invisible bands weighing her down, but every attempt to sit up sent hot stabs of pain through her body until tears gathered on her eyelashes.

"Whoa, stop. You're safe. I have a guard outside. I'm here, and I won't let anyone hurt you."

Amelia stilled and tried to clear her mind of the fog that was making her behave so irrationally. Her dark hair stuck to the sides of her face and itched, but she didn't dare try to move again to wipe it away.

"Where is Steve? Where is Ellie?" The words sounded like she was talking with her mouth full of marshmallows.

Travis hesitated and then took out his phone again and started typing while talking.

"I think Ellie is on the way. We both left at the same time . . . She should be here soon." He typed for a few more moments and then looked back at Amelia.

"Travis," she said, recalling his name more easily than the other details of her recent life, "where is my husband?"

"He was by your bedside for a while, but . . ." The plainclothes officer pressed his lips together like he was trying not to say something. "He was also injured in your . . . event, and the doctors made him go back to his room. I'm sure the nurse will contact him and he will be here soon."

"Steve was hurt? What happened? What's going on? Is Ellie hurt? What about my girls? Oh God. My babies." Fear started to act on Amelia like a drug, pressing down on her like a physical weight as her breathing turned rapid. Travis rushed to the side of the bed, shaking his head apologetically.

"Hey, hey, it's okay. Your children are safe; they are with Steve's parents. Mrs. Saxton didn't want to leave, but your daughters needed her. Ellie is helping with your dad, and Steve is okay, he'll be released soon, but, Amelia . . ." He got serious and looked her right in the eyes. "You were shot. Do you remember that? Do you remember being shot?"

Amelia searched her memory. It was like trying to remember a dream. At first, everything from the morning was blank, like it hadn't even happened. She remembered going to bed last night and then the curious feeling of needing to take her sister to school, but beyond that, everything was gone, erased.

"I can't remember," she said, shaking her head carefully and feeling like a failure. Steve was in the hospital, injured, maybe in front of her eyes, and she couldn't even remember it.

"That's normal. You've been through a lot. Take your time."

Amelia closed her eyes and ran them back and forth in the darkness. As she focused, brief flashes began to flood in. The car. The house. The lights not working. Then the Broadlands Roofing office and a man with a mask. A gun. Yes. A gun.

Amelia opened her eyes, panting.

"I don't know for sure, but I remember a man in the office, wearing a mask. He was holding a gun." She ran her tongue over her teeth, rough with tartar, trying to think past the man in the mask. "I don't know about anything else. It's like a wall, a black wall I can't get through."

"Don't push too hard. It will come." Travis rocked back onto his heels, nodding slowly. "We'll talk again soon, and Ellie has my number. She can call me when you have more input."

"Officer . . . uh . . . Travis. Can you call Ellie?" Tears started to run down her cheeks, and every sob stabbed at her chest. She didn't know what was more painful—her injuries or the heavy blanket of loneliness that covered her suddenly. "I need my family. I need someone."

"Yeah." He nodded, looking at her sympathetically. "It's probably good to check in with her anyway. I'm not sure what happened to her. Maybe she stopped by the ER first to see—" He cut off his sentence, which would've seemed odd to Amelia if she hadn't been so anxious to talk to her sister. Travis took out his phone and pressed a button. The phone rang loud enough that Amelia could hear it in her hospital bed. It seemed to ring endlessly, and she closed her eyes and focused on it, finding every thought and movement exhausting. Five, six, seven . . . then a pause before Ellie's brief but chipper voice mail.

Hi, this is Ellie. Leave a message or just text me.

Travis pressed the red button to cut off the call and stared at the phone.

"That's so strange," he said to himself, and then looked at Amelia like he was seeking answers. "She's been waiting to hear about you all day. Let me try again."

He dialed again and held the phone to his ear. Three rings and then a pause. Ellie's voice, thin and nervous.

"Hello?"

"Brown, where are you? I've got some good news." He smiled down at Amelia, his face suddenly bright and animated. This man didn't just work with Ellie; he liked her. For some reason the thought made Amelia swell with a bit of pride. She didn't blame him; her sister was beautiful and funny and strong . . . so so strong.

"Yeah? Everything okay?" Ellie asked, sounding hesitant like this was some kind of trick.

"More than okay. Amelia is awake. She's talking and coherent and asking for you. Are you close?"

Amelia couldn't hear her response. Gaining a little strength, she gestured for the phone.

"Here, I'm going to pass you to her." He nodded briefly and put the phone to her ear. Ellie's breathing was loud and shallow through the receiver and didn't sound right.

"Hey, L. You okay, sweetie?" She talked to her like she used to when Ellie was just a little girl and Amelia was the fill-in mom. Ellie gasped, and her voice hitched.

"M . . . you made it. Oh my God, I'm sorry I'm not there." A loud whimper muffled the rest of her sentence, and even lying in bed, Amelia ached to reach out and comfort her.

"Shhh, Ellie. It's going to be okay." In the background, behind Ellie's faint cries, she thought she heard a man's voice speaking sternly. Ellie seemed to respond to the voice by taking a gulp of air and swallowing loudly. When she spoke again, her voice was less emotional, more measured.

"Ellie, where are you?" she asked with a sinking feeling in her stomach that had nothing to do with the surgical incision there.

"I'm in the car, on my way. I'll be there soon. I promise." The voice in the background rumbled, and there was something about the tone of Ellie's comment that made Amelia bristle.

"You aren't in the car, Ellie. Who's with you? Who is that man?" As Amelia's alarm increased, Travis took notice. She could see the muscles in his arms tense and the corners of his eyes draw together. Ellie's breathing grew heavy again and thick.

"I'm at your house. I'm with Ste—" The words were rushed and spilled out fluidly until the last was cut short and the phone went dead. Amelia glanced up at Travis, who was still holding the phone to her ear. He was watching her facial expressions intently, leaning over the bed railing until the plastic casing creaked.

Ellie's last phrases went through her thoughts again, sparking a dim thought or memory. Her house. Her husband. Her sister's voice, strained and on edge. Then the bright flash of a gunshot and another. A man with a mask but another man too. A man she knew but couldn't quite make out.

"You need to find Ellie." Amelia turned her face toward Travis, knocking the phone over, the steady beeping on the machine turning crazy again. "I think she's in trouble."

CHAPTER 39

ELLIE

Wednesday, May 11
7:36 a.m.

Steve yanked the phone from Ellie's hand and pressed the End button. He placed it in the front pocket of his pastel button-up shirt angrily.

"Damn it, Ellie. What the hell?" Steve glared at her. "I told you that no one could know I was here. I have to get out of town, now. I shot a man. I can't stay."

Ellie put her hands in her pockets to keep them from shaking. Seeing Steve in the abandoned house was shocking enough, but then when he told her about shooting Randy and leaving town, her knees went weak, and she wondered how many more of her idols could fall in one day.

"It's Amelia. If anyone can keep a secret, it's your wife. Don't you think she deserves to know you're running away? Shooting Randy was self-defense. Everyone knows that. And all this stuff about that Tim kid and the fire—just speak up and tell the truth. It was *years* ago. We can work through it." Steve stared at her for a second when she mentioned the fire and then began to pace back and forth from the kitchen door to the hole he'd been rummaging through. If he hadn't seemed so frantic, Ellie would've taken him by the shoulders and shaken him.

He looked almost comical wearing his father's khakis and a light yellow button-up dress shirt. Steve pressed his lips together and nodded slowly as though processing the information as she said it. He coughed lightly and flinched back against the pain, blowing out several long breaths.

"It isn't just that, L. The only loose end with Tim was taken care of weeks ago. Amelia left her keys out; you were on shift . . . Chief is pretty easy to convince of things nowadays, so we took a little field trip. Those papers are safely here now"—he pointed at the hole in the floor—"and they will be going to Cuba with me."

Weeks ago. The explanation sounded so calculating and manipulative. It sounded like a mastermind who was proud of his deception. Every time she thought she'd figured out what was going on with Steve, another mask slipped into place. She wasn't sure if she could even identify the "real Steve" if she saw him.

"But you have to know this isn't about the fire," he continued. "It's the gambling stuff. Don't pretend you know nothing about it, because I know Amelia told you. You know she was divorcing me, right?"

A stab of betrayal went through Ellie's stomach. "No, she didn't tell me." So it was true. Damn it. Why didn't Amelia confide in her? She pushed the pain away and refocused on Steve. "I don't know much and I don't really want to know, but please tell me this robbery didn't have anything to do with that. God, Steve. What did you get yourself into?"

He shook his head and stopped pacing. Standing in front of her in the dark office, he reached out with his good side, placing a large, comforting hand on her shoulder.

"No, no . . . but once they start investigating, they are going to find out, and there are other things, money things that I could go away for. With what I had in the safe and the money my parents are willing to wire me, I can get away until this all gets cleared up." Steve gestured in a general way to the office as though it were a cancer that needed to be cut out. He continued talking in a low, deep, nearly hypnotic voice. "But Caleb has it out for me. He's going to tell all kinds of stories, and I . . . You must think I'm a coward, but . . . how am I supposed to support my kids if I go to jail? This way I can start over somewhere new and send money to my parents, and there's the insurance money . . ." He dragged his hand down her arm and took her hand in his. "I mean, she didn't want to be with me anymore, but I'd still take care of her. You know I would."

Steve was growing emotional, and though it all seemed a little convoluted and made Ellie's head swim, she couldn't stand to see him in such a state. He was always, always there for her. Green Jell-O, there for her. Ellie placed her left hand over their clasped fingers as Steve's tears turned to sobs. He leaned over, his forehead pressing against the pile of their hands.

"I don't know what to say," Ellie said, completely confused. Amelia wanted a divorce? Steve was still running his gambling business?

Steve pulled back; his face was wet but calmer than she expected. His eyes were clear, the whites brilliant. It was like some kind of clarity in his mind was being transmitted there.

"You should come with me, L. You've always hated this place. You deserve so much more. My dad has a friend in Cuba who's gonna take me in for a while. We can go there and then make a plan. Amelia wanted me to make this money thing right. You could help me. We've always made a great team, and Collin is no good for you, Ellie. You could find someone else, easy."

He squeezed her hand so hard, it almost hurt. Fear and a tiny pulse of excitement pounded in her chest. It was like the desire to walk into a burning building; you knew it was dangerous, lethal even, but it called to you. Not even just the saving-lives part; it was also the excitement, the adrenaline, the unknown. It was the part of her that didn't scream, "Go back" when the heat hit but crooned, "Push forward."

"Come with me," he begged, his body suddenly alive with energy. "You can be whoever you want to be. No more taking care of everyone else. No more giving up your dreams. This is your chance—leave Broadlands forever."

Those were the words, the ones she'd wanted to say for all twenty-two years of her life. *Leave Broadlands.* The phrase played in her mind like a lullaby. *Leave Broadlands.* Then, before she could stop it, the word that always followed that luscious, tempting phrase . . . *but* . . .

"You want me to go with you?" Ellie didn't struggle with words normally. She was bold and fearless most of the time, but Steve's request knocked the words out of her. Go with him? Go to Cuba? This whole episode seemed like some kind of bad reaction to the medication or maybe he hit his head after he was shot. This seemed like a very different Steve than the strong, experienced firefighter she'd always idolized.

A strange sensation made its way up her shoulders and neck and ears and to the top of her head, and she realized what it was. Fear. She wasn't safe with Steve. She needed to get out of here as soon as possible.

The phone in his pocket started to buzz, and she grabbed for it like a lifeline. Before she could wrestle it out, Steve's hand wrapped around her wrist, strong and vise-like. Her heart started to pound and not in the enjoyable, thrill-seeking kind of way. This was like when the emergency went wrong.

"I don't think you should answer that right now." He pried the phone out of her hand and glanced at the screen. "Rivera? Who is that? Wait, that's your cop boyfriend again, isn't it?" Steve pressed the red Decline icon on the screen and then held down the button on the side of the phone until it powered off, going from a living being to a cold, dead brick of glass and plastic.

Ellie stepped back once and then again, angling for the open door, trying to get some space between her and Steve. The part of her mind that had always seen him as an overprotective brother told Ellie to calm down, told her she was overreacting. But the part of her brain good at assessing dangerous situations told her to get out. Now. She took another step backward, the threshold within reach, but Steve reached around behind her and shoved the door shut.

"You don't want to go in there, I promise."

Ellie shoved her anxiety down, pressed her body against the metal door, and faced Steve, her feet squarely in a dried pool of Amelia's blood.

"You need help. Come with me to the hospital. Amelia is awake. You can talk to her about all of this. Come with me," she pleaded. She didn't care how great a mentor Steve was or how much she looked up to him—this was insanity. She put her hand on the doorknob boldly, like she wasn't afraid.

"L, I told you not to go in there or you'll be sorry," he repeated his warning, and this time there was a touch of humor in his voice ignoring her request. "The only place I'm going is out of this town, and I'm going now. This is your last chance."

"I'm not going with you." Ellie twisted the knob, taking a step back, but Steve lunged forward and grabbed her by her shirt collar, swinging her onto the roofing-office floor. She landed with a crushing crack, her father's brush snapping in half in her back pocket.

"Don't go in that room!" Steve roared, his face red and sweaty.

Ellie, in pain and awe, cowered on the floor, scared of the stranger standing above her. Some kind of insanity had taken him over. She tried to lean in a little closer to inspect Steve's pupils, suddenly worried about a bleed on the brain. He glanced at the watch strapped to his wrist, probably also his father's.

"Fine, stay here in this shithole of a town, but I'm leaving and you should get out too." He returned to the hole in the floor and the pile of cash and unlabeled blue folders. He continued to load them into Cora's purple butterfly backpack. "We're out of time, Ellie. You need to get out of *here*—now."

Steve was being erratic, scary, and potentially dangerous. He was also part of this strange fire cover-up at Nancy's, but then again so was her father. It would all be cleared up if she could get him to safety; she knew it.

"Come with me, Steve," she said, rubbing her elbow where it had hit the floor, blood beading up around the edges of the rug burn, and then sat up. "You know what trauma can do to a person. You saw your wife shot. You killed a man in self-defense. You need help. Let me help you."

Steve ignored her completely as he placed the last few items into the bag before reaching in one last time and pulling out a small revolver, snub-nosed with a brown handle. Ellie fell back onto her injured elbow, shocked, and her faith in Steve quickly dissolving into horror. She scrambled around on the floor, trying to get to her feet and knowing she was in an incredibly vulnerable position.

As Ellie flailed about, Steve tossed the sagging bag onto his shoulder and pointed the gun right at her. He was cool and didn't seem to be struggling against any demons. In fact, he seemed more serene than he had in the past twenty-four hours.

"I'll give you to the count of five to get out, then I'm leaving, and I'd suggest you not try to stop me. None of this was part of the plan, but I'm not going to go to jail forever because of Randy's mess-up. Get up and go. Now."

Talking to Steve was like throwing herself repeatedly against a brick wall until she was bloody. He couldn't hear her, or at the very least, he wasn't listening. Despite the paralyzing reality of having a gun pointed at her face, Ellie found a way to make her body respond to her orders. She stood up, blood trickling down her arm, and her legs started to shake.

"One . . . ," he started to count, and Ellie knew she was out of time. If you can't get the victim out of the fire, you don't let it consume you too. You run. "Two . . ." The gun shook in his hand, finger over the trigger. Ellie put up her hands in surrender.

"I'm leaving." She backed away, toward the Broadlands Roofing outside office door, the one that led to the driveway, developing a plan for escape. She'd run through the thick patch of brush and trees on the other side of the gravel driveway. She'd get in her car and start driving to the hospital and tell Travis. The police would find Steve pretty easily since he was dressed in his father's clothes and likely driving his car.

"Three . . ." He kept counting, holding the gun with two hands now like he was taking aim. He wasn't bluffing. She stopped planning and started moving as fast as she could.

With a hard twist and pull, Ellie broke the police seal on the other side of the door. The pop made her jump. She wondered if Steve's gun had gone off by accident, but she didn't dare look back. As the fresh spring air rushed through the crack in the door, Ellie pulled harder so that the door swung wide. No police officers or any other vehicles were waiting. It would only take a few leaps across the gravel to make it to the safety of the trees, but as soon as she turned her back and ran through the open area, she'd be a sitting duck. The relief of the fresh air and freedom was brief as Steve continued counting down.

"Two . . ."

Ellie let go of the door. It was time. Her ears were ringing, her feet struggling to move as fast as she wanted them to, but she had to do it; she had to turn her back to a man with a gun and run.

"One . . ."

The last shouted number echoed out the door, and Ellie leaped off the wooden front porch, skipping several steps and skidding across the gravel drive. It was hard to find traction, and she fell, the little stones embedding in her hand, but she didn't feel the physical pain. The panic produced by fearing for her life pulled Ellie up almost like hands under her arms, yanking her toward the sky. Without waiting to be steady, she took off again, covering her head and leaving a trail of dust behind her.

Once in the trees, she uncovered her head and risked a glance back over her shoulder. The door to the office still hung open, but there was no sign of Steve. He must still be inside, gathering more hidden cash or documents. Ellie wasn't going to wait to find out. She reached into her pocket and retrieved her keys, wishing Steve hadn't taken her phone. After driving an ambulance, driving Collin's Jeep at full speed would seem like driving a race car. Still, no time to delay.

She took off again through the trees, the side street where she'd parked visible through the thick underbrush. Just as she was about to break through the tree line, a loud boom pounded in her ears, and an invisible force shoved her down to the ground, her face raking against the needle-covered earth. A loud, high-pitched whine rang through her ears, and her head felt inflated with water or air. The world spun around her, and it took a moment to understand what was happening until she heard the unmistakable sound of fire.

Any attempt to stand made Ellie's head pound, but as she crawled across the ground, she saw it—her sister's house engulfed in flames, debris surrounding the structure like a skirt. She covered her mouth, shaking from the explosion, shocked at the devastation. What did Steve do?

Steve. Where was Steve?

Fighting through the pain and confusion, Ellie sat herself up against a tree trunk, resting her heavy head on the rough bark. If Steve was inside—he was dead. Dead. He'd done some terrible and confusing things, but dead? She'd spent so much of the past twenty-four hours worrying about her sister, she had no idea that in the end it was Steve who would end up gone. Even with all his irrational behavior, death wasn't what she wanted for him.

The heat of the fire lapped at her cheeks, and she watched it through the trees. Five more seconds, five, and she would've been caught in that blaze. The house was quickly engulfed in flames, the fire a deeper red than she remembered fire being, the heat so strong that the leaves closest to the house were starting to wilt.

Ellie thought she should feel panic, that she should want to run away, but instead she started to sink into the moist earth beneath her. The tears she'd been holding back since she first saw her sister, lifeless, covered in blood, started to pour out in hot streams. As she stood, crying, the mud took on a life of its own, pulling her down into the muck. When it hit the bare skin under her pant leg, a deep shiver vibrated through her already racked body.

The wind blew through the trees, sending goose bumps across Ellie's arms and making her bones ache despite the intense heat from the home. She tried to find the energy to get up, to pull herself out of the dirt and get help, but it seemed impossible to move any farther. She'd been trapped by Caleb, Steve, Broadlands, and her love for her father, but this was the first time she'd trapped herself. Ellie felt heavy, weighed down, not just with mud but also with despair. There had to be an explanation.

No answers came. Just silence and trees and her sister's house burning brightly in front of her. Sirens sounded in the distance. The Broadlands Fire Department, no doubt. They'd help. They'd fix things.

The wind picked up again, this time grabbing at the branches and sending the half-burned leaves from the trees near the house, along with a gust of hot ash and wind, down around Ellie. The ash used to be a home that her sister's family lived in. It used to be a safe place to visit and play and grow closer to the people she loved. It was one of the only reasons Broadlands was even bearable. And now it was gone, along with the image of the family that used to live inside.

The cooling ash brushed her face, cheeks wet with tears, and for one moment, reality and the questions that accompanied it floated away, and she enjoyed the beauty of the fire and the dancing embers around her. Fire was the same everywhere whether devastating a house, a city, or an open prairie. If so much trauma and danger could lurk here in Broadlands, was it really safer than anywhere else?

The sirens grew louder, so loud her already tender ears ached, but the closer they came, the more they warbled in her ears, the light around her going from red to black over and over again like someone was flashing the lights. Just before they went dark, she heard a familiar voice, and arms picked her up out of the seemingly inescapable mud. Moments later, she awoke to Travis kneeling over her, checking her pulse.

"Ellie, thank God you're okay." He touched her hand gently and then her forehead. "Did he hurt you anywhere?"

Ellie wasn't sure who Travis was talking about at first, but then she remembered Steve with a gun pointed at her. She spoke in a gravelly whisper. "Not really."

"Do you know where he went?" he asked.

"Inside," she said simply. Travis glanced over his shoulder and took in the ball of flames behind them, smoke leaving a towering trail into the sky.

"Inside?" he asked. "Are you sure?"

Ellie nodded and then closed her eyes again, her body forcing her to escape from the nightmare around her. Travis placed his balled-up sweatshirt under her head and ran off to a cluster of police cars. The world started to fade, and she remembered one more important thing about fire. Sometimes in nature, fire caused pinecones to open and prairies to bloom. Sometimes it cleared out old dead trees to make way for new life. Sometimes fire wasn't about destruction—sometimes it was about renewal. Sometimes fire was necessary.

CHAPTER 40

ELLIE

Friday, November 4
Eighteen months later

The sound of an e-mail coming through on her phone made Ellie wake with a start. It was dark, and the chill in the air was distinctly fall-like. She didn't know how to define the difference between the cold in the spring and the cold in the autumn, but they were opposite in their basic nature—one filled with promises of the future, the other filled with good-byes.

She actually liked both kinds of cold. Both were cool enough to make you want to curl under a blanket but not so cold you felt like your bones were going to break if you took too hard a step.

The clock read 4:45 a.m. It was still too early to be up officially, but sometimes when you'd been working twenty-four-hour shifts for so long, it was hard to get back to a normal schedule. Most mornings she'd just roll over and try to go back to sleep, but today she had class.

Ellie rolled over, rubbed Travis's back, and placed a quick kiss on the nape of his neck. She still loved the way he smelled. She sat up and adjusted her ring. It was a little oversize, and the modest diamond kept slipping around her finger toward the palm of her hand. It was strange wearing an engagement ring again. After breaking things off with Collin, Ellie thought she'd never get married, especially to someone from Broadlands.

But on dark mornings like this, when she wrapped herself in the pink fluffy robe she got when she was thirteen, she had this overwhelming sense of relief that she'd gotten out of that place. She might live in a tiny studio apartment in a slightly questionable neighborhood, but she was in New York and a full-time med student again, so it felt like a palace.

A lot had changed since Amelia woke up. After the house fire and the search for Steve's body, Ellie felt more trapped in Broadlands than she ever had. For a while she was full-time caregiver to not just her father but also her sister. She was also her family's only source of income. Amelia woke up as a single parent faced with bankruptcy, conspiracy, and potential fraud charges. It took a while for her recollection about what happened in the Broadlands Roofing office to fall into place. Caleb helped fill in his part of the narrative, but Randy's death and Amelia's actual shooting remained fuzzy, a common response to trauma and extreme blood loss. The only person who could fill in the blanks would be Steve, but no one knew for sure whether he had survived the blast. If he had, he'd left no trace of his escape.

It was universally acknowledged Steve was not the innocent victim he portrayed in the hospital, and if he ever resurfaced, there was no doubt he'd be arrested. But this idea of Steve as a criminal was hard for Ellie to reconcile. She still hoped there was some explanation, some way to reconstruct the picture of a man she'd held as a hero for so long. Amelia, on the other hand, liked to believe he was dead; it was easier that way. Although she wanted answers, she didn't want Steve.

Ellie was left a little off balance when Amelia filed for divorce from her hospital bed, not knowing whether Steve was alive or dead. Ellie really couldn't blame her. Steve had lied . . . a lot, and he'd hurt so many people. Ellie knew her sister deserved more. But another part of Ellie mourned her sister's relationship. Steve and Amelia had always been together, and when Ellie needed him, Steve had always been there. But it didn't take long for her to notice a new person who emerged from that hospital bed—a strong, determined woman who got her real estate license and started her own business within months of almost losing her life. This new version of her sister never seemed lonely, and soon Ellie wondered how she'd gotten to the point of seeing her sister as one of Steve's appendages rather than her own dynamic self.

Though Amelia was single, it didn't mean she was alone. Caleb was in her life more than ever, and Ellie and Travis had bets on how long it would be until they made it official. Cora and Kate mourned their father as though he were dead and came to love Caleb in a new way. When he wasn't taking classes at the university, Caleb was in Broadlands helping Amelia fix up the Slattery place, which she had bought in foreclosure.

Caleb helped by more than just swinging a hammer. When Chet decided to retire from firefighting and EMT work entirely, Caleb came to Ellie with an idea he wanted to offer to the experienced paramedic—Chet would serve as a full-time caregiver for her father in exchange for free housing and a generous salary provided by the savings Caleb had built up over the years. His only caveat was that Amelia never know and be told that Chet volunteered. Ellie tried to say no, but when the opportunity to leave Broadlands finally developed, she gave in, knowing she'd need to repay him one day. After the experience in the Emporium, Ellie didn't want to like Caleb, but that selfless offer for a man who had once accused him of murder moved her, and she knew that if Amelia ever decided to trust a new man with her heart, she and the girls couldn't ask for a more caring individual.

With her feet wrapped in the fleecy warmth of her slippers, Ellie grabbed her laptop and headed for the kitchen. The heat hadn't clicked on yet, and she adjusted the ancient thermostat up a few clicks, finding the few dollars more in utilities completely worth it.

As the heat kicked on and the coffee started to drip into the pot, Ellie opened the lid of her computer and flipped through the sites she'd left open, some of wedding dresses, others for her classwork and Facebook. After triple-checking to make sure her assignment had gone through to her professor and bookmarking the dress she was in love with that week, she had one browser window she didn't close.

In private-browsing mode, she typed in the web address for her e-mail. Not her main e-mail that dinged when it came into her computer or cell phone. No, this address was confidential. This e-mail address was for one person only. He'd opened it just for her. Using a stolen social media account, he forwarded her the information with a copious apology and a promise to send money. She didn't even know if it was really him; you could pretend to be anyone on the Internet. Or at least that was what she told herself.

She didn't know exactly why she checked that account and didn't just turn it over to the police, just in case. Maybe it was this secret hope that they were wrong, he wasn't dead, and if he wasn't dead, that he wasn't a monster. There were so many pieces missing. It was almost too painful to believe he could be so heartless. She didn't know how to believe that about Steve. She didn't know how to be the one to turn him in—yet.

Her heart always thumped as she put in her user name and password, hoping for and dreading an e-mail at the same time. As the page loaded, she went through the same thought process she always did. If he had written again, she would forward the e-mail to the police or she would tell Travis or . . . at least tell Amelia. She should tell someone. But she never did.

When the e-mails filled in, one at the top was highlighted in a bold lettering, and a simple numeral one stood next to the in-box icon. One new e-mail. It had been nine months since his first e-mail, and now her in-box held nearly two hundred journal-entry-like missives. The subject line read simply: *Update 192*. Ellie guided the on-screen arrow over the new letter and clicked.

The format was the same. Always addressed to her. One paragraph talking about activities and plans, the second reminiscing about better times, and the third asking about specific individuals, asking for forgiveness, and occasionally renewing his offer to help her leave Broadlands— forever. Then he'd sign it: *Always, Steve.*

She'd never actually considered going with him, but the knowledge that she *could* was enough. It probably wasn't a good secret, but then again, most secrets weren't.

Yet even in New York, she still checked the strange e-mails, compelled and comforted by them. Addicted.

Ellie shook her head, sincerely frustrated with herself. Because she was a bad sister? Because she was a bad fiancée? Because he was her nieces' father? Because she thought she could save Steve, bring him back from the dead?

Travis coughed from their bedroom, signaling that he was awake for his shift. Ellie jumped, her already racing heart beating harder. Always careful to cover her tracks, she signed out of the e-mail account, cleared the history, closed the browser, and snapped the cover shut. If Travis ever found out . . . She didn't even want to think about it.

With one shove she pushed the computer to the side of the counter and took out her favorite mug, the one Amelia and the girls had given her for her birthday that year. It had a picture of Ellie and Amelia showing their necklaces, Amelia still in her hospital bed and Ellie in her paramedic's uniform. Around the lip of the cup in black letters it said, *Thanks a Bunch for Saving My Life*. Ellie laughed so hard when she unwrapped that gift; the way her sister could make a joke out of something so horrible was just one of a million reasons she loved her.

Ellie filled the mug with coffee and pulled out another generic one for Travis. When he reached the kitchen, Travis was shivering in his tee shirt and reaching out for the warm mug. He stood next to her, close enough so she could wrap her arm around his waist, partly in an effort to warm and partly in an effort to be warmed. He kissed the top of her head before taking a long sip of the black coffee. In that moment everything felt normal. And she was happy. And she knew she could trust him with her future, but still . . .

Ellie turned her head to the side, listening to his strong, steady heartbeat. One day she'd tell. Really, she would. One day . . . when she knew the truth of who was writing to her, if it was really Steve and if he was beyond saving . . . when she knew Travis would understand, when Amelia was ready to face the ghost from her past . . . when Ellie finally remembered who carried her out of the brush fire the morning of the explosion.

But for now she'd wait. Ellie tipped her head back and looked Travis in the eyes.

"I love you, babe," she whispered. Travis looked down at Ellie as though she'd told him he'd won a million dollars, his mouth turned up on one side in a crooked smile.

"Nah, I love *you*." He brushed his lips against hers and then wrapped his arms around her waist until they were so close, it was hard to tell where one ended and the other began. She shook her head again. It wasn't time . . . not yet.

Ellie was finally out of Broadlands, but now she had to figure out how to get Broadlands out of her.

ACKNOWLEDGMENTS

Chris Hanson—thank you, first for your service as a Portland firefighter/paramedic and second for your willingness to share your knowledge and experience with me to make *Working Fire* as accurate as possible. Your stories and expertise are the foundation of this story. Thank you for donating so much time to this project and for that truly awesome tour of the cadaver lab that made me go "OH!" and "Ewww" at the same time.

I have the most amazing writer's group full of women who not only give great feedback but are strong, insightful, and a great example to me. Joanne Osmond, Mary Rose Lila, Kelli Neilson, Deborah Brooks, Paulette Swan, Tiffany Blanchard, and Candice Toone—you ladies are smart, beautiful, and the best support an author could ask for.

Thanks to my fellow Lake Union author, Catherine McKenzie, who reached out to me over and over again to provide support and advice and opportunities for growth. It has been fun to go from fan to colleague to friend.

To my fellow author Mallory Crowe, thank you for checking in on me, sending me the BEST songs to inspire me, and for showing me what it means to work hard and constantly seek to better myself and my work. You have no idea how much you have helped me over the years. Thank you for being my long-distance support. You deserve all the success you find.

Thank you to Kelli Neilson, author, critique partner, and friend. Thank you for being there for me professionally and personally. I can't explain how much I love attending conventions together and working through plot lines. Thank you for talking to me for endless hours and welcoming me in your home when needed most. I love how your mind works and how you help me grow every day.

Emily Hanson . . . to think I started this book leaning on Chris's expertise and ended it leaning on yours day in and day out. You are the BEST assistant any author could ever ask for. You are also just a stunning person and friend. I'll never stop being grateful you moved to Illinois when you did. I love you and who you are. Thanks for taking care of me, making it possible for me to balance writing and being a mom, and all the other experiences life has brought to us.

Thank you to the author team at Lake Union. I'm sure if I pulled back the curtain, I'd find a team of wizards at work. Gabriella Van den Heuvel and Dennelle Catlett and all the other hands, eyes, and brains that made this book possible—you guys rock . . . sincerely.

Tiffany Yates Martin, your hard work and input while editing *Working Fire* has been priceless. Thank you for helping me make this story all it could be and inspiring some crucial and truly beautiful changes. It was an honor to work with you, and I look forward to keeping a good thing going.

Danielle Marshall—my editor and guide—thank you for your patience, guidance, and empathy. Your faith in me and continued direction were not only well timed but also a tender mercy in my life. Thanks for your passion and hard work. I always love seeing your name in my in-box.

My fantastic agent, Marlene Stringer—you called me on a cold February morning and changed my life by offering me representation. Then called me again when I was at Scout camp with my boys and told me of the offer from Lake Union. Thank you for your patience and support. I love being on the same team together. You are a force to be reckoned with. I look forward to all of our future adventures.

All of you who read *Wreckage* and *When I'm Gone* and took the time to recommend them, write a review, or even write me an e-mail—you have inspired me. It makes my day when I open my e-mail or Facebook and get a message from someone who was touched by my writing. Thank you for loving my characters and their lives. I hope you love Ellie and Amelia just as deeply.

My parents—you have been there for me so much. Thank you for being there, being proud and supportive. Not to mention your endless bragging and for letting me know you love me no matter what. Thank you as well for all your help and love for my kids. I love you.

My siblings—you each have shown your love and support in your own ways. Katie and Michael, thanks for always asking for status updates and spreading the word about my writing. Philip, thank you for all your phone calls and never-ending understanding. Thanks for showing interest in my interests, and I look forward to reading your acknowledgments one day (where *you* will thank *me* profusely . . . right?).

And, Elizabeth, so much of the love between sisters that I talk about in this book I learned from my relationship with you. If I listed all the ways you've been there for me throughout the years and this year in particular, I'd run out of room. You have always believed in me and are a stunning CP partner on top of it all. Thank you for reading a million drafts of this story and giving me honest and constructive feedback. I can't wait to see what the future holds for you. I love you and believe in you. Always.

To my kids—you are my dearest friends of all. I love your spirit and authenticity. Your passion for life and your continued resilience are an example to me. Thanks for being my biggest fans and support. I love you guys with all my heart.

ABOUT THE AUTHOR

Photo © 2017 Amber Linderman Photography

Emily Bleeker is a former educator who learned to love writing while teaching a writer's workshop. After surviving a battle with a rare form of cancer, she finally found the courage to share her stories, starting with her debut novel, *Wreckage*, followed by the *Wall Street Journal* bestseller *When I'm Gone*. Emily currently lives with her family in suburban Chicago. Connect with her or request a Skype visit with your book club at www.emilybleeker.com.